I0783218

Journey To Distant Consciousness Remote Viewer Battles

By

Paul D. Escudero

WORKBOOK PRESS LLC
187 E Warm Springs Rd,
Suite B285 Las Vegas NV 89119 USA

Website: https://workbookpress.com/
Hotline: 1-888-818-4856
Email: admin@workbookpress.com

Ordering Information:
Quantity sales. Special discounts are available on quantity purchases by corporations, associations, and others. For details, contact the publisher at the address above.

ISBN-13:   978-1-963718-00-3 Paperback Version
               978-1-963718-00-3 Digital Version

REV. DATE: 01/11/2024

Table of Contents

***

Preface

Normally I do not put prefaces in my Novels because people usually skip over the preface and go right to the story. But this is a special case.

There have been books written and internet accounts of *Remote Viewers*. Many people have given interviews on radio shows claiming they were former employees of intelligence agencies or law enforcement agencies and discussed themselves or other people used as *Remote Viewers*. But one thing I've discovered in my research, it's not all the same. The methods, expectations, and results are significantly different on a case basis and certain users of remote viewers have no idea what other remote viewers are accomplishing.

Remote Viewers could be as deadly as nuclear weapons if you can learn all your enemy's intentions and the fortitude to act on information supplied by remote viewers. From my personal exposure to remote viewing and what remote viewing constitutes gives me an insight which I'll speculate about and probe in this Novel.

If what I've learned about remote viewing is true, then remote viewing could possibly have already been used against World Leaders. Thus, their enemies may be informed by remote viewers in advance of many of their planned moves. How else could you explain an inferior force devastating a more capable and advanced opponent?

What led to this Novel is a *Remote Viewer* came to me wanting to share a personal story and since I met this *Remote Viewer*, that person has become a technical advisor to guide me skillfully through this fantastic discovery and realization of how remote viewing accomplishes obtaining critical information.

Remember *Remote Viewers* come in all sizes and shapes and do not operate the same way, nor can they provide the same results. It comes down to the individual in how they obtained such extraordinary abilities and how people who exploit their revelations operate.

This book is fiction based on a plausible *Remote Viewer* experience by someone who ostensibly came to me from the stars. And if that person really did arrive, and walks among us, how would we know they did not originate on Earth? But thanks to someone who exposed me to remote viewing, this Alien explains it to me as I now explain it to you in a fascinating story.

A word of caution. In this story there are places and events that will grip you. It's not for the faint of heart. But if you want to know how something like this comes about then you must read those unpleasant episodes to understand how it evolved into what the remote viewer accomplished.

This remote viewer creates quite an emotion for me when I think about that person's story. There is nothing like it that I could ever imagine.

In my lifetime I went through some very scary episodes as my profession was very dangerous. Even though I had many experiences, filled with fear, intrigue, and numerous possibilities that could easily manifest, and a few close calls, I never experienced anything like this remote viewer did in my lifetime. I sense something very special about that person who will remain a friend and even though our ships will very seldom if ever pass close by, that person will know I appreciate and have great respect and admiration for such an incredible history.

Most people realize there are evil people that are brutal and disgusting and create victims and cause people great pain and suffering. This remote viewer experienced that and much more. Part of the story in this book depicts such events, but due to the harsh realities of the world, the real perpetrators cannot be identified. After enough time passes, such vile people escape any form of punishment as many like them do.

It may make you slightly uncomfortable reading that part of the story but since it's the experience that led to the remote viewer beginning her journey in the intelligence business, it must be told. In my private discussions with her she authorized me and asked me to write that. In a way it's closure for her.

In recreating the experiences of the remote viewer, from the ashes emerges an extraordinary person with extraordinary abilities that provides handlers with such vital intelligence, and unforeseen events, they ultimately had to take that person to an isolated location for protection. But due to the intergalactic nature of what remote viewers can obtain from unique intelligence, the handlers want that including the vision and sound of the target.

This remote viewer ultimately sees and hears with high fidelity what the handlers seek. By the time you complete this Novel your mind may transcend from an ordinary Earth-like experience to a journey in time and space that fascinates you and makes you think about a lot of things.

CHAPTER ONE
Meager Beginnings

Lingraw Arginin lived in a mountainous area of Difland, one of the outermost planets of the Crawflang Empire. People in this area lived off the grid, had no running water or electricity. Lingraw Arginin and the mountain people that lived in this forested area were modest people with great resolve and patience.

The mountain people produced leather goods made from Tomlars surpassed the quality and softness that other hides providers sold to marketeers who ventured into the area and traded manufactured goods for the various products including shoes, blankets, and topcoats. To a visitor from planet Earth the Tomlars had a striking resemblance to Thomson's Gazelles.

Conditions on Difland were not ideal for social development culture because of the long history of the Tyrannical government nearby just across the border in Tartarland. Occasionally, Tartarlanders would risk the long trek across the mountains that separated the continent in order to escape to Wenmark. The problem with such stragglers going across Lingraw Arginin's property is they often shot and killed Tomlars for nourishment during the trek. And since there were always more of the trespasser than Lingraw Arginin could handle in a one on-one fight, they had to be taken down one at a time.

Today was no different as the long moving battle that lasted a week commenced. One by one the males in the group were taken down by shots at ultra-long range that only a frontiersman could accomplish out of necessity.

It was kill or be killed. Lingraw Arginin understood from previous encounters between local people and refugees fleeing

Tartarland resulted in the deaths of locals, so it only made sense to kill them before they killed you.

Eventually Lingraw Arginin killed all but three of the Tartarlanders. Of those three a male and a female who then deserted the other female, left her behind as she was slowing them down and the couple wanted to get as far away from the kill zone and potential Tartarland militia people sent after them to arrest the defectors.

Lingraw Arginin enjoyed a Tartarland woman now and then when he could arrange to capture one, like today. He took the freezing deserted and crying woman back to his cabin well hidden in the forest that had another large room attached to it that housed all the Tomlars he took care of and in some cases milked to provide Tomlar cream for fermented alcohol drinks and a cheese like product to eat with meager winter foods stored for the long winters.

To a Midwest farmer on Earth the home seemed more like a barn than a home with several storage areas with food the Tomlars ate while trapped indoors during the long, horrible winter.

The Tartarland woman was very close to go into hypothermia because she was not well clothed against the elements. The man and woman who deserted her took all her possessions including her fur coat that would have kept her warm and protected her. It was quite apparent they left her behind to die.

Unfortunately for the terrible couple, they met their new masters as they went around the mountain with a very poor map that helped them get lost. The husband was killed by the mountain people and barbecued and fed to their dogs and the woman became a slave for the tribe quickly wishing she was back in Tartarland.

After warming up the woman and giving her some tea made from mountain substances and fresh snow, Lingraw Arginin gave her some Tomlar cheese and dried crackers created from mountain potatoes.

Lingraw Arginin was not an expert in Tartarland standard language but knew enough of the words for very basic communication allowing him to barter with explorers and hunters that passed by. Thanks to most of the explorers and hunters arriving almost in starvation, Lingraw Arginin was able to slowly accumulate important items such as weapons, binoculars, and explosive devices that could easily take down a wild bear that was charging. As soon as the other bears saw their brother blown to pieces, they fled back into the forest running away in great fear.

"What is your name?" Lingraw Arginin asked in basic Tartarland tongue.

"Maki Zorthun," the woman responded.

The woman realized she was past the point of not revealing her identity. This whole trip planned and executed by the "coyotes" not only depleted all her life savings but turned into such a disaster she was now at the mercy of this stranger.

In due time he explained to her he had a covered shed built on the side of the building that had a poop deck in it that dropped the human waste on a slide down into a small creek that had water running through it 10 months out of the year to wash it away.

This Frontiersman man also had something else that surprised Maki Zorthun, a large tub he got in a trade from other Frontiersmen that had enough room in it to bathe. He also used it once or twice a year to squeeze fruits to get the pulp used in ferments.

Maki Zorthun started feeling a little safer and warmer and content to eat some solid food. But also had great fear that real soon she would have to leave the cabin and go outside to the poop deck to urinate or have a bowel movement. Will he watch her and want to have sex afterwards after she exposed herself?

Lingraw Arginin had not been with a woman in quite a long time and simply enjoyed the female companionship.

Even though Lingraw Arginin knew the obvious, he asked the question to give a hint of decency and forbearance, "Why were you out in the forest not clothed for the harsh winter?"

"I was with a group traveling together that someone was systematically killing and eventually there were only three of us left. A man and a woman I traveled with said I was slowing them down, so they robbed me and took my fur jacket and left me behind to die."

"I'm sorry to hear about that," Lingraw Arginin responded not revealing he was the person killing those traveling partners.

After the discussion went on a bit the woman admitted, "We were escaping Tartarland where life has become unbearable with a Tyrannical government. It's a horrible place to live now."

"It must be pretty bad if you are traveling across the mountains in the wintertime."

The organizers of our escape said it's the best time to go because it gives us the best time to get away. The government can't fly their Vertical Takeoff and Landing (VTOL) aircraft to track us down to kill us like they normally do with all defectors because the mountains are usually cloud covered this time of year."

"Your group was very foolish because sometimes we have storms that last a couple weeks. You all could easily be stranded and covered with snow and perished."

"Everyone was willing to take the risk because life in Tartarland is so hellish."

Even though Lingraw Arginin had a thick dialect, Maki Zorthun was able to effectively communicate with him and each passing hour felt safer as he made no attempt to rape her. Maki Zorthun knew Lingraw Arginin looked rugged and strong and could probably mount her with brutal strength if he wanted and there really wasn't much, she could do about it since she wasn't armed, and he would no doubt subdue her and make her pay the price if she ever appeared to instigate any form of violence.

Maki Zorthun thus knew she was at his mercy and the price to be paid was her life. Hopefully one day when it warmed up and the snow melted, he would let her continue her journey to freedom like all the other refugees that were now stuck on the mountain and most of them perishing.

Lingraw Arginin only had one connection to the outside world. He traded gold nuggets he obtained in rivers and streams over the year and obtained a radio receiver that was battery powered and had a solar panel to recharge the batteries. He also had a box of spare batteries to last him the winter, but he only listened to news reports for an hour a day and that was it. No entertainment or music was ever played on the radio. After the small talk died down and Lingraw Arginin acting quite humane showed Maki Zorthun to the poop deck and even had some innovative sections of Tomlar hide she could clean herself afterwards.

He then gave her privacy and went back into the home and grabbed a bucket and went outside and obtained a bucket of fresh snow and took it inside to dump into a pot he had by the fireplace keeping the home above freezing.

Lingraw Arginin always made tea using a large store of dried wildflowers he harvested during full bloom. That made the water far more pleasant, and the scent was quite appealing and increased the fresh smell of the home.

He also had to feed and give water to the Tomlars. In the days to come, Maki Zorthun would discover there was a special relationship between Lingraw Arginin and the Tomlars. They were almost like an adopted part of his family it seemed. After the sunlight came out in the morning Lingraw Arginin would take all of them outside to do their bowel movements and the Tomlars were trained not to do it in the home.

It seemed no different than a person walking their dogs in the morning and again in the afternoon before it got dark. Once in a while the Tomlars would call out making a shrill sound. To Lingraw Arginin that was a signal they wanted to go outside to urinate or discharge their bowels. While there was a lot of snow on the ground there wasn't much purpose in them hanging outside and they preferred the warmth of the home barn section portion they lived in.

But when the snow melted and the grass and wildflowers appeared, they wanted to be outside most of the day.

This astonished Maki Zorthun that Lingraw Arginin would let them out of the barn unsupervised all day long and she asked, "Are you not afraid they will run away or get lost?"

"I have a way of communicating with them."

"How is that?"

"I do remote viewing."

"What do you mean by remote viewing?"

"It's something everyone can do, but most people are unaware they can do it."

"And what exactly is that?"

"I can see what they see or hear what they are hearing."

"That seems rather impossible."

"This is a large mountain area, I do not want to have to go search for them, so all I have to do is the remote viewing and I know exactly where they are or if they are in fear from say a bear or wolf or some dangerous animals, they contact me, and I go rescue them."

This remote viewing seemed far-fetched to Maki Zorthun who thought perhaps Lingraw Arginin was toying with her mind. But as time passed and since she was always with Lingraw Arginin, she discovered he never went out looking for the Tomlars and when he went out to get them in the late afternoons, he always walked exactly to the spot they were grazing and led them home.

Lingraw Arginin's travels were remote, the Tomlars were never at the same place, and he knew exactly where to find them every time! Maki Zorthun slowly became a believer.

The first night Maki Zorthun stayed in the rugged cabin, it was cold even though there was a fireplace and there was only one bed. It was a large bed and could easily accommodate the two of them. At a certain time in the evening, Lingraw Arginin announced it was time to go to bed and it would be nice that night to have another person helping keep him warm. He directed Maki Zorthun to get into bed which she meekly complied now fearing the ugly part of Lingraw Arginin would surface and she assumed she would soon be raped but realized there wasn't much she could do to prevent. There was a strange type of candle next to the bed and as soon as they were in bed, Lingraw Arginin blew out the flame making it totally dark.

The next room was quiet, as the Tomlars were all now sleeping in a very satisfactory manner, feeling at home with their wonderful master.

There was no attempt for sex. Lingraw Arginin held Maki Zorthun in his arms. Her body heat and nice feeling in his arms allowed Lingraw Arginin to easily obtain sleep and by morning felt he had not slept so good in all his life.

Maki Zorthun was slightly agitated by Lingraw Arginin loud snoring. But when he didn't attempt to rape her and kept her warm, she eventually figured out how to get sleep despite the snoring as loud as a hurricane.

The Tomlars liked the snoring. It made them feel safe because they knew their master was nearby to protect them. Lingraw Arginin's snoring was pleasing to the Tomlars as it gave them faith their safety was assured.

Lingraw Arginin's brain was almost a chronometer. He slept and woke up usually within a minute or two from normal, almost as good as an alarm clock.

Maki Zorthun slept very well as she had been cold and scared for the previous two weeks and suffered severely from sleep deprivation. This was an equalizer sleep she desperately needed. What she didn't know is she too was cutting logs with her snoring in the night and he Tomlars seemed to enjoy the synchronizing of the two snorers nearby.

Trying not to disturb Maki Zorthun, Lingraw Arginin eased out of bed and thanks to the one window he had by trading the plexiglass panels with Frontiersmen, the double pane window that was letting in some of the morning sunlight. He quickly dressed and put a log on the remnants of the fire from the night. There were barely enough sparks and smoldering wood to light the fire with the new log.

Despite being careful, Lingraw Arginin managed to wake up Maki Zorthun who was far more tranquil because Lingraw Arginin did not force himself on to her during the night.

Maki Zorthun then wondered; *how long will it be until he seeks some sexual gratification?*

Even though Maki Zorthun was dressed primitively due to her circumstances she still had alluring features, her beautiful face, blue eyes, blonde hair, perfect teeth since she worked as a dental hygienist and had cosmetic work on her teeth that created a perfect smile. She knew she also had breasts of the size and shape that drive men to sexual release. Her slender body was movie star quality and her lack of sex left her body in almost pristine condition. *Maki Zorthun was the low hanging fruit ready to be taken* and she knew it.

With the fireplace going, Lingraw Arginin had two pots brewing they would enjoy in a while, but it was important to let his Tomlars out now so they didn't create a mess in the barn he would have to clean up.

"We have to let the Tomlars out for a short while, then we'll come back and have something to eat."

All they had to do was put on their boots and the fur topcoat. Maki Zorthun instinctively followed Lingraw Arginin into the barn and observed the Tomlars were still laying down next to each other keeping them warm in a cluster. The Tomlars knew what to expect but enjoyed their warm condition and did not budge until the door was opened and knew they had to get up and go take care of morning business, otherwise Lingraw Arginin would use subtle force to get them moving. They also knew after their morning outdoors they would have something to eat afterwards and water.

The Tomlars did not venture very far outdoors, but they all knew to go down the hillside and not enter the pure snow area up the hillside as Lingraw Arginin trained them not to go up the hillside and pollute the snow needed for their drinking water.

Lingraw Arginin grabbed a bucket as he was leaving the barn and went up the hillside and packed it full of snow. In a few more months when the snow started melting, he would simply go down to the creek with a bucket for his own use and the Tomlars would then drink from the stream to get their water a couple times a day.

As soon as he had all the snow, he wanted in the bucket Lingraw Arginin informed Maki Zorthun, "I'll be right back, keep an eye on the Tomlars."

Lingraw Arginin took the large bucket into the home and placed it next to the fireplace where the good heat would quickly melt the snow and heat the water up a little because the Tomlars didn't like drinking extremely cold water.

Maki Zorthun observed the Tomlars take care of their morning business and soon afterwards gathered near her knowing she would soon lead them back into the barn where they were anticipating the food and water that Lingraw Arginin was placing for them in feeding trays along the wall spread out where they would soon line up and eat without crowding each other.

In five minutes Lingraw Arginin came out of the barn and approached

Maki Zorthun and said, "Let's go back into the barn they will follow us back in."

As soon as the two walked towards the barn all the Tomlars got in line and followed them like obedient children. Once they were all inside, Lingraw Arginin shut the door. The barn also had a plexiglass window that allowed light to get in and the animals to see their feeding trays and went to work eating the food Lingraw Arginin had stored in the hay loft above fully packed for the winter. By the time all that was depleted there would be food out on the hillside the Tomlars could graze.

Shortly afterwards during summers, Lingraw Arginin would harvest plenty of wild grass and barley and store it up in the hayloft. He realized this year would be far easier because once the hay was staged in the barn, he could hand it up to his new partner and she could place it in piles he would reorganize for the winter's need. He would also teach Maki Zorthun how to milk the Tomlars and make cheese and ferments to allow periods of enjoyment during the long harsh winter.

Lingraw Arginin realized it would only be a period before Maki Zorthun would attempt to escape and get back to society. When or if she did escape, he would follow her with his powerful hunting rifle to kill wild animals or Frontiersmen who might try to capture her and make her a slave. Slave girls that were as beautiful as Maki Zorthun sold for a large amount of gold.

After the animals were fed and provided with water, it was now time to take care of their own needs and the soup and tea that Lingraw Arginin was boiling near the fireplace was about ready for consumption.

Despite being alone, Lingraw Arginin kept his remote cabin in relatively decent condition. This was his home and he constantly made improvements by trading with Frontiersmen, gold, hides, and fresh meat from either a Tomlar he butchered or a bear or wild deer that made the blunder of getting too close to his cabin. If he got hungry enough, he would go out and find a deer or a bear to provide substantial food for the late winter.

The bear and deer meat were dried and cured almost like jerky. When put in a soup with wild mountain potatoes, mushrooms, wild onions, and assortments of wildflowers and greens.

The food Lingraw Arginin tasted amazingly well, and the tea helped hit the spot and quench thirst.

Lingraw Arginin explained to Maki Zorthun, "We have to boil all the water you drink otherwise you may get sick."

"I don't mind drinking boiled water," Maki Zorthun stated as the quietly ate their meal including some dried crackers made from mountain potatoes.

Lingraw Arginin listened to the radio while they ate their meal catching up on all the global events and hearing about turmoil in the world, usually manifested by despot leaders always attempting imperialistic expansion.

After the meal was completed, Lingraw Arginin stated, "We need to go out and chop some wood to make sure we'll have plenty in the future."

"Alright, I can probably help chop some wood." Maki Zorthun responded.

As they were leaving the house with Lingraw Arginin carrying a rope coiled around his body and a large axe, he made the comment, "Two of my most important items I own is this nice heavy-duty rope and this large axe that helps me keep warm in the winter."

They walked about a quarter mile from the home where Lingraw Arginin was clearing an area of trees so he could have better visibility towards the trail that came near his cabin to spot Frontiersmen and strangers approaching.

Lingraw Arginin had very strong muscles living as an outdoorsman in the far reaches of a forest. He quickly approached the tree he had singled out for harvesting. After sitting the rope down, he went to one side of the tree and started cutting away to make sure the tree would fall in the direction he wanted.

"I've sharpened the blade on this axe so it will cut nicely today."

Lingraw Arginin was an expert lumberjack and had hired on with lumber companies in the past to help harvest trees, so he knew the most efficient ways to fell a tree. To the tree it was death by a thousand cuts. Lingraw Arginin cut out chunks of lumber paying attention to wind direction. After chopping away nonstop thirty minutes, Lingraw went to the opposite side of the tree and began chopping a notch, there as well.

Lingraw Arginin then asked Maki Zorthun, "Please walk about 100 feet away from the tree in a cleared area so you will not possibly get injured when the tree finally falls over."

As soon as Lingraw Arginin saw Maki Zorthun was far enough away he put those final cuts in the side the tree would fall towards. Finally, the tree fell over and landed horizontally near where Lingraw Arginin stood.

"Alright, you can come back here," Lingraw Arginin said.

As Maki Zorthun approached, Lingraw Arginin was already at work starting to chop away at the branches that also added to the fuel harvested. After a dozen branches were chopped nicely off the main tree trunk, Lingraw piled the branches up and tied one end of the rope to them, he then created a harness out of one of the tree's branches he tied the rope too.

Lingraw then said to Maki Zorthun, "We are going to drag these branches down to the house. You get on one side of the tree branch, and I'll be on the other side, and we'll drag these down to the house where we will cut them down further."

Moments later, just as if they were a team of horses, they drug the pile of tree branches down near the cabin where a makeshift carpenter's table was set up to allow further work on the tree branches in a more comfortable position.

There were piles for everything including bark and pine needles. The tree branches were cut up into really good size logs for the fire pace and subsequently piled up where they would cure and dry out for months. Next winter these portions of tree branches would be a source of fuel for the fireplace.

Now they went back up the hill and cut off a ten-foot section of the tree trunk and tied the rope to it and the makeshift pulling rig the two of them would use to drag the log to the cabin where they could work on it.

Lingraw Arginin had some steel wedges he pounded down into tree trunks to split them into ten-foot beams. If the tree trunk was significant, it would be split into four parts. The idea was to get them small enough to where they could be lifted by one person up onto a log housing used to dump in all the chopped-up wood components where they would slowly dry out and become next year's firewood.

Lingraw Arginin would take a sledgehammer and start a steel wedge into the tree trunk. That usually created a notch where another steel wedge could be hammered into the gap which usually loosened up the first. As the process was copied and the wedges worked down the length of the tree trunk log, the gap widened and eventually repeating the process going backwards split the log.

The next two tree trunk halves were quicker to split and then stacked up on a makeshift platform to keep the lumber off the ground to enhance drying. Time passed and a lot of the felled tree was harvested in a similar manner leaving half of it to do tomorrow.

As soon as Lingraw Arginin felt hungry, he said, "It is time to let the Tomlars out of the barn to them to do their business then feed and water them."

The process the Tomlars did in the morning was repeated and soon after the Tomlars were fed and drank all the water they needed, they were slowly finding their places in the barn to lay down and rest and build up heat for the bitter cold night that was coming. Had they been outside in the harsh weather, they would end up wet and ice sheets forming on their backside and with wind chill possibly 40 degrees colder. The barn was obviously a much more pleasant place for the Tomlars to be.

Today was bath day. Lingraw Arginin was looking forward to this and started getting buckets of snow for the tub. He simply dumped the snow in the tub and heated up water by the fireplace. With the fireplace going the room temperature got up to as high as 65 degrees, which for arctic people was quite warm. The temperature of the room slowly helped the snow melt.

Lingraw Arginin had a system. He would heat up a metal bucket of water sitting beside the fireplace and when he felt it was getting really warm, as hot as 120 degrees he dumped the water in the tub that instantly melted a lot of the snow. He then dipped the bucket down into the tub and filled it with water from the tub and sat it next to the fireplace on a rock shelf to heat it up.

Through trades with Frontiersmen and women, Lingraw Arginin built up a supply of nearly a dozen bars of soap. He liked the way he smelled when he was done. After bathing he washed his clothes in the bath water and hung them up on lines near the fireplace to help them dry. He had a change of clothes to put on. Some of his clothes, though sparse, were actual denim jeans imported from the free areas of the planet.

The bath water was systematically being heated up while they had their next meal. Again, it was made from dried meat and dried mountain vegetables and plants. Some of the pine nuts and other ingredients increased the flavor nicely. Salt and pepper were available thanks to barter and trade. The bath water heating took long enough for them to enjoy their mean and take care of business if they needed to freshen up after the meal.

Maki Zorthun enjoyed the privacy she was given on the poop deck, and it seemed to her that perhaps this situation might be tolerable after all until the spring and summer came when she planned to escape and get back to society.

After her trip to the poop deck, it was now bath time. Lingraw Arginin, being the gentleman, he was informed Maki Zorthun she could take the first bath and would thus get the clean water to bath. Lingraw would take the second bath already soapy water from Maki's turn.

At first Maki Zorthun didn't know what to do and realized Lingraw Arginin might look at her and get notions to rape her while she was nude and was frightened. While she was procrastinating Lingraw informed Maki, "If you do not quickly get into the tub, I will have to help you."

"Are you going to look at me while I'm bathing?"

"Absolutely. I consider it my entertainment."

This was the moment of truth. Maki Zorthun would now know what kind of savage Lingraw Arginin really was and she assumed she would be raped at any time so she might as well get it over with.

Maki Zorthun disrobed and sat down in the tub which had a small man-made table next to it with a bar of soap, deer skin wash cloth and a towel to dry off. As she's sitting down in the tub, she knew that Lingraw Arginin saw her body and she would soon be forcibly raped if that's what he wanted to do, and she knew there was nothing she could do to stop it.

Lingraw Arginin enjoyed looking at Maki Zorthun's womanhood, but he was never going to mistreat her. If there ever was going to be any type of intercourse it would have to be mutually desired. Maki Zorthun took her time bathing feeling the wonderful warm water that was perfect for her body temperature.

Lingraw Arginin stood up walking past Maki Zorthun putting great fear in her that the savage act might soon start, but instead he walked over to his makeshift shelf and had some clothes another woman left behind who also thought she was going to escape but instead ran into some Frontiersmen who were not kind and gentle like Lingraw Arginin was and was used in the most disgusting fashion passed around the campfire by the miscreants who took out all their pent up sexual needs on her. He would never divulge that to Maki Zorthun as he didn't want her to suffer with anxiety over the situation, she was now stuck in. He grabbed those spare clothes he thought one day might come in handy and placed them on the small table next to the towel.

"I'm going up to take care of my business. When you are done bathing put those clothes on and we'll wash your clothes after I get done bathing."

To Maki Zorthun's utter surprise Lingraw left the room and went up on the poop deck to do his business and he liked to take his time.

By the time Lingraw was finished taking care of his business and returned into the large one room cabin, Maki Zorthun was dressed and sitting on the side of the bed wondering what was going to happen next.

Lingraw wasted no time in undressing and sitting his clothes aside and barely fit in the large tub and began cleaning himself, first washing his hair then his body. Since the tub was near the fire place the water had remained relatively warm in fifteen minutes Lingraw was finished and stood up using the same towel Maki used to dry himself and put on a change of clothes. He felt much better. Today was a happy day for him.

After Lingraw was dressed he had a couple buckets going up onto the poop deck dumping the bath water that ultimately cleaned the residue off the Shute down to the creek. After a couple trips, the tub was mostly empty, so Lingraw picked it up and dumped the residual water into one of the buckets to take it upstairs and dump.

After that the tub was moved back to a storage location and filled with numerous items to help reduce the congestion of the room. It was suddenly bedtime and Lingraw indicated to Maki Zorthun they would now go to bed. It was a repeat of the previous night with Maki agonizing over Lingraw's snoring until she finally felt compelled to start sleeping and was soon adding to the cacophony of sound that made the Tomlars happy they were near their protectors.

Fully bathed and smelling good the two enjoyed the night's sleep. In due time, light started coming through the plexiglass window in the morning hitting Lingraw in the face and eyes and waking him up. Again, Lingraw tried to get out of bed without waking Maki Zorthun, but his slightest movements caused her trip wires to go off and she was quickly wide away feeling quite satisfied a back-to back night of good sleep happened.

A repeat of the previous day happened. First involved taking care of the Tomlars. Today was an interesting day as up until now, the Tomlars seemed to avoid Maki Zorthun. But today, one of the juvenile Tomlars approached Maki and came up close and started sniffing Maki. Out of reaction just like petting a dog, Maki reached out and petted the young Tomlar who seemed more interested in Maki and gave the appearance it enjoyed the petting. Other Tomlars approached Maki without any apparent fear. They knew the additional snoring the past couple nights were Maki's noise and started thinking she might be a new member of the family.

Maki Zorthun suddenly enjoyed the affection of the Tomlars, but when they were all done taking care of their morning business, they had food on their mind and started moving towards the barn door because they knew Lingraw was preparing their meal and fresh water. As soon as the barn door opened, they made their way inside and if it was filmed, one would detect Tomlars went to their specific location along the feeding trays every day. It was as if they had their territory staked out.

Soon after Lingraw and Maki had their morning meal and listened to the radio a short time, they were back up the hill cutting what was left of the tree trunk in half and hauling the two sections down to the work area and splitting the logs into four pieces.

Lingraw's cabin was built with logs that were slightly modified on two opposite sides to give a flat edge to accommodate better placement and insulation.

Not far from where the cabin/barn was built the side of the hill was exposed after a landslide. The Difland Mountain people and

Frontiersmen knew based on explorers that came through the area, some of the calcified material found in large quantities on the side of the area exposed with landslides could be heated up with a fire to a very hot temperature and used as an ingredient later for a mix producing extraordinary insulator as well as survive weather over generations.

Building the log home was an engineering challenge and primitive minds came up with innovative procedures. It was backbreaking work but building the cabin to last generations would well be worth it and there were plenty of trees around in this plush forest area.

The Cabin had to have a strong foundation log laid down in trenches served that purpose. Bags full of rocks brought up from the stream nearby helped to greatly lock in place the logs made from big tree trunks. Ingenious leveling tricks were used simply by utilizing gravity to ensure everything was built level.

In order to build a tall building and get the logs into position, many yards of dirt from the hillside were dragged in large bags made from deer skins elevating the dirt to the sides of the building on each layer of logs brought in allowing the next layer of logs to be installed simply by dragging them in place. The sides of the building and the dirt mound and ramp slowly grew as the log cabin grew in height.

The wall in the middle of the building separating the barn from the living quarters allowed great support for the very sturdy roof that went up last built using split logs and filled in with the calcified cement like mixture, to create water tightness and keep the cold winter out. This was a multi-year project, but after the first year with a temporary roof put on, Lingraw easily was able to survive the winter since he had the wisdom to make sure the fireplace was completed before winter set in. Harvesting the trees for the log cabin produced large piles of debris that became excellent firewood for the winter.

The dirt mounds on over half of the log cabin remained. The surfaces of the logs in this area were coated with the calcified mixtures ultimately creating a moisture barrier and protected the logs, thus there was no reason to remove the dirt which acted as a huge insulator helping to keep the building warm in the winter.

The front of the log cabin that had the door to the barn and the door to the living space, had very elaborate doors installed using primitive tools and methods, but they worked extremely well and when shut had a good dear skin seal to keep out the cold air. In due time two windows were installed allowing in sunlight for the barn and the living spaces. Habitability was thus assured.

The roof made from split planks and sealed with the calcified mixture heat treated was very rugged and would withstand high winds from any storm. The living quarters and the barn area all had split plank floors cemented in place with the calcified mixture, allowing a very clean environment where people could live in relative cleanliness despite being in the back woods. Training the Tomlars to go outdoors to defecate was a huge time savor as there usually was never a mess to clean up.

Lingraw had Maki do some of the wood splitting and chopping this day. He would gradually work her up in due time but didn't want to overwork her early on as he realized she would eventually grow into that outdoors person, or in the summer attempt to escape. At this point he had no idea how she would change if any.

Maki Zorthun didn't have a hairbrush or a comb or anything to do for her hair. As Lingraw was watching her chop some wood he remembered he had a sack of things he collected over the years and suddenly remembered he had a few things in there he could give to Maki to help her with her hair and more importantly, there was a thing called a toothbrush with some commercial paste to go with it.

Lingraw would never use that stuff so when they went indoors, and she sat down on the bed staring at him wondering what was next he went to a shelve where he knew he had those items stored for a rainy day or possibly a trade with Frontiersmen and grabbed it and walked over to the bed that was currently made up thanks to Maki's help and dumped the contents on the bed

"There are some things here that you might want to use. You can have any of it and I'll clear off a shelf for you to put your items."

Maki Zorthun started looking at the items on the bed and suddenly felt some humanity and the thought she could do something simple like comb or brush her hair made her quite happy. She saw something else in the pile of items that got her fancy real fast, a pair of scissors. Maki didn't like ultra-long hair and now knew she could give herself haircuts. Small things like this out in the middle of a forest can be uplifting to someone. Another interesting artifact was a small mirror and a compact case with mirror and powder. Another item that Lingraw had no idea what its purpose was a red lipstick.

***

CHAPTER TWO
Creating a Remote Viewer

L ife slowly continued in the modest and most backwards manner. Maki Zorthun was a cultured woman. As a concert fiðluleikari (violinist) she was used to dressing up and looking like a princess. Unfortunately, Maki Zorthun was pretty and vulnerable, and she was tagged to satisfy rich men who worked directly for the despot Dictator Illtnaut.

When Maki Zorthun refused to give her body to the creep, one of her special friends with connections with the security apparatus loyal to the Dictator Illtnaut warned her she had to disappear, or the *apparatus* would grab her, and she would end up out in the countryside at a private Dacha working on her backside whether she liked it or not.

Maki Zorthun virtually had hours to spare to go into hiding. While she was in hiding is when she got tied in with the group scaping that blundered into a region where the Frontiersmen killed first and asked questions later to protect their meager lives.

Lingraw Arginin had no idea he had an exquisite woman living with him now. But he enjoyed her company and liked to watch her bathe but never forced himself on her. He was polite and respectful towards Maki Zorthun who slowly grew appreciation for his decent behavior, though it didn't please her that he watched her bathe. But as long as he continued showing restraint and decency, it's the least she could suffer to stay safe and well-treated.

Another development was the Tomlars grew affection towards Maki Zorthun. Tomlars are emotional animals with facial recognition as good as birds. As the days went by more and more of the Tomlars demanded Maki's attention and the warm-hearted woman was happy to give them all the affection they sought.

What Maki Zorthun didn't know was Lingraw had remote viewing with the Tomlars and thus knew their emotional peaks and idiosyncrasies. He thus knew all her interactions with the Tomlars and how they took a distinct liking for her. Maki didn't know this, but they brought her into their family. They cherished her.

The routine didn't deviate for almost four months, then finally the snow was melting, and larger patches of ground were exposed, and the spring green slowly emerged. The Tomlars really loved this time as they went out foraging getting some of the new growth that was appearing and supplementing their diet. It also meant they were not cooped up in the barn most of the time.

This is when Maki suddenly started to learn about the remote viewing as about an hour before dark, Lingraw would walk out to the exact location where the Tomlars were grazing, and he would tell them to follow him back to the home. They expected this and knew he had some additional food for them to which they looked forward to. They were getting their water from the creek so delivering them water each day became less and less a burden.

In a few weeks spring flowers started blooming and Maki was taken back by the splendid beauty she now saw that didn't know existed. It had a surreal effect on her, and she was ovulating and suddenly feeling horny. She wasn't a virgin, but she didn't sleep around and could count on one hand the number of sex partners she had in her entire life. She wasn't well experienced, but her heart was damaged a couple times by Noble Savages that gave her a false impression of what their true intentions were.

Maki's heart was hard, and she didn't give it out recklessly. But she was feeling a strange attraction to Lingraw that was rough around the corners but sweet on the inside. He couldn't read, but he acquired several books though trade with explorers and Frontiersmen and thought one day he would learn how to read, but he never had a teacher. Suddenly he had a teacher, and asked Maki's, help. It was during those training sessions that Maki grew even closer to Lingraw.

That evening afternoon when Lingraw was heading out to get the Tomlars and bring them back to the barn to feed them, Maki made an excuse why she couldn't go, relating to her digestive track. While Lingraw was away she put together a candlelight dinner and found a radio station that played soft Fiðlu and

Klavier music. She had everything prepared just in time for Lingraw and the Tomlars returning. The Tomlars and Lingraw had never heard these sounds before, but they did sound rather appealing as they approached the cabin that had the barn door and the cabin door open allowing the sound to escape and flood the valley.

It was almost a spiritual experience for Lingraw hearing the strange music sounds that he would investigate as soon as he put the food out for the Tomlars who all seemed rather pleased hearing the music.

After giving the Tomlars food he went into the cabin living spaces and was now mesmerized looking at the candlelight dinner and the woman wearing red lipstick with her hair made up into a classic style that young lovers often did to enthuse their mates. Lingraw approached Maki very slowly, totally absorbed in her exquisite beauty.

Lingraw knew she put on a candlelight dinner that conveyed there was more to it. Lingraw decided he would allow Maki to conduct affairs because he was too emotionally twisted now to know what to do. He was like a fish out of water flopping around. The almighty heavens had reached down and touched him somehow. He knew there were absolutely no princesses anywhere in the valley or anywhere in these mountains, and here was staring at one.

"Please have a seat so I can serve you your dinner."

"In a few days prior, Lingraw had shared some of his ferments with Maki because he was feeling good, and Maki knew where Lingraw kept the stock and had a glass of ferments for him next to his plate with very nice-looking food prepared in ways he never seen before.

Lingraw sat down and tasted the food and took a drink of the ferments and then suddenly felt he could talk. He was no longer in a trance.

"This food tastes good. Thank you for this wonderful meal."

"It's my pleasure Lingraw."

Lingraw knew his remote viewing could work bi-directional. While he was eating and enjoying the fabulous meal that Maki made for him, he remotely viewed the Tomlars and quickly noted every one of them were done eating, laying on the floor with their heads pointed to the door wondering about the source of the music. Lingraw then gave all the Tomlars the vision he was looking at the beautiful Maki.

The Tomlars felt Lingraw's happiness, and they also had the pleasure centers of their own brains now impacted by this vision. The combination of music and Lingraw's vision and sound created a strong quintessential feeling in each of the Tomlars. They collectively wished they could reach out to Maki this minute and show her their love.

This was quickly turning into a magical night. As soon as Maki saw Lingraw finished eating his meal she said, "I will take care of all this in the morning, for now I want you to go to bed with me."

Lingraw went to bed like he usually did, dressed to keep warm but now that it was warming up, he didn't need to wear so many layers to bed and Maki surprised him by saying, "Take off all your clothes. I will keep you warm tonight."

Lingraw in a state of awe meekly complied with Maki's instructions and laid down in bed nude starting to feel cold and hoping Maki would come quickly and put the covers over them. And she did.

They were soon lying in bed facing each other and the candle on the table was still burning so they could look into each other's eyes.

"Do you know how to kiss a woman?"

"I've never kissed before."

"Let me teach you."

In teaching Lingraw basic reading skills, Maki had made an impression on him that she knew what she was doing, and he was her willing student and tried to do as she asked him.

Now Maki kissed Lingraw's lips and she had brushed her teeth and used the paste he provided her, and her breath smelled very sweet, and she made it a point not to eat much to alter that scent. She wanted the best she could provide in such primitive conditions.

Maki's red lips were quite compelling. It changed Maki's persona completely and the kiss sent a lightning rod through Lingraw.

Lingraw had never experienced this before and the Tomlars were sensing everything and enjoying this expression of love their human family members were expressing. Every single Tomlar loved Maki with all their hearts. She was their beautiful sister they would always cherish now.

The next big shock that hit Lingraw was when Maki grabbed his manhood and squeezed it quickly making it rock hard. She knew what to do and took charge of the situation.

"Just lay back and relax, I will show you how to do this."

Maki now knowing for a fact Lingraw had no sexual experience climbed on top of him and took his rock-hard manliness and inserted it into her very wet and well lubricated womanhood and slowly started making love to Lingraw who very quickly started feeling an intensity like he never felt before in his entire life time. Within two minutes he exploded inside Maki giving a huge release of gratification.

Maki could feel the warmness of Lingraw deposit and the abundance of it. She was filled, mission accomplished.

Maki had her own gratification triggered by Lingraw who had lost control of his body as his motor functions were completely in a parallele universe from his cognitive awareness.

Because of the huge psychological release, Lingraw and Maki both succumbed to a neural quiescence and were soon sleeping holding each other in their arms.

From this day forward there were many more such episodes of emotional and physical bonding. Lingraw now knew Maki owned his heart. The Tomlar family was completely on Maki's side and always felt good to be around her.

In due time as Maki suspected would happen, she became pregnant. As she's teaching Lingraw reading she explained her maternal situation and what was going to happen in the not-too distant future. Lingraw was now in a totally different psychology as this woman who came out of nowhere on her trek to freedom just turned his life upside down.

Their emotional bonding became complete. Maki was now irrevocably in Lingraw's life. And she had her plans too. She knew he could get her to freedom on the other side of the mountains and if he agreed she would help him adjust to that new world and help educate him in ways that would allow him to survive in that rat race and live a life of freedom with modern conveniences.

Maki Zorthun also knew she did not want to make such a trek until the child was at least a couple years old and able to cope with the journey.

This was a dream come true love. It was an impossible love, but it happened. Maki Zorthun became Lingraw's willing partner and always did what he requested in a cheerful manner and as such completely seduced Lingraw and she had the backup of all the Tomlars who could get into his head if they wanted.

Maki Zorthun's pregnancy advanced and the day was coming it would be time to deliver the baby. Maki, being well educated, explained to Lingraw what he had to do and had the scissors on the table next to her bed to cut the umbilical cord of the baby and to wrap it up right away and she would then feed the child.

Some women are not predisposed for childbirth. Maki was one of them. It took her last breath to deliver the baby and a moment later she was dead.

It took Lingraw several hours to realize Maki Zorthun had died in childbirth. He was devastated. Worse yet, how would the baby survive?

The Tomlars were also devastated. They precisely knew the moment Maki Zorthun's spirit left her. They too were all very saddened by her departure.

It was due to Lingraw's remote viewing and the ability to the Tomlars to feed back to him, they provided the solution. A couple of the Tomlars now had young ones of their own, but they felt they had sufficient milk to share it with Maki Zorthun's baby. And so, the child survived and flourished.

Maki Zorthun didn't have enough time to really educate Lingraw before her death, but she taught him enough to where he could teach the child the very basics. He knew that Maki would want her daughter educated so he went about it the best he could. He slowly raised the child he named Tavishien Arginin.

Maki Zorthun was buried next to the tree stump she first helped cut down after she arrived. This was a special place for Lingraw as it signified the essence of the beginning of their relationship.

Life went on and the girl slowly grew up.

***

28

CHAPTER THREE
War Games

The mountainous area of Difland where Lingraw Arginin lived in was a disputed territory, but seldom fought over due to the difficulty of conducting warfare in that mountainous region. Nevertheless, the Tartarland military conducted training exercises in the area, sometimes hoping to get the Western Alliance involved in live fire combat where they felt they had a strategic advantage over the Alliance in numbers and location of nearby bases.

The tyrannical Dictator Illtnaut shoved his military into this operation somewhat ill-prepared. There was a lack of food and shelter, even though it was not in the deep of winter where such remote conditions would create cataclysmic failures due to the lack of logistic support. The Tartar soldiers had no option but to rummage for food, sometimes that included exploiting and mistreating Frontiersmen in the process.

Lingraw had no idea these horrible excuses for human beings were anywhere close or he would never have sent his daughter Tavishien Arginin out with the Tomlars by herself that morning. This time of year, the Tomlars ventured further and further away from the log cabin and barn as there was untouched vegetation the further, they traveled.

***

There were two delightful images that Tartar soldier Rockovnar observed through his high-power binoculars: a small herd of Tomlars and a young pretty blonde headed woman that appeared to be a teenager. Rockovnar and his filthy dirty disgusting group had been foraging for food for several days and were on the verge of starvation. Due to piss-poor planning the batteries in their hand carried navigation equipment had run down and they had no idea where the hell they were. The Tartar soldiers realized they were hopelessly lost and on the verge of starvation.

Rockovnar and his five men worked out a plan to surround the girl, capture her and butcher a couple of her Tomlars and barbecue them. After they filled their bellies with that wonderful Tomlar meat they would then pass the young girl around the campfire and molest her.

It all unfolded quickly and had it not been for remote viewing Lingraw would never have known what became of his daughter. He immediately got his weapon and plenty of ammunition and took off running in the general direction where he knew Tavishien was located receiving her pleas for help and the Tomlars were also in terrible emotions watching a couple of their brothers get killed by the vicious men.

It took a while for Lingraw get to the location and approach safely and from a distance. Lingraw could see there were six heavily armed men, and his daughter was in her last stages of consciousness as one of the evil men decided he had enough of her screaming and hit her over the head with his rifle butt to knock her out. Just as he stood up bragging to his buddies, "I shut the little bitch up," a bullet went through the middle of his head, and he fell over dead.

Seeing his daughter nude and the man hitting her savagely really upset Lingraw. Having exposed his position with the first shot he was on the move and the fact they were now chasing after Lingraw meant his daughter might be left by herself and if she came to, she could put on her clothes and attempt to escape.

These were capable military people, having experienced live combat in the past, were efficient killers. Had they been facing the typical Western Alliance soldier, in a short period of time, they could have tracked him down and killed him.

But they had two things going against them. Lingraw was a much better shot and could hit them at longer range, plus he knew where he was and every possible escape route to maneuver around as he lured them systematically into killing zone traps.

Some of the surviving Tomlars soon joined Lingraw and they would be at risk, so he directed them to a safe area to remain until all this was over.

Tavishien was unconscious and now in a coma. She was in bad shape and needed medical treatment and Lingraw knew of such a place, but it was thirty miles away. He could get her there, but it would take a couple days and she might not last. He was very saddened by the extreme viciousness these Tarter soldiers exhibited towards a helpless child. He would make them pay and the very last one he would wound then torture him in a way he deserved by cutting off his manliness after he had him bound and tied up.

Lingraw knew a lot about these men as he was sensing them almost in a telepathic means. Even though they were a distance away, they became close enough a time or two to Lingraw's hiding spots where he was able to sense their Aura which then allowed him full remote viewing of them. He thus knew exactly where they were and where they were heading.

Lingraw would wait in ambush and as soon as one of them got into a kill zone, he would take out just the one person and not stick around for another shot. In doing so he became invisible and as time went by the men chasing him became more and more desperate as they were watching their buddies get killed one by one. By the time they started thinking of using the girl as a human shield, it was too late. Lingraw had them relocated several miles away and they had no idea where they left her behind. It would take them hours in the heavy forest to relocate her for that purpose.

Finally, Lingraw nailed four of the six men leaving just the two who considered just walking back to their temporary camp and hopefully lose the person shooting at them in the process. They had no compass or radio to call for help. They truly were on their own in the most hostile area they could imagine.

Just before the two men turned to go back to their camp one of them received a bullet in the head and fell over dead. That left one person, Rockovnar who made that fateful decision in molesting the girl when they had just killed a Tomlar and ate it, all of them would still be alive now. Doing what they did to Tavishien cost them their lives and Rockovnar was in fear because he knew he was facing a deadly opponent who just killed all his men.

Rockovnar didn't know what to do but he knew back at the camp all his survival equipment was there. He had to get back there, or he too would soon be a dead man. Rockovnar also needed the reloads as he had shot most of his rounds and his soldiers were almost out of ammunition, so they didn't offer much in rearming.

Now there was a running gun battle between Rockovnar and Lingraw who was showing himself just enough to get Rockovnar to fire shots wildly and run him out of ammunition. Lingraw wanted to capture him alive and make him pay for what he and his men did to his daughter.

The moment of truth came as Rockovnar wildly fired his weapon and suddenly realized he was out of bullets. He then started to run back in a panic towards what he thought the camp was and had to go through some heavy brush. While pushing himself along through the heavy brush he became suddenly unconscious as Lingraw nailed him over his head with his rifle butt.

With a few feet of rope Lingraw always took with him out into the forest in case he captured an animal to tie him up to bring home for slaughter and butchering, Rockovnar was quickly tied and bound and unconscious.

Lingraw threw Rockovnar over his shoulder just like a fireman's carry and called all his Tomlars to guide him to precisely where Tavishien was laying nude in the camp.

It took a half an hour to reach the camp where Lingraw dropped Rockovnar down on the ground which jolted him back to consciousness. Rockovnar quickly realized he was bound good and the hope for escape was extremely low.

Lingraw reached down and checked his daughter, he could see she was bleeding from her vagina where she had been raped by all six men in the most savage manner. She was alive but unconscious. She desperately needed help.

Lingraw put Tavishien clothes back on and cleaned her up using water from several of the Tarter canteens. He knew he needed to leave right away to get her help but when he saw what those evil bastards had done to his daughter Tavishien, he felt obligated to render justice to Rockovnar who he did not know his name or his rank. He pulled out his hunting knife that was very sharp, walked over to Rockovnar, undid the belt to his military trousers and unbuttoned them.

Rockovnar didn't quite know what to expect, at first, he thought that he might just be stealing his clothes. Then Lingraw grabbed the man's penis and cut it off and threw it into the fire where it started to burn. Rockovnar went into shock and was slowly bleeding to death. Lingraw cut Rockovnar into a few more spots to make sure he quickly lost a lot of blood and would never regain consciousness.

The Tartars had rope canvas and some polls in their camp used for mounting weapons or surveillance equipment. Lingraw knew he had a long walk ahead of him to get his daughter some medical treatment and informed the Tomlars they would pull the sling like gurney he built out of the materials on hand to carry her the distance. He would thus be free to use his weapon if necessary to protect them from further danger or any other military people. The long trek began.

***

CHAPTER FOUR
Rescue

Western Alliance INTEL people were ten miles away being vectored into the area where the six Tartars were located. These six Tartars traveled almost Fifteen miles further west than where they were to stop and do surveillance and make sure no Western Alliance troops were around to observe their operation. But when they went too far, they crossed over some trip wires that got the Western Alliance interested in why they were way beyond the artificial border between the two military powers. Hence, they were presumably behind enemy lines and didn't know it.

The Western Alliance scouts were going through the forested area heading toward an area where drones had picked up the infrared from the campfire that had started to barbecue one of the Tomlars they butchered. Eventually the drones detected Lingraw and the herd of Tomlars pulling the makeshift gurney. Through drone video they could see a man was armed and the person in the makeshift gurney did not appear to have consciousness.

The decision was made to fly a VTOL craft out to the caravan and survey what was going on. They had recorded gunshots with their big ear system and knew there had been some fighting in the vicinity of where they were interested.

Lingraw had seen flying machines before and while Maki Zorthun was teaching him how to read, one of the books had a picture on the cover of a flying machine and thus they had a discussed the VTOL.

When the VTOL aircraft flew out and landed near Lingraw he didn't react as he understood such things existed. A couple cleanly dressed individuals got out of the VTOL and approached Lingraw.

"Good afternoon, sir, if you have a few spare minutes we would like to talk to you."

"I do not have time to talk, I need to get my daughter to some medical help right away."

"We can take her; would you mind coming with us and answer a few questions?"

"Sure, if you can get my daughter some medical help, I'll do whatever I can to help you."

"What about your animals there?"

"I'll tell them to go back to my cabin and wait for me."

"Will they be, okay?"

"Yes, it's summertime there is water near my cabin and plenty of food for them to forage."

"You can talk to your animals?"

"Yes, as soon as we take down this sling all of them will walk back to my cabin."

Within moments the kind men helped carry Tavishien to the VTOL which had plenty of room for her and Lingraw.

The pilot reported to the base camp the situation and they were flying directly to the Western Alliance medical compound set up to support the pending operation.

The doctors did a quick triage and asked Lingraw what happened.

Lingraw then informed the doctors all the grizzly details including watching them hit his daughter over the head with a rifle butt.

That was vital information because they immediately did a CATSCAN and discovered Tavishien had a severe trauma to the head and was now in a Coma. Lingraw also informed them how the

Tartar's repeatedly raped his daughter, and she needed some medical attention in that area as well.

Doctor Hannah Barrymore started crying when she commenced cleaning up Tavishien and determining what kind of surgery she might need to repair her severely damaged cervix.

Professional INTEL officers debriefed Lingraw on how he and his daughter escaped from the Tartar military members.

"I was never captured, but they did capture my daughter. I killed them one by one until they were all dead then proceeded to attempt get my daughter to medical help when the VTOL came down and met us."

"There were no other Tartars around?"

"No, just the six."

"Do you know why they were there?"

"They were lost. They had no idea where they were."

"How do you know that?"

"I'm a remote viewer."

"What do you mean, remote viewer?"

"I know what they are seeing or hearing."

"How do you do that?"

"It's something I learned from my father in order to be an effective Tomlar herder."

In due time, the INTEL people got reports from the doctors who corroborated everything Lingraw said happened to his daughter. They then asked Lingraw if he would guide them to the camp where the Tartars had been.

"I want to be here when my daughter wakes up."

"The female nurse will be by her bedside while we are gone. According to the doctors they may have to keep her in a coma for a while during her brain healing. She's sedated now and will be sleeping while we are gone."

"Alright then."

Soon Lingraw was traveling for the second time in his life in a VTOL. The step up in technology was huge.

With Lingraw guiding them it did not take long to find the camp. The remnants of the barbecue pit still burning also helped to locate it with the infrared sensors. The VTOL landed 20 yards from the campfire in an open area. Once out of the VTOL, Lingraw was able to remote view what was left of his Tomlars now waiting inside the barn. Some of the survivors had been trained to shut the doors. An outside view indicated the place was shut up and secure. The Tomlars could also open the door if they had to get out and make a nature call.

The Western Alliance troops could see that Rockovnar was dead, and his penis had been cut off.

"Did you do this to the man?"

"You saw what he did to my daughter right?"

"I suppose we should bury him."

"I have a better idea."

"What's your idea?"

"We can throw him into the fire it along with the Tomlar carcass they didn't barbecue and throw on some more firewood and let the fire take care of him and all the debris."

"That works for me, its best we get rid of the evidence because some of my superiors might otherwise want to charge you for a crime of dismembering the soldier."

"Fine."

"Help me carry him over to the fire."

Soon they piled on everything except the spare ammo they departed a short time later. With all their camping equipment blankets and sleeping bags, a good size fire was soon burning up the Tartar Soldier body and the Tomlar carcass with all their other equipment including expensive radios and navigation devices.

"You said you killed five other men. Would you like to take us to them?"

"They are scattered all over the forest and it would be impossible for you to get your craft anywhere near them."

"How did you kill them?"

"A single gunshot wound to the head."

"Can't you show us just one of the bodies?"

"There was one that is probably close to where you can land the VTOL craft, but we'll have to walk a half a mile."

"That's not a problem, we are willing to go."

Lingraw showed the Western Alliance men to the best landing zone nearest the last man he killed leaving Rockovnar as the sole survivor.

It didn't take long for Lingraw to cover the half mile with the INTEL guys to the kill zone. The body was there unmolested by wild animals, but there was a bear lurking in the shadows nearby that was going to partake in a fabulous meal until the group came upon him and scared him away.

When they came up to the man, the leading INTEL officer asked, "Did this man rape your daughter?"

"They all did. I was too far away to stop them, but I saw him take his turn and he was the one who hit her on the head."

"Alright," the INTEL man said then pulled out a knife and started cutting some of his clothes away near the man's penis.

"What are you doing?" Lingraw asked.

"I'm getting the DNA evidence to substantiate you statements these men raped your daughter to make sure some prosecutor is disarmed and doesn't try to go after you for killing them. Based on the doctor's reports, they all probably deserved what you did to them."

"Sure."

As soon as the INTEL man cut the blood-stained briefs off the man that had obvious Tavishien's vaginal fluids and bleeding results, put them into a plastic bag to take back as evidence, but he was already convinced the dirty rotten bastard did the evil deal.

"Can you take us to your cabin so we can look around?"

"Sure, I don't have much there but if you want to see it, I'll gladly show you."

"Yes, we want to see it and take a couple pictures if you don't mind."

"The Tomlars will be glad to see me. They were shook-up seeing a couple of them killed and my daughter raped."

"Alright, us get into the VTOL."

Soon the men were flying to Lingraw's cabin that had a good landing zone making it easy for the pilot.

Once they all got out of the VTOL, Lingraw said, "I'm going to go have my Tomlars come outside and see you and me to help them calm down a bit."

As soon as Lingraw opened the door to the barn he directed all the Tomlars to come outside so they could meet his guests.

The Tomlars slowly came outside still somewhat nervous but feeling good that Lingraw was there and acting normally.

They also reacted by seeing everyone was calm and friendly.

One of the INTEL guys approached one of the Tomlars who stood there not moving because Lingraw informed him via the remote viewer ability to remain calm, the man is friendly and would not hurt him.

The Intel guy started petting the Tomlar and feeling good about the animal. The other Tomlars approached out of curiosity. While this was all ongoing the INTEL men were photographing everything and soon Lingraw asked, "Would you like to go look inside, and perhaps have a drink of my ferments for getting my daughter to the doctors quickly.

The INTEL man felt for Lingraw because he knew his daughter had been terribly treated by the six apparent sub-human individuals who were despicable in the eyes of society for the crime they committed. At this point in time, he agreed to have the ferment as a way to show respect as it affected him emotionally knowing the trauma Tavishien experienced.

In the INTEL world it's always a two-man rule, the agent would not go into the cabin alone even though he felt no fear, it was simply policy, so another man went with him indoors and they were invited to sit down at the table that had two chairs.

Lingraw poured the two INTEL men each a half cup of the ferments and poured himself one as well and they all drank it together in a most somber manner.

"Would it be okay if we take a few pictures of the inside of your cabin?"

"Sure, I have nothing to hide. I'm not rich, but I'm happy."

The lead INTEL person nodded at the other who had a small handheld device like a cell phone and quickly photographed the inside of the cabin, then nodded at his boss to indicate he got it all.

The INTEL man then said, "We should probably leave now to get you back to your daughter."

"All right, I'll tell the Tomlars to go back in the barn and we can leave."

"Who's going to take care of the Tomlars if you do not come back for a while?"

"I've trained them to open and close the barn door. They will let themselves out tomorrow and go graze and drink water from the stream then let themselves back in the barn at the end of the day when they are ready."

The men exited the cabin. There were no locks because it was pointless as there really wasn't anything of value inside the home to steal.

Standing by the Cabin, Lingraw gave the commands to his Tomlar herd and just like clockwork one of them went over and opened the door and the rest followed him in. Once the Tomlars were all inside the barn, Lingraw said, "We can leave now. They are all situated for the night."

In a few moments all the men were back aboard the VTOL, and it took off heading back to their base and the hospital.

Back at the hospital, the staff approached Lingraw and said, "We know you had to travel to get here through the forest and we have arranged for you to have a bath and a shower and if you want, we can give you a haircut. We'll launder your clothes, and they will be available tomorrow."

Lingraw was cleaned up significantly and did not look anything like the way he arrived after the shave and haircut, he looked completely civilized in the change of clothes.

The next problem was where he would sleep. He didn't want to leave his daughter so after a little wrangling, the medical team brought in an extra bed for Lingraw to sleep in so he could be next to his daughter.

Just as expected, the DNA analysis came back the next day, and the dead man had substantial amounts of Tavishien's DNA in the blood and mixed in with her vaginal liquids deposited in his underwear. It was now confirmed what Lingraw alleged, these men gang raped his daughter and almost killed her in the process. No prosecutor would ever touch on such a case.

The six missing men simply became another mystery in the Tartarland military history.

Tavishien stayed in a coma for eighteen months. The doctors and nurses almost gave up on her and were about to suggest to Lingraw he allow them to send her to Tomorrowland. Of course, that was something he would never agree to.

At the end of eighteen months Lingraw's hair had turned completely gray but his crystal blue eyes remained the same along with most of his facial features. Then suddenly, Tavishien awakened and saw she was in an unusual situation in a strange place she did not recognize and an old gray-haired man sitting next to her weeping because they were just about to turn off life support and call it quits.

"Who are you?"

Lingraw rose immediately when he heard Tavishien's voice. He was utterly stunned. SHE WAS ALIVE!

When Tavishien saw Lingraw she recognized his face and his eyes and said, "Papa is that you?"

Lingraw stood up and walked over ang grabbed Tavishien and started crying profusely.

"Yes, my dear Tavishien this is Papa."

Tavishien then embraced her Papa, feeling so much better coming out of the nightmare she experienced. But at the very end of the nightmare an angel appeared and said, "Tavishien, you now must go back to your world. Your Papa needs you now more than ever. If you do not go back now, he will be heartbroken for the rest of his life."

That's when Tavishien woke up and here he was in a strange place she had never seen before and because of the neuro monitors and other instruments monitoring her activity, suddenly doctors and nurses came into the room. Doctor Hannah Barrymore, who first treated her and stayed on for eighteen months to make sure she was given a chance at life now had tears streaming down. This was one act in her life she would be grateful to the graces of God to help this poor woman who had endured such a terrible trauma.

During those eighteen months, Lingraw spent most of his time back at his cabin with the Tomlars looking out for them and regrowing the herd to replace those lost in the vicious attacks.

The Western Alliance gave Lingraw a battery powered radio they could contact him with, or he could call them in case conditions changed, and up to just a few moments ago they had given up hope then suddenly for no explained reasons, Tavishien came back to life, though weak and in serious need of some physical therapy. Sadly, the Tartar soldiers had ruined her uterus and she now could never have children. Her whole life was now irrevocably altered.

There would be no discussions today of anything of importance, but Lingraw explained to Tavishien: "You have been sleeping for a long time and you were in a coma. You are in a medical facility called a hospital where these people are helping you with your physical issues."

"Papa, I had a terrible dream."

"Tavishien, we are here with you, and you are safe, and you will be well taken care of."

"Where are the Tomlars?"

"They are home and patiently waiting for you to return."

"The Tomlars contacted me in my dream."

"What did they say?"

"They wanted me to wake up and come back to them."

"Why didn't you wake up?"

"I was scared to wake up. People were hurting me and as long as I stayed sleeping, I was safe."

"Then why did you wake up?"

"Papa, you may not believe it."

"Tavishien I will believe anything you tell me. You have always been accurate in everything you ever said to me."

"Papa an Angel, just like in the book you showed me, came to me and told me I needed to wake up that people needed me."

"I'm glad the Angel came to you because I really missed having you with me."

"Are we going home soon? I want to see the Tomlars."

"The doctors said you need to stay here for a while to get rehabilitation."

"I want to see the Tomlars to thank them for saving me."

"I'll talk to the men who give me transportation back to the cabin if when I come visit you the next time to bring one of the Tomlars with me."

"Alright Papa, when you go home one of those Tomlars will approach you, bring that one."

"In the past eighteen months, the INTEL people had numerous discussions with Lingraw as they investigated the case further. One of the INTEL specialists had seen a couple cases of the use of remote viewers and studied all the information he could find on the matter. Some of the remote viewers were highly successful, others were dismal failures and some only worked some of the time. There was no rhyme or reason to it and there were no measures they could take to determine if there was a catalyst or something that manifested the successful examples that were far and few.

In discrete checks doing extensive surveillance on Lingraw, the INTEL officer realized there indeed was something going on that could not be explained in any terms that a complicated intelligence agency could cope with. There simply had not been enough successes to suggest this was something worth pursuing. But as the INTEL officer became more and more acquainted with Lingraw who seemed to not have any agenda, preferred to live a simple life on the mountain where conditions were not palatable to most citizens.

This intelligence agent was different. He also accompanied Lingraw out to get the Tomlars to bring back to the barn, and just like Maki Zorthun realized long before her death, there was only one explanation. Lingraw had remote viewer abilities. Lingraw's problem was he was old now and not the kind of person they could integrate into a new program to exploit this remarkable capability. Then the INTEL officer discovered Lingraw had taught his daughter Tavishien remote viewing and according to Lingraw her remote viewing was as powerful as his.

There was never any hope that would develop into a feasible opportunity for the intelligence gatherers, until suddenly Tavishien woke up.

The INTEL officer heard the conversation, plus the room was bugged. All the conversations were recorded in the event something of value was said.

The next day, Lingraw was scheduled to be flown back to his cabin so he could take care of essential business such as preparing for winter approaching. The INTEL official informed the transportation people he would accompany Lingraw to his cabin in the woods. He knew this would be a test. If the one Tomlar went directly to Lingraw, that would give an indication Tavishien did remote viewing and communicated long distances to the Tomlar.

Tavishien had never seen a woman before and only saw drawings her papa made of her mother. Lingraw was a fantastic artist and the herd of Tomlars helped him remember Maki's face and draw it picture perfectly. Doctor Hannah Barrymore had somewhat adopted Tavishien and had a strange resemblance to the pictures Tavishien's father drew of her mother and she was so very nice and sweet and convinced Tavishien that she would take good care of her, and it was important her father go back to the cabin in the woods and prepare for winter.

The trip to the cabin would be a lot shorter than Lingraw imagined. Two VTOLs were flown out and men with chain saws were sent to expedite winter preparation to get Lingraw back to the hospital as soon as possible as this new situation was taking on a life of its own as the Intelligence Officer, a man named Agent Lucika convinced his superiors to allow him to further investigate this remote viewing and find out if there could possibly be useful applications for the future.

As soon as they arrived and Lingraw opened the door to the barn, all the Tomlars walked out and into the area around the barn nibling at the growing plant life that now accelerated expansion in the later stages of summer. But there was one Tomlar that walked directly up to Lingraw and there seemed to be an interaction between the two the INTEL Officers could see but didn't understand.

After that brief episode Lingraw directed the Tomlar to go graze with his brothers and sisters but he would be going on a trip with him in the flying machine. Lingraw turned to the INTEL Officer and said, "I need to take that Tomlar with me when I go back to the hospital. Tavishien communicated with this animal and feels it saved her life and wants to personally thank it."

Agent Lucika then informed Lingraw the work force was there to cut the lumber for him so they could get him back to the hospital today as the doctors felt it would be best if he was near his daughter for the next few days as she is slowly removed from medications and comes fully back to reality.

Lingraw had no objections to the men cutting winter firewood for him and was soon utterly fascinated that in the span of four hours these men created as much firewood as Lingraw did all winter long. They also set up ingenious piles so that firewood was off the ground and would dry in time for use in the winter. By 4:00 P.M. everyone was ready to go back to the base and the hospital.

All the Tomlars were put into the Barn with some ample feed laid out for them which would take several days to eat along with what they got grazing. And just before they took off, Lingraw got into the VTOL and a Tomlar followed him up into it showing no fear. Lingraw thought the animal would behave better if it were laying on his lap, so he situated the animal that way, who showed peacefulness on the entire flight.

The VTOL landed near the hospital at the conclusion of the trip and now there would be a problem figuring out how to take care of the Tomlar. However, that was soon solved as base workers quickly constructed an oversized doghouse where the Tomlar could sleep at night. To their surprise Lingraw insisted on staying with the Tomlar which made Tavishien feel good since she could remotely view the two of them sleeping just outside the window of her hospital room.

The INTEL Officer, Agent Lucika, was fully convinced this remote viewing worked and all he needed to do is figure out how to employ it for his intelligence agency.

***

CHAPTER FIVE
Rehabilitation

D octors and Psychiatrists were teamed up to deal with Tavishien. Once the director of the Intelligence Bureau gave Agent Lucika the go ahead to put efforts into this new experiment. Medical and psychological treatments were given priority to Tavishien almost above any other citizen or official. She was not just VIP she was SVIP. The doctors and the psychiatrists assigned were systematically chosen and briefed, *do not get involved in anything the Intelligence Agency didn't require their* participation.

This *remote viewing experimentation* was going to be severely compartmentalized. The medical team and intelligence support staff were all given cover stories and told to stick with the propaganda and to assume Tavishien and her father would be constantly monitored and recorded.

The medical staff quickly understood if they asked the wrong questions or did what counter to the Intelligence bureau's desires, then planned for uncomfortable future events. Agent Lucika from the Western Alliance Intelligence Bureau was now the conductor and the chief orchestrator of all events surrounding Tavishien in particular, but to some extent her father as well.

A couple days after Tavishien regained consciousness, she was informed she was going to be put in a wheelchair and taken outside for some fresh air.

As soon as Tavishien was wheeled out of the hospital and over to a nice park bench where patients' relatives could sit and unwind after stressful events, here came her father with the Tomlar now on a leash. With all the uncertainty between pedestrians and traffic, Lingraw felt the Tomlar would be safer if he had on the leash and could be controlled.

The Tomlar pulled Lingraw along as it seemed to be utterly in need of

Tavishien's personal affection. It was a grand reunion and the two spent several minutes with Tavishien sobbing and holding the wonderful Tomlar friend who saved her life by understanding it was critically important to notify Lingraw that evil had descended upon Tavishien.

Had Lingraw not showed up as soon as he did to the crime scene the evil bastards would have killed his daughter and put her into a shallow grave since they already got their jollies off and as soon as they had their fill of the Tomlar carcass, moved off into a direction based on the direction of the sun to where they thought friendly forces were bivouacked.

The Tomlar connected all his brothers and sisters and gave reports on the lovely Tavishien. The herd was now happy for the first time in a long time since they now knew Tavishien was alive and well and survived her terrible ordeal.

The Tomlar was like medicine to Tavishien. She was feeling better at the moment as if mother nature was sending her ethereal strength through the combined mental power of the entire Tomlar herd.

Lingraw sat down at the park bench next too Tavishien's wheelchair. Lingraw had been briefed by the Doctors and the Psychiatrists they didn't want to bring up the crime until Tavishien's body and her soul had a chance to heal. When they thought it would be time to inform her, she would be a barren woman they would do so and be prepared to sedate her as necessary to get over that terrible episode. But first they needed to get her to walk and be able to start doing things for herself such as utilize the toilet and take showers and baths.

Doctor Hannah Barrymore was Tavishien's godsend in that she acted as a surrogate mother and coddled her in a manner a teenage daughter especially one that had gone through such a terrible trauma.

They were going to visit and allow Tavishien to get some sunlight to build up some natural vitamin D in her body to help create the vitamin cocktails she now received.

The small talk lasted a while and the nurse informed everyone they would soon be going to the cafeteria. An animal handler from a Zoo was brought in to assist with the Tomlar so that Tavishien and her father could enjoy a meal together. Tavishien's meal was highly crafted because she had been intravenously fed for eighteen months while in a coma. Now her digestive track needed to be prepared for eating real food so that when she went back into the world she would survive.

However, Agent Lucika, the Western Alliance INTEL operative had no intentions of ever allowing Tavishien to go back to the cabin and barn. Based on Agent Lucika's expectations of the outcome of this experiment, his superiors would soon learn how valuable she could be and thus would be relocated far away to get indoctrinated as well as programmed into the operations they would use her.

The carrot they would use to get her to agree was they promised to take care of her father for the rest of his life. He would never have to toil again or live in a cold home needing another human to help him stay warm at night in the harsh winter conditions. But the two would soon be separated for life as Lingraw was growing old and reaching that age where life expectancy matched his age.

The emphasis on restoring Tavishien where money was not an issue, and her Rehabilitation was the priority over all other patients coming down from high up in the government meant she had the best of the best even if they had to fly them in. Between the physical therapy which included several hours a day spending time with her Tomlar and her father, slowly restored Tavishien's vigor and she was feeling great and wanted to be discharged.

Then came the slam dunk. There were no less than three psychiatrists in the room with Tavishien, one of which had sedatives as this was going to be a very rough conversation, they wished to hell they never had to do or ever had to do again in the future.

Now it came out. A recapitulation of the crimes against her by these six terrible excuses for human beings. The conversation brought back gaping holes and when she discovered he dirty rotten bastards eliminated her ability to ever have children, she was devastated. Everything was planned for this special day. She had previously been fed a very nice meal.

So, when the three psychiatrists thought it was time to sedate her and give her a period of tranquility the signal was given and a few moments later, the poor Tavishien was put back in her bed now enjoying her travel to another dimension.

All the Tomlars and her father received her remote viewing thoughts. They too were deeply saddened. Lingraw wept, there was nothing he could do, he was just as much a victim as his daughter. Now years later Lingraw wished he had the foresight to take Maki Zorthun to a hospital for childbirth. He felt responsible for both disasters he could have mitigated.

If it were not for Tomlars that was there to help Tavishien, who now was helping Lingraw, he might not have survived the day. The sorrow was overwhelming. But one thing Lingraw felt was his time with Maki Zorthun was precious and she gave him a wonderful daughter in the end that provided him so many years of joy. Every day of his life he missed Maki Zorthun. And now that his daughter had gone through such misery because of his negligence, it hit him in the heart.

Something happened in the night. It was good Tomlar was there for Tavishien. The Tomlar called upon the rest of the herd to help. They stayed awake all night long pouring out their love to Lingraw and Tavishien. Thanks to the remote viewer interactions, Tavishien was slowly psychologically made whole again. She might not ever have children, but she would live and survive and help her father and look out for the Tomlar family she cherished who helped her get through this very difficult period in her life.

In the morning when Tavishien awoke she smiled and exhibited characteristics of someone who was not suffering from any psychological disorders. Her favorite doctor and protector Hannah Barrymore was there with two of the psychiatrists. The third could not be here this morning as she was having a serious mental problem of her own trying to figure out how to deal with this tremendous catastrophe in the life of a young woman.

Doctor Hannah Barrymore did a quick medical check of Tavishien and quickly determined she was medically satisfactory considering her physical condition was changed for life. The two psychiatrists were two of the best and were always diagnostic long before they would get trigger happy dishing out the drugs and soon engaged Tavishien in a conversation and was quickly relieved at her display of forbearance. It seemed like a miracle happened during the night and now Tavishien was very contempt in her appearance. There was no sadness and there was nothing heavy to digest and analyze.

"You seem very happy today," the first psychiatrist stated.

"Yes, I feel a lot better, and I've gotten over the bad news I received yesterday. I can deal with it."

This was the most intriguing experience the two psychiatrists ever experienced.

Agent Lucika of the Western Alliance Intelligence Bureau listening in on the audio he was secretly recording, knew precisely what happened. Unfortunately, due to operational directives he could not divulge his speculation to the two distinguished psychiatrists. But he knew quite well that remote viewing played into this. He didn't know exactly how that worked but he knew one day he would find out.

The clinical analysis came to an abrupt ending when Tavishien surprised them with her next statement:

"I'm getting kind of hungry; can we find my father and go to the cafeteria and get something to eat?" Tavishien asked.

Doctor Hannah Barrymore was always spot on and said, "I will get your father and we'll all go down to the cafeteria and see what they have for us."

"Thank you."

"You are most welcome dear."

The Zoo handler who had received a special briefing by Agent Lucika stayed with the Tomlar and Lingraw all night and offered, "I'll stay here with your Tomlar while you get something to eat."

"Thank you I appreciate your help."

"My pleasure."

Soon the three were in the cafeteria eating a nice breakfast where Agent Lucika arrived to join them began his agenda with Tavishien and her father.

Doctor Hannah Barrymore was uplifted in spirit because she had watched Tavishien recover from her brutal and deadly episode to once again a vibrant person.

The psychiatrists were reporting to Agent Lucika, Tavishien's Temperament appeared very positive and exposing she was full of life. That's because Tavishien had a growing sense she would soon get released from the hospital and be allowed to go home with her father where the seclusion was alright because the Tomlars gave her great joy as well as the wild nature that abounds.

Agent Lucika knew he didn't have a lot of time to seal the deal. He wanted concurrence to his plans prior to Tavishien released from the hospital. With her positive psychology and her improving physical health it would soon become problematic to keep her trapped in the hospital even if they could coerce the doctors to keep her there as a patient.

After everyone started eating Agent Lucika began his pitch to Tavishien. His numerous discussions with Lingraw led him to believe that he would go along with this project because it insured someone would look after him when he got older in a few years as he already learned the hard way disaster could strike and take his daughter away.

"Tavishien, you lived in the forest all your life and never had a chance to see what society offers including an education, if I could arrange for you to get an education and exposure to the world and the universe, would you be interested?"

"Thank you but when I leave the hospital, I need to go home with papa to take care of our Tomlars."

"I know you want to help your father and I have a proposal. If you allow me to take you somewhere that can offer you an education and a new way of life so you no longer must endure the harsh life in the forest, we will provide people to take care of your father for the rest of his life. He'll no longer have to break his back cutting firewood or fear trespassers as we'll have a security detachment there to protect him."

"I think I just want to go home and be with my Tomlars."

"If you let me take you to a place that has ideal weather and wonderful facilities to enrich your life, you can bring along a couple Tomlars if you want so that you can be with them and enjoy them as we continue with your rehabilitation and start your education."

Agent Lucika had spent hours psychologically conditioning Lingraw for this moment and Lingraw was indoctrinated in how Tavishien went through her brutal ordeal because he really wasn't an ideal parent and allowed her to be placed in a situation where something like that incident could manifest.

Tavishien didn't understand she had master handlers working her over and her father was in fact coerced and felt the pressure to go along with the plan.

He almost wanted to cry about it, but he had his dignity and knew Agent Lucika made perfect sense *that to take Tavishien back to the forest when she had this wonderful opportunity would be more of his mishandling of her future*. He thus caved and went along with the scheme.

The discussion went forward, and the plan was all laid out. Tavishien looked at her father looking for affirmative backup to take her back to the cabin in the forest. But she quickly discovered "Papa" had decided what was best for her was to accompany Agent Lucika to a faraway city to start her education and complete her rehabilitation. One of the benefits of going along with this plan included the wonderful female Doctor Hannah Barrymore who was also coerced into coming along for a while. Her quid pro quo was to be reassigned to a location closer to her family instead of near the mountains where if war broke out, she would suddenly be in harm's way.

The big event was just about to happen. Tavishien had no idea she was now deeply involved with INTEL people and how swiftly they moved.

After breakfast, Tavishien was taken back to her room to freshen up not knowing what to expect and as soon as she was laying back in her bed wondering just when all this was going to unfold, her father and the female Doctor Hannah Barrymore which was possibly another Jane Doe type fake name came into the room and said they were going to put her back in the wheel chair and take her outside to visit with the Tomlar, then go for a little ride.

Tavishien was slightly surprised that after she visited with her Tomlar friend she was then wheeled over to a van with a ramp to easily push her into it and the Zoo technician came along with the Tomlar and placed it into the Van. The Van had windows she could look out, but Tavishien had never traveled anywhere consciously so this was all quite a unique experience for her.

The van drove to the airport where a transport was waiting for her. They all got out of the Van together and one of the orderlies pushed the wheelchair up next to a short ladder to the aircraft's access.

Somehow Tavishien suspected all this activity might be goodbye to her father. She wondered if she would ever see him and the Tomlars herd again in her lifetime. Tavishien could walk to and from the bathroom now from her bed and was asked if she wanted to attempt walking up the few steps or they could carry her.

"I want to try walking."

Through the remote viewer ability, she had she knew "Papa" wasn't coming with her, but the Tomlar was. She understood her father had to go back to the cabin and barn and take care of the Tomlar herd. That was his existence. At his age, he didn't contemplate changing his life in any way.

Agent Lucika knew it would be best for Lingraw to continue living his life the way he did, but he would now have help and protection. Whether he would ever see Tavishien again depended on a lot of factors, many of them unknown at the present time. It would all come down to how valuable Tavishien's ability manifested Intelligence Bonanza's. The other factor was that getting her as far away as possible from her father meant they would more than likely be able to control her more effectively and not have any external types of interference.

After a couple hugs and some brief tears, Tavishien climbed the few stairs into the aircraft, and as soon as she was seated with her Tomlar staged in the two seats next to her somewhat tied down for its own safety, the aircraft was ready to depart.

The seats on this aircraft could swivel around so Doctor Hannah Barrymore had her three chairs turned around facing aft towards Tavishien. There was also a veterinarian and a psychiatrist on board to sedate Tavishien and the Tomlar if necessary. But as it turned out that wasn't necessary because the interaction between Tavishien and the Tomlar kept them both calm.

As the plane slowly turned around to head for the end of the runway, Tavishien looked out the windows and observed her father standing there next to the van with a couple agents onlooking. This was the beginning of a new chapter in Tavishien's life.

What life was to be bestowed on Tavishien was uncertain at this time but knowing Doctor Hannah Barrymore would be nearby made her feel safer and more secure. No one in her entire lifetime had affected her like Doctor Hannah Barrymore other than her father. The bond between the two appeared solid and

Tavishien would always remember Doctor Hannah Barrymore as someone special in her life, even though as time passed, she realized they would never meet again after her rehabilitation was completed.

Even though the aircraft flew supersonic, it still took almost five hours to get to their destination. Looking out the window Tavishien saw the city they flew into and all the modern skyscrapers that dotted the landscape. It truly was a sight to behold, especially for someone that never left the forest her entire life.

After the plane landed, it pulled into a hanger and the door was suddenly opened and several people in suits boarded the aircraft and asked Tavishien, "Do you need help climbing down the stairs of the plane?"

"I think I can make it down the stairs but hold onto my arm in case I slip."

They were soon off the aircraft and into a Limo. The Limo driver thought he had seen everything in his life, but when the Tomlar went into the back of the Limo with the passengers, he realized this was going to be an unusual day for him.

The Limo driver was directed to go to the nearest park to allow the Tomlar to take care of business after being cooped up for five hours on the plane.

Everyone got out of the Limo at the park which was very nicely designed and landscaped. The Tomlar did its business then came right back to Tavishien just like it was her personal guard dog. Once Tavishien stated the Tomlar was finished doing what it needed to do, they all got back into the Limo and were soon driving out to the countryside and eventually pulled up to what appeared to be a mansion. Indeed, it was, as the Western Alliance Intelligence Bureau ran its most important spies out of this building. The place was situated to allow numerous doctors perform cosmetic surgery on patients to change their facial recognition and disguise them.

Tavishien had some damage to her face they planned on correcting. After twenty-four surgeries, Tavishien, thanks to computer graphics had an image like how Tavishien appeared prior to the brutal attack. Since one side of Tavishien's face had not been severely damaged, computer processing could then extrapolate how the other side should appear and they performed their magic. Also, the INTEL people had photographs of the drawings Lingraw made of her mother Maki Zorthun that clarified any part of the image they were uncertain about.

It took months to do the facial restoration and healing. At the same time the staff slowly added to Tavishien's daily workouts and rehabilitation.

The first part of Tavishien's rehabilitation included time swimming in a heated pool. Tavishien had never been in a swimming pool or deep water. She had no concept of swimming, but with her swimming instructor she slowly mastered it to get her body back in shape to walk and run. Tavishien also had a weightlifting coach, and an exercise instructor with a massage routinely to help her aches and pains she generated with her workouts.

Interspersed in all the physical therapy, Tavishien had private tutors and education experts to help take her from the dark ages up to modern times. That education in itself proved to be a painful process because Tavishien had never been taught basic reading and writing skills.

After six months of physical therapy, it was time to train Tavishien in martial arts. Tavishien's martial arts instructor Gabriel. During their first session Gabriel threw Tavishien against the wall and slapped her around to get her fired up and upset. The big cat fight ensued and Tavishien went after Gabriel with ample vigor and rage. Gabriel allowed the fighting to continue for twenty minutes when she yelled out, "All stop."

A couple other assistants in the room then grabbed Tavishien and held her while Gabriel explained it to her.

"I had to get you fired up to get you to expose your fighting spirit. Now I know you have a fighting spirit which I do not need to work on. All I need to do now is teach you the techniques, some of which are deadly and in fact, you will get to demonstrate that on real prisoners."

"What do you mean by that?"

"From time to time, we capture Tartarland spies and saboteurs. They know what happens to spies when they are caught. We give them a chance to live. What they must do is fight you when we think you are ready and if they defeat you, which means they killed you, we let them walk out of here free.

"You would let me get killed by one of those spies?"

"No, I'll prepare you so that will never happen. You are a woman, and they will never expect you to be as deadly as I will train you. Some of your training may seem to be disgusting to you, but in the future, you need to be able to protect yourself in case we need to send you to a dangerous location."

This would not be the first time, nor the last time Gabriel initiated a fight with Tavishien by *bitch slapping* her and initiating fowl contact including goosing her rear end that got Tavishien really upset.

As Tavishien received indoctrination and training and had full access to worldwide computational and data resources they taught her to navigate, she put forth the effort to learn the essence of espionage and sabotage. At the conclusion of her self-training, she realized the seriousness of the business she was now in and wished she was back at the mountainside cabin with all her Tomlars and her father.

Tavishien also knew her timeline, when she was knocked out into a coma and when she came to was approximately eighteen months. It became clearer to her as each day passed that her father sold her out. *What was his motive? Was her "Papa" quid pro quo so great he would give up his own daughter?*

The one thing that Tavishien had was her remote viewing. She could investigate her father's world anytime she wanted and so now she did with great interest to see what the price was to give up his daughter.

At first everything seemed out of the ordinary. Then it all started to unfold. Government people were there taking care of a lot of his needs. He was no longer hunting bears and deer to dry for use in the winter. He wasn't out picking berries, mountain potatoes and wild onions or for that matter gathering up food for the Tomlars. Vehicles in the winter with tracks on them like a bulldozer arrived routinely delivering sacks of food for Tomlars and groceries for him. They carted away all his old makeshift furniture and brought in new things.

Government construction crews built a shed, installed a generator in it and had a propane gas tank installed. He now had electricity. He soon had water piped into his home from an underground storage tank to help prevent it from freezing along with a reverse osmosis machine to provide him and the Tomlars with very clean water. The government workers dug a cesspool and hooked it up to a bath and toilet installed in an extinction to the home allowing these modern conveniences and more storage for food and necessary items.

Lingraw was no longer living off the grid, in the wild in the most austere conditions. There could be no other explanation, than her father sold Tavishien to her handlers. Tavishien wept upon the realization.

The Tomlar she had with her was very unhappy being away from the herd back at the cabin and barn. Each passing week the Tomlar became more and more unhappy to the point Tavishien was worried it would give up the reason to keep living and die. The Tomlar no longer desired to live and it was time Tavishien had to do something about it.

Several times a week, Tavishien met with Agent Lucika of the Western

Alliance Intelligence Bureau. She informed him at their next meeting, "The

Tomlar is not doing well and wants to die. I would like you to send it back to

"Papa" so it can be back with its brothers and sisters."

"Would you like to go with it and visit your papa?"

"No."

"Why wouldn't you want to go?"

"I'd rather not discuss that if you don't mind."

This change in temperament and attitude quickly got two psychiatrists involved in figuring out exactly what was going on with Tavishien. She had had absolutely no contact with her father, so how could Tavishien suddenly turn what apparently appeared to be cold towards her father?

After reading through the reports full of speculation and no clue in the world, Agent Lucika came up with a theory. Tavishien had used her remote viewing and discovered some things about her father that upset her. Just exactly what was that? He then asked the watchers who were assigned to Lingraw's cabin detail to send pictures of it, inside and out and give a summary report on a typical day in the life of Lingraw.

Nothing earth shattering came back except the massive change in the

Cabin and all the modern conveniences Lingraw now enjoyed. Agent Lucika had an outstanding knack at putting two and two together. That's why he rose to the level he did.

Agent Lucika guess turned out to be highly accurate. Tavishien was upset with her father because she felt he sold her down the river to get all the opulence he now enjoyed. In a way this was a good development as far as Agent Lucika was concerned because as he predicted, she never wanted to go home again, and they never had to worry about losing Tavishien in the process. The planets had aligned and created a situation that Agent Lucika could never have created even if he tried.

As soon as transportation was arranged, Tavishien spent time with the Tomlar informing him that he would now go home and be back with his brothers and sisters. The Tomlar was happy and would fully cooperate and conduct itself in such a reasonable manner, the handlers would not dread taking it back.

"Are you coming with me?" The Tomlar asked in a remote viewing frame of mind.

"No, I'm staying here."

"When will you come back and see Papa?"

"For now, I'm staying here because I have some serious amount of learning I need to do."

"The herd will be unhappy you didn't come back with me.

"I will remote view them in the future and we will stay in touch."

When the men received the Tomlar to ship it back to Lingraw, Tavishien was there to say goodbye to it who was sad she wasn't coming with him. But his spirits were now lifted he could go home.

The men were very close to Tavishien, and she read their aura and would monitor them on their journey to make sure they didn't mistreat the animal.

Halfway to the airport one of the cargo haulers said to the other, we should take this animal some place and butcher it and barbecue it, I think it probably tastes good."

Tavishien detected that conversation monitoring the two cargo men and immediately went to Agent Lucika to report she was fearful of what those men were about to do. Moments later one of the men hauling the animal, received a phone call from Agent Lucika who asked, "Did you guys just talk about barbecuing that animal you are hauling?"

The men were stunned and denied it, but Agent Lucika knew better and said, "Be advised, if any harm comes to that animal, you will get lie detectors and neuronic sonification."

The Tomlar had no further fear of anything, and Agent Lucika just got more confirmation of Tavishien's capabilities. Because this was such an important revelation, within two hours the cargo haulers were being interrogated by the master himself, Agent Lucika who broke them and they admitted having the conversation.

Tavishien's remote viewing ability was now fully confirmed. All that was left was training and deployment, not perceived as an easy task.

Having gone almost twenty years with no academic learning, Tavishien's education was slow and painful to the instructors. Gabriel also received a lot of injuries as she slowly trained her student to become a deadly spy.

Tavishien's espionage would be different than anything ever experienced before. Agent Lucika understood the reality of deploying Tavishien's skills. What Tavishien brought to the table was probably as destructive as nuclear weapons.

If the Intelligence Bureau could ever get Tavishien close enough to Tartarland's tyrannical Dictator Illtnaut, they would know every move he planned to make in the future, and they could quickly mitigate any opportunity Illtnaut thought he could exploit.

As Tavishien got stronger she spent less time in the swimming pool and now started running with Gabriel. Gabriel explained, "You need to run eight miles every day as we get up to that level so that you can survive a prolonged fight if you get into one.

"If you can do eight miles, I can do eight miles," Tavishien said as she made it her point to beat Gabriel every step of the way now, no matter how much it hurt.

Gabriel loved it when Tavishien challenged her because it helped improve her training regiment, but also gave her the sadistic opportunity to beat her ass again.

During the next training session, the two women started out on an eight-mile course. It was simple to figure out distance because the normal route they took was two miles per lap. This would be the first time Tavishien ran eight miles in her life. For the first four miles Tavishien kept up but from then on Gabriel slowly pulled away until she was almost a full quarter of a mile ahead after six miles. Gabriel knew she would be happy confronting Tavishien and letting her know she just beat her ass again. Tavishien remote viewing Gabriel was disgusted with the thought Gabriel would make such a comment.

Something happened around the six-and-a-half-mile mark. The Tomlar Herd back at her father's cabin in the forest remote viewing Tavishien started to encourage her. Their combined energy filled Tavishien with an inner strength she didn't know she had so she put forth a significant amount of effort.

After checking behind her at the seven-mile mark, Gabriel knew she was so far ahead of Tavishien there was no point in checking again until after she crossed the finish line.

The volume of the Tomlar remote viewing was now at a very loud amplitude resonating with all Tavishien's brain patterns. Tavishien's motor functions were now in overdrive. Any stress or discomfort she previously had was quickly replaced by added vigor and fervor.

Tavishien's velocity quickly matched and exceeded an Olympic runner desperately wanting to win that gold medal cruising into the finish line. With less than one hundred yards left and Agent Lucika now standing at the finish line observing the efficacy of the workout observed it all for himself. Gabriel in her cocky attitude was gliding to the finish line and out of nowhere Tavishien passed her. The race was on!

Anyone watching now would assume these were two Olympic class runners in a hundred-yard dash giving it their utmost effort. Gabriel gave it all, but Tavishien pulled ahead of her slowly and soon passed Agent Lucika standing there smiling realizing the impossible had just happened. No female ever beat Gabriel in a running race, period. And Tavishien just cleaned her clock.

Gabriel was mildly shocked that Tavishien made up such a deficit so quickly. She also knew something else, few runners in the Bureau ever completed Eight Miles this quickly. And she knew something else was coming and expected it real soon. Tavishien did not disappoint her.

"Looks like I beat your dumb ass."

Under normal circumstances, Gabriel would have *bitch slapped* Tavishien and they would soon be grappling on the ground, but today, she simply took the insult and reflected on it because she truly wanted to know what happened. She also knew Agent Lucika secretly filmed their workouts to later critique Gabriel on her techniques and approach towards developing Tavishien. She would later be in a critique and ask to see the replay.

Agent Lucika also wanted to know what happened because the extraordinary explosion of speed came out of nowhere and the video showed Tavishien had been slowing down and showing signs of stress.

To Tavishien's surprise Gabriel answered her verbal rubbish with a complement.

"You did well today. I'm always happy to see you achieve stellar performance in your activities."

***

In the days and weeks to follow there was more martial arts taught and poor Gabriel had to have more frequent messages and pain reducers as her success in training Tavishien also made her damaging attacks more lethal and devastating.

Tavishien knocked Gabriel out a couple times in their self-defense training. Gabriel loved to start it with either a *bitch slap* or throwing Tavishien up against a wall and sometimes choking her until Tavishien could escape. Because this phase of the training was so deadly and Tavishien might accidentally kill Gabriel on purpose, there were now two training assistants always present to protect Gabriel when Tavishien reached that point she was moments away from killing Gabriel.

Now came some of the most dangerous training. They could not risk Gabriel getting killed in some of these technique developmental activities, so they had to bring in Cadavers. The Cadavers had surgery to keep their eyes open allowing eye puncture training for Tavishien. Poking an assailant's eye out with a fatal blow might be the only way Tavishien could save her own life. They also wanted her to get a feel for how deeply she needed to penetrate the eyeball socket to do the fatal damage that would save her life. It would be a last-ditch effort and failure to succeed would mean her death and loss of an important asset.

They went through 25 Cadavers before Tavishien perfected her eyeball attack methodology. It only took one eyeball penetration to kill the opponent, but Tavishien wanted to nail both eyeballs which would eliminate the other person from observing her if she didn't manage to kill him. That meant he couldn't point a gun or know where to lunge with a knife. Also, an assailant would be in such tremendous pain, he most likely would go into shock and be temporarily immobilized allowing Tavishien to escape.

During their numerous training sessions, especially when Gabriel did her famous goosing of Tavishien, there were head butts to follow. Eventually Gabriel learned to avoid goosing Tavishien because the head butts were getting far more painful. It was becoming clear to Gabriel and Agent Lucika, it didn't matter how much it hurt Tavishien, she would carry out her attacks on Gabriel or anyone else despite the self-pain it created.

Eventually the training got down to escaping from several men who might be able to take down Tavishien and put her into a situation that meant she would likely die in the end. The flashbacks of the six Tarter soldiers and the support Tavishien received from her dear Tomlar herd, seemed to invigorate her and in training episodes, it appeared she was doing a great job at egress from such capture and confinement.

It didn't make sense to Tavishien why she was getting all this self-defense training, but when Agent Lucika thoroughly studied Tavishien and her remote viewing proficiency, it simply came down to the fact she would have to get physically close to the target to read his Aura so she would be able to remote view him safely later at a remote distance.

The enemy knew about remote viewing and knew they had to prevent a remote viewer from getting physically close to their target. As soon as the enemy became aware of one of their leaders was the target of remote viewing, they would provide sufficient bodyguards to keep a remote viewer away from that individual. Hence, Tavishien would have to break through security and in those cases possibly disable the security apparatus to get close enough to tag the subject of their planning and operations.

Agent Lucika was in fact one of the best spies in the world. He seemed to have an element of clairvoyance because he figured out situations nobody else could including the discovery and exploitation of Tavishien. As far as her father was concerned the amount of financial costs for him was considered chump change considering what his daughter was expected to soon start providing.

As the physical therapy and workouts continued, Agent Lucika devised his plan on the exploitation of Tavishien. Like anything in the spy business, they stick their toes in the water first and check the temperature before they jump in. Because Tavishien was recovering from emotional trauma as well as a severe physical attack, Agent Lucika would have to go slow with her at first until he spotted eagerness and intensity in her actions.

First and foremost, there would be a series of tests not so much to test Tavishien's commitment and endurance, but more so to evaluate her ability as an information provider. Agent Lucika's speculation was the quality of the data would surpass anything a team of spies could do for him.

There was one more aspect that made all the cost and effort worthwhile. A single spy has a much smaller footprint than a team of spies and is less likely to be detected. Spies must be present to intercept and acquire the intelligence directly. The problematic aspect of that approach is, a lot of spies got captured, tortured, and sometimes turned into double spies that often become very destructive to an intelligence bureau.

Now it was a matter to do real world tests of the remote viewer capabilities. The tests could not be done behind enemy lines because Tavishien probably was not far enough along to put her into those situations. But she could do remote viewing in the safety of the city where she was being trained. Agent Lucika had two types of targets he could do validations on. First is people working in financial services organizations. The other was organized crime. Information that Tavishien provided could be checked over time and evaluated for accuracy. Even though financial services had their own security apparatus, and known to have bruisers to deal with problems, Tavishien might sustain injury or severely beaten but unlikely she would get killed.

Organized crime on the other hand would waste no time killing her if they viewed her as a threat. And since Tavishien's reports would be compartmentalized and only go through Agent Lucika, there would be a very low chance any of that would get compromised and put Tavishien at risk. Once she tagged the individual, she could then do her work remotely in the safety of bodyguards in secure facilities.

Tavishien's first tests would soon commence while her training and rehabilitation continued.

***

CHAPTER SIX
The First Mission

A day of martial arts training and boxing had just finished. Tavishien was all smiles because today right after Gabriel did her *bitch slap* to kick off training, the fierce battle commenced. Without the two assistants present, its likely Tavishien might have killed Gabriel today. Tavishien was soaked in sweat after the epic battle, and she was all smiles because she just knocked Gabriel out before the assistants grabbed the raging woman and held her down until she calmed down.

It took several minutes and while they were holding Tavishien, so she didn't get up and put the finishing touches on Gabriel and talking to her in a fashion the two psychiatrists explained they had to do for this special woman, especially after what she had been through.

Finally, Tavishien's muscles relaxed, and she calmed down and simply said, "You can let go of me now. I'm okay."

Gabriel was soon lying in a gurney getting ready to be carried to a nearby medical office.

Tavishien walked over and looked down at Gabriel who was now double visioned and could not really focus on Tavishien or even know who she was. Her brain was in a half-conscious state where she could partially see but not be able to comprehend what she was looking at. Gabriel was messed up pretty bad today and a short time later the two assistants going through a critique had to explain why they waited too long to intervene. That would not happen again.

Agent Lucika had entered the room halfway through the fight and saw the intensity of the battle. It was fierce and it was deadly, compared to many spies these two women were no pushovers. They easily could make grown men cry.

After Gabriel was carried away, Agent Lucika approached Tavishien and said, "Tavishien, I would like you to accompany me to my office, there is something I need to talk to you about."

"Is it about me beating up Gabriel?"

"No, it's unrelated, but we need to discuss it in private."

"Alright, lead the way."

Tavishien had no idea the level of surveillance she had. Everywhere she went and everything she did was filmed and recorded. Agent Lucika observed every bit of it and sometimes when he got busy, his assistants reviewed the recordings and made briefs on what they observed and highlighted those segmented videos they thought Agent Lucika should see. He didn't miss anything. Now he was going to do his first major experiment with his new operation.

When they went into Agent Lucika's office they were scanned by hidden sensors to make sure nobody secretly planted a bug on them, which happens quite often in the spy business. Even though Agent Lucika would never engage in espionage against his own intelligence bureau, they had to be certain a double spy or someone paid well didn't slip him a micro bug which sometimes happens while traveling.

When they sat down at Agent Lucika's desk, had there been a detection of any devices, security people would be coming into the room to escort everyone out while they scanned the room and took the two individuals back for secondary screening. Today none of that type of activity was in the cards. Agent Lucika had not traveled recently or gone into the public. Tavishien had been in house arrest and trapped within the confines of the facility and therefore was not likely to have picked up a bug. However, they had to be vigilant because a bug in the right place at the wrong time could be very damaging.

"Please have a seat."

Tavishien had no idea what this conversation was going to be about and made no assumptions. One thing she did sense was that Agent Lucika had always been decent to her and helpful. Agent Lucika had built up trust in Tavishien and was always friendly and never demanding. Agent Lucika probably had a hand in having Gabriel beat the crap out of her for such a long period of time, but today when she knocked out Gabriel, she realized she had been well prepared and had a guess as to what she might be doing in the future.

Agent Lucika got right to the point. "We brought you here because I had every reason to believe your remote viewing was substantial. I still believe that."

"Alright," Tavishien responded.

"I know you are still rehabilitating from your injuries when we first found you, but you have come a long way and healed up quite a bit, wouldn't you say?"

"Yes, I'm considerably better off than what I was a year ago."

"I've decided now would be the time to start deploying you on missions."

"Are you going to send me behind enemy lines?"

"Not for a while. I want to assess your abilities here locally where you will not be under a lot of potential hazards and risks."

"How would you do that?"

"My plan is to bring you up in stages. Your first stage will test your ability with low risk. After we evaluate that mission then we'll take you to the next level where you will be exposed to entities that will no doubt pose hazards and some risk."

"When do you anticipate all this occurring?"

"First we need to get you a cover story and plausible identity where you will fit in with your targets."

"And what would that be?"

"You are an attractive woman. You have a body shape that men enjoy, your hair, eyes, and your face all are up there at the same level as fashion models."

"And how would that fit into your plans?"

"Your workouts with Gabriel will be reduced now so you can spend your time in training for this new role. Plus, I think after today, Gabriel needs some rest and relaxation because you beat her up pretty good."

"Well, you know it is either beat her or get beat."

"I'm not saying you did anything wrong. You did as I expected you would and demonstrated that under certain circumstances you would put forth maximum effort, which may one day save your life."

"Okay so how does Gabriel fit into all this?"

"She doesn't, I mentioned she needs a rest because you worked her over pretty good today, and that's ok because for several days while she's resting and enjoying some time off you will get that training in you cover role."

"And what precisely is that?"

"You will become a fashion model. I will use my special connections to make sure you get put into exhibitions and get seen so that it will be easier for you to encounter your target."

"Who's my target?"

"You will get all the details in your OPPS Briefs, but I will tell you what he does. He's a high-ranking executive in a financial services company."

"What kind of information about him do you want?"

"We have no specific need for his information. But because of the business he's in, there are obviously probably a lot of dubious details you will discover, inform us about and we'll check it out via appropriate means to vet the information you give us." "That doesn't sound too scary to me.

"Society believes these financial services guys are all nice guys and play decent. But, if they discovered you found out some of the shady deals going on, they might probably hire contractors to attempt to silence you."

"How would they silence me?"

"They would kill you."

Suddenly the enormity of it all became clear to Tavishien. She could potentially be playing with some rough cookies if conditions caused such an awareness to her target.

"When does all this start?"

"You can take the day off, go visit Gabriel in the hospital if you want and tell her you are sorry even though I know that would be a lie. Then tomorrow morning, your trainers will be here to teach you how to do modeling in front of high-end clientele."

"I'll be ready."

"After you get cleaned up from your workout, if you want, I'll take you to the hospital to visit Gabriel so you can tell her a sweet lie."

"What if I suddenly get the notion to beat the crap out of her?"

"She's in bad shape. I think when you see her, you may not feel like beating her up."

"I'm kind of hungry."

"After we visit Gabriel, I'll take you to a nice restaurant and buy you a meal you would like."

"Do they serve roast Tomlar at that restaurant?"

"I'm not sure, but they definitely have some good, barbecued meats."

"I suppose I need to celebrate beating the crap out of Gabriel today, so I'll give it a shot."

"I'll be here working, come by when you are ready to go."

"Sure."

Tavishien stood up then walked out of the office and proceeded to her private dormitory room where she took a nice long hot bath. She had a few aches and pains because Gabriel did not let her win. She fought her off every moment until that last punch did Gabriel in.

The bath felt so good that Tavishien would have stayed in longer, but her hunger pains got her moving.

Tavishien didn't have any clothes that would be considered beautiful. All she had was casual clothes that would not in any way convey to anyone she was a fashion model. She didn't even have a clue how she would look when they gave her a makeover. She had no idea how beautiful women could be with the right fashion designer, makeup artist, and hair designer.

When Tavishien was ready to walk back to Agent Lucika's office, she qualified as a plane Jane with no makeup or anything to suggest she had any alluring qualities. That was alright with her because she had no expectations or knowledge of what was in store for her.

Tavishien entered the building walking towards Agent Lucika's office, and she was sent through because Agent Lucika had informed security Tavishien would be coming to his office. They would be leaving his office to go to the hospital and visit Gabriel.

Some of the females she encountered going through security gave Tavishien strange looks like never before. Tavishien thought it was odd the way they were looking at her but news travels fast and no other woman had ever knocked out Gabriel.

There was a receptionist working not far from Agent Lucika's office who was expecting Tavishien and said, "Agent Lucika is expecting you. Let me notify him that you are here."

The receptionist then paged Agent Lucika who then shut down the video he was watching reviewing today's events, then exited his office closing the door behind him that automatically locked and approached the two women standing there.

"Alright Tavishien, please follow me to my Skycar, we'll fly it to the hospital parking."

Tavishien had no idea what a Skycar was, but she was familiar with VTOL military aircraft observing them coming and going when she was rehabilitating in the hospital before she was moved to this Intelligence Bureau Campus.

It was a short walk out the door to the assigned parking and since Agent Lucika had the semaphore modulator in his pocket, the onboard artificial intelligence detected his presence and two persons approaching and immediately rotated two doors upwards allowing them to enter the craft.

"Get in on the other side and you have a seat belt to hook up. Just watch me."

Agent Lucika stepped into the Skycar and sat down on the seat and hooked up his seatbelt. Tavishien thought that was simple enough and copied his actions. Once the seatbelts were secured in place, the two doors pivoted down and shut and locked. The crafts instrument panel was lit up and looked very modern, almost like the medical instruments in Tavishien's hospital room.

The Skycar flew itself and had voice activated commands.

Agent Lucika then directed the Skycar artificial intelligence, "Take us to

Coloson General Hospital."

"You wish to go to Coloson General Hospital, Sir?" the artificial intelligence asked to confirm.

"That's correct and park in guest parking."

"Now departing for Coloson General Hospital guest parking."

The Skycar took off a lot smoother than the aircraft that Tavishien had flown in. Soon it was in Sky-traffic and heading towards the city center then suddenly diverted and soon landed in a half empty parking lot for Skycars. Artificial Intelligence, knowing this was Agent Lucika's destination, opened the two doors for him and his passenger.

The two were met inside the lobby by one of Agent Lucika's assistants who informed him, "She came back to consciousness about an hour and a half ago. They just gave her something to eat and drink and I was advised to come back to her room in about fifteen minutes which was a while ago, so we can probably go there now."

"Alright take us to her room," Agent Lucika responded.

The agent led them to an elevator, and they were soon up on the fourth floor heading towards Gabriel's private room. While she was unconscious, they did Cat Scans and other medical procedures to determine what if any serious injury existed. The conclusion by the medical staff was, she only had a concussion but decided to hold her over for a couple days to monitor her to catch any issue that might arise.

Gabriel had two black eyes, a broken nose and a split lip that was glued together and being held in place by a special tape that would dissolve as soon as the doctors decided the bonding materials applied fully reconnected the split lip and would not be an issue with the tape removed.

Tavishien wasn't a bad person, she just got over animated during the fight and turned into an animal for a brief period of time and did the damage. Now looking at how Gabriel's face was messed up, she felt bad at what she did.

Without prompting Tavishien walked over, bent down and hugged Gabriel and said, "I'm so sorry I got carried away."

"That's okay Tavishien, I pushed you really hard and you finally cracked. I didn't back off when I should have so this is not your fault."

Gabriel witnessed some minor sobbing that Tavishien was doing and felt the love and compassion she now gave her in the hug, and she hugged her back. They would now be soul sisters forever.

Agent Lucika observed all this and suddenly had a much greater understanding of the two women and felt good they had this emotional bonding under the circumstances, because it resolved a lot of issues quickly. It also released a lot of burden off Agent Lucika, because the game he was playing would ultimately turn deadly and a more cohesive team that cared about each other would be significantly easier to work with.

The women talked a bit, then the doctor who was in the room with them said, "I gave Gabriel a sedative and a sleep inducer as she needs to rest because of her injuries. I think she is about ready to fall asleep, so I think it would be prudent if you guests would now depart her room."

"Alright doctor. Gabriel, we'll come back tomorrow and visit you. Is there anything you want me to get you?"

"The doctor probably may not like it, but can you bring me a baked bread spread."

The doctor frowned as Agent Lucika said, "Sure I'll sneak one in for you, and you can put the hospital food in the box, and I'll get rid of it for you."

Agent Lucika then smiled, and the Intel people then left the room leaving Gabriel with a doctor and a nurse.

The assistant would remain in the hospital over the night and check in with the nurses every hour to get an update on Gabriel's condition. The nurses were glad someone was there that cared about Gabriel and didn't mind him coming every hour for an update. Finally in the morning, he was informed she was awake and feeling good. They suggested he now leave, and they would contact Agent Lucika if there was anything to be concerned about.

Right after visiting Gabriel, Agent Lucika took Tavishien to his Skycar and gave the Artificial Intelligence the name of the restaurant to take them. Artificial Intelligence had all of Agent Lucika's prior trip destinations stored in nondestructive memory and in milliseconds had an electronic map to guide the Skycar to the ultimate destination.

In a short time, they were inside a restaurant and the only thing that came close that Tavishien ever saw was the cafeteria in the hospital and later at the Intelligence Bureau Campus.

One thing Tavishien discovered right away was the scents were overpowering which added to her hunger.

Since the restaurant was half empty due to the timing they were promptly seated, and the waitress stood to take their orders. Tavishien was still learning to read and really didn't know what any of what the menu meant because she had never experienced it before. She simply said, "Mr. Lucika, could you please order for me because I have no idea what any of this means."

"Alright."

Knowing that Tavishien grew up as a meat eater he ordered them each.

Brakaloff which was much like Venison is on Earth. The meat would be cooked with a special sauce that would add tremendous flavor to it. The meal also came with other items that would fill them both up easily.

Agent Lucika looking at Tavishien knew that because of her up bringing and her relative existence up to now, she appeared like a plane Jane that most men would not find attractive or put much effort into courting her. But he had seen in the spy business where plane Janes could be made to look elegant and had seen Gabriel dolled up so nicely, he wouldn't had minded having a special intercourse with her, but as a shrewd spy knew the first rule of espionage: *Never dip your pin in Company Ink.*

When Agent Lucika looked at Tavishien he knew that over the next few days they would transform her into a fashion model and she would appear far more glamorous and become irresistible, meaning the financial service guy he picked to test her remote viewing would salivate over her allowing her to get so close to him she would totally absorb his Aura and be poised to start reporting on everything he did.

This was going to be an interesting experiment, to the point there would be two additional transcribers assigned to this mission. The transcribers would not be there to gain useful intelligence, because it wasn't really an intelligence matter. They were firmly briefed this was going to be weird and not to ask any questions, that the accuracy of their report was more important than what it contained.

Agent Lucika ordered a nice elixir to help make the experience more pleasant and ordered one for Tavishien to see how it affected her because very soon she would start getting educated on taxology and how to detect possible drugging and how to mitigate the effects. She would have some special antidotes, but time was critical, she had to get those antidotes down fast or the drugs would do their trick and she would be disabled and possibly in severe danger.

The meal was soon served, and it wasn't that Tavishien was a pig, she simply had not completed all the etiquette training she required to operate around the elite she would soon experience. She had a lot to learn with not much time to do it in.

Agent Lucika could tell by the way Tavishien woofed down the food it was good, and she was hungry. Based on her body language and the display of satisfaction it was apparent she liked the food. The elixir seemed to also make her seem strange and out of character.

Agent Lucika took his time and ate his meal at a pace he enjoyed and was only half done before he realized Tavishien was staring at him wondering why he ate so slowly.

But Tavishien was patient and didn't say much. In fact, at the present time, she was remotely viewing her Tomlars back at her father's cabin and they of course were very happy to hear from her. She knew every one of them loved her as they were a part of her family. She could not help but think about what would become of them when her father passed away. With his gray hair and aging, it could happen unexpectedly.

Tavishien also thought about her mother and felt sadness she never got to meet her. She had her name and information about her life in the Tartarland civilization. One day she might be able to go there and explore her beginnings. It was just hope currently due to the global situation.

Eventually Agent Lucika finished his entrée and asked her if she wanted some dessert. Tavishien wasn't sure but in the hospital and later in the Intelligence bureau Campus cafeteria she learned about deserts and felt blessed she could have them.

Tavishien asked Agent Lucika to pick a dessert and soon ice cream with a lovely cookie appeared.

Eventually the meal was over, and it was back to the intelligence bureau Campus. Agent Lucika escorted Tavishien to her private dormitory room and they said good night, and, in a while, they were snug in their own beds slowly succumbing to the effects of the meal and elixir, Agent Lucika had thoughts of Tavishien and how she was going to soon demonstrate what he knew she was capable of.

***

82

CHAPTER SEVEN
From Savage to Fashion Model

The next morning, Tavishien was awakened by her handlers to get her ready for the big day. A woman who had been used on many covert operations to dress and prepare women for their roles and knew how to keep her mouth shut because of the financial rewards, would arrive at 8:00 A.M. sharp ready for a long day.

Ljótunn bon Swartzler working with the top fashion designers for over a thirty-year period knew the insides and outsides of the fashion industry and had great insights in now to utilize a model. The first lesson she learned was it was all about the model and not the garment.

The garment was the billboard, but the model was the message. The message is what really mattered because purchases of expensive designer clothing and fame associated with a designer always came down to emotions and how the designer triggered them. Without the finesse of the model, the designer would simply just have another garment hanging on a rack.

In preparation for the conversion of a savage into a model, she requested Agent Lucika provide pictures and video of her candidate to allow her to figure out what wardrobes and makeovers would be most appropriate to create the image she wanted. In the case of Tavishien, she had numerous limitations. The first obstacle Tavishien had was a lack of education that could create issues.

Not all fashion models are rocket scientists, and Ljótunn bon Swartzler had to deal with a few that were not so bright, but they had great bodies, pretty faces and hair that allowed the hair designers to create wonderful hair designs.

The way to mitigate the issue of education is to condition the model in what to say and what not to say. In some cases, silence is golden and as she would later explain to Tavishien, you communicate by the way you show your body. Men in particular, do not care so much as to what is in your head, they are more interested in how you would appear disrobed.

A good spy is taught to use any weapon and any talent possible for the moment of need. One of the tools of the trade is seduction and the paramount lesson is desire is ten times a greater influence than gratification.

Female spy techniques for Tavishien were a part of the curriculum. Some or a lot of it was displeasing to Tavishien because it articulated the evil in society and how far powerful men would go to achieve their gratification. Tavishien also started realizing that Agent Lucika was probably a purveyor of some of that evil and now she was in over her head and no way out. Eventually she made her way out of the spy and remote viewer business but two years later found herself right back at it.

When Ljótunn bon Swartzler marched into the large conference room that had just a few people, Tavishien had no idea how much that woman was going to change her life. The process was starting now and her assistants coming in with several wheeled containers appeared like a mild spectacle.

Tavishien didn't know enough about what she was observing and sat back taking it all in. She was sitting on one side of a table by herself, and Agent Lucika was in a chair at the end of the table, master of ceremonies and arbiter of the unknown but obviously dubious transcendence.

Ljótunn bon Swartzler had plenty of pictures and video of Tavishien and didn't need an introduction and walked directly up to her and said, "Hello Tavishien, I'm Ljótunn bon Swartzler and I'm here to train you to be a fashion model."

Out of primordial respect, Tavishien stood up and said, "I do not know how successful I will be at it, but I realize I need to learn this for a future assignment."

"Tavishien my dear, I hate to be the bearer of bad news to you but knowing where you will probably be assigned in the future, you need to understand from this day forward you will always have to be a fashion model of some sort, because you interface with any possible client or customer, will require you to utilize the skills I'm going to teach you."

"I'm ready."

"I think the first thing we will do is show you a video I've constructed that will show some of the women I've trained and at a fashion show how they perform."

Before Tavishien could even begin to think, some of the workers had pulled out a special projection screen and set it up about ten feet away from Tavishien. From her seat it would be the same definition as a movie theater for someone sitting in the middle of the audience.

A projection device was place on the table, offset a couple feet from Tavishien and the technicians who had worked with Agent Lucika in the past knew where the lights dimmer controls for the room were located and right on the signal from Ljótunn bon Swartzler the lights were dimmed, and the video and sound started.

Part of the essence of a fashion show included sound as a psychological inducer. Tavishien was slowly coming out of the stone age into a modern society and even things like music that everyone takes for granted, was a real eye opener for her. Since Agent Lucika's team understood the essence of this remote viewer and what she had never experienced in life, they spent a couple hours per day exposing a lot of society to her. It was indeed a mind twister for Tavishien, and the high-fidelity three-dimensional music provided by the projection system was something that went beyond anything Tavishien had experienced in life.

Even though some of the models were not beautiful, their figures and their composite picture was a billboard for the clothing apparel design they were showing. The fashion models calculated movements almost like a ballet dancer was carefully choreographed not so much to make the woman look spectacular, but to exemplify the clothing apparel. The designer was not selling the women they were selling the design of what they were wearing.

Tavishien sat there open minded taking it all in as this was something new to her, but what she observed the women doing didn't seem like they were doing much but walking along showing the clothes. She would soon be taught the reason why people focused on clothes is how the fashion model did the carefully choreographed act. They were indeed high-tech actors with a script just as complicated as anything in the entertainment industry.

At the completion of the video, the lights were turned on and Ljótunn bon Swartzler who had personally trained many of the fashion models shown in the video, started the questions and answering session that would kick off the activities.

As always Agent Lucika would be there just some of the time, but he had every bit of it recorded for later playback and analysis.

One thing that Agent Lucika knew most emphatically was that Ljótunn bon Swartzler knew what she was doing. She was one of the best in the business and had already facilitated the training of a dozen Intelligence Bureau spies.

To be a great spy required a female to be a master of seduction, a fashion model, a lethal martial artist, and a very intelligent person. The foes Tavishien faced were equally devastating, and the wrong move would cost them their lives. There simply was no room for error as they operated on a razor's edge of the difference between life and death as well as success and failure.

"Tell me Tavishien what did you think about the women in the video and how they performed."

"It didn't seem overly complicated to me."

"I have some fashion shows I will soon be taking you on to get your feet wet and see how it all unfolds."

"I'm sure I'll be ready for it."

"We often record our training sessions so that we can critique the girls as we prepare them for the next show. It requires a lot of attention to detail because once they walk out on the stage it's all right then and there exposed to the prospective customers. Just one minor screwup and you might have killed the deal. Bear in mind some of these garments start out at 20,000 credits."

Tavishien had no foundation about the value of money and what 20,000 credits related to. Agent Lucika wrote down on his notepad a bullet to have the trainers spend an hour or two with Tavishien and indoctrinate her on the currency and what relative value it was for various products and services.

Agent Lucika knew he couldn't take anything for granted, Tavishien lacked exposure to most of society. This was not going to be an easy chore to prepare her for dealing with a financial services person who was above average intelligence and very experienced in life matters.

Now the schooling started and Ljótunn bon Swartzler said, "We have set up cameras so that we can record your activity then do a playback side-by-side with one of these fashion models to see how you performed in comparison to them."

"Alright. It doesn't seem like they did that much."

The room was a good fifty feet long and from the conference room table to the wall behind Tavishien was at least ten feet with plenty of room to walk around which would be a case during break times when people attending meetings could have their private side bars or utilize their personal communicators to contact their boss, their wife, or someone business related.

The room's open area was perfect for a fashion model runway. A camera on a tripod was set up at the end of the room where it could film Tavishien walking towards the camera.

Soon Tavishien was taking walks down the runway after reviewing each model before her launch. She then came back to the table sitting next to Ljótunn bon Swartzler who gave her great description of all the movements and things the fashion model did.

"Remember, we don't want them looking at your face, we want them to look at your body because that's where the clothes are we want to sell."

In due time facial expressions and actions were gone over and in the span of about half an hour Tavishien was amazed at how technical it was. Then came the big surprise: "You have to synchronize yourself to the music just like an ice skater does."

Agent Lucika was now writing more notes: "Show Tavishien some ice-skating videos."

After a couple walks down the conference room, being filmed, Tavishien quickly discovered by no way did she compare with the women in the video. And she had an attitude. Aside from wanting to beat the crap out of Gabriel, she now wanted to show those starlet fashion models, she could do it as good as they did. And now she knew she had a lot to learn. So, it was all ears and concentration.

Ljótunn bon Swartzler spotted the eagerness in Tavishien and her sudden thirst for knowledge. It's always more efficient when you have a student that wants to learn.

So now as Tavishien made those treks down the conference room, Ljótunn bon Swartzler standing in the middle gave her constant instruction just like a Karate instructor would. This was no different than a Karate Kata or an ice skater routine, every move was designed and specific. And as Ljótunn bon Swartzler is teaching she's explaining the purpose of each movement, which is based on showcasing the clothes, not the woman.

Tavishien totally understood it and her realization caught on quickly and discovered fashion models walking down the runway were acting or making complex movements, no different than a Karate Kata, ballet dancer, or other arts and crafts people. It was a surreal awakening.

With Ljótunn bon Swartzler guiding her along she was doing all the moves perfectly.

Agent Lucika noted in his notebook, *make sure Tavishien has an earbud, and we have Ljótunn bon Swartzler giving her the coaching remotely via closed circuits.*

The training went on until noon time then it was time for Ljótunn bon Swartzler to depart because Tavishien had physical training and lectures to attend for her education.

By evening mealtime, Tavishien had received condensed education and a good physical workout with Gabriel's assistants. She went back to her dorm room, took a shower, changed, then hopped over to the cafeteria and got a healthy meal. Then it was bedtime and dreams about her Tomlar herd and her father. She slept well and in the morning her handlers woke her up to get her ready for her next Ljótunn bon Swartzler session. She had a slight meal, drink, and was ready for training.

This time there were more people. It was going to get more interesting today.

"Tavishien, we do not know for sure how best to dress you for your exposure to your future contacts. Therefore, we must experiment by giving you several hair designs until we find the right style."

The hair shampoo that Tavishien was using was replaced secretly while she was away to apply the substances deemed necessary to promote good hair style. It smelled the same and she would never know.

When Tavishien arrived the next day in the conference room for more training, she discovered far more equipment there than ever before and another half dozen people and racks of clothes. It was mildly disconcerting, but Tavishien handled it.

Ljótunn bon Swartzler started the conversation:

"Good morning Tavishien. We are going to step up your training into high gear. You did well yesterday, but it was as if you were casually dressed. From now on you will be dressed as a model because you need to have the psychology of the fashion model as you walk down the runway and demonstrate the clothing, and in your case to entice the targets of your missions. We learned a long time ago to train just like you would in a real mission, which means you need to be dressed for the training exactly like you would for the real event."

"I do not think I need all that, I think I can train like we did yesterday." Tavishien said.

"Tavishien, why do you think major sports athletes wear their specific equipment while they train? You must be accustomed to dealing with these expensive clothes just like you would be walking down the runway. I'm sorry, but I can't teach you how to do that in your workout clothes. Today when you put on these designer clothes you will discover it adds an element of the requirements for your training. "

"Alright I will cooperate the best I can."

"In your specific case it's another requirement we must work on. You are not only going to be selling the clothes to the target of your mission, but you are also going to have to sell yourself. This is going to be much more difficult than training a fashion model because they only need to sell the clothes. In your case you also must sell your soul."

"I'll do what I have to do."

"Back behind those dividers is your temporary dressing room. This is Sumi who will dress you. We already have your first wardrobe there to change into as well as a hair designer that will work on your hair. A makeup artist will be there as well to convert your image to what we have designed to specifically mesh with the fashion design you will be wearing."

Tavishien had no idea what was going to happen next and simply went along with it. She had some curiosity about what was going to happen but knew to wait to see the results and simply said, "Sure. I'm ready to do what I need to do."

The fashion experts led Tavishien back behind the room dividers and sat her down in what appeared to be a barber's chair that could be lifted to the best height for the technicians now starting to work on her.

The hair designers were not going to shorten her hair as they realized her elegance would better shine with longer hair in a nice design. The new shampoo product Tavishien used that was designed specifically by Ljótunn bon Swartzler, made her hair ultra-soft and manageable. At the same time the hair designer was working on the hair, a makeup artist began the facial transformation.

"Tavishien, I'm going to put some facial products on your face now that will allow up to put on makeup to change your appearance. Once we get done, nobody will know who you are."

"That's good, maybe it will enable me to sneak out of here later," Tavishien remarked.

Tavishien sat there like a good soldier and the crew went to work. In thirty minutes, Tavishien was sporting a new hair style and luxurious makeup that completely morphed her into an entirely different person. The fashion designers did not let Tavishien look into the mirror until they had her designer dress and shoes on. Then one of the fashion designers turned a large full-length mirror around to allow her to see herself.

It was clear for a few moments Tavishien was in a state of shock. The video's showed women can be made to look beautiful, but here she was looking at herself and the transformation. She had no idea she could be made to look so exotic and so beautiful.

Ljótunn bon Swartzler now inspecting the fashion designer, hairdresser, and makeup artist creation felt pleased with what she saw and after she had Tavishien put her ear bud in one of her ears.

"Tavishien, we are going to simulate that Agent Lucika is your target. Assume there are others there to watch you walk down the runway. You are to conduct yourself exactly like you did in the later portion of our session yesterday," Ljótunn bon Swartzler said.

"Sure," Tavishien replied.

"Do not make eye contact with anyone in the room and follow my directions as I will coach you in how to move with this specific garment on."

"Understood."

"This will be a tough one because when you go out there you will elicit emotion out of some people in the audience and you are going to have to learn to not allow them to capture your attention."

"I'm sure I can stay focused."

"You have a job to do, and you are the purveyor of all the emotions for the next ten minutes. You are going to walk down the runway, do your modeling, then come back to this dressing area, where we will change your clothes within five minutes, just like at a fashion show."

"Why such a rush?"

"Timing is critical, you cannot allow the audience to cool down before you hit them with the next imagery."

"Alright, I think I can do it."

"Good. I'm going back to my spot at the conference table and as soon as the music starts, walk up to the other end of the conference room, count to twenty, stand there during the count, then begin your movement down the runway, synchronized with the music, and I will coach you once you start."

"Alright, I'm ready."

Ljótunn bon Swartzler walked out of the dressing area, then stepped up to the center area of the table next to the sound technician ready to start the music. She smiled at Agent Lucika because she knew for a fact, he had no idea what was coming next. And she loved to surprise Agent Lucika.

After nodding at the sound technician, the music started playing and as expected Tavishien walked out behind the room divider and walked casual to the other end of the room, stopped, and turned around and counted to twenty.

In the room sitting next to Agent Lucika, was Gabriel who was brought in to observe her student. She wasn't physically fit to fight with Tavishien any time soon, but Agent Lucika respected Gabriel's insights and comments. He would talk to her privately after the fashion show.

At what Ljótunn bon Swartzler thought was twenty seconds, she spoke softly in her microphone: "Begin."

Tavishien walked down the full length of the runway taking directions from Ljótunn bon Swartzler then turned around at the end and walked back up the improvised runway, just like she would do at a fashion show and exit to the backstage area.

In this case, she was directed to simply turn around and walk casually back to the dressing area, to change into her next outfit.

Ljótunn bon Swartzler looked over at Agent Lucika and Gabriel. Ljótunn bon Swartzler was highly trained in studying body language since customer reaction was a huge impact on fashion shows.

Ljótunn bon Swartzler could tell that Agent Lucika and Gabriel were both stunned and, in a semi, trance reacting to how much Tavishien had changed as well as how glamorous she could be made to look.

To Agent Lucika this solved a lot of issues because a smoking hot woman like Tavishien would have no troubles in motivating the little heads of despots wanting to feel the invigoration of experiencing the splendor of such an elegant looking person.

The music stopped for five minutes since that would be the signal to recommence once Tavishien was prepared to model the next dress. When they completed the change, one of the fashion designers stepped part way out of the change area and nodded, then the music started again.

The transcendence in Agent Lucika's emotions also began as he was slowly mesmerized at what he now saw. Tavishien's first wardrobe was alluring, now she was almost hypnotic and walked the runway again leaving Agent Lucika speechless.

During the next change, Agent Lucika took Gabriel with him to his office to have a private discussion.

"What do you think?" Agent Lucika asked.

"To be honest I was shocked," Gabriel responded.

"I think she is slowly developing the credentials in many ways, that will make it plausible to deploy her on some field tests in the weeks ahead," Agent Lucika.

"What do you have in mind?"

The plan was unfolded to Gabriel and at the end of the discussion Agent Lucika said what he had in mind for Gabriel.

"Since this is her first time out and I'm more concerned about her ability to deliver me the information than her ability to protect herself. Just in case she's not ready to fully defend herself, I want to send you along as a backup to make sure she gets out of there without getting hurt."

"I'm sure between the two of us, we'll be able to handle whatever they dish out at us."

"You will be well armed, and the backup team will have additional firepower just in case this turns ugly."

"It would not be my first time I left my mark on a person of interest."

"Remember in our business, the idea is to get away with the goods without them knowing. You will swing into action once you determine it's a case of last resort. I don't want Tavishien injured in any manner during the mission."

"What you are doing to her is placing her in high risk, the way she's being dressed up she will tantalize the dude's little head and he'll want some action."

"Let him think he's going to get all the action he wants, but the two of you are to exit immediately after Tavishien indicates she can remote view him."

"Understand all."

At noon, when the fashion consultant was done training Tavishien for the day, Agent Lucika entered the room with some last-minute instructions.

"Gabriel, escort Tavishien back to her dormitory room. She needs to shower and get all the makeup and hair design out before she goes to the cafeteria to eat. I want her to maintain her normal appearance until she's prepped for the mission, then we'll leave immediately for our destination."

"Right away, Agent Lucika."

Tavishien was in her plane Jane clothes but her hair and makeup did make her look like eye candy to people at the intelligence bureau

Campus would pick up on rather quickly if she went to the cafeteria or to workout in that appearance. In the spy business, subtlety is everything.

One thing that crossed Agent Lucika's mind was he hoped one of the women didn't *bitch slap* the other and have a fight before they got to the cafeteria. He relied on Gabriel's professionalism, but one never knew how much pent-up emotions Tavishien had for frequently receiving abuse by Gabriel until the recent fight that put Gabriel in the hospital.

The women arrived at Tavishien's dormitory room. Tavishien knew what her instructions were, to wash off all the makeup and wash her hair to undo the hair design, she didn't need Gabriel's help.

"I can take it from here." Tavishien said.

"Sure, call me when you are ready to go to the cafeteria there is something I want to talk to you about."

"Alright."

Tavishien took a bath, washed her hair and cleaned off all her makeup and was soon looking in the mirror at the plane Jane again. But she was thrilled at the way she looked earlier and intrigued why Agent Lucika looked at her the way he did. Was she reading too much into what she was thinking, then she did the big NO-NO. She started remote viewing Agent Lucika and soon wished she hadn't, but now it was too late. She would be getting his thoughts and his visions in the future regardless of her desires.

When she was ready to head for the cafeteria, she called Gabriel using the communicator Agent Lucika gave her that had a lot of other features that would eventually help her in the spy business.

"Alright I'll be right there," Gabriel said soon after answering her communicator.

Moments later, Gabriel, who was dressed modestly met Tavishien at her door to her dormitory room. The women then walked the short distance to the cafeteria and had their talk on the way.

"You looked very pretty today; it was amazing how nice you look."

"Thank you."

"You will be going on a mission soon. I will be going with you, so I don't want any hard feelings between us to exist."

"I have no hard feelings towards you. After I beat your ass in the fight, I lost all my anger."

"I must admit you did a great job. I was proud of you even though it was painful."

"How can you be proud of me for beating your ass?"

"Remember, you are my student, I trained you well enough to beat my ass, which means you can beat most women and a lot of men."

The women had their lunch and chatted about trivial things and then it was time to dress for some physical exercise. They were soon in the gym ready to go to it.

"What are doing today?" Tavishien asked.

"As you can imagine, I'm not in good shape to work out with you in martial arts so we are going to work on your endurance. You are going for a run, and I will follow you along on a bicycle." Sure enough, Gabriel had a bicycle parked at the entrance to the gym and as the two went outside to start Tavishien's run, which Gabriel quickly hopped on and the two took off heading out on that two-mile loop Tavishien was very familiar with.

The course has some slight hills in it. As they were heading up small hills Gabriel was standing up on her bicycle putting in some hard peddling, but as they started down the hill se sat back and coasted, keeping a distance behind Tavishien who was pouring on the coals.

Tavishien who was slowly working her condition up to a point where most top athletes operated didn't feel her body kick in adrenaline, noradrenaline, and cortisol until the two-mile mark. Then she felt like she obtained her second wind. After the six-mile mark, Tavishien was starting to feel more stress and discomfort and her breathing became more pronounced.

Tavishien's body was not able to give her any more of those stress hormones so for the next two miles and the last lap it was all *willpower*. It was moments like this she forced herself to remember what the six monsters did to her before her father killed all of them. Her *willpower* then increased a full magnitude.

The bicycle had a speedometer on it plus Gabriel's wristband holding her personal communicator had satellite navigation coordinates logging once a second, building an image she could play back later that showed her location on the bicycle, speed, acceleration, or any other positional measurement including distance measurement and rate of travel.

Tavishien was keeping up a velocity of ten miles per hour running, but when she ran down the hills, she increased to eleven to twelve miles per hour. Finally, they came up to the last quarter mile and Tavishien knew she was almost done and felt the fury of her heart and her psychological transcendence as she forced herself to uncover her mental wounds and increased velocity to thirteen and fourteen miles per hour, just like she was a sprinter at a track meet. Her body was also drenched in sweat.

After passing the well-known start marker she then decelerated to a walk and continued for a bit walking and breathing hard. Tavishien knew her legs hurt, and it was hard to breathe for a while as she was sucking for air. But she also realized she had to be in great shape to fight off evil *bastards* that would do to her just like the Tartar soldiers.

Later when Gabriel observed the computer display in her office automatically created by the macro processing function the artificial intelligence plotted color coded on each lap. The first lap was baby blue, second lap pink, third lap lime green, and the fourth lap a light purple. The distance plotted above the simulated street gave a visual representation of speed. There was separation of a few feet on the image that appeared canted at about a fifteen-degree angle, just as if it were filmed by a drone.

When Gabriel placed the cursor over the top of any of the colored traces, the instantaneous velocity and the ten second average also displayed. If she wanted, she could select exponential averages that allowed a fast build up and slow bleed off the data. That was good to look at as well since it showed areas during the run where significant acceleration occurred which also resulted in the line becoming thicker and more pronounced.

During the last quarter mile, the line plotted became very thick and the numbers climbed. In the exponential average display, Gabriel could see the exact spot where something triggered Tavishien's acceleration. She soon forwarded that information to the chief psychiatrist overseeing Tavishien's mental health profile and performing mitigation when required.

Mindful that Tavishien's terrible experience led her to coming here was one of those psychological wounds that would not heal anytime soon. So, the treatment was to treat the wound with more out of sight and out of mind and to do things to help erase those memories.

In due time during counseling sessions the Psychiatrist learned this was a point when Tavishien uncloaked those memories and used that psychological inducement to increase her performance by twenty-eight-point five percent.

That report was sent to Agent Lucika who then forwarded it to Gabriel who now was starting to realize what made Tavishien tick and know what to use in the future if they were in a serious scenario and they needed every prayer of a chance to get out of a bad situation.

***

CHAPTER EIGHT
Showtime

Besides more fashion model training, workouts, a few more weeks went by then it was showtime and general education ended for a while. Tavishien received special briefings directly from Agent Lucika on the mission that was ready to launch. They would soon be leaving the intelligence bureau Campus, get on an airplane and fly a long distance to where an investor's conference was taking place in a lavish resort/hotel.

There were certainly many examples of eye candy floating around the hotel. Nevertheless, Tavishien was well prepared, and her stunning imagery placed her on equal footing as all the other eye candy flown there to give the financial genius and company economists their inducements for being loyal to the investment cartels. Half of the women navigating the resort hotel and the swimming pool in revealing bikinis were girls for hire, extremely well-paid corporate concubines role playing to make the sugar daddy believe they were there for their love and emotion.

The cold-blooded snakes were there for the money and access to insider trading. Any influencer brought in would have to exceed the luster of all those play bunnies roaming around. Half of the play bunnies were mildly uneducated, and the investment cartel people were only interested in the three "F's" so there was no need to be banging a rocket scientist.

Tavishien's target, Thurston bon Katterberg liked them young. His old hag wife was left home like usual to cry in her beers while the illustrious financial wizard went off to do his work. To Mrs. Katterberg, her dull husband who was always discussing numbers and investments to his inner circle which she overheard, had no idea he lived a secret second life where he acted out his lust and desires for fine looking young women who proved time and time again hey were experts of eliminating "soft offs."

At most of these investment conferences, the master of ceremonies for the concubines was the illustrious Maxine Causwell. Thurston bon Katterberg directed his administrative aid, a young twenty-eight-year-old woman named Sandra to contact Maxine Causwell to make arrangements for a lovely young woman he would soon be feasting over on a theme from Paganini.

Long before that meeting two women showed up unexpectedly in the hotel that were dressed so well, they could be an inherent risk to Maxine Causwell's concubines, so she naturally took interest in them. They didn't need to work for Maxine. All Maxine had to do was make the arrangements and Thurston bon Katterberg would pay her nicely with Ponzi scheme funds he raked off simple minded investors who thought he looked out for their financial interests.

Maxine Causwell was not bad looking herself and in fact had sex with Thurston bon Katterberg a time or two when there was no appropriate young lady available to satisfy his needs.

Today Maxine Causwell was wearing a purple dress that went down to approximately five inches above the knee which was appropriate since she was a taller woman about six inches taller than most women. Her cleavage was showing through the nice slit in the middle of the dress top. A darker purple sash around her mid-section with a gold medallion on the front gave Maxine an image that would get a lot of men reacting with their little head.

Maxine's only issue was she had now reached forty years of age and no longer had that wonderful soft skin of a twenty-five-year-old. Her other attributes showed signs of significant activity, so she knew she wasn't a spring chick and learned early on to become the Madam of the concubines to insure she maintained her level of income.

Maxine Causwell was resourceful and conniving. There were many a young lady who ended up in bed with men like Thurston bon Katterberg who had no intention of giving it up that were slightly drugged up and suddenly working on their backs in ways they never planned. Since they had no idea how they ended up in the strangers bed it would be hard for them to complain to law enforcement who illogically thought the young ladies were working girls being pimped by Maxine Causwell. In some cases, Maxine bribed undercover agents with money and girls to get them to go along with the program.

The bankers and investment advisors that attended these financial conferences were untouchable. Any young lady who wanted to go the extra mile to have them prosecuted over a flimsy rape charge, would be harshly dealt with, including sometimes by corrupt law enforcement.

Tavishien wore a light blue dress and had her hair pulled to one side that allowed her designer earring to show on the other side. Her makeup and red lipstick accentuated her makeup and her blue eyes. She had very nice eyebrows that conveyed luster. One could say her nose was in perfect geometry for her face size.

Even though Tavishien worked out every day, she still had a feminine looking body. She had nice breasts that would encourage any mere mortal, and the strapless dress covering only half her breasts allowed enough to be seen that men and women alike enjoyed looking at Tavishien. The dress came up to just a few inches below the crotch, hence she had to be careful sitting down to cover up that area with her hand to avoid giving men a free look at what she bestowed in that area including a tantalizing undergarment that left little to the imagination.

Ljótunn bon Swartzler an older woman and out of the range of the dirty old men who wanted younger flesh, was impeccably well dressed. Ljótunn bon Swartzler would be always close by to give Tavishien and Gabriel directions as to accentuate their bodies in a way to make men start using their little heads in overdrive.

Some of the resort hotel clientele enjoying the pool, the bar, and the eye candy were Agent Lucika's men and women. They masqueraded as couples even staying in the same hotel rooms together to give the appearance, they were on a lover's tryst and enjoying life. All the team members knew who Tavishien and

Gabriel were, but not necessarily the opposite. Sometimes it's best a spy does not have awareness of the support staff, so they do not accidentally blow their cover.

Gabriel had a nice makeover as well. This was not her first nor would it be her last time to dress up for a clandestine operation. Only she, Agent Lucika, and Ljótunn bon Swartzler knew what Tavishien's mission was. The mission was compartmentalized, and the team only knew one thing, to make sure nothing bad happened to Tavishien.

Tavishien wore shoes with bugs in them so she could be remotely monitored in the event she went in the room with Thurston bon Katterberg. If the investor wizard tried to rape Tavishien and she was not able to get away from the attacker, she had her trip wire code word that would send people flying to her rescue including what appeared to be hotel maids with a cart load of weapons.

Thurston would always go into a room with two bodyguards hanging outside to prevent anyone interfering with what he planned on doing to the young woman. Knowing he would attempt to drug Tavishien as that was his modus operendus, she would have the antidote ingested before they had their casual contact.

Gabriel wearing fake blonde hair today, had on a short moth colored dress with shoulders but a bear spot on the chest that showed her cleavage. Her dress barely covered her crotch as well and she had hips with perfect geometry that would help most men's little head think hard.

Purposely Braless in her dress to entice men, Gabriel's areola and nipples were apparent in the dress even though there was no color that could be seen. With her superb makeup done by world class makeup artists, she appeared as a woman in her early 30's instead of a woman pushing 40.

The stage was set, all they needed to do now was be seen, especially by Thurston bon Katterberg resulting in him contacting Maxine Causwell to arrange a rendezvous. If he suggested a three way with both women, Maxine would work on it knowing it could be potentially very expensive if these were actual working girls that penetrated hotel security to latch onto wealthy clients.

Usually, hotel security was very successful at keeping out working girls unless they worked for Maxine Causwell who bribed them quite well and it would not be the first time Maxine slept with the chief of security to ensure her girls could operate unmolested.

The conference was underway and the first day events were just concluded shortly after Tavishien and Gabriel arrived. Thurston bon Katterberg had just successfully conned a few neophytes who appeared desperate to make a killing off their investments because they had such lackluster success in the past.

Neophytes were proving investment doesn't pay, that if they wanted to make big money, they either had to start trading securities which they didn't have the acumen or go to a specialist like Thurston bon Katterberg operating hedge funds that reportedly returned stratospheric growth in investments.

When it comes to a Ponzi scheme, the operators knew the axiom of investments: Greedy get killed and Pigs get slaughtered. By producing vast gains year over year, the Pigs and the Greedy never had the common sense to stop and think, *If it's true good to be true, it probably is.* As the neophytes watched their investments grow, they had every reason to leave the investment parked for a few more years to get the huge return on their investment.

Testimonials by the shrewd ones who cashed out added to the luster of the Ponzi scheme which tended to coerce more neophytes to invest, and the ones already invested to keep dumping more money there chasing contrived gains. Because so many investors were hooked, there was always more money coming in than going out so there was never any issue of paying someone who was cashing out and bragging about the profits.

The seemingly impossible mission operation is highly choreographed and based on past activity. Agent Lucika's team was briefed that Thurston bon Katterberg would soon be escorting a new group of suckers to the resort/hotel bar and flood them with drinks and elixirs to enhance their satisfaction of dealing with such a great financial wizard. Chief among the new suckers were fund managers and banksters. The banksters were just as bad as Thurston bon Katterberg and were simply trying to multiply the wealth they stole out of clients' accounts.

After quite a few of the seminar attendees settled into somewhat a huddle at the bar toasting and talking BS to each other, the two glorious women would make their grand entry, just like they were walking down the runway at a fashion show.

Ljótunn bon Swartzler following a distance behind knew these two women would get the attention of the men in the room and simply slithered in with an escort and sat down at the rear of the bar where she could talk into her secret microphone and give the appearance she was talking to her escort. The women wearing a well camouflaged ear bud on the side of their head covered up by the hair style would take directions from the master who could also hear the conversations which would help to create new pathways towards seduction.

All they had to do was get Tavishien alone in the room with Thurston bon Katterberg to read his Aura then they could all depart and allow Agent Lucika to perform the next phase of the operation that included the remote viewing and the follow-up to determine the accuracy. Part of the plan was a support staff set of couples had a reserved table enjoying drinks waiting for their clue to get up and leave.

The women marched in just like on the fashion model runway and as soon as they were right at the table near the bar, the two couples stood up and left with their half empty glasses sitting there and Tavishien and Gabriel quickly took the chairs in this high visibility portion of the bar that was now getting crowded as more and more investors left the conference room and made their way to the bar to bolster their ego's with alcoholic and elixir drinks laced with BS stories to impress the others. A lot of these investors liked to brag how they did a major score in their investments and were now diversifying the wealth through a hedge fund operator like Thurston bon Katterberg.

Thurston bon Katterberg was always looking for eye candy and he knew that Maxine Causwell would soon be contacting him, and he speculated the eye candy delivered as short distance away, was manifested by her great finesse.

In due time as his little head was focused on the girl in the light blue dress, he stepped away from the bar and walked over near a window where it appeared he was simply having a business call which was expected especially at a conference like today.

"Hello Thurston."

"Maxine, those are two lovely women you brought in here."

"I didn't bring any women there. Are you at the bar?"

"Yes."

"Let me go take a look to see what you are talking about."

"The girl in the light blue dress is the one I'm interested in. She's sitting across from another nice-looking woman wearing a moth-colored dress."

"I'll be there in a minute."

Thurston went back to his place at the bar where he was giving a neophyte, pointers on investing and how he saw the market going in the next six months.

Even though the bar was getting crowded and rowdy, Maxine Causwell was able to find a table across the room where she could analyze the women that Thurston mentioned. Maxine Causwell knew Thurston bon Katterberg's pecker was on over drive the minute she laid her eyes on Tavishien. The other woman wasn't too bad either and the fact she wore a dress that showed off her nipples and aerials led Maxine to evaluate Gabriel she would soon meet, as a tramp looking for some action. *If she's looking for action so is her friend,* Maxine concluded.

In a moment she called Thurston who walked back over to the window looking like he was taking a business call.

"Thurston, I do not know who those two women are."

"That's alright, can you help introduce the lady in the blue dress to me."

"Certainly, but standard rates and conditions apply even though they are not my girls."

"You get the girl in blue up in my room, I'll even throw in a bonus."

"She turns you on that much?"

"When she stands up and you see how short her dress is and now nice her legs are, you will know why I have such enthusiasm."

"I can tell from here; she and her slutty friend have on short dresses."

"Alright, you know what you need to do."

Thurston went back over to his place at the bar and continued schmoozing the greenhorn-neophyte that was eager to hand over a large amount of cash chasing investment dreams.

Right about the time the waitress approached Maxine Causwell's table and saw the women had not given orders to any waitress and were still sitting there waiting for service, stood up and said, I'm going to relocate over there to that table with the two young ladies. Give me a minute to introduce myself, then come over and I want to buy them a round of drinks.

"Alright Madam Causwell," the waitress said who know Maxine quite well and understood she was the madam because she had been here many times before.

Maxine then walked over to the table and said to Gabriel, "That is such a pretty dress you have on."

"Thank you."

Maxine then turned to Tavishien and said, "I didn't think God made such beautiful women like you anymore, where did you come from?"

"Actually, the mountains. That's why I'm so healthy."

In their earbuds, Tavishien and Gabriel were simultaneously alerted, "This is Maxine Causwell who arranges young women for Thurston bon Katterberg, invite her to sit down and have a drink with you."

Gabriel immediately responded, "Would you like to join us?"

"Certainly, you have the best seats in the house."

Part of their spy training included using their real first names so that they would not accidentally blow their cover story in the future by accidentally stating the wrong name.

"I'm Gabriel and this is Tavishien."

"I'm very glad to meet you. My name is Maxine Causwell."

"Thank you, Maxine," Gabriel stated hoping that Tavishien would soon spring into action to get the focus on her.

About that time the waitress who knew Maxine Causwell's motives approached the table and asked, "Ladies may I get you something to drink?"

Maxine Causwell quickly responded, "Yes, and I would like to buy these ladies a drink."

The waitress who liked girls over men, looked down at Gabriel's breasts and enjoyed the view and said, "Madam what would you like to drink."

"I'll have a Kanill Grasker elixir."

Tavishien briefed on what types of elixirs and drinks that would work best with the anti-dote she just swallowed before coming to the bar in case she was drugged, responded, "I'll just have some red wine."

"And you madam?" the waitress asked as she turned towards Maxine Causwell, knowing what her usual drink was, but had to ask the question out of decorum.

"I'll have a Gæsaber elixir."

The Gæsaber was a double fermented elixir that contained about twenty percent alcohol and gave Maxine Causwell a nice kick which she often needed knowing she secretly felt bad pimping the young women.

Maxine Causwell, who needed the income knew the axioms of the business she was in. Either pimp or be pimped. The former was always more pleasant than the latter.

Tell me ladies, what brings you to the Grand Xenix Resort?

Gabriel chimed in quickly because she knew Tavishien would have to think about her cover story for a moment that would end up looking suspicious and said, "We are fashion models. We are here to look over a few venues in the city for the designer to put on a show in the future."

"Why don't you just put on the show in this hotel, it has all the amenities you would need."

"I'm sure the fashion designer wouldn't mind putting on the show here, but quite frankly I think she would be more interested closer to the center of the city because people must take transportation to get out here to the Strip and back," Gabriel responded.

"I would think people with a lot of money would not mind coming out here even though it's out of the way," Maxine Causwell said.

"Part of the issue is everyone working the show that must be involved. We must use local talent and having a venue closer to downtown also solves their transportation problems," Gabriel said.

Thurston bon Katterberg knew there were a dozen horny guys at the bar now that would be making a play for the eye candy sitting in front of him. He knew his teammate Maxine Causwell would facilitate his approach and enrapture of the two young ladies and it would cost him, but since he had quite a bit of that Ponzi scheme money available to spend, her costs would be trivial to him. He needed to beat his contemporaries to the battle zone, the ladies table.

Thurston also wanted to get a closer look at Tavishien who now had her back to him. He let the lady's chit chat a while longer and knew he was running out of time an option if he did not strike now and beat the other horn toads to the lady's table. Right in the middle of a bunch of dumb questions by the Neophyte who had transferred large sums of money to him only a short while ago, Thurston said, "Excuse me a minute I want to go say hello to my friend Maxine."

Based on what was discussed already, Maxine Causwell assumed it would take another thirty to forty-five minutes before it would be appropriate to introduce the two stunningly attractive women to Thurston bon Katterberg. Then suddenly out of nowhere for reasons she didn't understand, Thurston approached the table and said, "Hello Maxine, how have you been?" "Thurston, I've been quite well. Thank you for asking."

"Thurston, this is Gabriel and Tavishien," Maxine Causwell said and pointed with palm upwards to each woman as she mentioned their names."

"I'm really glad to meet you Gabriel and Tavishien."

Then to play along as if this was a spontaneous effort Gabriel and Tavishien made to make it look like an accidental meeting, the language gave that innocent impression as this chance meeting was a big surprise.

"Ladies, Thurston here is my financial advisor. He tells me where to invest my money and so far, has done an excellent job of assisting me in managing my portfolio and creating nice gains for me so I can enjoy life."

"That's very nice of him," Gabriel said.

Tavishien sat somewhat quiet and was now just starting to learn a little about investments with her training she was getting to bring her up to modern times. Life on a mountain in the middle of a forest usually has no relevance to investments, nor were there really any good legal documents as to saying who owned the land. The frontiersmen simply believed in the philosophy: possession is nine/tenths of the law in these matters.

The Frontiersmen and people that lived a few miles away from Tavishien's father viewed him as the landowner since he had been living there fifty or more years. They also traded with him and now and then there was a community party where Frontiersmen and women came from miles away to get together, eat, drink, and tell stories.

Therefore, there was plenty of backup to the notion Tavishien's father owned that mountain land, just like his neighbors own their land, and if there was a dispute, they would settle it among themselves, or someone would end up dead.

It was a hard life, but they all lived in the same conditions, so nobody felt sorry for anyone. This whole notion of securities and investments was quite a huge awakening to Tavishien. And now she learned they were paying her well and putting funds into her trust fund where it would be managed by professionals and grown to keep ahead of inflation and build her equity for her future life where she would not be destitute nor need to move back to her father's cabin the day her remote viewing ended.

Tavishien had somewhat come to the realization there was more to life than staying buttoned up in a cabin in the winter with a herd of Tomlars in the Barn attached to the home. Tavishien's income was considerably higher than most citizens. However, that could abruptly end if she was found not to have promising remote viewing ability.

Tavishien could almost get Thurston bon Katterberg's Aura while he stood next to her checking her out carefully. It only took Gabriel and Maxine Causwell five minutes to figure out Thurston bon Katterberg was interested in Tavishien who cast a spell upon him. Thurston bon Katterberg was already slightly lubricated from the elixirs he enjoyed at the bar a few minutes ago. Some of the elixirs accelerated his libido to a certain extent. His concentration and his focus were being guided and prompted by messages his little head sent to his big head.

Thurston bon Katterberg had tasted a few young women who looked very similar to Tavishien, and he knew that if he could get her out of the bar and into his hotel room, he might just travel down that road to ecstasy again together with this gorgeous creature.

Little did Thurston bon Katterberg know, Tavishien had no interest in sex. Her experience with those six terrible soldiers prevented her from ever having such desires in the future. But she would go to his room at the appropriate time so she could read his Aura then promptly leave the Grand Xenix Resort with her handlers and likely to never come back.

Since Tavishien and Gabriel were wired up, any conversation would be immediately available for coaching and modification of actions based upon conditions that transpired.

"Thurston, why don't you join us for a drink?" Maxine Causwell suggested overstepping the boundary of her relevance since she was invited to the table occupied by Gabriel and Tavishien.

"I would be delighted."

Tavishien started reading Thurston bon Katterberg's Aura as soon as he sat down between her and Gabriel.

Tavishien realized she probably didn't need to go to his hotel room to be able to do remote viewing in the future, but the bar was noisy and filled with people that were blurring Thurston's Aura, so it wouldn't be pure and could cause some scattered success in the future. She would have to be alone with him for a short while.

The four sat there enjoying drinks and talking. Thurston was a charmer but Gabriel and Tavishien were all professional. Thurston's charm was not going to work on the two women, but in the dangerous game they played, they gave adaquate feedback to make him think otherwise.

Tavishien started receiving special instructions in her ear bud: "Inform Thurston you need to go to the lady's room and when you get up be sure and walk down the runway just like you were taught."

A moment later, Tavishien said, "Excuse me for a minute I need to go visit the lady's room, I'll be right back."

Gabriel, under normal conditions, would have volunteered to go with Tavishien to the lady's room to enhance her physical security, but she also heard the special instruction which meant to go put on a show. It was all about seducing Thurston by Tavishien to get him in the room where the careful Aura reading could be done with no distractions or excess noise that currently surrounded them.

Tavishien was halfway down the bar/restaurant center entrance way before, Maxine Causwell realized she had screwed up and not offered to go with Tavishien. However, the effort already paid off as Thurston under video surveillance and not knowing it was focused on Tavishien's tush and watched intently as she walked down the runway and his focus on her was easily noticed.

Thurston was captivated at what he observed and the people watching him including a psychologist very advanced in body language dynamics determined he was infatuated, and the result would be he would succumb to his libido and put maximum effort into getting her alone where his fantasy could come true.

Support staff immediately went into the bathroom to provide a layer of security for Tavishien to make sure she was not molested or mistreated in the bathroom, but most likely she could defend herself from anyone who attacked her there and she was not in the mood to let someone mistreat her.

Tavishien wasn't there to use the bathroom. Her only reason to go to the lady's room was to walk down the runway and give Thurston bon Katterberg the imagery to work on his psychology and his libido to entice his future actions.

After a delay to simulate a woman's time in the lady's room, Tavishien was prompted, "Go back to the table wearing the alluring subtle smile we trained you to do."

Tavishien nodded at the support staff and exited the lady's room and walked down the runway towards her target. She was in fact beautiful, and she knew it, but she also knew she had made every dick hard at the bar, Thurston included. As a trained fashion model, she knew how to look forward and towards her destination and not make eye contact with the horny men at the bar. They might be rich and loaded and here to get richer with Thurston's help, but they were not in a position to get any of this pussy cat.

Thurston had gathered great appreciation for when Tavishien left to go to the lady's room but now as he observes her body from the front view, he felt utterly speechless. The makeup artists, fashion designer, and Ljótunn bon Swartzler had trained Tavishien extremely well because they had a unique person unlike anyone they ever encountered before.

And now it was starting to show as Ljótunn bon Swartzler watched her perform and didn't have to give her a single instruction as Tavishien traveled down that runway to her table where she would now complete the seduction of Thurston bon Katterberg.

Maxine Causwell was in awe. She trained a lot of concubines in her days and none of them came close to Tavishien, nor did she know Tavishien could probably kill most of her clients.

When Tavishien returned to her seat, Maxine Causwell already knew the obvious, Thurston bon Katterberg was panting like a dog and if he could leg hump Tavishien without causing a scene he would already be doing it.

Maxine Causwell wasn't nosy; she was just terribly smart at investigating people to find their weakness and strengths in allowing her to find pathways for exploitation. Once the line of work the women did was out in the open, it was a topic Maxine Causwell knew a lot about and asked questions to steer the conversation in the direction she needed it to go to get Tavishien up into Thurston bon Katterberg's Grand Xenix Resort penthouse to give him an opportunity to bang her and allow Maxine to earn a large pile of money out of the transaction.

Since Tavishien's handlers had artificial intelligence to research everything being discussed and real time transcribing of Maxine Causwell's statements, information went into Gabriel and Tavishien's ear buds in parallel including statements Tavishien was to make in response to Maxine's statements or questions.

Half of the information Tavishien received was about things she had no knowledge of. But thanks to the real time feed she elucidated locations and people and personalities in the fashion industry that was totally fiction because she really had no involvement, but it gave Maxine a false sense these two girls were the real deal.

Since Tavishien had worn dozens upon dozens of designer clothes during modeling training, and getting her picture taken against a portrait frame, numerous fashion pictures were loaded up on her personal communicator which would convince the unsuspecting like Maxine Causwell this was the real deal, and these two women had an extensive career in modeling.

As Maxine asked about certain designers and their creations which she personally had seen in places like the Grand Xenix Resort being worn by mistresses of the banksters, Tavishien had pictures of herself wearing those splendid wardrobes. It blew away Maxine Causwell. There she was sitting next to a couple of the top fashion models in the world, and she had Thurston bon Katterberg sitting there taking it all in and panting like a dog wanting to hump Tavishien so badly he would pay any price.

Thurston suddenly stood up and said, "My communicator just buzzed me, excuse me, I need to take this business call."

Thurston walked over to an area by a window that had nobody around so he could appear like he was taking a business call. What he did instead was send Maxine a voice message saying, "I will pay you triple our normal agreement, if you get the blonde up to my room right away."

He then went back to the table and sat down. Suddenly, Maxine stood up and said, "Excuse me for a minute, I need to go to the ladies room."

That wasn't a total lie as she did need to tinker. When she reached the bathroom stall and sat down and pulled up her communicator to get her voice message, she knew Thurston likely sent her, she smiled, knowing it was going to be a good pay day.

Thurston didn't stay much longer as he knew he could count on Maxine to do her part in this transaction and excused himself saying some nice goodbyes to the women and went up to his room to prepare for his transcendence into a tryst on a theme from Paganini.

Meanwhile, Maxine shot Tavishien and Gabriel a deal: "I know someone who would pay you lavishly for your modeling services and is here in the Grand Xenix Resort doing a financial seminar for the next couple of days. I'm sure he would pay you handsomely to show up in designer clothes every day and mingle with his clients. Are you interested?"

The women didn't know how to respond, but their handlers certainly did on the affirmative and shortly the three women were heading up to Thurston's room. When they arrived outside the door to his resort room there were two goons outside in suits obviously part of his security detachment.

One of the goons knew Maxine quite well and knew she was bringing the girls up for Thurston turned and opened the door for them and they smartly marched into the luxurious penthouse.

In their earbuds they knew they were going into Thurston's room and there he was sitting wearing a smoker's jacket with a it up cigar and all smiles.

"Please come in." Thurston was all smiles thinking he would be humping Tavishien in just a few moments after he offered the quid pro quo.

Thurston knew to play along with Maxine as she had a scheme to get the women in the room and would soon do her other scheme to get Gabriel out of the room with her allowing Thurston to be alone with Tavishien.

After they conducted their financial arrangements for the modeling services, Maxine said to Gabriel, "I would like you to come to my penthouse because I have another job that I would like to offer you exclusively."

In her ear bud Gabriel heard, "Go with Machine."

Soon after the two women were out of the room the great octopus started in on Tavishien with his arms around her and groping her and saying all those splendid lies coming from his little head.

In her ear bud Tavishien is directed, "Tell him to go into the bathroom because you do not like undressing in front of men."

As soon as Tavishien said those words to Thurston bon Katterberg his smile and face lit up and he responded, "Okay as soon as you are undressed and under the sheets, yell out to me you're ready."

"I will."

Like a good gentleman, Thurston walked over to the bathroom, went inside and shut the door. The support staff saw the door close through the video camera mounted on the broach Tavishien was wearing and she heard in her ear bud, "Leave the room now. A security detail is approaching the room now to make sure your egress is safe."

Tavishien promptly walked to the room entrance and during the time Thurston was fondling her privates, she got a complete read on his Aura that was not cluttered by anyone being in the room with them. Tavishien would now be able to remote view Thurston with great accuracy.

When Tavishien walked out the door the four men in Agent Lucika's security detachment had just arrived and were facing the two goons guarding Thurston. They were distracted by the four men wondering *WTF* are they doing.

Tavishien walked between them and headed right over to the elevator which had a door open and Gabriel holding it open. Gabriel was smiling because she took the time to *bitch slap* Maxine Causwell after she was touched Gabriel inappropriately and offered a nice lesbian soiree that would never happen.

As soon as Tavishien was in the elevator, Gabriel hit the closed door and they were soon on the way down to the lobby. When the door opened the girls walked out of the elevator to discover Agent Lucika and five agents were there to meet them and intervene at the penthouse if there was a need.

At Thurston's Penthouse door, the four men stared down the two bruisers who suspected these were four guys not to tangle with and the odds were not in their favor. The four men suddenly turned and started walking towards the elevator which arrived just as they arrived there and when the door opened there were a couple more gun slingers there in case there was a need.

Two vehicles pulled up in front of the entrance of the Grand Xenix Resort. Agent Lucika and several of the men escorted the two ladies to one of the vehicles and opened the passenger door for them. After they got in the car and the door was shut. It pulled away and Agent Lucika got in the next automobile with Ljótunn bon Swartzler and followed the first car to the airport where they got on a private Jet and flew back to the Wenmark area where the Intelligence Bureau Campus is located.

By the time they arrived at the Intelligence Bureau Campus, artificial intelligence and staff on hand had put together a significant briefing for Agent Lucika of what all transpired, including the incident between Gabriel and Maxine Causwell.

"I suppose if I were in your shoes, I would have done the same thing," Agent Lucika expressed to Gabriel during her private debrief.

"Nobody is going to touch my privates without my permission including another woman." Gabriel said with a strong tone.

"As it turned out, it allowed you to depart Maxine Causwell's Penthouse at the perfect time to be in the elevator to assist Tavishien egress."

"I was a little concerned about Tavishien getting out of Thurston bon Katterberg's Grand Xenix Resort penthouse."

"As soon as you left the room, we sent up four security detachment men to intervene if Thurston started molesting Tavishien."

"How would they get into the penthouse to rescue her?"

"They had hypodermic nights out pistols with them. The two goons would quickly sleep sitting against the side of the wall, and we have keys to every room in the resort. Thurston would also have received his nights out hypodermic and awaken in the morning with his arms around his two bodyguards."

"I would hope you at least undressed them before you put them all together."

"Luckily we didn't have to do that emergency egress because your departure out of Maxine Causwell's Penthouse and the security guys showing up at the precise moment, alleviated all that."

"What now?"

"I'm going to debrief Tavishien in a few moments. After that it's going to be business as usual, training for your next mission which will be tougher, and we'll be dealing with some bad hombres."

"People that could easily kill us?"

"This will test your teamwork to the utmost. Now that you have recovered from you last boxing match with Tavishien, you can get back to your physical regiment."

"All right."

"One other thing."

"Because of the surveillance we must put on you for your own protection, we know that a couple times a month, you and a couple of your friends go out to various locations and socialize and mingle with others. Would it be possible for you to take Tavishien along a time or two so that she can start to get the feel of what a normal society is like?"

"Sure, that's not a problem. She looks cute when she dresses up. I'm sure a lot of guys will come on to her."

"She's probably not ready for them or a relationship after what she's gone through in her life with her terrible injuries. So be sure and be a good sister and protect her."

"Of course."

"Thank you."

"You are most welcome."

***

The training continued. But Tavishien knew the more she learned the amount of knowledge about the world she lacked. She knew she lived in the stone age with her father. Her only exposure to technology was her father's radio he listened to about an hour each morning, getting the news. Electricity, running water, and having her father stare at her while she took a bath in the same tub her mother bathed in made her feel icky at times. One time when she confronted him as to why he had to watch her bathe his reply was: You look just like your mother. Through you I see her.

Now she was gone. What did he have to look at besides the picture he hand drew many eons ago?

There were a couple more days of Gabriel riding the bicycle, but soon she was back running and working out with Tavishien just like old times.

Tavishien had to warn her, "Listen Gabriel, I know you are a wonderful person and everything and we'll be doing a lot of work together in the future, but I have to warn you, if you *bitch slap* me, I will have to kick your ass again."

"Not to worry, we need to train you now for other types of people you will have to contend with and the only way we can do that is you will soon have to deal with multiple men at the same time. You must learn escape techniques with these guys because your life may depend on it."

Now there was a change of routine that caught Tavishien by surprise. After she showered after her workout and was cleaned up ready to go to the cafeteria for lunch each day, she was taken to Agent Lucika's office where just the two of them met.

"Alright Tavishien, I know it's been a couple days since you met with Thurston bon Katterberg. But I want you to tell me what he's doing now."

"Alright, it will take me a few minutes. While I'm remote viewing you must be absolutely quiet or leave the room or I can't do it."

"I'll be quiet, please proceed."

Tavishien sat back into her chair and let her mind do what she knew it could do. It somehow connected to Thurston bon Katterberg through the ether and was now viewing a holograph that constituted her awareness and physical understanding of the world and those minds she probed.

Tavishien had no idea how it worked. All she knew is it worked and because Thurston touched her inappropriately and was physically close to her. Tavishien received a very strong readout on Thurston's Aura which enabled her now to seek him a long distance away and suddenly see and hear what he was seeing and hearing. After fifteen minutes of total silence and what appeared to be cognitive departure, Tavishien seemed to come out of that blank look on her face. She started telling Agent Lucika information she discovered during the remote viewing.

"Thurston bon Katterberg is in the bar with Maxine Causwell sitting at a table and having an argument. Maxine Causwell wants paid and Thurston said he didn't receive the services requested and thus refused to pay. Thurston had just finished talking to a person named Grondyker who gave him large sums of money to invest. Grondyker is patiently waiting at the bar for Thurston. They were in a big discussion on some of the finer points of the investment before Maxine Causwell approached and demanded Thurston's attention.

Agent Lucika didn't have to take notes, it was all being recorded and the spies they currently had in that bar had secret video recorders on lapels and other devices and hidden microphones. Artificial intelligence working in the background took all Tavishien's comments and transcribed them and stored them into computer memory to be used in developing the AudioVisual-and fact checker report that would be at Agent Lucika's data terminal shortly after Tavishien left the office to make her way to the cafeteria to get something to eat.

While Tavishien was eating, it all started to unfold for Agent Lucika. He had expectations for all this and now it was the come to Jesus' moment. It would take Agent Lucika weeks if not months of dissecting the information to come to conclusions, but with the help of artificial intelligence, he was getting it all 30 minutes later laid out in a concise manner to make it very easy to figure things out.

Artificial intelligence laid out two columns. One was the conversation that Agent Lucika had with Tavishien, the other was the events at the bar which included the secret microphone pickup of Thurston bon Katterberg's and Maxine Causwell's private discussion.

On a column between the two sources of study was a correlation factor readout.

In past remote viewing exploitations studies, they hoped to measure forty percent correlation. In preparation for this project Agent Lucika had poured over those records and case studies over the eighteen-month period Tavishien was in a coma, to determine if this was something they wanted to devote the resources to exploit.

Agent Lucika was convinced but knew it would require field tests to get a handle on the applications and accuracy.

In some of the more successful reports, their best remote viewers at best achieved fifty percent correlation with facts and reality.

First attempt reports showed Tavishien achieved a ninety five percent correlation coefficient. It was utterly stunning to Agent Lucika. But he also had been trained by some of the best psychoanalysts and probability and statistician experts and understood the vivid truth. Tavishien was the real deal and just one conversation had utterly convinced him.

The evidence was almost surreal in nature. But due to his training, he reluctantly kept with the game plan. As desperate as they were with galactic conditions, it was very important he got the information and the results done correctly and even though it now looked very promising, time has a way of quantifying results.

These pre-lunch sessions would continue for a while to determine Tavishien's accuracy and the endurance of the remote viewing for a specific target. Was there a duration Tavishien could successfully sustain remote viewing Thurston bon Katterberg?

These were important questions to resolve because there is a good chance that if Tavishien succeeded in remote viewing an enemy, she might not get a second chance to get near the person for Aura reading especially if they had to kill someone in the process of obtaining access to the target.

The following day around the same time Tavishien arrived at Agent Lucika's office as requested and they began another session. "What is Thurston bon Katterberg doing now?"

Moments later the information started flowing.

"He's at the Grand Xenix Resort lobby approaching an employee at the counter."

Agent Lucika sat quietly listening as Tavishien continued describing what she was seeing and hearing.

"He's now checking out of the resort and said goodbye to the resort employee. He's now walking to the front entrance escorted by two individuals I've seen before. They were stationed outside his penthouse door when I went there."

Agent Lucika looked at Tavishien observing all her facial expressions as she conveyed this remote viewing information.

"Maxine Causwell just approached Thurston bon Katterberg and it appears they are having a small argument about him not paying her for services he did not receive. He just said to Maxine Causwell, 'since you didn't provide me with any girls, you should have offered yourself if you wanted to get paid.'"

"Thurston you know I don't do men."

"That's a terrible shame."

"Maxine Causwell is very angry, and made a physical attempt at Thurston bon Katterberg, but one of the bodyguards intervened as the other got him into the Limo and shut the door. The two bodyguards got into the driver and passenger side in the front seat and the car is now moving."

Tavishien then began to describe the buildings and landmarks they passed as the Limo drove to their destination. Then suddenly Tavishien said, "They pulled up in front of a private jet hanger. Thurston and one of the bodyguards are now walking into the building through a hallway and through a door and into a large hanger area with an aircraft located there."

"Anything else?"

"A blonde flight attendant is at the steps of the aircraft and is welcoming Thurston bon Katterberg as he steped up the aircraft's ladder into the cabin of the craft. There are six nice comfortable seats in the cabin. Thurston is sitting down in a middle seat that has another facing him. The flight attendant shut the door to the plane, walked over to the pilot and informed him the passenger was onboard and they could leave. She then walked over and sat down in front of Thurston bon Katterberg. The bodyguard is sitting in a chair across the aisle from Thurston being quiet."

"The flight attendant asked Thurston how his day was going. She smiles because she sees Thurston is looking at her legs and she knows she has a short dress, and that Thurston is hoping to see a lot of her. She did not disappoint him."

"The morning suddenly got better," Thurston said while looking at the flight attendant who has a name tag Casandra.

"The plane is now out of the hanger and the pilot is doing some lastminute checks and it has started moving down the runway access."

Tavishien didn't say anything for a couple minutes then she suddenly said, "The plane is taking off now. The flight attendant Casandra asked Thurston if wanted anything to drink. He declined and said he was going to lay back and take a nap. He reclined in his seat and shut his eyes. I think he's trying to sleep now."

Agent Lucika knew the discussion took quite a bit of time and thought he should turn Tavishien loose now so she could get her lunch because she had a busy afternoon planned. "Alright Tavishien, thanks for the report, go ahead and get some lunch."

"Thank you."

"You're welcome."

Tavishien ran into Gabriel entering the cafeteria. She didn't know Gabriel was bird dogging her to get into position to have lunch with her then spring the invite on Tavishien.

"Could I join you for lunch?"

"Sure, why not since you didn't make me beat your ass today."

"With the training we have lined up for you, it's unlikely we'll be fighting again for a while. You will be working with the two male assistants again."

"I hope I didn't hurt the guy too badly yesterday."

"He informed me he was okay after the pain killers and the ice he put on his groin area."

The women selected their food which was free and made their way to an empty small table with four chairs and sat down and started eating.

Gabriel noticed Tavishien still enjoyed her food the way savages did, but she was making some improvement and using less fingers thanks to her daily knife and fork schooling in her etiquette class.

Sitting close to Tavishien, Gabriel could study her face and skin. Tavishien was truly a beautiful woman. Her skin was very fair, and she had the most perfect complexion because those long winters couped up in her father's cabin meant she had far less skin damage than people in the city from outdoors activities. Also, it wasn't truly apparent because people do not know what she used to look like, because of the cosmetic surgery she received to correct the damage the vicious soldiers did to her when they gang raped her.

One thing that struck Gabriel was how Tavishien was slowly coming to life and grasping her new world and seemingly showing more and more signs of enjoyment and pleasant demeaner.

When Gabriel was half done with her entree, she decided to bring up what Agent Lucika asked her to do. "Tavishien, a couple times a month I get together with a couple of my girlfriends, and we go to a club where we have drinks and do a little dancing and socializing. I'm going tonight, would you like to go with me?"

"I'm not sure. I've not done that before; I might feel awkward."

"You will be in good hands, because one of these other ladies is a martial artist and does high level security protecting diplomats and wealthy clients. And with me at your side, you will be perfectly safe and get the chance to meet men and possibly have a good time."

"I don't really have any nice clothes to wear to an event like that."

"If you agree to go, I will use my influence over some of Ljótunn bon Swartzler's employees and get you fixed up nicely for the event."

"If you can arrange that, I suppose I could go."

"Alright, we'll leave her around 6:00 P.M. and I'll have the makeup girl with an evening gown for you to change into around 5:00 P.M. to give them plenty of time to work their magic on you."

"Well, if I do go out to some place like that, I would want to be beautiful."

"You will be the best-looking woman there; I promise you that."

"Alright, I'll try something once."

"This will also be good training for you when you go on assignments where you have to meet individuals in a social scene such as this."

"Great. I'll view this as a training session."

The women finished their meal and went their separate directions as

Tavishien was getting more etiquette and socializing skills training. In due time Tavishien would slowly evolve into a very capable woman her peers and enemies would find a challenge by underestimating her.

***

CHAPTER NINE
A Time for a Party and a Time for Death

As promised at 5:00 P.M there was a ring on her dormitory doorbell announcing someone had arrived.

Tavishien was slightly taken back to see four of the fashion experts there to work her over with several pieces of luggage to haul all their equipment. In the span of the hour, they made Tavishien a beautiful princess again. To sex it up for her a notch or two, they selected a black strapless dress that was relatively short but well below her crotch.

For ultra-short dresses Tavishien had been trained to wear shorts under her to hide the privates. This dress was long enough so she didn't need to put on shorts. Near the waste of the dress the designer had silver and gold metallic circles bonded to the fabric giving it a surreal three-dimensional appearance.

Tavishien had a very nice light tan from working out, running, and exercising that made her legs appear quite sensational and fit the dress most completely.

They even brought with them matching shoes her size. The fashion experts were simply doing more style training with Tavishien with the caveat, she got to display the goods in public and arouse the little heads of men. She would also have protection there.

Gabriel was asked for specifics about the evening affairs and Agent Lucika put a small task force together to ensure Tavishien had no issues. Today was a game changer for Agent Lucika because he got another ninety five percent correlation to Tavishien's remote viewing of Thurston bon Katterberg's trip on the private jet.

Between security camera video and secret interviews with the flight attendant who was more than happy to accept some nice bribe money, Tavishien had indeed recreated every single event including departure from the Grand Xenix Resort and his flight home. It was now crystal clear to Agent Lucika they now had a super weapon to use for the appropriate target.

Gabriel took Tavishien out to the parking lot for skycars. There was a Skytaxi there waiting. It was a company car and the driver worked for Agent Lucika. Gabriel knew this but she was not going to divulge it as it was for Tavishien's best interest to not know a lot of the security apparatus, otherwise she might feel uncomfortable and possibly claustrophobic.

It took fifteen minutes and the Skytaxi pulled up in front of the night club venue and the driver said to Gabriel, "Text me if you would like a ride home."

"I will certainly do that, thanks."

The two women looked good, but there was no doubt in any of the men who observed them coming into the club that Tavishien was smoking hot.

Once they got into the club, Gabriel introduced Tavishien to her good friends Brynja and Freyja. The two women were pleasant looking with brunette hair but in no way compared to the luster Tavishien now displayed.

The women got into mild chitchat enjoying hanging out and soon received drinks to help adjust to the club's atmosphere.

There would no doubt be an element of promiscuity with some of the women present in the club that night and men were there waiting to get their opportunity for introductions and possible start of romances.

As the night passed, and several introductions and requests for dances, some of the men present probably had more to drink than what they should have. One of the men saw the eye candy in front of him and decided to risk rejection by making a fool out of himself. He didn't realize he was going towards the wrong woman or what she had experienced in her life that caused her fast response.

When the stranger grabbed Tavishien and wrapped his arms around her from behind, do to Tavishien's training and reactions, she responded just like she would if an enemy grabbed her. Memories of the six soldiers grabbing her tripped her trigger and she immediately swung into self-defense and did an evasive maneuver and put her fingers into his eye socket immediately killing him.

Most people didn't see all this unfold because it was so blazingly fast, but the artificial intelligence immediately notified the security detachment to get her out of there fast. Artificial Intelligence analyzed Tavishien probably killed the man now laying on the floor not moving or showing any signs of life.

Two of the men dressed in suits immediately approached Tavishien who now had Gabriel at her side and said, "Gabriel, you and Tavishien must leave with us immediately."

Gabriel then turned towards Tavishien in somewhat in shock and half belief and said, "Tavishien, I know these men, we must leave now, you are in serious trouble."

The women followed the men out the door of the club to the curb where a Skycar had just landed. The doors swung open, and everyone entered the Skycar and immediately after the doors automatically shut, flew to a safe house.

Luckily for Tavishien, her appearance had been so radically altered by the fashion people, the security camera video would not be able to identify her.

Agent Lucika showed up with a change of clothes for Tavishien and had her bathe and removed all her makeup. After she changed into less descriptive clothing, she was taken out to a Skycar and whisked away to the airport where she was put on a private Jet and flown a great distance away. The Intelligence Bureau didn't want

Tavishien anywhere near where prosecutors could get to her to interrogate and break her because she killed someone who had connections and would want that person prosecuted with the full weight of the law.

It was just Agent Lucika and Tavishien on the plane. Agent Lucika didn't want anyone to know where he took Tavishien and in fact took her to one of his most obscure hideouts.

This was an island where people lived a meager life but were engaged in extracting gold out of seawater. It was a slow a meticulous process, and only provided enough funds to pay for some of their basic needs since over half the food they ate had to be imported.

Agent Lucika found this island and befriended the people and acted as a trusted courier from time to time to take their small amounts of gold to the market to facilitate trade and income for things they needed. This would not be the first spy he dumped in their laps and since they had very little outside communication nor the desire to undermine Agent Lucika in any way, he felt good nobody would ever come here looking for Tavishien.

On the plane they had their bid discussion in how and why Tavishien killed the man. Agent Lucika felt somewhat responsible because had she known she had protection there, she would have just waited for the man to be confronted by the security detachment just seconds away.

After they came to an understanding, Tavishien stated, "I'll never let that happen again, because now I know more about the situation, I'm in."

"There may come a time where you have no choice but to kill a man to allow you to get to the target to read his Aura. And if we must sanction a killing how that will be dealt with will be carefully planned so that you are not made into a criminal."

"Do you think authorities know who I am?"

"No, your disguise was rather clever. Nobody knows what you really look like. Even the best facial recognition software will not be able to identify you."

"What about the other two women?"

"They were removed from the club right after you left and were told never to reveal anything about you to anyone, otherwise they might disappear. Also, they will not be going back to that club, they have been warned to stay away from it, indefinitely."

"But they still might be able to identify me to authorities?"

"No, they don't know your name. Gabriel gave them your Alias. They are on our watch list and if they talk to authorities, we will have no recourse but to help them disappear."

"Would you actually kill them?"

"No, we would hand them over to some bad guys we know of. We would not be interested in what they do with them, but I'm sure they would not be able to talk to authorities any time soon."

In due time Tavishien had settled in with the leader of the fishing village who would be paid nicely to look out for her. Plus, with her martial arts ability just now proven to be effective, it's unlikely there would be anyone in the village to do bad things to Tavishien. Agent Lucika then left and flew back to the Intelligence Bureau Campus to do any damage control necessary and to remove any evidence necessary.

The first thing that happened that made the crime investigators unhappy was when they learned all the surveillance video was damaged. Either the equipment malfunctioned or worse yet, due to negligence, it was never turned on as the tape in the machine was blank and not recorded on.

All leads simply dried up and the case went to a file of unsolved cases. The man that was killed was somewhat an unsavory character with a police rap sheet, so the National Police drew the conclusion organized crime killed the dude for something only they know about that will never surface because organized crime never let out any information for any reason. Organized crime's own survival was based on being ultra-quiet about their affairs.

Since the dead man was perceived as another slimeball, the chief inspector didn't have the desire to spend vast sums of money on a dead-end case with no leads. Hence the investigation withered at the vine rather abruptly. In due time Intelligence Bureau Agents infiltrated the National Police with agents that seized any records of the event, and they disappeared after Agent Lucika received the special package. The National Police would never know the files were missing nor was there a tickler to have someone review the case. Since all records disappeared so did the case.

Tavishien only spent three months with the island people but immersed herself in their gold production. This activity interested Tavishien so greatly she started researching in great depth the technology required to extract the gold out of sea water. She researched to determine who were the leading experts in everything associated with extracting gold out of ocean water.

Since Tavishien was a trained spy plus she had the remote viewer ability, all she needed to do is get close enough to read the expert's Aura, she could slowly absorb all the person's thoughts and activity developing the technology. But to Tavishien the question was how she could ever get to such a person. In her training Tavishien learned a lot of approaches including blackmail and coercion and ultimately the quid pro quo.

Tavishien opportunity for such an opportunity to get physically closer to gold extraction experts was coming sooner than she realized, but she would have to pay the price because sometimes quid pro quo exacts a painful price.

At the end of her three-month sojourn to the remote island, Agent Lucika suddenly arrived and took Tavishien back to the Intelligence Bureau Campus where she was soon back in her dormitory room that appeared to be left exactly the way she left it.

Nobody had entered her dormitory room, except the maids would come in now and then to clean and inspect it as well as search for bugs that might have been planted via nefarious activities.

Because of the spy business, fifty percent of the maid's work was searching for bugs. They were not just maids, that was their cover. They had to do the dirty work to masquerade for their real purpose in life: hunting down moles and spies. It seemed kind of counter intuitive that enemies would be involved in planting bugs in the Intelligence Bureau Campus, but they had help with double agents, moles, and people via coercion. The Intelligence Bureau Campus was one of the most fruitful locations to gather INTEL since it was the heart of the apparatus where ninety percent of all the INTEL collected resided in one form or another.

After a couple days of getting back into her daily routine, Tavishien was back in Agent Lucika's office going through some more remote viewing of Thurston bon Katterberg. Today, like all others, she reported on what he was doing with some of his customers who didn't know they were being fleeced in a Ponzi scheme. This was an INTEL operation, not a criminal investigation. One thing the Intelligence Bureau always stuck by; they would never allow a criminal investigation to get in the way of their INTEL apparatus.

Even though the Intelligence Bureau knew Thurston von Katterberg was a crook and taking advantage of gullible people, they could not initiate in criminal procedures, simply because right now he was the only viable entity to really quantify Tavishien's remote viewing capability and measure how long it lasted and how accurate the reports remained. If Thurston bon Katterberg got busted for operating a Ponzi scheme it would be by some other entity other than the Intelligence Bureau who had other agendas.

Just like all previous remote viewing results that Agent Lucika reviewed, Tavishien maintained a ninety five percent correlation. This was a good development in that since her remote viewing of Thurston was delayed three months since the prior sessions, the fact that Tavishien was able to provide the information helped Agent Lucika to surmise, it was possible she could retain that ability to remain in contact with her target for a lengthy period. That would be crucial if war started. Because once the shooting started, it would be impossible to get a remote viewer anywhere close to enemy leaders.

Today was a little different than before. Agent Lucika said, "Your afternoon training has been modified a little to give you a little extra time to come back in my office for a conference, I want to discuss something with you."

"Sure."

Tavishien didn't know what to expect but with Agent Lucika, the unexpected was typically the expected.

On the way to the cafeteria Tavishien met with Gabriel who asked, "May I join you for lunch."

"Sure, after the good workout you gave me this morning, why not."

The women went inside, obtained their food trays and drinks, and found an empty table where they could sit, eat, drink, and not be bothered with others.

"You look healthy, it appears you got a nice tan while you were gone."

"My entire body is tanned because the people in the village didn't wear many clothes and after a while, I adopted their grooming standards."

"The men on the island were not attracted to you?"

"A couple days after I went full native and took my clothes off like the rest, one of the men there tried something with me and after I beat him up so quickly, the rest of the men decided to stay the hell away from me."

"What about their women?"

"When I talked to their women and they asked me questions about sex, I informed them I was not interested in sex. Had no desires at all. They seemed to like me more afterwards."

"Now you are back, so we can get back to the training and get you back to where you were three months ago."

"When I was at the village, I worked out hard because I could swim in the ocean and became friends with some of the animals. The villagers thought those animals were going to eat me. They were shocked I became a friend of those vicious sea animals that no doubt could kill me very quickly."

"Maybe later when we are in private you can tell me how you did that."

"If I did it would cause you a lot of trouble, its best you do not know."

"Kind of like the things we did at the Grand Xenix Resort?"

"Yes, along those lines."

The women finished their meals, and they were soon heading in opposite directions because Tavishien had an appointment with Agent Lucika.

***

CHAPTER TEN
Correlation and Connectivity

When Tavishien arrived in the offices; the receptionist was already waiting for her thanks to artificial intelligence prompts.

"Please go in, Agent Lucika is waiting for you."

"Thank you."

The receptionist walked Tavishien to Agent Lucika's door, opened it and announced, "Tavishien is here for her appointment."

"Thank you, send her in."

Tavishien was soon sitting down looking at Agent Lucika wondering what was next.

"We have a new mission to perform."

"Alright."

"You will not have to travel far, they are nearby."

"That shouldn't matter."

"This will be your most dangerous mission and will go a long way to prepare you for operations in very dangerous circumstances."

Agent Lucika then explained to Tavishien that her target was the head of the organized crime syndicate for this part of the country. The head of organized crime, Karl Vlasson, was well protected and well-armed. The National Police were never able to locate him and arrest him.

The Intelligence Bureau that avoided getting involved in national law enforcement issues to protect their spies' identities, but they knew how to locate Karl Vlasson, but that ability would never see the light of day in the criminal justice system because they would not be willing to give up their sensitive sources and methods to the criminal justice system that was fully penetrated by organized crime and enemy spies. The criminal justice system was such a leaking sieve so bad you might as well call it Swiss Cheese.

Agent Lucika laid out the high-level plan to Tavishien and over the next month they would train for this specific mission. They would in no way alter organized crimes operations and even though they did some highly illegal and nefarious activities no different than Thurston bon Katterberg, none of that would be affected by this operation which was nothing more than more penetration training for Tavishien whose nerves and forbearance would be tested like never before.

It would take them almost a year of quality control checks before they would determine that Tavishien's remote viewing was ready to step up to the challenge where a lot more sensational activities took place. But even so, the current status indicated her exceptional ability was ready to weaponize and organized crime was going to give them a lot of opportunities to test Tavishien.

Sometimes spy agencies must employ unsavory characters to do certain dirty deeds. As an example, the Intelligence Bureau would never kill someone intentionally because that could lead to some serious criminal investigation and the National Police had an ongoing antagonism with the INTEL boys. But they did indeed need to have someone killed now and then such as a mole or a double spy to stop a serious information breach.

Most of the time the moles and the double spies lived beyond the means of normal citizens placing them in a good position to get whacked when they were often in remote areas enjoying the fruits of their espionage. Hanging out at a beach community was not a wise choice because it made it easier for unsavory characters to help them disappear in ways there would never be a body to locate in an investigation, they simply just disappeared, and it became a missing person case. When the enemy lost contact with their mole or their double spy, they concluded such an operation occurred.

This relationship with unsavory characters is how Agent Lucika planned to insert Tavishien to get near Karl Vlasson to read his Aura and start the remote viewing.

A particular person working in the special projects section of the Intelligence Bureau was that exclusive interface to one of Karl Vlasson's goons where special procedures and methods were used to hunt down and eliminate moles and double spies. They would meet in very innocuous locations that would be the last place the National Police would look for them.

A fashion show would be such a great place. Once the two made eye contact, there would be a rendezvous in the venue to discuss business. The meeting would take place in a bathroom or an outside smoking area, where full control over the environment was possible to ensure privacy. Discussions about the terms of the contract and transfer of credits were the only thing ever done during such meetings.

Karl Vlasson had a reputation of getting young women through his operatives always on the lookout for new flesh.

Ljótunn bon Swartzler had her marching orders to make Tavishien appear far more attractive than her other models at the fashion show. Agent Lucika wanted Tavishien to be extremely alluring to get Karl Vlasson's goon focused on her to create the ambience and follow-up activity he anticipated would come from this fashion show.

The stage was set, and the operation was soon put in place. Tavishien was escorted by Ljótunn bon Swartzler to the Grande Perstroyan Divergency Hotel and Resort Ballroom that had three-dimensional seating for one thousand guests. A temporary walkway that provided the models runway to show the luxurious gowns had been constructed and decorated with video displays along the entire platform to produce surreal images the fashion designers and consultants created before the show that appeared during their model's performance.

The seven sloped balconies also constructed for this show allowed density of views and closer positioning to the model's runway. Since this was the big show of the year, models would arrive from all over the planet with their fashion designers and staff. Just outside the venue were Grande Perstroyan Divergency Hotel and Resort rooms access hallways on three wings that intersected at the ballroom entrance for models to change their wardrobe components.

The balconies laid out using the finest artificial intelligence ever used allowed all observers from every level to effectively see the fashion models and their wardrobes. The models trained to avoid eye contact would feel apprehensive observing so many close-up eyes on them. Even though models played a significant role in exposing the essence of the garments they were wearing, it also helped to be attractive to encourage attachment to the view by the observer.

In today's fashion show there would be an exception for Tavishien. As part of her training, she would be making eye contact with the gangster Tolar Seia who provided the interface between the Intelligence Bureau and the organized crime syndicate called the Blue Gang.

The Blue Gang group of vicious killers and racketeers would split a live baby in half with a butcher knife for the right contract. Sometimes business rivals that entered internecine warfare sometimes kidnaped small children and did that for revenge. A package would arrive at their mansion with a note: *concerning your missing child……*

Agent Lucika understood the levels of viciousness Karl Vlasson's Blue Gang would go to for the right number of financial rewards. He also knew he was placing Tavishien into the most danger she ever experienced in her lifetime, including when the Tartars gang raped her. Hence there was no room for any screwups or inadvertent disclosures.

As far as Ljótunn bon Swartzler's staff knew, this was just a fashion show with nothing of importance to it, other than getting Tavishien more exposure and experience for future engagements.

Thanks to the awesome power of the Intelligence Bureau, they were all inside the Resort/Hotel room just 3 doors down from the main entrance to the ballroom. Before Ljótunn bon Swartzler took Tavishien to the hotel room to change into her first modeling outfit, she took her out onto the runway where other fashion designers had their models to get a feel for the runway and the multi-level balconies. Right off to the right side of the end of the runway on the second level is where Tolar Seia would be seated with an Intel Bureau Spy.

Tavishien received training including Tolar Seia's rap sheet and numerous images to help her be aware of his appearance and how he operated. She also knew his upcoming reserve seat selection and as promised as she was walking out on the model's runway, Agent Lucika was sitting in the reserved seat that Tolar Seia would be sitting in about forty five minutes from now as the crowds were let in by the fashion show staff.

"I'm going to stand here, and I want you to walk the runway so I can watch your performance," Ljótunn bon Swartzler said to Tavishien.

Other fashion designers were coaching their models as well to help them adjust and eliminate all stage fright. This was a very important show, and a lot was at stake because in the fashion business it seems the winner take all.

"Alright," Tavishien responded not feeling any concern.

With Agent Lucika watching quietly and trying to act simply as an unknown observer, Tavishien went all the way back to the double door entrance, which is the unwritten official starting point. In reality, the starting point is where the audience first detects the fashion model and starts analyzing the design.

Tavishien made her majestic walk down the runway just as she had rehearsed it one hundred times. The Intelligence Bureau had copies of the plans for the runway and the guest seating and had constructed mockups for Tavishien to practice and get the feel for the geometries to focus on her movements.

The first pass was pretty good but Ljótunn bon Swartzler had some pointers and recommendations to Tavishien's body movements and the way she moved her hips. Another part of this final training at the venue included practicing making eye contact on Agent Lucika who was acting the part of Tolar Seia including facial expressions and anthropomorphism that exemplify Tolar Seia's typical conduct because of his personal self-evaluation partially built on his life as a high-ranking gangster.

The second pass down the runway a mere ten feet ahead of another woman also practicing her movements for the upcoming show, seemed to resolve any issues that Ljótunn bon Swartzler discussed after the first pass.

"That looked quite satisfactory. Do you think you can do it exactly like that in the show?" Ljótunn bon Swartzler asked while looking very seriously at Tavishien.

"It should be close enough to what you want, I'm sure," Tavishien responded in a somewhat respectful tone with an edge of rebellion in her delivery.

Even though Agent Lucika was sitting 25 feet away he could hear the conversation with great fidelity because both women were bugged and didn't know it.

As soon as the two women left to go back to the Resort/Hotel room used as a dressing and rehearsal room, Agent Lucika stood up and walked out of the ball room and headed for the elevator to take him up a few floors to a series of Resort/Hotel rooms with interconnecting rooms used as a local command center tied in via artificial intelligence back at the Intelligence Bureau Campus nerve center that had compartmentalized special operations sections behind steel vault doors where a team would work in shifts around the clock until Tavishien was finished and brought back to the Campus and debriefed by Agent Lucika.

Shortly after Tavishien arrived in the Resort/Hotel room she was taken back behind temporary room dividers to relax for a few minutes, get a touch up on her makeup and hair, then about fifteen minutes before she was scheduled to walk down the runway with her first designer outfit, she was dressed in the luxurious garment.

First impressions are important. Ljótunn bon Swartzler was going to use her nuclear option in the first salvo. She had Tavishien dressed in the finest creation the world will have ever seen. The design on this spell binding outfit was a guarded secret and a culmination of Ljótunn bon Swartzler lifelong dreams and ambitions. She held off showing it because she never had a spectacular model, she wanted to convey the artistry. But tonight because of her lucrative contract with the Intelligence Bureau and being at one of the most important fashion shows for the year, it was time to display it to the public for the first time.

Tavishien was not the first fashion model to walk down the runway, there were a dozen before her and just before she was scheduled to proceed down the runway, Ljótunn bon Swartzler arranged through the exhibition operators to change the music with a new sound full of advanced psychoacoustics that planned for this dress. She had worked exclusively with Tavishien to pull this off and now she would find out just how well it turned out.

Right on cue from Ljótunn bon Swartzler, Tavishien started down the runway with the magnificent music playing that added tremendously to the luster. All eyes were on Tavishien including Karl Vlasson's representative: Tolar Seia. This grim-faced poor excuse for a human being at first wasn't too excited going to something stupid like a fashion show with his Intelligence Bureau contract, but they had great seats. Nobody blocked the view and suddenly he was a mere fifteen feet away from the illustrious Tavishien. Unexpectedly Tolar Seia was satisfied they were at a fashion show and not at a boxing or martial arts arena watching dudes beat the crap out of each other.

Under his breath Tolar Seia whispered to the Intelligence Bureau Rep (IBR), I'd just about give anything to Boink that girl. Tolar Seia didn't know it, but his comments were recorded because the IBR had high fidelity recording ability and even with the music in the background, the artificial intelligence was able to read and produce a transcription of the comments.

The lure and the bait were set. Agent Lucika heard what artificial intelligence transcribed through his ear bud a safe distance away where he could observe Tolar Seia with the IBR watched intently the body language and the reactions.

The crowd was animated at Tavishien. It didn't matter what she wore for the rest of the night. She knocked the ball out of the ballpark so far with this first dress, she could wear a rag for the rest of the night and the audience would adore her greatly.

There was some noise from spectators in the ballroom that few if any of the fashion models received.

Before Tavishien turned around to make her way back to the entrance of the ballroom, there was her target, Tolar Seia. Up to that minute Tavishien had not made eye contact with anyone, which was part of the game plan and is how the fashion designers wanted it. They wanted the girls to sell designer clothes and not themselves.

Ljótunn bon Swartzler who had special briefings from Agent Lucika, was a little apprehensive. She didn't like dealing with organized crime, especially the crime boss Karl Vlasson and his *Blue Gang*. But being the risk taker and a professional, she knew how to bury her fears for the moment and get the job done, hoping that Agent Lucika would be in a position to help her if bad things transpired.

There was an area on the second level where the fashion designers had exclusive area set up for them to stand and observe their models on the runway to get a feal for how they were performing and discover any discontinuities or possible flawed movements to critique later.

Under normal circumstances the eye contact between Tavishien and Karl Vlasson's representative Tolar Seia would not be tolerated. But this was all part of the staged performance.

Ljótunn bon Swartzler was getting a double paycheck tonight. First, Ljótunn bon Swartzler would be making money selling that garment to the fashion industry that would waste no time in copying it for retail investors. And then she would also get an insane pile of cash for supporting this Intelligence Bureau mission.

Absolutely nobody on Ljótunn bon Swartzler's staff knew what was going on or that the IBR man was there coaxing Tolar Seia into a psychological whirl wind to get him set up to be an unsuspecting surrogate in a foray of clandestine pursuit of a critical measure in remote viewing and testing the agent's ability to penetrate the enemy to read the Aura for the outcome.

Tavishien also had some aspects of her she had not quite fully revealed to Agent Lucika because she herself was slowly coming to grips with it. Besides remote viewing Tavishien felt she could also get into people's minds to influence their emotions. Tavishien felt uncomfortable revealing that, because it could really cause her a lot of grief if Agent Lucika felt she might be a risk to him and others in the Intelligence Bureau. Such an ability could be ten times more damaging than remote viewing, which was maybe one hundred times as important as nuclear weapons.

When Tavishien made eye contact with Tolar Seia she applied some of her unique telepathic ability in that regard. Some people might consider it mental telepathy, but she wasn't communicating.

She was controlling emotion and working over Tolar Seia really good.

Tolar Seia had no idea what hit him. He was utterly astonished to the point as Tavishien turned away from him, she could see he had tears in both eyes. She had emotionally moved him unlike any woman before or after.

It's hard to affect the emotions of a gangster who kills people for a living and likes young girls not of legal age and does a lot of highly illegal deeds. Tolar Seia had a heart that was as solid as concrete and as cold as steel. As he wrestled with his emotions, he said to himself, *it's a terrible shame I will never be able to enjoy a woman like that in my lifetime.* He knew she was clean and beyond approach, and at best he was a Noble Savage nowhere in the stratum to allow a transcendence to a bonding of some sort with the lovely woman. Nevertheless, he now felt significant emotions as his feelings were captivated.

The IBR saw the eyes water up and knew they had zoom lens cameras on them and during a critique afterwards, the tear episode would be discussed.

Tolar Seia had mildly pitched a fit about coming to this fashion show. He wanted to go to a strip club or a boxing match. But the IBR informed him, for his own safety and plausible deniability to law enforcement they had to go to a venue like this. Had they shown up in a strip club its likely authorities would be there to bird dog them. Probably the same could be said for a boxing match.

Now the IBR thought quickly and came up with the idea to test Tolar Seia to be able to write the impact that Tavishien had on him. This would certainly be of substantial interest to Agent Lucika.

"Hey Tolar, I know you are kind of bored, if you really want to leave, I suppose we could."

"Actually, I'm enjoying this, us just stay and see some more."

"Sure, if that's what you want."

The IBR had now confirmed the behavior in Tolar Seia that Tavishien had altered in a major way including causing him an emotional spike. *This is getting more interesting, the IBR thought.*

The fashion industry was ablaze. Ljótunn bon Swartzler was approached by two very condescending uppity women who were not the friendliest in the world, but when they see extreme success, they obviously like to give credit where credit is due. These two women were the most vicious fashion critics in the industry who everyone always listened to. To get a complement out of them, especially in front of others, is truly an accomplishment.

Some of the other fashion consultants and designers standing by the three women overheard it and based on that conversation they knew and so did Ljótunn bon Swartzler, she just hit a home run on the first dress. It would be smooth sailing for the rest of the night because Tavishien had set the bar.

While they were all back in the Resort/Hotel room changing gowns, Ljótunn bon Swartzler explained to Tavishien, "I received some very nice complements from two of the toughest critics in the fashion industry. You did a marvelous job, and you made my design flourish tonight. You were perfect on the runway and the special event we planned for was a huge success according to our friend Mr. Lucika. Congratulations, you have just proven tonight you are as superb as any fashion model in the industry."

"Thanks for your nice complements. I owe it all to you because your training was especially good."

"When you go back out on the runway, all you need to do is exactly what you did before. It doesn't matter what you wear now, people will focus on you. You are a designer's worst nightmare; a model people would rather look at than designer clothes. If I ever take you to another fashion event, I'm going to have to make you look ugly so people will look at my clothes!"

The two women chuckled and Tavishien could not help but grab and hug Ljótunn bon Swartzler who reciprocated in her own heart felt hug.

One thing that Ljótunn bon Swartzler knew that none of her staff knew was Tavishien was being groomed to be a super spy. Here she was being hugged by a woman who no doubt would help write history. That made it feel even more special.

The slight makeup adjustment, hair repair, and new gown suddenly had Tavishien shining again. This garment did a better job of exposing her breasts and hips that were the perfect pear shape of a slender woman. All the excess weight was in her breasts that were what men would consider that absolute perfect size, not too big and not too small.

Just like before, Ljótunn bon Swartzler had the music changed. Other models didn't do this and just cruised out with the existing sound which did nothing more than blend them in with everyone else. The brilliance in the change up did a couple of actions that gave Tavishien once again the focus of the audience. First it broke up the monotony of hearing music that probably had been played to long where it had lost its sizzle. Secondly, this music was picked by Ljótunn bon Swartzler because the beat and tempo would embody the essence of Tavishien's movements on the runway.

Just like before when Tavishien walked down the runway, she had all eyes focused on her with great attention. She had previously blown them away with her performance, so their brains were pre-wired for the next tumultuous allegro that now enveloped everyone helping them transcend to a greater curiosity and amazement.

Tolar Seia might have been a tough lion in the gangster business, but tonight Tavishien was turning him into a mere pussycat. He was weak at the knees and captivated far more than any nude strip dancer ever did for him dancing around a poll in a darkened room where the spotlights were on the gorgeous creatures that earned the crime boss Karl Vlasson a twenty five percent cut in the action.

Tavishien did not make eye contact but out of the corner of her eye and in her peripheral vision she could see the genuine interest and affection now exposed by an appreciative audience. That garment was sold before she even got it off her body.

Now down at the turn at GROUND ZERO, Tolar Seia sat there in utter expectation. Not even one of the fashion models made eye contact with him as they were doing as they were trained to do. But when that gorgeous creature arrived right at the exact spot she did her turn around, she did two things. One of which Agent Lucika knew she did because it was caught on camera. She did the other thing nobody but her would ever know, she infiltrated the dirty mobster's mind and placed an enormous amount of influence into the emotional and pleasure centers of his brain.

It was probably the first time in Tolar Seia's life and most likely the last time he would have a penis erection and tears in his eyes at the same time. He could have taken triple doses of Damiana and Larginine amino acid and would not have his body jacked up like this.

Once again Tolar Seia was caught on camera. The efficacy of using Tavishien in non-traditional methods of spy craft had just run its course and would write a new chapter in special methods and procedures. If Agent Lucika only knew the other half of the formula, the entire spy apparatus would be turned upside down overnight.

But just like Tavishien feared, she might be viewed as an existential threat for the future and must be eliminated before she might do some serious damage to the wrong person, including Gabriel and Agent Lucika.

Tavishien wore two more designer outfits before she was done for the night and as Tolar Seia stewed because she was long gone before he could manifest a private meeting, it did open some discussions for quid pro quo.

Sometimes quid pro quo works in the opposite direction when the contractor needs something from those who pay them, and in this case, it was the IBR he would pursue creating a rendezvous with the young woman.

The path to the head of the organized crime syndicate, Karl Vlasson, was through Tolar Seia. Now the plan unfolded. Tolar Seia wanted something the IBR man could help him get, but the IBR man wanted to personally talk with Karl Vlasson about a contract that was so secret, they didn't want anyone else in the room with him when the contract was offered.

The quid pro quo that would soon develop in the next few days: If Tolar Seia would set up that rendezvous with crime boss Karl Vlasson, the IBR would bring the young woman with him to the meeting to personally introduce him.

What Agent Lucika figured out with his clairvoyance was once Karl Vlasson laid his eyes on Tavishien, he would want her for himself. That dynamic created the window of opportunity they sought. Tavishien would get in close with Karl Vlasson without any outside noise and read Karl Vlasson's Aura and would be able to remote view him indefinitely.

Agent Lucika didn't know that Tavishien now somewhat a wild card of her own wanting results she could obtain as to not have to waste too much time with these crooks putting her life at risk would also do to Karl Vlasson the same exact thing, she did to Tolar Seia and get him so jacked up she would have him eating out of her hand when she did the ultimate actions allowing her to get lost forever.

After several exhaustive meetings between the IBR and Tolar Seia, a meeting was finally set up.

To facilitate this meeting, the model trainer and clothing designer Ljótunn bon Swartzler and her crew were brought in to do the hair, makeup, and prepare Tavishien with the best designer dress available nobody had seen.

Tavishien was fitted with a shoulder less full-length black dress with floral designs that created an exquisite ambience that would no doubt make mere mortals' knees weak when they observed Tavishien in the dress, plus she would work on their minds and get them so horny and jacked up they would be in a frenzy soon enough.

Tavishien's safety was built around the concept that crime boss Karl Vlasson would want her so badly he would prevent Tolar Seia from obtaining her sweet nectar and he will have designs himself and plan for a rendezvous with Tolar Seia out of the way.

This would be a meet and greet and hopefully Tavishien could read Karl Vlasson's Aura and not have to make a repeat trip.

The IBR and Tavishien were put in a sky car. There would be some nearby backup if necessary and Agent Lucika would be orbiting in a Skycar a short distance away to be in position to lead an attack if the situation got out of hand.

The destination was a mountain top mansion that was extremely hard to access or escape from. The circular driveway leading to the mansion had plenty of parking and the parklike landscaping gave a spectacular image to anyone who had never seen it before. From the air you could see adjacent pool, tennis court, arbor, and other adjacent buildings that were no doubt bunk rooms for the security staff and the hired help such as maids, cooks, landscapers, etc.

There was a welcoming committee waiting in the circular driveway and the IBR assumed from the air they were standing next to a parking stall they wanted him to land in.

The seductive perfume as well as all the fashion application to Tavishien had its impact on the IBR man. He knew the rules of the game, *never stick you pen in company ink*, but for this woman he would be willing to violate those unwritten rules.

The Skycar landed and the IBR and Tavishien stepped out of the Skycar to meet the half dozen people waiting. There were two women and four men, all meticulously dressed. The women were most likely crime family *Hostitutes*. Their dresses were short and provocative, and no doubt had been offered to the IBR man in the past, but as far as he was concerned, they were *crime boss company ink*, so the prohibition still applied.

The group collectively welcomed them and then the leader of the group said, "Let me escort you into the mansion. Mr. Vlasson is eager to meet you."

"Thank you."

The IBR man had a legitimate contract for Karl Vlasson. It was another sad day for the Intelligence Bureau, as they had discovered another mole. It was a pretty lady who everyone liked and she, like people before her, had a price as well as a revengeful attitude because the Bureau had done her wrong in the past. The Intelligence Bureau had not yet determined how the malcontents got identified by the Tartars, but one day hoped to figure that out and Agent Lucika was already thinking of ways to use Tavishien to help penetrate who and how it was being done.

The mansion was huge and the beams overhead the front entrance alone exposed the majestic quality of the architects who designed such an extraordinary structure. Opulence was obviously everywhere they looked. Besides money earned via nefarious activities, some of the money Intelligence Bureau paid the crime syndicate helped in construction costs.

They were led through three very large rooms used for a variety of purposes, but mainly to indulge their guests and possible business associates. The handlers led the two all the way and out the rear of the building to the pool area. Over in a shaded area wearing a swimming robe and surrounded by a couple of gorgeous *Hostitutes*, was none other than Karl Vlasson.

You could almost smell the evil a mile away. Just like the former President who had his over sexed sister murdered for being an embarrassment and almost ruining his political journey, Karl Vlasson had no restrictions on himself to kill anyone if it meant business and extravagant income.

One of the female *Hostitutes* escorting the IBR and Tavishien introduced them to Karl Vlasson who was wearing sunglasses and gave a generous smile as he eyeballed Tavishien who was dressed up by one of the best fashion designers, Ljótunn bon Swartzler in a way to increase the activity in his libido and start his little head thinking.

And here she was, the woman who had captivated his representative Tolar Seia and the IBR man standing there.

Just like on cue, here came Tolar Seia, dressed in an expensive business suit and very expensive designer shoes and approached Karl Vlasson and said, "The conference room is all set up for our discussions."

"Alright, let's go do the deal."

Karl Vlasson stood up and said, "Would you please follow me to where we can have a private discussion."

Only Karl Vlasson, Tolar Seia, the IBR and Tavishien went to the conference room. Once inside they were ushered over to a table where Karl "Vlasson said please have a seat."

"Alright what is the deal you wish to make?"

The IBR pulled out a briefing stick out of his pocket and handed it to Karl Vlasson, who then took it and handed it to Tolar Seia and said, "Put this into the projector so we can see what's on it."

Next to the table was a smaller table with several items on it including the sophisticated projection system that had sound and video capabilities that could be used for business or pleasure. Karl Vlasson sometimes observed video and sound of women screaming getting raped by his men just before they killed her. He always liked to see how they dealt with people he sanctioned.

Very soon the video started showing an attractive woman secretly filmed with her Tartar lover and controller. The fifteen-minute video gave a biography on the woman and various views of her to help the assassins easily identify her.

After the video ended, the IBR then gave a few pieces of information concerning Ileana's travel plans.

"She is scheduled to go on vacation in two weeks and we know her controller Dmitri Gergiev has reservations at the Grand Xenix Resort where we expect them to meet."

"You want us to whack her there?"

We'll pay you a bonus if you can manage to take the two of them to another destination."

"That's simple, we expect the bonus to be equal to the contract."

"Understand. We know this will be a cost-plus contract because you will have to deploy people."

Karl Vlasson then turned to Tavishien and asked, "What is your name my lovely dear?"

Tavishien was now playing with Karl's mind and answered, "I'm Karoline."

"That's kind of an unusual name, not sure I've ever heard it before."

"I come from a mountain tribe far away from humanity, we have strange names and speech there."

"Sounds very interesting, maybe perhaps one day you can find time to spend with me and tell me all about it."

"I'm sure we can work something out."

Karl Vlasson then turned towards the Intelligence Bureau Rep and asked, "Is it appropriate for this fashion model to be privy to our discussion."

"Yes, I personally recruited her to be used in a variety of ways.

She knows to keep her mouth shut."

"May I ask you why you brought her along?"

"Yes, I brought her at the request of Tolar Seia who I think would like to get to know her better."

"Why would Tolar want to get involved with a fashion model. He prefers strip dancers and female wrestlers."

"There is a lot of energy that goes into a fashion show, and I think Tolar recognized the artistic aspect of it and thought Karoline's appeared like a nice woman, and she is."

"I'm sorry but I have to say I think that is utterly ridiculous. I think Tolar's mind is in the gutter, and he is only interested in BOOM-BOOM."

"You will have to ask him."

"I'm sure he and I will have some discussions about it. But I want to ask you the simple question why you would want to introduce him to such a nice-looking woman. I would think you would want her all to yourself."

"Karl, first of all I believe in the wise policy of *never dipping my pen in company ink*, secondly, since she's the person who identified the double spy that is covered by the contract, I felt it only fitting for her to meet the principal parties who will carry out the contract."

"Does she know what the contract implies?"

"Yes, and she simply wanted to meet the people who are going to execute the contract, afterall it's her achievement to discover this person who did a lot of damage to us."

"So, she's more than a fashion model. Is she a spook too?"

"That she is."

"Maybe I might want to get to know her."

"That's up to her."

"I have an idea."

"Such as?"

"Usually, you have an eyewitness to observe the execution of the contract to report back it actually happened and the results, how about send her to my Grand Xenix Resort penthouse and I'll arrange for her to be your observer for contract validation."

"If she's available it's up to her. She may not get excited watching you carry out the contract, but she may get interested in knowing Tolar Seia better. I think she has developed a feeling for Tolar Seia."

Karl and Tolar sat there stunned at the revelation, but was it real or a con job? Spooks never tell the truth.

Tavishien was sitting right next to Karl Vlasson. There were periods during the discussions where it was silent and no conversations going on while everyone was thinking about the situation and Tavishien in particular. This was a lucky break for Tavishien because she was able to get a quality read on Karl Vlasson's Aura. There would be no need for her to ever come back.

Karl looked at Tolar and understood he had been instrumental in getting Karoline (aka Tavishien) here at the mansion and he was a loyal a good assistant. To steal Karoline away from Tolar could cause some problems with his business model, so he decided to step back and give Tolar the chance to pursue the romance. No doubt he would love to have sex with this beautiful woman, but there would always be beautiful women, but not necessarily reliable and loyal assistants.

"Per our arrangements, I've sent one third of the contract funds to your account at the Wenmark Regional Bank. When the contract is completed, you will receive the remainder of the funds."

"You have always been spot-on in the way you handle our transactions. I do appreciate the way you operate."

"Thank you."

"Tolar will escort you and Karoline out to your Skycar. I do hope she is sent to the Grand Xenix Resort. I'll work with Tolar on his manners, so he doesn't blow it with her."

"I appreciate that. It's always good to have good working relations with your business clients."

Tolar escorted the IBR and Karoline (aka Tavishien) out to the Skycar and said goodbye to them and added, "I appreciate you coming here today, Karoline, it means a lot to me."

"Thank you for your curtesy."

Moments later the two were in the Skycar heading back to the Intelligence Bureau Campus along with the air armada sent and prepositioned close enough to intervene if required.

Tavishien would know what Tolar and Karl had to say after they left because she was able to remote view Karl with high fidelity.

Upon arrival back it the Intelligence Bureau Campus, the IBR was first debriefed and interrogated by Agent Lucika who had received real time transcripts of the conversation at the organized crime mansion.

At this point in time, it was undecided how they would deal with contract validation. Tavishien's report would weigh heavily in on that decision.

The debrief with Agent Lucika went down just like usual with a new twist to it.

"Are you up to traveling to Grand Xenix Resort to get a close up with Karl Vlasson?"

"During the meeting I was sitting close to Karl Vlasson, and he physically moved close to me checking me out. There were brief periods of time where there was no discussions or noise. I believe I got a good read on his Aura at that time."

"Do you want to try remote viewing him now?"

"I already have."

"And what did you discover?"

"A few disgusting things he said to Tolar Seia after we left."

"Such as?"

"He informed Tolar Seia that it's unlikely he would ever have a real relationship with me, and he wouldn't mind fucking my brains out when we meet down at the Grand Xenix Resort."

"How did Tolar Seia respond to that?"

"He responded: Go fuck yourself." He then stood up and walked away.

"Did you by any chance read Tolar Seia's Aura?"

"Yes, I did, I can now read them both."

"That's rather interesting. We've never had the number one and number two leaders of a major crime family under such great surveillance."

"I read him because I felt that if there was any future involvement possibly with him, I would want to know whatever he is planning."

"It seems to me there is no point in sending you to Grand Xenix Resort with these results."

"No there is no reason to go, and I'm not interested."

"It would be kind of interesting to see what would happen if you were there in the bar at the same time with Thurston bon Katterberg and Karl Vlasson."

"I'm sure it would get kind of ugly fast. Thurston has some firepower and Karl Vlasson has some guns to bear."

"Maybe we can use you to inspire a gangland shootout between them, to eliminate a lot of filth at the same time."

"I think my services would be better put to use against the Tartars who made my life so horrible."

"That's coming. We will spend the next year training you while you do the remote viewing on Thurston bon Katterberg and Karl Vlasson."

"What about this woman you are planning to have Karl Vlasson knock off?"

"She's a double spy, we have to get rid of her."

"Perhaps you can put her into my training package. She helped the Tartars: I would love to kill her for you."

"I would seriously entertain having you do the killing, but we have a policy not to get our fingers dirty. We have one hundred percent deniability in case the National Police investigated us for allegations we murdered someone."

***

CHAPTER ELEVEN

Luthor Braxleon and Commander Bull

It was back to school and physical training. Every now and then the National Police who have a jaundice relationship with the Intelligence Bureau get into a difficult position and must bury the hatchet for a while and call upon their services.

A criminal enterprise existed and every time the National Police got close to making the bust on major drug and illegal elixir smugglers, the entire enterprise vanished. People high up in the National Police organization knew there was a dirty person among them, but they could never figure out who it was, because whoever it was seemed to be rather slick and never left behind any traces of possible involvement.

Nobody in the upper echelons of the National Police showed signs of unearned wealth or something that would raise a red flag to indicate they were being paid off. None of the upper echelon had any financial transactions to track that might suggest who was involved in tipping off the criminals.

When things get so bad that the National Police must suck up their pride and ask the Intelligence Bureau for help, you know a crime must be wicked.

Illegal drugs and elixirs had a corrosive effect on society. People like Karl Vlasson capitalized on the readily available source of such narcotics and illegal elixirs. No doubt Thurston bon Katterberg laundered money for criminal activity. Unfortunately for the criminals, they would only get back twenty percent from Thurston's Ponzi scheme.

The National Police had one person of interest. Since he had his own private transportation and an early warning system, the few trusted partners who knew of the treachery among them kept that information close to themselves and after meetings with the head of the National Police, the combined task force that would include only a couple members of the National Police to keep compartmentalized and the Intelligence Bureau would be involved. This was such a hot potato it ended up as Agent Lucika's project.

The National Police and most of the Intelligence Bureau had no idea Tavishien existed or her talents. The stage was now set. The Intelligence Bureau would infiltrate Luthor Braxleon. Tavishien will identify the mole in the National Police. The small group of National Police Officers that were sick of getting beat by the insider pleaded with the captain to not inform anyone including his deputy of this operation. The National Police struggled hard and long not wanting to blow this opportunity to finally nail the mole.

Hence, Commander Bull was not briefed or informed that such a major operation was underway utilizing the Intelligence Bureau to assist their very small task force. Unfortunately, these National Police Patriots could not risk exposure and thus could not bring any significant number of agents to work on the case. They swallowed their pride and informed the Intelligence Bureau, *the only way we can achieve our goal is we will have to rely on your heavy guns.*

The two National Police members present in the conference room with Agent Lucika were not happy when he informed them of the way he did business.

"I know the way you guys operate. You want to be duly informed and follow the operation from cradle to grave and have an insider's view. We have sensitive sources and methods we cannot disclose to you we'll use in this operation. The only thing I can give you is information but not how we obtained it."

The two National Policemen were naturally disappointed they would not have access to the eye candy, but reality had set in. They were desperate and it was to the point this was a national embarrassment if the public discovered it. The National Policemen reputations was at stake as well as the public's perception. Solving this case was such a priority they would eat humble pie and let events occur in the way the Intelligence Bureau dictated, if they obtained the end results desired, identification of the Mole.

The Intelligence Bureau completed the planning for the clandestine operation and Tavishien started her refresher training in modeling and soon put her to the task.

Tavishien now had the pleasure of traveling to another resort in a faraway location. The Grande Emerald Resort was currently the location where Luthor Braxleon had taken up residence in a Penthouse.

Luthor Braxleon didn't have the firepower or the security detail that Thurston bon Katterberg or Karl Vlasson enjoyed, but he did have a bodyguard that would be part of the security apparatus they would have to penetrate to get Tavishien near Luthor to tag him for remote viewing. Arresting Luthor Braxleon would provide no benefit because he had no idea who the Mole really was, but his connections did. By penetrating Luthor Braxleon they would discover the membership of the crime family and in the process discover the mole.

The plan unfolded with the help of Ljótunn bon Swartzler and the two fashion critics she managed to befriend; a fashion show was arranged for the Grande Emerald Resort. Ljótunn bon Swartzler didn't need to sell any garments at the fashion show since Agent Lucika provided her with ample funds to do the show and bank some money in the process.

Luthor Braxleon was under constant surveillance as the Intelligence Bureau greased the palms of the hotel security to allow them to put in their toys. Some call it *Cash in Advance*.

One thing could be said about Luthor Braxleon was he was a combination of Whore Munger and frequent use of call girls. He liked pretty women and spent time at the Grande Emerald Resort looking for targets of opportunity. One phrase could size him up for what he was, a pussy hound.

Luthor Braxleon would soon enough be given a spoon-fed introduction to a fashion model. At the bar the night before the fashion show, Luthor Braxleon was enjoying some elixirs and had no idea the kind gentleman talking to him who claimed to be a businessperson that owned a *couture manufacturing company* was here to look over some of the fashion designs the next day. He was invited to the fashion show with Douglas Draske who had reserved seats located next to the runway to best see the fashion models well.

The hook that Luthor Braxleon swallowed was, "Often these models end up in the hotel bar where we get to meet them and schedule some play time."

"What do you mean by play time?"

"Creative positions."

The next day Luthor Braxleon was sitting in a seat where Agent Lucika had helped Tavishien practice her performance that was coming up real soon.

Just like in her previous fashion show Tavishien was groomed with special care and made into an exquisite woman, and just like she did with Tolar Seia, Luthor Braxleon was left speechless. The eye contact was very powerful.

Once again, Agent Lucika had no idea Tavishien was flooding Luthor Braxleon's pleasure center and emotional center of his brain causing him significant psychological transcendence into a unique emotional state that would resemble almost total brain washing. The stage was set because as Tavishien knew from her vast training, desire is always ten times more powerful than gratification.

After displaying four profoundly beautiful designer outfits, each time with different musical ensembles to invigorate the passions, Luthor was addicted and disappointed the fashion show ended abruptly.

"This was utterly fantastic. I would never have considered coming here had I not met you at the bar. Let me take you there and buy you a drink. I appreciate this."

"Not a problem," the Intelligence Bureau Rep responded and soon they were at the Grande Emerald Resort bar and grill now filling up with a much larger crowd than normal thanks to the fashion show just completed.

Luthor was very excited and soon was getting lubricated by some very expensive fine elixirs he ordered for the two of them.

The Intelligence Bureau Rep had a lot of good training in the past to pull this off since he had been at other fashion shows. Soon the magic was to unfold that captivated Luthor Braxleon like seldom he experienced, because dressed up in another outfit looking well enough to make every man in the bar toungues drag on the floor came the illustrious Tavishien. In the company of Ljótunn bon Swartzler, Tavishien displayed her utter arrogance because she knew she was the *best-looking bitch* in the room bar none.

Since this was all staged, two Intelligence Bureau Rep's sitting at the bar simply holding the seats for Ljótunn bon Swartzler and Tavishien simply stood up and walked away at the very moment the women were poised to grab those seats. Tavishien naturally grabbed the seat next to Luthor Braxleon which soon caused sexual volcanic tremmors in Luthor.

Luthor entered a state of quintessential obsessions sitting next to the fashion model that just captivated him on the fashion show runway and her eye contact drove thousands of ethereal darts through his heart. He was utterly stunned that here she was sitting on the bar stool next to him.

Tavishien didn't like going into hotel rooms with men because there was undue risk, and this guy was a dangerous criminal. She read his rap sheet. He would twist the heads off puppies for thrills. He truly was a bad dude. Tavishien really didn't want to go up to the hotel room with this creep even though she knew she could probably kill him so mixed in with the chit chat she read his Aura the best she could then tested her remote view.

After Luthor bought Tavishien a drink and she drank half of it, she excused herself to go to the lady's room where she could be in a quiet area and test her remote viewing to see if it would work. Tavishien sat down on the toilet in case other women came into the bathroom would think she was taking care of business. Instead, Tavishien was remote viewing Luthor and discovered she was able to read him.

Tavishien then left the stall and looked around noticing she was alone and called Agent Lucika on her personal communicator and said, "I was able to tag Luthor, I can remote view him, us get the hell out of here."

Moments later Agent Lucika walked up to Ljótunn bon Swartzler and said, "Ljótunn, I have a client that would like to purchase one of your gowns, could you please come with me to meet them?" *That was the coded phrase to convey, mission is complete or aborted, we are now leaving.*

"I would be delighted."

The support staff had a couple beautiful women to get into those seats and keep Luthor occupied so he would not look for Tavishien. In due time with the charm the women poured on, Tavishien quickly escaped his thoughts and after they bought him a couple drinks and drugged him while he went to the men's room, they soon departed the scene and left with the last of the Intelligence Bureau Rep's.

Two hours later Tavishien was in a private debriefing with Agent Lucika and the remote viewing results started, but due to Luthor Braxleon's inebriated state, it would not be for another couple days before the INTEL gathering would commence.

The National Police Officers were not happy they had no instant gratification, but under the circumstances, they had no choice but to be patient since all their prior leads had been blown by the insider mole.

Finally, around forty-eight hours later when Luthor Braxleon was coherent and involved in activity the INTEL bonanza started flowing.

Agent Lucika was shrewd. There was no way in hell he was going to tell the National Police who the Mole was. He knew they would screw it up like everything else they did.

Agent Lucika had a bona fide solution. He wanted to now test Tavishien to see if she was capable of contract killing.

The Intelligence Bureau Rep was once again visiting Tolar Seia on the beach far away from microphones or other and the discussion began.

"I have another contract for you and if you do it you will be able to spend some time with Tavishien."

The mere utterance of Tavishien's name sent shock waves through Tolar Seia who was all ears now.

"What's the contract?"

"You are to kidnap the person we'll identify and take him to a good location where Tavishien will kill him."

Tolar was mildly rattled with the last statement and asked, "Is she a real killer?"

"Yes, she is very deadly. Normally as you know we hire you to do the killing, but her boss wants Tavishien to do this for training purposes."

"Well, I'll be god damned."

The stage was set.

Commander Bull didn't do anything extravagant to raise any concerns or issues. He was an outdoorsman and liked to go on long walks into the forest.

Because Commander Bull was high up in the National Police, he always had a well-armed and corrupt bodyguard.

Today was another one of those days when Commander Bull and his bodyguard who also got paid by criminals were walking in an open area a few hundred yards wide in the middle of a forest on the foothills of a mountain range.

Commander Bull and his bodyguard had no idea the amount of surveillance they had on them walking through the waste high grass on their way to a tree line with nobody in sight. There was no reason to be concerned.

As the two walked along talking about normal life and situations, they found themselves in society, the bodyguard's head suddenly exploded with several high-power rifle shots through the head. To the astonishment of Commander Bull, a dozen men stood up from the grass pointing their rifles at him. He turned around to look for an area to run to and quickly discovered he was surrounded. He was soon bound and gagged, and a VTOL aircraft came out of nowhere and landed in the tall grass where he was escorted and put on board.

Inside the helicopter was Tolar Seia and a few of his goons in suits.

The VTOL lifted off and soon flew to a safe house in the middle of nowhere set up for this mission.

Commander Bull was led into the safe house and told to sit down in a chair that he was soon tied too and really could not move since the chair was bolted to the floor.

"You will have a visitor soon."

Fifteen minutes later Commander Bull could hear the noise of a VTOL landing nearby. Momentarily Agent Lucika entered with the captain in charge of the National Police, and a very attractive woman, Tavishien.

"Commander Bull, I suppose you are interested in why you are here. You are the Mole we have spent countless months looking for. Since we can't reveal sensitive sources and materials used in detecting your fraud, we must deal with you in another manner."

"And how is that?"

"The public will be informed the police are looking for you in the forest a few days from now when you come up missing," The captain of the National Police stated.

Commander Bull looked on knowing he was in a very serious situation that might end up painful soon.

"Goodbye, Commander Bull," the captain said and was soon out the door and VTOL sounds could then be heard.

Moments later there was more VTOL sounds as more craft were arriving to fly Tolar and his gang away.

"Tolar, we'll handle it from here. Thanks for your assistance."

"You are welcome and thanks for the money."

Tolar and his crew then left the safehouse leaving only Tavishien and Agent Lucika present to do the *Tasatsu*.

Tavishien looked at Commander Bull when they were suddenly alone and said, "You compromised yourself with your crimes. You are despicable garbage and society should not waste any money prosecuting you. So, I'm going to take care of you to save money."

Tavishien then looked at Agent Lucika and said, "Would you mind stepping outside."

"Sure." He was soon outside waiting.

Tavishien then took off the gag so that Commander Bull could speak.

"Do you have anything to say for yourself to plead for leniency?"

"Fuck you bitch."

"That's the wrong thing to say to a *bitch* like me."

Tavishien then emptied her clip into Commander Bull's face flowing out most he the brain matter out the back of his head, then Commander Bull's head bent over.

Tavishien then walked out the door and meeting Agent Lucika then walked over to a VTOL and left. Moments later the safe house was engulfed in flames.

A manhunt started for missing Commander Bull. He was never found. But due to his stature and position within the criminal justice system, all of his personal matters were investigated and soon enough a lot of damaging information was detected in his personal finances, and he was an embarrassment to the force which they had to cover up.

The fact Commander Bull vanished with all those assets gave the investigators the idea that he probably ended up disappearing with the help of individuals who had to silence him for some issue his involvement created. Since the conclusion was, he evidently got caught up with some negative issues with organized crime, they no doubt made fish food out of him or eliminated him in such a way his remains would never be found.

The head of the National Police was the only officer who knew Commander Bull was taken to the Intelligence Bureau safe house. They had no idea if Commander Bull was killed or what happened to him as they were not around to observe the killing. The safe house was destroyed by the fire and could never be used again.

Commander Bull's disappearance was a cold case they knew was never going to be solved as the files went to the dead case storage with only yearly ticklers to re-examine which would turn up the same results. The National Police Chief and the two specialists had a good speculation of what happened to Commander Bull and the spooks that captured him didn't exist as they used an alias and temporary facial identity change during the mission.

Tavishien a temporary red head wearing a mask with an appearance of a young Lucile Ball who would be considered no less than Elegance and Ecstasy in the eyes of mere mortals by her very short dress and appearance showing a lot of cleavage that night. The

National Police Captain wondered, w*as the woman an organized crime operative?*

***

CHAPTER TWELVE
Learning How to Drive

Moving up rapidly from the stone age to modern times in the span of a couple of years created an educational challenge not only for Tavishien but also her handlers.

What do you do with a woman that knows nothing about modern society? What basic things does a Spy need for survival?

One item of interest is private transportation. Aside from Skycars that were appearing more frequently as society shifted with more technological advances, there were still ground vehicles and hovercrafts used all over the planet.

In some tropical areas where the landscape was predominately marshland. Hovercraft was used instead of ground based, vehicles. Skycars did appear in a few of these areas, but mainly ground based transportation existed for wealthy clientele in well secluded holiday resorts. The bulk of the freight came in by hovercraft of various sizes and shapes.

Inter-island transportation was via Hovercraft Ferries, some of which also carried vehicles to a few of the towns that had a local road network. Also found in substantial quantities in the small towns and villages that had road access, were motor bicycles. Since most of the driving was local, dependability was more important than speed. Half the motor bicycles were hydrogen powered; the remainder were all electrical.

The next phase of Tavishien's training was safe operation of these types of transportation devices. In due time she would almost become a stunt woman as she had to improvise and save her own hide from angry men who do not like to get bested by a female spy.

Agent Lucika had the alias of Marti for this mission, as he took Tavishien to the small remote coastal town Perland via a Skycar.

Agent Lucika had visited Perland often in the past for a variety of reasons such as utilizing it as a staging area for operations elsewhere. Perland was out of the way and organized crime as well as Tartars would never travel to Perland looking for trouble since it didn't pop up on anyone's radar.

Through years of interactions and ample quid pro quo and dealings existed between Marti (aka Agent Lucika) and Elnar Harkensen in this small village of Perland. This private business relationship would now facilitate Tavishien's training.

Elnar Harkensen was also the proprietor of a rental company that rented boats, bicycles, scooters, and electric powered cars. He also owned a bed and breakfast resort. Hence, Elnar Harkensen was a one stop shopping just about for all of Agent Lucika's needs for Tavishien training activity.

As the Skycar landed in the middle of Elnar Harkensen's Bed and Breakfast Resort parking lot, he was standing there waiting for Agent Lucika who had contacted him in advance to arrange equipment accommodation and plan the series of rentals. Gabriel and another Intelligence Bureau Rep (IBR) by the name of Tristan Karjal were along for the operation for security as well as training and to give the appearance they were two couples enjoying a holiday.

The six-seater Skycar had plenty of room for the four travelers, a driver who would soon depart with the Skycar back to its base, and all the luggage they required for a two week stay.

The doors to the Skycar rotated upwards and the passengers all exited. The driver also got out and walked to the rear of the Skycar that had a cargo area for luggage or freight shipments if necessary. He opened the access door and started removing all the luggage and sitting it up on the pavement next to the Skycar without being prompted.

"Greetings Elnar," Agent Lucika (aka Marti for this mission) said warmly with a smile.

"Glad to see you back here, Marti," Elnar Harkensen stated and always enjoyed the Cash in Advance he always received when Agent Lucika came around.

Elnar didn't need introduction to Gabriel or Agent Tristan Karjal an Intelligence Bureau Representative (IBR) who often helped Agent Lucika (aka Marti) for previous missions to this town) during past trips to this location for other types of training sessions including clandestine deployments off hovercraft.

"Let me introduce you to Tavishien who you will get to spend some time with over the next couple of weeks," Marti (aka agent Lucika) said.

Tavishien walked over to Elnar Harkensen and held out her hand and said, "Pleased to meet you sir."

"Thank you Tavishien, just call me Elnar."

"No problem, Elnar."

Elnar Harkensen looked at Gabriel who was appearing cute today in her touristy like clothes and said, "Gabriel, you are looking really nice today."

"Thank you Elnar, you are always such a sweet talker."

Elnar then looked at Tristan Karjal who still had a youthful appearance even though he was starting to develop some leathery skin from exposure during harsh environments on missions.

"You are looking in good shape, Tristan."

"Well, Elnar, I do manage to get a good workout every day. One must keep in shape in the line of business I'm in."

"I can imagine," Elnar Harkensen who knew the obvious, he was looking at a tough character who had killed people before in the line of duty and lived the life of kill or be killed. He also knew one other fact. Tristan Karjal wasn't needed here for Tavishien's training. It was obvious that he and Gabriel both considered bad asses were here for security and to protect Tavishien, someone who was a special person. He also didn't buy the cover story Tavishien's a fashion model they were training up for public relations for the Bureau.

"Let me take you guys inside to your rooms."

"Thanks," Agent Lucika stated as he went to go grab his luggage."

"Let me help you carry some of that," Elnar stated as he went over to the pile of luggage and grabbed one of them. The driver also helped, and between the six people all the luggage was carried in one trip to the two reserved rooms with double beds. It was obvious to Elnar, none of these people were lovers but they had to put on a show to convince any possible trailers who were sent to do surveillance on them.

As soon as they were settled in their bed and breakfast rooms, Elnar said, "As you know Marti (aka agent Lucika), I serve breakfast in the morning, but for lunch or dinner you will have to go to some of the restaurants here."

"Not a large choice since there are only three of them," Marti said.

"You are lucky we have these three. We barely get enough tourism to support the restaurants in town."

I suppose I should feel grateful since some places I've had to work only had one restaurant that was open when the owner felt like coming to work."

"How did you cope during the days the restaurant wasn't open?"

"My boss was perturbed at the cost of the meal deliveries via Skycars. They had to fly 100 miles to get there so it was expensive.

"What could he do about it?"

"Nothing, he knows I do not work on an empty stomach, nor do I expect my crew to either."

"You want to start the hovercraft training in the morning?"

"Yes, we do, however we would like to try out your motor bicycles this afternoon."

"No problem, but remember, you break them you own them."

"Didn't I always pay up in the past?"

"Yes, you did, but I lost 4 Hovercraft, 3 electric bicycles, and two electric cars in less than 4 days and it took a few weeks to get replacements."

"Well, we wrecked old junk, and you got new models out of the deal so why are you complaining?"

"I'm not complaining, but you sir sometimes can be a disaster."

"True."

"How many electric bicycles do you want this afternoon?"

"Four of course, one for each of us."

"That's all I can spare now. Can you do me a favor and try not to wreck any today?"

"When we go out, we'll probably wreck one or two this week, not to worry.

I'll have new ones flown in to replace those we damage."

"If that's the case please damage them all," Elnar said with an evil grin.

Elnar walked the four IBR's down to the bicycle stand in front of the bed and breakfast and unlocked them and said, "Batteries are all charged up will last you past lunch time. When you bring them back, plug in the charger cable and put the locks on them." "Sure thing," Marti said.

Tavishien had preliminary training back at the Intelligence Bureau Campus and could get on and do basic riding. Today they would step it up a notch because she needed to learn how to avoid automobiles attempting to run her over and kill her.

"The trick is to make the evasive maneuver at the very last second to make sure the automobile driver was committed and did not have enough reaction time to hit you," Marti said.

"What if I'm on a busy city street?" Tavishien asked.

"Anywhere someone drives a bicycle has maneuver opportunities including turning down a narrow walkway a car can't reach or around an obstacle. Worse case, get up on the sidewalk so the car must mow down dozens of people that will instantly get the police after them."

Gabriel chimed in, "That is unless operating in Tartarland, where it might be a police chase."

The group headed out driving in the small town that had a two-foot dyke around it to prevent flooding in high tide scenarios. The road passing through the town had a slight hill going over the built-up area, but the rest of the town was built on flat land that no doubt used to be marshland, filled in with truckloads of dirt and rock from nearby mountains fifteen miles away with majestic peaks covered white in the wintertime.

Marti took the group around town driving these electric bikes with pedal assist for human power when desired. It appeared like a group of tourists out having fun on bicycles which was totally innocuous to the residents who saw tourists all the time do this kind of behavior.

With a population of less than 1000 it did not take a lot of time to see most of the town on bicycles, including the main throughfare which had all the storefronts for a small country village. Most of the buildings on Main Street appeared just like going through a

European town in the 1930's. All the stores were also homes with residents living upstairs.

The only hotel in town that was not a bed and breakfast was on Main Street. The lower portion was a bar with a restaurant and upstairs was eight rooms to rent, some of which came with a woman at an inflated price. The woman was usually willing to provide *special services* but expected a generous tip after she made the customer fully satisfied.

During the drive around town, Marti reconnoitered a lot of places where they could train Tavishien egress techniques. There were some narrow alleys and places easy for a bicycle but would be very difficult or impossible to get through. There were also other natural physical barriers. Part of the dyke that surrounded the community had asphalt cover for pedestrians but was too narrow for vehicles.

There would be places like this where Tavishien could get on and simply casually drive away from her assailants who would be stuck behind and must find another means of reaching her. As such Marti took them along the dyke walkway and other areas, he deemed great for egress techniques. As they were riding along Marti schooled Tavishien in what he had in mind.

With about one hour before lunch time, they exercised the first escape and Marti gave Tavishien direction and said, "I'll follow from behind and simulate being an automobile traying to capture you."

As soon as they were ready, Marti said, "Take off."

Tavishien started her electric bicycle up and used the foot petals to help accelerate the speed to slightly above the speed limit in town. After waiting enough time to give a distance likely to match a real-life scenario, Marti began the chase.

Tavishien was a fast learner. She had the physical acumen as well as the spontaneity in her to emulate sportsmanship by the best athletes. Even though sometimes her memory had issues from the brain trauma she received from the Tarter soldiers, when it did work right, she had great analytical skills and acquired the techniques Marti (aka agent Lucika) taught her.

Just like before in their drive around the town, Tavishien found those narrow alleyways and darted through them to escape her trailer, Marti on the chase electric bike. Gabriel and the IBR Tristan Karjal followed along on a loose trail trying to guess where the chase was going. By staying in the center of town they were able to see where the two were going.

Marti simulating a vehicle could not get on the dyke and chase Tavishien from there, he could only travel down the nearest parallel road. Suddenly Tavishien's electric bike went down the side of the dike facing the water. Marti (aka Agent Lucika) turned at the end of the block fearing she had fallen into the water and might be in trouble. By the time he got up onto the dyke looking for Tavishien, there was no sight of her. Then he heard a whistle. There she was 100 yards away back on the dock looking back momentarily and laughing. She had totally spoofed Marti!

Marti did what the enemy would do, went back down on the street giving chase and soon saw not a trace of Tavishien. Right in the middle of town was Gabriel and IBR Tristan Karjal.

"Do you know where she went?"

They both shrugged their shoulders with that look on their face like *we do not know*. Marti waited a few minutes then called Tavishien on her private communicator and said, "You can come out from hiding now, we are going back to Einar's Bed and Breakfast now."

Down a narrow alleyway Tavishien suddenly appeared with a grin on her face. She just bested one of the spies in the business.

"The electric bicycle appears to be in one piece. I'm sure Elnar will appreciate that," Gabriel remarked sarcastically.

"Good job evading the assailants," Marti said feeling good that Tavishien just proved she was cunning and resourceful in figuring out the move she made. Her electric bicycle was a little dirty from scaling the dyke picking up a lot of dirt and debris, otherwise had no bent parts or noticeable scratches.

It didn't take long in a small town to get back to Elnar's Bed and Breakfast, park the electric bicycles, plug in the chargers, and lock them up.

"What are we doing for lunch?" IBR Tristan Karjal asked.

"Why don't we walk over to Elijah's he usually fixes a good lunch," Gracie said.

"Alright," Marti (aka Agent Lucika) responded.

The four Amigo's walked a block and half to Elijah's Diner, where food for this part of the country was considered superb and would be frowned upon in most cities. But out of sight and out of mind often alters one's palate.

Tavishien immediately felt at home in Elijah's Diner. It had a hint of backwoods nature to it and Elijah, and his wife dressed simply enough and were not out to impress anyone in a town where everyone knew everyone plus everyone knew everyone else's business.

The group looking at the menu knowing they were around where a lot of good fish catching went on ordered fish entrees and had some nice elixirs to wash them down.

There was no shop talk at the lunch table but all four had special ear but type devices that were very well disguised and they were wired for remote assistance including guiding conversations in a public setting to enhance the imagery in ways to make them look more tourist like and city folks. Small town people are usually bored to tears unless they are hiding out here for nefarious purposes. Quite often they want to know what you do and sometimes how much money you make. They are also interested in where you live and how you live.

All four had cover stories and for Tavishien her story was very easy since her private communicator was loaded up with fashion show pictures of her that she had been in.

As expected, it didn't take long before the Elijah's started asking questions out of boredom. Elijah knew Marti, Gabriel, and Tristan Karjal from prior trips, but was smart enough not to dig too deep into what they did, and their cover stories were rather innocuous. But this new person was quite different, and she stood out because her table manners were not quite as sophisticated as the other three. In some cases, she ate with her hands! And she didn't waste time playing with her food as she whooped it down!

Elijah approached the table and asked, "How's everyone doing, would you like another drink?"

"I'll have another one of your special elixirs," Tristan Karjal said.

"Anyone else?"

Nobody responded so Elijah came back moments later with the special elixir he knew that Tristan Karjal was already having a good buzz with.

As Elijah stood next to Tristan and Tavishien, he looked at the fine-looking young lady and asked, "What's your name misses?"

"I'm Tavishien, glad to meet you."

"Just call me Elijah."

"Sure, Elijah."

"What are you doing here with these characters?"

"I'm a fashion model, and they are helping me to explore the wilderness, learn a little self-defense, and just rest for a few days."

"Interesting. Where do you do fashion modeling?"

"All over in most cities, would you like to see some of my fashion shows?"

"Sure."

Tavishien pulled out her personal communicator that spread out a holographic presentation several times larger than the communicator so that individuals could look at video or holographs. She started playing the video taken when she was seducing organized crime people. As expected, Elijah was extremely surprised how beautiful Tavishien looked in the video and he could tell it really was her.

Tavishien could tell that Elijah was mesmerized and she did one more thing the rest of them had no idea she could do. Tavishien used her mental telepathy to affect the pleasure center of Elijah's brain which soon had an impact on him which caused him to become more verbose in his response to the holographic video he now observed.

"Would you like to see some more?" Tavishien asked.

"Oh yes, please." Elijah said with utter expectation.

Elijah's wife was soon standing beside him also watching the videos and their body language showed they were enthused to be standing next to a top fashion model.

Marti (aka Agent Lucika) knew this couple was gossip galore and was pleased that Tavishien had immersed them with the knowledge she was a fashion model which went a long way towards eliminating any speculation on other roles she might play.

In due time, the group finished their meals and elixirs, and Marti (aka Agent Lucika) paid the bill with great tips and left.

Mrs. Elijah soon discovered her husband was happy for a change. Lately he had been kind of cranky and now suddenly, he was being soft, gentle, and helpful. If that fashion model was responsible for her husband's shift in moods, then she hoped they would come back often for meals during their stay.

As the group walked back to Elnar Harkensen's Bed and Breakfast, they found him outside by the electric bicycles apparently cleaning them as water was running down the gutter and all the electric bikes appeared sparkling clean.

"I'm glad you didn't bust up my electric bikes but one of them needed some extra cleaning."

"Not a problem, give me a bill for extra cleaning," Marti responded.

"You can plan on it."

"Since you are not going out on the Hovercraft until tomorrow, what do plan on doing this afternoon?"

"Still running that small tourist bus?"

"Sure am, but I do not have any reservations for today."

"You have four for this afternoon. Let us go up and get freshened up then we'll meet you down here, say in 30 minutes so we can show Tavishien the countryside."

"Alright, meet you here in 30 minutes."

After everyone was ready, Elnar Harkensen pulled out onto the country road with the four passengers. Since there were only four tourists on the bus, each person had a window seat. The vehicle was cool and comfortable.

Elnar Harkensen had a circular route he took people on which allowed them to see the marshlands, the fishermen, and the planters and fish farm operators.

At first glance at the local landscape and homes Elnar Harkensen drove past gave the impression the area looked impoverished. Close to the road most of the buildings had no paint and the roofs appeared quite primitive. What struck Tavishien the most was the roofs on these buildings didn't look as well as he father's cabin built at the mountainside forested area.

Elnar Harkensen knew that the first observations are important, and he didn't want tourists to believe this entire area was full of insular poverty. Hence, he diverted off the main road into some estates that were obscure by trees and foliage where he knew the owners quite well and pulled through their circular driveway to show there were significant opulence in the area, but it was purposely out of sight and out of mind, as to not attract attention of potential criminals.

There was a whole different world just 500 yards off the main road. After touring a few of such manors, they came up to a construction zone.

"You can see the trucks are hauling in a lot of rock and dirt," Elnar Harkensen noted.

"What are they building?" Tavishien asked.

"A wealthy person from Pango Tango is building a mansion here."

"Where's Pango Tango?" Tavishien asked.

"Pango Tango is the closest major city about thirty miles North of Perland," Elnar Harkensen replied.

"Where's all that dirt coming from?" Marti asked.

"There are mountains about fifteen miles away that are the source of that material. When you have a lot of money you can afford quite a few truckloads of rock and dirt." Elnar Harkensen replied.

"How long before this place will be finished?" Marti asked.

"They are a few weeks away from completing the fill of the marsh area, then they will start installing foundations and install piping and external connections to services they need."

"Will they have electrical hookups?"

"Yes, all the power lines are buried along the sides of roads inside pipes to keep out the moisture."

"Is that why we do not see any power lines back in your town?"

"Yes, that's right our power lines are all buried underground running through pipes."

The trip continued and thanks to Elnar Harkensen, Tavishien had a growing understanding of the area. Agent Lucika, Gabriel, and IBR Tristan Karjal already knew the area from previous trips and Elnar's tours.

As the car drove down the main road a few more miles they passed a few fish farms that looked rather spectacular, then they came upon a wide area that was totally green and appeared to have plant life waste high. After traveling a mile past all this green flora, they came upon several people working in a muddy field and Tavishien asked, "What are they doing?"

They are planting Beikoku. That's a grain that is a main staple for people in these parts of the world.

How do you use it?

They use it in many ways. They create types of breads, noodles, wines, and other substances out of it.

"What does it look like when they harvest it?"

"Remember the large green areas we just passed?"

"Yes."

"That is Beikoku farms and in another month the plants will turn brown, and they will harvest it."

"Can you show me how Beikoku looks?"

"Sure, there is a roadside canteen ahead we can stop for refreshments and see some of the products they make with the Beikoku."

After passing a few more Beikoku farms there was suddenly a stand of native tropical trees and a parking area in front of a local constabulary.

"We can go in here so she can see some of the bakery items and the other products made with the Beikoku," Elnar Harkensen said.

Soon the vehicle pulled up into one of the dozen empty parking spots in front of the constabulary with a Billboard stating "Food, Spirits, and General Merchandise."

As soon as they all exited the vehicle and entered the building to a friendly reception, it was apparent to Tavishien this store sold about everything the community wanted or needed. There was a bar with stools and two tables to serve diners who ordered food.

"This place is more of a takeout than anything. People would come here to do their shopping and take edibles home with them," Elnar Harkensen said.

Two older residents were sitting at the bar drinking elixirs that were nothing more than strong tea that helped them keep a clear head but at the same time enhance social engagement.

These men were dressed like many of the locals and appeared they could go to work at any time. Their work clothes were their social clothes. Only on special occasions would they dress up differently and that was rare for events like weddings and funerals.

Tavishien was still grappling with the notion of religions. She had her Arctic religions that were passed down from her Papa who received his from his parents and grandparents. There were no similarities at all. City people thought the mountainous Frontiersmen were nothing more than a Cult that believed in the most ridiculous paranormal and supernatural surrounding their belief system. From an outsider looking in one would conclude the religions that people practiced in the cities was just as farfetched. What really mattered the most is who indoctrinated a person and how well they did it.

Half of the building was a restaurant/bar/grocery store. The other half was a hardware store that would qualify as a primitive retail store that sold shoes, clothes, and everything not hardware someone might need in a home.

Despite the small size the *Food, Spirits, and General Merchandise* store had a wide variety of items to purchase. It was apparent to the visitors that tourists helped this store flourish as there were a lot of items tourists would need for outdoor recreation such as insect repellant and suntan lotion.

In the grocery section of the store, besides the strange items that were on the shelves, there were also several large barrels heaping full of white substance in one barrel, brown in another, and a strange green in the other.

Marti noted to Tavishien standing next to him about five feet away from the barrel full of white substance pointed at it and said, "That is Beikoku after it's been processed."

"It looks interesting," Tavishien stated realizing this is just one more item in her life she had no knowledge of being raised so remotely.

"Those scoops and bags by all the barrels are for the customers to fill a paper bag to the amount they want, and the store owner weighs it and charges them," Marti noted.

"Back behind the person operating the bar and talking to the two local gentlemen, are a dozen barbecued animals hanging by string."

"Do the customers buy them and take the meat home like that?" Tavishien asked?"

"Yes. But if a person sitting at the bar requested, they can order some of it and eat it there while drinking. If they want to take one of the carcass home, the bartender will cut the string with his knife and wrap the barbecued animal in butchers' paper and put it in a bag and hand it to the customer who would pay for it when they checked out at the counter."

"What's in all those boxes on the shelves back behind the counter?" Tavishien asked.

"That's a mini pharmacy. Instead of shelves of bottles, they have those wooden boxes full of substances the employee who is also a *country pharmacist* puts into a bag for a customer for a particular ailment such as upset stomach, headache, or other issues."

"How well does those substances work?" Tavishien asked.

"This is a country pharmacy and what you see there has much more potent medicines than what is normally allowed in the cities." Marti said.

"Is that legal?" Tavishien asked.

"The government learned a long time ago to leave country people alone as they do a great job of taking care of themselves and by the nature of how they live their lives they have much fewer medical issues. Should a serious medical condition arise, people in the town would call in an ambulance that would take them to Pango Tango City for more modern treatments," Marti said.

"Do the wealthy people that live in some of those mansions we saw use this stuff too?"

"They would simply get in their Skycars and fly to a hospital or a doctor in the city. Traveling via their Skycars they can be at the doctor's office in 15 minutes or less."

"How well do those people in those mansions live?"

"Quite well. I know some of them. They have cooks, maids, landscapers, midwives, and whatever they need."

"Is the food better out here in the country?"

"Far better and fresher. And it's in abundance, unlike some of the cities where prices are steep."

The amusement of a *country store* soon wore down and it was time to leave. They all hopped back in Elnar Harkensen tourist vehicle and continued their sightseeing trip.

They drove through a couple fishing villages and saw several dozen parked boats.

"This is the time of the day the fishermen start coming back with their daily catch. They would be back out again early in the morning heading out to deeper water before sunrise. The fishermen take care of their catch, sell it to the middlemen, if necessary, then clean up eat, have a few elixirs and be in bed sound asleep several hours before midnight and repeat the same thing again in the early morning," Marti noted.

Tavishien didn't know this yet, but she would be coming back to one of these fishing villages in the morning to hop on Hovercraft to learn how to operate them in the thick marshes nearby.

For an outdoors person like Tavishien, she learned the lay of the land quickly. Back in the mountains living with her Papa she had to learn a lot to stay alive. Her one mistake was being complacent just because the Tomlars were not reacting to the approaching Tartar soldiers who were trained well in how to sneak up on their enemy. With six men, they could converge on Tavishien from all directions at once and attack before she could figure out an escape route.

Even if Tavishien managed to escape, the Tartar soldiers might have shot her in the leg to disable her for their ultimate satisfaction. Perhaps because of that experience she was keener now in noting her surroundings and possible egress locations. With the training she has received it would not work out too well for the same six Tarter soldiers if they ever met up again, had her father not killed all of them.

The tour concluded and Elnar Harkensen pulled up to the driveway spot with a sign "Tour vehicle parking, please do not park here."

The group then got out of the vehicle and went up to their rooms with plans to meet later for dinner after everyone had a chance to relax and freshen up.

Gabriel invited Tavishien to use the facilities first because she didn't want to leave behind a nasty smell that might take a while to dissipate out the open window. Tavishien took care of her business promptly, just like she ate her food, she didn't fool around. Out in the forest when crouched down taking care of business in a forest, one never knew if there was a bear or other vicious animal around so if one needed to take a dump in the forest, it was prudent to get the job done quickly just in case.

The ceiling fan in the bathroom did a good enough job to clean out any residual smell and by the time Tavishien had her clothes back on ready to walk out of the bathroom any trace of the nasty smell was long gone.

After she left the bathroom Gabriel went in and wasn't in such a rush. She took about three times as long, so it was good she was generous allowing Tavishien in first.

Tavishien was learning more and more about her communicator and what she could do with it. It was nothing short of a huge information supplier. Moments like this Tavishien scanned information she wanted to explore deeper and learn more about civilization. It was more than an educational exercise; it was also a great awakening and exposure to a modern society just as if she walked out of a cave man era.

There were so many things to explore, animals, geology, history, and technology. It was mildly disturbing to Tavishien what she didn't know, so she was very practical and time conscious to make good use of her time off to explore new information and become better informed about the world around her. There was so much to learn, but Tavishien knew one step at a time she would learn a lot.

All of society was at Tavishien's fingertips on her personal communicator. Tavishien's communicator was now everything to her. Her access to credits for purchases, pictures if she chose to take any. She was advised not to take any pictures of IBRs because if she was ever captured since the enemy knew many of the IBRs they would no doubt torture her to make her explain how she knew them and exactly what they did and her relationship with them.

Tavishien's handlers and trainers explained to her: "The more pictures of people you have on your personal communicator will multiply the special procedures they will do to you to extract information. It's in your best interest to never photograph any IBR personnel."

After killing the high-ranking National Police official, Tavishien knew how serious the business was and to the extremes enemies would go. Tavishien took her special briefings with great care and understood the need to practice those methods as they were taught for her own survival.

Through her earbuds she could hear the audio content of her communicator and in evenings and during trips where she was trapped on airplanes or in vehicles or Skycars for the travel, she often surfed the *data universe*.

Sitting in the bathroom doing her business, Tavishien was always engaged in surfing the *data universe* and any imagery that caught her attention caused her to drill down deeper into the details and information.

On this day she discovered something from the *data universe*. It was a land-based transportation system to deliver large quantities of products to cities and towns around the nation. It wasn't anything like a vehicle she had seen before, and it appeared to have several very large transportation devices connected and traveling at moderately high speeds.

As Tavishien drilled down she discovered videos of these transportation devices called *Maglev Freighters*. What surprised Tavishien was that on priority freight shipments the *Maglev Freighters* traveled at four hundred miles per hour when they were running in air stabilized tubes.

Air stabilized tubes sucked the air out of the tunnel in front of the *Maglev Freighters* at an incredible rate to eliminate most of the wind resistance. Because of the air evacuation out of the tunnel, the *Maglev Freighters* were moving along as if they were in a vacuum since there was very little wind resistance. Hence the only friction holding down velocities was the hysteresis in the maglev coils. If they could eliminate the effects of hysteresis on the A.C. power to the maglev coils, they could achieve much higher *Maglev Freighters* velocities.

Tavishien observed some of the *Maglev Passenger Trains* and said to herself, *one day I want to take a trip on one of those Maglev Passenger Trains.*

The world which Tavishien grew up in without mechanical devices, was now changing rapidly including the fascination of the *Maglev Freighters* in her a growing knowledge as she learned more.

Since Tavishien's study of geography and maps showed where she grew up was only fifty miles away from a major city. She was perplexed that her father never made the effort to take her to society and show her what that was all about. *Perhaps he feared if I saw the city life, I may not want to go home with him?*

Tavishien was not a talkative woman. Because of her utter isolation growing up, she had no friends. All she had was Papa and the Tomlars. As such she didn't have the need to talk to others, gossip or overtly interchange with people. Hence, she was the perfect spy since she had virtually nothing to say to anyone. But at the same time when someone spoke to her, she was polite and appeared to simply be an introvert nobody would suspect as a deadly spy that she was slowly becoming.

Gabriel had learned Tavishien's traits and knew she did not like to be sucked into a conversation. It was not a fact that Tavishien didn't have empathy, she was a loner because that's all she knew. Her social development was in such poor preparation it was now a high priority for Agent Lucika.

One thing Tavishien thought she wanted to do if peace was ever struck with the Tartars, she would want to go and investigate her mother's roots and family and if there were any surviving members of the family disclose the journey her mother went on and her final resting place.

Tavishien didn't have to be coerced into going to sleep at night, so she didn't affect Gabriel, her temporary roommate's sleeping tendencies. Tavishien always seemed to go to bed early, just like she did out of habit when she lived with her father.

Just as the rooster crows Tavishien was wide awake and while Gabriel snored, she went to the bathroom and took care of business and took a shower and dressed. By the time she finished dressing Gabriel was just waking up and was amazed that Tavishien was already dressed, and spit polished with her growing prowess of learning how to apply makeup effectively to make men's little heads think.

"You look great this morning." Gabriel said.

"Thank you, I feel great since I didn't have to run eight miles yesterday and beat your ass." Tavishien responded.

"Over the next couple of weeks, we need to work in some exercise time, otherwise it will be tougher when we return to the Intelligence Bureau Campus."

"I don't mind working out, schedule it when you want. I like working out as it helps me take my mind off everything."

"Alright, let me get dressed and let's see what breakfast surprises Elnar Harkensen has for us."

A while later the two ladies went down to the breakfast lounge area that had entertainment displays, music devices, a small library, and an assortment of board games and other materials to placate bored to tears tourists whose reservations extended long past when they were done enjoying all the local activity the village and surrounding area had to offer.

Marti was there already with the IBR Tristan Karjal drinking a morning tea and waiting for the women.

As soon as the women sat down at their table, Elnar Harkensen approached and asked the group what they would like for breakfast and gave them choices one through four which covered the bases. They all settled on number one which included meat, eggs, Beikoku, fruit, and drinks.

While their meal was served, Marti said, "This is quite a bit of food. It will probably hold me until dinner."

"Yes, it tastes pretty good," Gabriel responded.

Tristan said, "I'd like to know what this meat is, never tasted anything like it before. It tastes pretty good."

About that time, Elnar Harkensen walked by the table and Tristan asked,

"Excuse me Elnar, can you tell me what kind of meat is in this serving?"

"Sure, it's Hǎiguī. It's an aquatic type of animal that lives in the marshland and the bay area in large numbers. Normally they are hard to catch but people in this community have figured out how to do it," Elnar responded.

"And how is it they catch them?"

"It's their trade secret, they will not let anyone know," Elnar lied knowing quite well they used sticks of explosives to create a major shock wave to knock the animal unconscious then they would drag it aboard their fishing boat that had a deployable ramp to bring these things aboard with a winch as they weighed 100 to 200 pounds.

The group poked away at their food and sipped their drinks all wondering how today would turn out. This would be Tavishien's first exposure to Hovercraft.

***

CHAPTER THIRTEEN
Hovercraft

After breakfast, Marti rented one of the tourist cars from Elnar Harkensen. These were rugged four-wheel drive vehicles designed to go off road and climb steep trails. On the dashboard was a note Elnar placed there with large letters saying, "Only drive this vehicle on roads or registered trails in case you get lost we can find you."

After they all hopped in the rental, Marti (aka agent Lucika) headed south in the vehicle out of town heading about 10 miles where he knew he could get Hovercraft Rentals. The owner of the business was more than happy to rent Hovercraft to Marti because in the past when Marti's students severely wrecked the Hovercraft, the IB bought him brand new ones of equal or better performance. Nothing sweeter than to have a 20-year-old Hovercraft on its last leg getting replaced free of charge by brand new ones in a situation that was not taxable.

Around the time Marti pulled into the Hovercraft Sales and Rentals parking lot a representative was there waiting. The Sales and Rentals representative he dealt with in the past was waiting for him because of the appointment made ahead of time.

As soon as Marti exited the vehicle Norman Swansen who owned the Hovercraft business approached Marti and said, "Hello Marti, how you been?"

"Busy as usual."

"I can imagine."

"Are those two Hovercraft ready to go?"

"Yes, please follow me."

Marti and the others followed Norman out to the piers where the Hovercraft were parked. People would leave here on water, but no doubt they would soon be traveling over seagrass and shallow water.

The two Hovercraft were tied up next to each other at the pier. Marti said, "Gabriel, you and Tristan get in the first boat. Tavishien and I will get in second. I will guide Tavishien to the seagrass area I like to train in. You follow us there and as soon as you hit the grass, assume the chase is on."

Marti turned around looking at Norman and said, "We are leaving now, see you in a couple hours."

"Marti, can you do me a favor?"

"Sure."

"Try not to wreck the Hovercrafts today."

"You know I always treat them very gently."

"Yea just like the last time, you demolished two Hovercraft. Not sure how the hell you survived."

"We were lucky, I told my student to jump with me at the right moment when the Tartar's crashed into the Hovercraft."

"You never informed me about that part of the story."

"At the time it was considered somewhat sensitive until our government and the Tartar representatives hashed it out and we explained why their bodies were burned so severely when the hovercraft exploded into fire because they sliced open our gas tank and ignited it."

"How did you make it back to land?"

"While we were being chased, I called for help, but they didn't arrive until it was too late. They plucked us out of the water and brought us back. That's how I showed up the next day wearing clean clothes to let you know your Hovercraft would not be coming back."

"Any chances you will run into any Tartar Agents on this trip?"

"No, we are out just training, they have no idea we are here. Plus, when we had that unfortunate run-in with them the last time, we were here observing their activities and their agents detected our surveillance that led to all that."

"If you do manage to destroy them, you know what kind to buy me to replace them."

"That we do," Marti said and chuckled and walked over to the Hovercraft.

Marti led Tavishien onto the Hovercraft and directed her, "Strap yourself into the pilot's chair. I'll tell you what to do."

Marti strapped himself into the chair next to the pilot's and turned towards Norman who was on the pier, "Norman, would you mind giving us a shove off to make it easy for the rookie pilot?"

"Sure, no problem."

Norman took his long pole designed for such a purpose to help people more safely get away from the pier by shoving the front of the Hovercraft out towards the saltwater marsh lake, and as soon as the boat was perpendicular from the pier shoved the rear end of the boat which got it moving slowly out towards deeper water.

Norman had the Hovercraft warmed up on idle speeds so all Tavishien had to do now was push the throttles forward.

"You steer the Hovercraft just like you do a vehicle. It will respond the same," Marti said.

"Alright," Tavishien responded.

"See this lever?"

"Yes."

"That's the throttle so when you slowly move it forward you will pick up speed. Go ahead and move it forward a little to where my hand is."

"Okay."

As Tavishien moved the throttle forward the big fan on the rear of the Hovercraft increased RPM and they would feel more wind going past them even with a plexiglass cockpit shield.

The body of the Hovercraft was black, and the flotation devices were rubber bladders filled with *plasterene balls* the size of peas. The *plasterene balls* were strong but contained mostly compressed air in the process they were manufactured. The rubber body of the Hovercraft was solid and ridged and built with 30 small compartments filled with these *plasterene balls* making it essentially impossible to sink, but also allowed it to maintain a very shallow draft allowing it to slide up on a beach where it could be moored for the night if necessary.

More experienced Hovercraft drivers would drive up to the beach travelling at high speed and as they hit the beach do a 180 degree turn so that when they were ready to depart, they were facing the right direction. When they went back into the water, passengers and cargo were removed to make it lighter to make it easier to get it waterborne. Once in shallow water the Hovercraft could then be repopulated with people and cargo.

The big blue fan on the back of the Hovercraft was powered by a powerful lightweight turboshaft engine which added to the horizontal thrust. It also blew a lot of water behind it and as it sped up creating a wake, more water and water vapor would flow in the slipstream behind it at high velocity. Therefore, if you were chasing this Hovercraft, you could not follow directly behind and would have to chase from the Port or Starboard quarter.

There were rollover bars that went over the pilot and passenger seats that had an aerodynamic sunshade to keep everyone out of direct sunlight allowing them to remain outdoors all day long. The sunshade surface was mounted with photocells used to charge up the Hovercraft's batteries while parked next to the pier. The photovoltaic cells on the panels were very efficient and could do a battery recharge in a few hours.

The turboshaft engine used to drive the big fan assembly was brought up to speed by an attached electric motor that acted like a generator while in motion.

A power module bolted onto the turboshaft engine did electrolysis producing hydrogen fed into the turboshaft that added tremendously to the horsepower and significantly reduced fuel refills significantly.

The Hovercraft looked new, and it was and as Tavishien pushed the throttle forward approximately a half an inch bumping into Marti's hand, she could feel the acceleration.

Tavishien felt a thrill as the Hovercraft moved out towards the center of the huge lake that connected to the ocean.

There wasn't much boat traffic this morning, so the risk of collision was low. Marti said, "This is the throttle. When you push it forward, we'll go faster. That dial is the speed indicator." Marti then pointed to the speedometer.

"The Speedometer says we are doing twenty knots. Push the throttle forward to speed up to forty knots."

Tavishien complied with Marti's instruction and the turboshaft engine now spinning the fan at twenty thousand RPM accelerated and they were flying across the water.

The computerized stabilizer put a fin down into the water deeper that kept the pitch of the Hovercraft perfectly level despite any wind or wave action. It was a smooth ride. At the time there was no wind or waves, so it was ultrasmooth.

Marti looked behind and saw the other Hovercraft was now chasing them as planned.

"See you have the rear-view mirror?"

"Yes."

"Notice you have another Hovercraft chasing us?"

"That's just Gabriel and Tristan."

"They are too far away for us to know for sure, so we must assume it's a deadly threat and now we will start to take evasive courses. If they follow our course change, then you know they are coming after us."

"Understand."

"See the compass indicator on the dashboard with the auxiliary digital display?" Marti asked and pointed to the instrument display.

"Yes."

"It shows we are going on a course of 025."

"I see that."

"Change your course steer left slowly to 340."

"Alright."

Tavishien turned the steering wheel slightly and the Hovercraft seemed to tilt and slowly curved left.

"Keep a good eye on that Hovercraft following us."

"Alright. But I know its Gabriel and Tristan."

"How do you know that? They are too far behind to identify?"

"I just did a remote view on Gabriel she's in the boat talking to Tristan and just informed him of our course change."

"Alright, you know the obvious, but this is a simulated attack. Forget that's our friends. They will act like Tartars chasing us."

"Okay. I'm all for playing games especially if I can kick Gabriel's ass again."

"Good spirit."

"Now that you have identified a simulated threat what do you think you should do to try to evade them?"

"Not sure."

"Behind us is a large area of seagrass. The boat chasing us could be faster, we don't know. We must assume that is a possibility, so we must use tactics to evade."

"Okay so what do we do?"

"We are going to make another course change now to 270 degrees. As soon as you see the other Hovercraft gets back behind us after the course change, then change your course to 210 degrees. We are going to slowly make a circle and eventually go on a course of around 140 degrees that will take us into that large area of sea grass that has a few mangrove patches in it to hide behind."

Tavishien complied with all of Marti's course change instructions and then as she was nearing the sea grass Marti said, "Pull back on the throttle, we need to slow down some to navigate in the sea grass."

"Alright."

The Hovercraft at forty knots started to slow since there was no propulsion shoving it along and when it finally hit the outer area of the seagrass, it was now down to twenty knots.

"The idea is to go ten to twenty knots in this sea grass area so you can make sure you don't crash into a mangrove."

"Alright."

During the slowing down, the other Hovercraft got closer to them, but they were still a long distance away.

"See that mangrove over there off the right side?" Marti pointed to the growth.

"Yes."

"Try to steer behind it in a way to block the view of the other Hovercraft."

"Alright."

In a couple minutes Tavishien steered the Hovercraft behind the mangrove and was now steering on a course of 145 degrees.

"Intermittently look in your rear-view mirror and if you spot the other Hovercraft steer to put it back behind the mangrove then we need to find the next one to hide behind."

The chase continued and the Hovercraft slowly got into thicker and thicker seagrass and more abundance of mangroves and finally Marti spotted a thick mangrove and said, "See that mangrove up ahead?"

"Yes."

"We want to pull up to it and try to hide there and hopefully lose them."

"Sure."

Tavishien conducted the maneuver in impecable skill now having a really good feel for the control of the Hovercraft.

Moments later Tavishien announced, "We've lost them."

"How do you know that?"

"Gabriel just informed Tristan they had no idea where we went."

"Do you know where they are at and what direction they are going?"

"They are not very close because Gabriel's Aura does not appear strong like it would if she were near. But she just looked at the compass on the dashboard and they are going on a course of 090 at five knots. Gabriel is now searching for us with binoculars."

"No sign of us?"

"No, we completely lost them."

In a few minutes Tavishien announced, "They have given up the chase and are now on a course of 340 to go out into open water."

"In a real-life scenario, the enemy would do that and wait for us to leave our hiding spot. We would thus not leave until dark to help hide our exit. But since this a simulation, we'll leave now and find them."

"Sure, what course do you want me to go on?"

"If they are going on a course of 340, we'll copy that course and hopefully spot them soon."

"Sure."

After a while the mangroves and seagrass started thinning out and Marti said, "Go ahead and speed up to about fifteen knots."

"Alright."

After running for about ten minutes with Marti looking through his special binoculars, he spotted the other Hovercraft and said, "pull back on the throttle, slow to about two knots so we maintain headway. Us give them a chance to outfox themselves."

Tavishien sat there taking it all in and Marti handed her the binoculars and said, "Stand up so you get a better view."

After Tavishien steadier herself she scanned the horizon and in due time found the very small image off to the distance that was probably the other Hovercraft.

"I think I see it."

"Hand me the binoculars so I can show you something."

Tavishien handed Marti the binoculars who then said, "See this circular piece going over the eyepiece?"

"Yes."

"That's the focus for the binoculars. When it's totally focused it gives an estimated range. See this red button on the side?"

"Yes."

"Once you focus in on the target and you press that red button several things happen. This set of binoculars is linked to a satellite that sends telemetry from the binoculars back to the IB Campus where computers there and artificial Intelligence proceeds to help."

"That seems rather cleaver."

"With the built-in compass and the spatial ranging, it does when you focus in on a target it starts calculating range and relative motion. Look through the binoculars again and twist the dial and look at the graphics you will suddenly see presented to you as a holograph which will give you target specifics such as range, estimated course, and speed of the target."

"Does it continuously track the target?"

"No. Each time you want an update, you press the red button and computer algorithms back at IB Campus will calculate new range coefficients to let you know where the target is and what you are actually tracking."

"Alright."

"Tavishien, go ahead and track the Hovercraft for a while and every few minutes when you refocus hit the red button and watch the updates."

"Marti let Tavishien press the red button a few times before he asked for information."

"What is the estimated course and speed showing in the binoculars?"

"It says speed seven knots and a course of 045."

"They probably think we are drifting up the coastline looking for an escape route."

"What do we do now?"

"Go ahead and speed up to four knots and change course to 290 degrees. I think we can put more distance between us and the other Hovercraft before we make our grand exit."

Tavishien changed course and sped up to four knots as Marti said. She was looking for obstacles in the water to make sure she didn't bump into something as she felt Marti would be monitoring the other Hovercraft and would advise her to do the next maneuvers when the time came.

As the sea grass got less and less, Marti knew their silhouette would be more exposed but when he saw the other Hovercraft speed up ostensibly chasing a false clue, Marti knew it was their chance to get away.

"Stay on this course but speed up to twenty knots, they just made a big mistake and are chasing after some other boat now."

"Why just twenty knots?"

"At twenty knots we will not leave behind such a rooster tail they can spot. After we get some more distance between us and the other Hovercraft, we'll increase the speed more."

In five more minutes of running, they were out of all the seagrass and into open deep water.

"Increase speed to forty knots."

"Alright."

Now the Hovercraft was leaving behind a rooster tail, but the other Hovercraft was so far away now, the only way they could spot it would be to make an intensive search in this direction. Since they were looking for something a lot closer, they would not be doing such a search. At forty knots they opened the range quickly.

Marti was Navigating off observation from mountain peaks and knew about when to change course towards the boat docks and said, "Change course to 090 degrees. We are going to return to the boat dock. As soon as the boat dock came into view Marti said, "Slow down to twenty knots and change course to 110 degrees."

Tavishien maneuvered the Hovercraft as directed and soon spotted the boat dock. At around 100 yards to the dock Marti said, "Bring the speed down to zero. We'll coast the rest of the way."

At about thirty yards the Hovercraft was going still too fast, so Marti said, "We are going to put it in reverse to slow down some. He then pulled back on the throttle to the point he thought would be best and the Hovercraft slowed more abruptly and was soon only traveling at one or two knots. At the appropriate time Marti put the throttle back to neutral and the Hovercraft gently came up to the dock where Marti said, "I'm going to grab the line and hop onto the pier to help tie it up."

After getting the forward line on the cleat and wrapped around it, Marti yelled to Tavishien, "Throw me the after rope."

Tavishien threw the rope to Marti who then pulled the rear of the Hovercraft up to the pier and tied it down on the cleat just like he was an expert.

"What do we do now?"

"The bait shop serves drinks. Us go over there, get some refreshments, and sit down at one of the tables with a nice canopy and I'll call our associates and tell them to return to the pier."

In twenty minutes, the other Hovercraft pulled in and tied up.

Gabriel and Tristan walked over to the table and Marti said, "Why don't you guys get something to drink, and we'll talk about it for a few minutes then plan our next outing."

"Sure," Gabriel said, and Tristan followed her over to the bait shop and purchased a couple bottles of refreshing drinks and joined Marti and Tavishien.

There was nobody around so they could have a private conversation.

"You guys did a great job of giving us the slip," Tristan said.

"Tavishien figured out how to do it, I was just along for the ride," Marti said with a smile.

"That was pretty good for her first time out," Gabriel said.

"Well Gabriel, you should know by now, I like beating your ass every chance I get," Tavishien said in a way conveying she enjoyed the competition.

"You will not get many chances." Gabriel responded.

"I'll enjoy every chance I get." Tavishien said.

"Marti liked the rivalry but wondered what Tavishien really thought. Perhaps he would get one of the psychiatrists to figure it out.

After they finished their refreshments, Marti gave them the big challenge.

"Alright gang if we go back out now and do another scenario and skip lunch, then we can finish go back get cleaned up, have an early dinner and relax for the afternoon."

"I can go for that," Gabriel responded.

"If she can handle it, so can I," Tavishien chimed in.

Marti looked over at Tristan who knew better than to insert his desires into the conversation and simply smiled.

"Alright. Tavishien and I will take off. In Five minutes come look for us."

"Will do." Tristan said in a very affirm manner.

Moments later after Marti cast off the lines and hopped on the boat, he said, "We will not always have someone to push us away from the pier. Turn left on your steering wheel and put it in reverse at two knots. We will curve away from the pier. As soon as you think we are perpendicular to the pier then center your steering ."

"Understand all," Tavishien responded.

After the Hovercraft moved for a while, the nose was soon pointing to the pier and Tavishien centered the rudder and continued backing at the same time pointed the pier.

At about fifty yards from the pier, Marti said, "Turn right and continue in reverse until the bow swings around to open water, then put the throttles in the forward direction and speed up to twnty knots pointing the middle of the bay."

"Understand all," Tavishien stated.

In due time the boat was pointed outbound and Tavishien steadied up course and threw the throttles into the forward position. Tavishien then ran the throttle forward and sped up to twenty knots.

Marti then said, "Turn on a course to 330 degrees."

Marti then handed the binoculars to Tavishien and said, "Here, I'm just riding along to observe. You will do everything on your own. I'm only here for safety now. Just like the last time, they will give us a chase you are to evade them and lose them like we did before."

"Sure."

The operator chair of the Hovercraft was up a foot or so above the passenger seats, so Tavishien didn't need to stand to look for the chasers. Tavishien knew they were coming thanks to her remote viewing of Gabriel. But to become more adept at manipulating the binoculars she grabbed them and raised them up into position and looked behind and could see the white rooster tail coming from the other Hovercraft.

Tavishien confirmed they were going forty knots via remote viewing and at that speed would not take long to catch up with them. Tavishien shoved the throttle forward and soon the Hovercraft was shaking slightly as it hit 45 knots bouncing along in the small waves kicked up by the onshore breeze.

Tavishien knew from her childhood days not to get boxed in where wild animals could surround her and attack as a group, so she looked for a location where the mangroves were not to thick but thick enough to hide in. It was touch and go from her distance to know for sure, she would have to get closer and changed course to 040 and only looked back a few times because she already knew what Gabriel was seeing.

Marti made a mental note that Tavishien wasn't looking through the binoculars very often and after the scenario was completed would ask her why in the critique.

The second Hovercraft had a slight angle on Tavishien's and was slowly closing the range even though Tavishien was doing about five knots faster. When the second Hovercraft eventually reached about 170 degrees relative to Tavishien's Hovercraft, the range rate went positive and Tavishien was slowly gaining space she knew now she could change course towards the seagrass and mangroves to get a better look at where she wanted to enter.

Ahead Tavishien saw patches of thick and thin mangroves as she was now gliding along on a course of 095 after the latest change. She would slowly get nearer to the sea grass and man groves and at the exact moment she desired she would cut in a sparse area then head for a denser marshland seagrass and mangrove area that would reduce her Hovercraft silhouette and make it harder to be tracked.

When Tavishien finally made her spectacular more she yelled: "Hold on tight."

Marti was already holding onto railing and when Tavishien made her unexpected maneuver he was suddenly glad she warned him because the Hovercraft tilted a good 45 degrees in the snap roll that easily could have thrown him out of the Hovercraft.

The new course of 175 degrees put the Hovercraft heading between too closely spaced mangroves that barely had enough room between them to allow the Hovercraft to pass. After a slight course change the silhouette of the Hovercraft was greatly reduced along with the speed which pleased Marti who had just experienced all the thrill, he wanted that day. Little did he know Tavishien had other ideas. This was the beginning of Marti realizing he had a wild cat on his hands with little fear of anything. It was almost as if Tavishien had a death wish.

Tavishien maneuvered around about as fast as she could navigating the mangroves and avoiding getting any closer to the shoreline. She knew the shoreline of the bay in this area tended to continue along at about a 30-degree angle and she was soon following that general course bouncing around the mangroves sometimes shifting towards the open bay because the mangroves got too thick. She was hoping Gabriel would make the wrong course change and go into an open area with no way out except the way she came in burning up precious time.

In due time, Gabriel steered into a dead end and traveled almost two miles before she had to reverse course and find a way out.

Tavishien precisely knew the time to maneuver as she approached a solid mangrove she said, "Hold on tight."

Within a few seconds Marti experienced another 45-degree snap roll and didn't want to display himself as a coward and held back the notion of telling Tavishien to slow down a bit. But the mountain girl genius had figured it out. She turned toward 350 degrees out into the open bay and threw the throttle forward and once again they were cruising along at 45 knots heading directly into the onshore breeze of 5 knots giving the sensation of a lot of wind.

As she figured Gabriel took a while to navigate out of the mangrove trap and by the time, they got around it they were looking in the wrong direction as Tavishien now had her Hovercraft at 240 degrees relative to where Gabriel was now navigating at a reduced speed trying to remake contact.

As Tavishien slowly approached the Northern area of the bay she turned on a course of 260 degrees slowly putting the other Hovercraft far behind.

Being a mountain girl and having navigated off mountains many times before, Tavishien instinctively knew when it was time to change course to 080 that would take them back in the general direction of the Hovercraft boat piers.

Without any input from Marti, Tavishien pointed the piers and slowed down at the appropriate time as if it were a copy of the first time, she approached the pier. Just like before Marti hopped off the Hovercraft to help tie it down.

As soon as the boat was tied down, Marti called IBR Tristan Karjal on his communicator and said, "We are back at the pier now. The exercise is over come back to base."

"Understand all, proceeding back to base," Tristan responded. In twenty minutes, Gabriel steered the second Hovercraft up to the pier. Marti and Tavishien were there to help with the mooring lines.

Nobody had anything to say. Marti would talk with them later after he had first a private conversation with Tavishien to figure out why she took all the actions she did. He had his suspicions.

As they were leaving, Norman Swansen who had sufficient time to look over the Hovercraft approached Marti and said, "I appreciate you didn't wreck my Hovercraft today."

"Not to worry, we'll try again tomorrow. After I teach Tavishien how to do loop to loops she might wreck one." Marti said with an evil grin.

They all piled into the four-wheel drive vehicle and made their way back to Elnar Harkensen's bed and breakfast to relax for a few hours before they would walk to Elijah's Diner for their evening meal.

The women each wanted to shower and change clothes before dinner and took their turn and spent most of their down time preparing themselves. The men were used to being grimy on the road and had nothing special planned for the evening, went as they were.

With the generous tips the night before, Elijah was glad to see this group back the next evening.

After they all sat down, guys on one side of the table and ladies on the other for some strange reason, Elijah was there ready to take care of these wonderful customers.

Would you all like a nice drink before I take your orders?

"Yes, please, I'll have that elixir you served last night," Tristan stated in a jovial tone.

"Give me what he's having," Gabriel added.

"Me too," Tavishien said as she wanted to try it as well.

"I might as well have what they are having," Marti said.

In a short while Elijah's wife came back with a tray of drinks and Elnar started recording their meal requests as they were being served their drinks.

In due time the group was mildly alone and could briefly talk shop to add on the critique they all now had. Just before they went to dinner, Marti met with Tavishien to ask some poignant questions. He now knew how she was able to defeat two of the best SIS agents and allude them.

It was still a big mystery to Gabriel and Tristan how they had been severely beaten twice today. But they assumed Marti (aka Agent Lucika) was engineering the escape plan. Now the bomb shell was released while they were alone.

"In case you are unaware, I helped a little in the first scenario today, but in the second scenario once we left the pier, I did not say anything until we pulled back up to the pier at the end." Marti saw stares of almost unbelief.

"Remember there are always sensitive sources and methods we employ. This is one of those cases. Don't ask because we will not tell. But you just experienced what we came here to do."

"Interesting," Tristan said in a rather concentrated effort.

"We will do more scenarios tomorrow because I want to get a better feel for our techniques before I write a report to my boss."

The three others simply looked at Marti taking it all in, not really knowing what he was hoping to achieve. What this really added up to was Agent Lucika had further evidence of Tavishien's special talents. It was also important to him when they had their brief discussion before dinner to let her know she had reached the point where her talents were state secrets and Gabriel, and Tristan were not cleared high enough to know all about that.

Furthermore, it was in Tavishien's best interest of survival not to reveal any of this to anyone. She had to keep this profound secret to herself. Only Agent Lucika (Marti) and his supervisor would ever have the details to this super woman and how she had developed these awesome capabilities unlike anyone they ever ran as spies before. This could be a game changer. But it also meant Tavishien was now in far more danger than she realized. During serious moments she would be employed at critical moments and possibly even sacrificed if the need deemed great enough.

Marti (aka Agent Lucika) had a distinct liking for Tavishien. It hit him in the gut looking at this beautiful creature that he knew one day he might have to send to her death.

Unfortunately, the riff between them and the Tartars not only existed on this planet, but a similar riff also existed on various territories and colonies on other star systems and planets. One day the big showdown was coming. It was unnerving to think that this area of space was controlled by a planet that was split and the outlying regions were also split and at the verge of galactic warfare.

It seemed almost insane that two powers from the same planet were fighting and thus all the nearby stars with habitable planetary system were also poised for the fight. There seemed to be no end in sight. The logical conclusion was the day was coming when they would come to blows.

Marti had a growing problem and didn't know it because Tavishien hid it from him very well. She knew what he was thinking anytime they were around each other. In some ways it became unnerving. At other times it became taxing as Tavishien could not block out Marti from her mind. It gets on your nerves when you know what the other person is seeing or thinking all the time.

Tavishien knew she could never have a relationship with another person because it would get dreary after a while knowing all their thoughts. She knew there was no way she could block it out.

But she knew how to fake it greatly. She also knew things about Gabriel she wished she didn't know such as how she sometimes had faked orgasms in the past to make her male companions happy. The more she knew about Gabriel, the less she liked her, but she knew she was trapped in a situation with no way out. *Would she ever get used to it?*

It was times like this she saw only one solution to end the anxiety and suffering all this brought on: suicide. *Could she, do it? Would she, do it? She always wondered.*

The meal was very pleasant. Elijah's wife seemed captivated by the crowd. The truth of the matter is after Elijah discussed Tavishien with his wife and informed her she was a famous fashion model; Elijah's wife went to the worldwide data consortium application available to her on the computational and communications terminal she and Elijah used for business and private matters including communicating with friends and relatives.

Elijah's wife checked up on Tavishien and since she was someone interested in new fashion designs, she looked over several of the shows Tavishien put on. Elijah's wife was stunned that sitting in front of her was this gorgeous fashion model. *But what was she doing with these spooks they knew better than to ask questions about?*

***

The next day the crew did three more scenarios. In one of them, Tavishien got boxed in. This was a good example for Marti (aka Agent Lucika) to gauge what Tavishien would do in a helpless situation like this where it meant capture and probably her death after they extracted all useful intelligence out of her.

The surprise was on everyone as Tavishien threw the throttles forward yelling "Hold on tight."

There were two mangrove patches very close together that made the only plausible escape route. At first Marti had no clue what Tavishien had up her sleeve, but after the hard 45-degree snap roll she cleared herself just enough from the other Hovercraft to make a run at it. It was a good case there was another Hovercraft on site to pick them up if this maneuver turned out not to be successful.

The first thing on Marti's mind was, *here we go again, I'll be buying another Hovercraft today.*

Thanks to the design of the Hovercraft with a large propulsion fan that pushed them along like an aircraft engine and the slope bow designed to allow them to beach the craft or negotiate over thick sea grass at low tide, and the numerous plant life that existed in marshes, when they hit the shallow area between the mangroves, the Hovercraft went airborne and landed more than fifty feet away from the impact point.

After things settled down a bit and they were open throttle heading out to the center of the Bay, Marti expressed his concern, "You realize you almost got us killed back there?"

"I hope you understand I was training with the same vigor as I would have to in a real event. I think the best way to stay alive is to take those kinds of risks. Worst case I would be captured and tortured anyway," Tavishien said.

"I suppose you have a point there. I've never trained someone before that would have tried what you just did."

"Nor have you had a student kill someone before."

Marty was stunned by that statement, but he knew it was true. It also conveyed to him what he should have realized all along, Tavishien was also remote viewing him. Suddenly he felt uncomfortable, but in the spy business there are plenty of times to get uncomfortable, so this is just another."

Gabriel and Tristan were slowly starting to develop a realization. They were amid their equal. Tavishien was a fast learner and had done far more than they were aware of. If Gabriel knew Tavishien emptied a clip in the skull of the double spy, her skin would be crawling now. Even without that discrete knowledge she knew Tavishien was quite capable of doing many things and she had no knowledge of Tavishien's remote viewing abilities. If she did, she would be feeling a lot worse than Marti right now.

Tavishien was genuinely a pleasant person to be around. She had no bias or political alignment. She was a free spirit without the slightest idea what she wanted out of life. The only thing she knew quite well that existed now was the fact she had no intention of going back to her father's cabin. Those days were behind her and the Tomlars would eventually have to learn to live without her.

The Tomlars missed Tavishien but in every passing day, their memories of her slowly faded. Tavishien would eventually no longer be in their hearts or minds. Their days were numbered because when Papa passes, they would be released on their own and must learn how to live and struggle in the outdoors. Their best bet would be to be captured by other nearby Frontiersmen.

The next day's events required another trip to another rental. This time it was going to be motor scooters. Motor scooters were available in most cities and would be an essential part of Tavishien's private transportation at various possible target areas.

The motorized bicycles were just a tool to help Tavishien move up to scooters. She would eventually get her shot at terrain followers, a hybrid aircraft and motorcycle. But for now, the necessity of learning the ability to handle a motor scooter was necessary for her training in how to survive and get away from potential assailants.

Today was different than before. It was just Tavishien and Marti. Gabriel and Tristan were left behind at the Elnar Harkensen Bed and Breakfast because they were not required or desired nor did they know what was in store for Tavishien.

Upon reaching the motor scooter rental, a man was waiting for them. His name was Ulger Kroft and looked handsome and exposed a lot of muscles by the shirt and shorts he wore. Ulger Kroft. was a stunt man used in movies. Nobody ever figured out how to get the most out of motor scooters like Ulger Kroft. Agent Lucika knew he would probably be buying a couple new motor scooters before the day was done because Ulger Kroft would take them to the limit, and he had no doubt Tavishien would prove she could surpass those limits.

Tourists rented these motor scooters. The owner of the motor scooter rental, Escterbina Kropolis knew Marti quite well and just like others had the same concerns as to how he and his people treated his motor scooter rentals.

"Marti, I'm sorry I have to charge you an additional fee because my insurance company will cancel me if I put in for replacement if you wreck my scooters."

"Not a problem. We'll replace the scooter if we wreck it."

"I expect you too, but I can't afford the down time waiting for a replacement."

"I'll tell you what. If we wreck one, I'll fly you one in today to replace it."

"I don't want a crummy substitute."

"You will get an exact model or a newer one."

"Alright, but please don't get injured."

"We do not intend too."

"Alright. I'll be waiting for your return."

"See you later, Escterbina."

Marti and Ulger Kroft explained to Tavishien how to operate the motor scooter that had controls like the motorized bicycle she used a few days before. Therefore, it wasn't such a steep learning curve.

After driving around, the parking lot of the motor scooter rental for a few minutes, Tavishien stated, "I think I got it, I'm ready to go."

"Follow us, we are going somewhere that Ulger can train you on some special handling of the motor scooter," Marti said.

"Lead the way, I'll be right behind you," Tavishien responded.

Marti headed out with Tavishien following him. Ulger Kroft remained behind Tavishien to act as a rear guard to make sure traffic passed them without any issues.

About ten miles down the road, Marti made a right turn and the other two followed.

They were now going down a dirt road with lots of foliage on each side. During parts of their travel, they went through what appeared to be almost like a triple canopy tropical rain forest. After a couple curves and twists in the road they finally came out to an opening that would be impossible to see from the road.

Ahead was a small building, where Ulger Kroft operated out of. He trained other stunt men for specific stunts and a few spooks like Marti's people from time to time. He also practiced for his own stunts.

They stopped and got off the motor scooters next to the building where Ulger Kroft had a marker board he could write on. There were a couple chairs for Marti and Tavishien so he could talk to them about what specific actions they would next attempt.

After Marti and Tavishien were seated and ready to learn, Ulger Kroft then said, "In order to reduce or prevent injuries, I must take you one step at a time. It might seem boring at times, but I don't like to rush things. When we rush, someone ends up getting hurt.

Ulger then lifted the first sheet of the marker board covering up the details of their first training scenario.

"This is a diagram of the obstacle course. Take a good look at this diagram then stand up and look out there. Just like on the diagram you see colored flags the correlate to points on this diagram."

Tavishien nodded and looked around and quickly gauged everything in the vicinity of where she was standing in the open area. The obstacle course was laid out in a clear and concise manner.

There were hills, deep depressions and other obstacles laid out along the path.

"When you go out the first time, you will notice a blue stripe has been painted on the obstacle course roadway. That is the nonintrusive passage through the obstacle course. In a few minutes we are going to go out and drive the blue loops and while we are traveling around that very safe blue loop, we are going to notice the yellow, orange, purple, green, red, black, and gray turnouts. As we move further up in difficulty, you will divert to the colors designated to attempt that maneuver.

"I think I understand," Tavishien stated.

"The first couple will not seem too difficult, but when you start the purple run, you will discover it becomes challenging from then on," Ulger Kroft said.

"I'm ready to try," Tavishien said.

"Alright, we are going to do the blue route now then come back and I will brief you on the yellow turnout and what's expected of you."

The three were soon on the motor scooters driving around the blue line on the obstacle course which gave them a closeup look at all the turnouts and what was in store for them. Tavishien noted very quickly the yellow turn out went to a brick wall. This was obviously training for when you get chased down to a dead end, which means probably soon you are dead.

When they drove back to the makeshift classroom, Ulger Kroft lifted the sheet on the marker board showing the next sheet that was specified for the yellow turnout towards the wall.

"There is a possibility one day you may have to put the motor scooter down on its side and slide into the wall. Your leg will probably get skinned up badly unless you are lucky and wearing the right clothing. But in real life we can't predict when something like this will happen so we can't plan our wardrobe."

"That's understandable," Tavishien responded as she understood she was the student and Marti was just an observer.

When we do the turnouts to the exercise, we don't need to drive all around the course. We can just drive directly back here for more briefing."

"Understand."

"If you look at the board you see the four pictures that detail what we achieve in what we are doing."

"Yes, I see that."

"Over on that post is a pair of leather trousers for you to put on as I think we'll do at least one slide into the wall. Just put them over the top of the clothes you are wearing."

"Sure."

As Tavishien was putting on the extra thick leather trousers, Ulger Kroft said, "I will demonstrate the maneuver first. I'm going to show you three times. First will be a slow approach where you simply turn around. The next time will be a faster approach where I want your scooter speed up to twenty miles per hour until you cross the yellow line I have down before the wall."

"Alright."

"I'll let you make as many twenty-mile hour runs as you wish to get your confidence up and then we'll move onto high speed which will be forty miles per hour."

"What if I can't stop fast enough?"

"That's when you have to lay the scooter down and slide into the wall."

Tavishien had slid down the sides of mountains before and scraped her skin up badly. She was a tough girl; she could handle it. She only wished Gabriel was out chasing her.

They commenced the exercise and Ulger Kroft proved very quickly why he was a well sought after stunt man. At the forty mile per hour maneuver, he laid the scooter down and slid into the wall and stopped. Then he got the scooter back up and blasted out like he was evading the enemy then drove back over to where Tavishien was sitting parked on her scooter.

"During your slow and medium speed runs, use your scooter, but when you get ready to do the forty mile an hour run, I want you to use this scooter, so we don't scratch up too many today."

"Alright."

Tavishien did the slow speed approach and never thought much about it. Then she started the twenty mile runs which were a little more complicated, but she didn't have to lay the scooter over and barely touched the wall once before she turned around and accelerated out of the kill zone as fast as she could. After three runs at twenty, she decided to tempt her fate.

"Alright, I'm ready to try the forty, us swap scooters."

"Here you go."

Tavishien got on the other scooter then got in position and headed towards the wall and at the yellow line she already knew what she had to do, lay it over. The scooter slid to the wall and had a small bump. Her leg hurt but nothing was broken so she picked the scooter up and shot out of the kill zone like a scared rabbit and drove out then came back around and faced the two amazed men. "I'm glad I didn't have to take you to the hospital," Marti said.

"I think I got a scrape, but it's not as bad as sliding off the side of a mountain and take a good fall."

"That was pretty good for your first time. Do you want to do it again?"

"No, I think I know what I need to do. No reason to skin up my leg."

"Alright, we'll move onto our next objective, drive over to the classroom."

Tavishien was now getting her next indoctrination, jumping over ditches and other man-made obstacles.

"We are going to do the orange maneuver next. We have a simulated canal. You need to gauge how far you need to go and try to get an upward movement if possible. Obviously, if your life is in danger, you will likely take on more risk. You must make that decision at the time since no doubt you will be on your own and the people chasing you will do you harm if they catch you."

"For this jump over the ditch there is a small ramp that helps you gain some altitude before you and the scooter descend on the other side. Beside the ramp and the simulated ditch is a drive by zone. You need to look closely at your speedometer and if you are not going at least 40 miles per hour do not go up on the ramp, do a drive by or you might get injured."

"What if I'm going faster?"

"With this scooter and what you will likely encounter in your travels, you might get lucky to get up to fifty miles per hour. When you rent a scooter or steal one in the line of duty, you should open it up and see how fast it will go in case you need speed. Never assume the speedometer implies how fast it can really go."

The three drove over to the orange turnout where Ulger Kroft said, "I will do the first jump then if you feel you are ready to try it you can, but if you just want to do a forty mile per hour drive past first, that's ok."

Ulger Kroft jumped this simulated canal many times training stunt men in the past and knew it by heart. He purposely set it up for forty miles per hour so that students would see that round number on their speedometer and have confidence they were going at the right speed. His performance was as expected for someone that performed it often.

Now it was Tavishien's turn. On her first attempt she hit the ramp at forty miles per hour and came down equally as gracefully as Ulger Kroft had demonstrated, then returned for further discussions.

The rest of the maneuvers were done equally well without scratching up the scooter.

"Alright, you did well Tavishien. Go ahead and take off the leather trousers and we'll drive back to the scooter rental."

The next day it was time to learn the Terrain Follower. This was one craft that could get Tavishien killed fast. They traveled to a base where experts assisted in the training. This base was not too far from where her father lived. Terrain Followers is how she might get into enemy territory in the future.

With a two-seater with dual controls her instructor led her through a day of basic training and the following day they went back for additional training. As a follow-up, Agent Lucika decided to have terrain followers staged near the base where Tavishien was first taken for medical treatment after the Tartar attack. She was urged to fly to her father's cabin for a visit a few times to build proficiency in her terrain follower piloting skills.

Agent Lucika escorted Tavishien in an identical terrain follower thinking she would fly directly to her father's cabin. Instead, she diverted and flew a mile away from it and landed shifting to the all-purpose surface mode. Agent Lucika wondered why she did this and followed along waiting for the surprise.

A quarter of a mile into the forest dodging a few trees and debris they came up to the herd of Tomlars. Not far from the Tomlars was her father, Lingraw Arginin with his rifle and almost ready to shoot when the Tomlars notified him it was Tavishien. He lowered his gun shaking realizing he had almost shot his daughter. Lingraw Arginin slowly approached Agent Lucika and Tavishien.

"Hello Papa."

"You know it's dangerous coming into a forest like the way you did."

"I had nothing to fear, the Tomlars were here."

"Yes, and that was a good thing."

The Tomlars slowly gathered around Tavishien sniffing her and enjoying the closeness to their dearly departed friend they almost forgot about.

In a short while Tavishien's father, Lingraw Arginin asked, "Would you like to go to the cabin and get something to eat?"

"The Tomlars are not expected to go back for a few more hours. I brought along some sandwiches and drinks we can eat sitting in the Terrain Followers and let the Tomlars continue doing what they are here for," Tavishien said.

The Terrain Followers could carry four passengers so there was room for all three of them to get in Tavishien's Terrain Follower to eat their picknick lunches. Soon the Tomlars were back at grazing and ignoring the activity of the Humans.

The sandwiches were rather pleasant for Lingraw Arginin as they tasted good as well as alleviating the need for him to make his next meal.

"How's life in the city?" Lingraw Arginin asked his daughter sitting next to him in the front seat of the Terrain Follower.

"I spend most of my time at the Intelligence Bureau Campus, but I get out now and then and do things."

"Did you find a mate yet?"

"Not yet father, plus I'm not sure such activity is in the works for me."

"Why did you come here in that contraption?"

"I'm out learning how to drive it and build up my proficiency. I might make a few more trips out here in the future as part of my training. If there is something you need me to bring, let me know."

"I pretty much have everything I need, but thanks for asking."

Tavishien knew her father almost killed her a while ago being finger trigger happy. She owed her life to the Tomlars. She would not surprise her father again. She knew an Intelligence Bureau Rep was always nearby. Next time she would preannounce her intentions for a visit.

After an hour of talking and visiting, it was time to depart. Tavishien had some Terrain Following Training left to do for the rest of the day including gliding down the sides of mountains at treetops where the slight error could mean instant death.

"Alright papa, we must leave now. I think I will be visiting again in a couple of weeks."

"Alright Tavishien, looking forward to your next visit."

In a matter of minutes, the Terrain Followers were gone with Tavishien and Agent Lucika. The Tomlars were sad about Tavishien's departure. Her father had similar emotions. It was a somber rest of the day for the Tomlars and Lingraw Arginin who would not be quite so lonely these days had he not been so negligent with Tavishien when she was a young woman and vulnerable.

Lingraw Arginin of all people living around all the Frontiersmen should have had tighter security measures to prevent what happened to his daughter. He would carry that burden to his grave. But in the meantime, because of how that incident redirected Tavishien's life she left a gaping hole in his everyday life. Lingraw Arginin's life was so much sweeter when Tavishien's mother or she were always nearby.

As soon as Tavishien and Agent Lucika maneuvered out of the thick forest into an open area, they transcended into the flying mode of the Terrain Follower. They both wore ear buds and a throat microphone to communicate.

As they were about five miles from the forest they left behind with papa and the Tomlars, Agent Lucika said, "I want you to fly up the side of this mountain as low to the trees as you think you can go, then when you go over the top, fly down the other side to the valley below it while I film your craft for replay later."

"Understand fly over the mountain," Tavishien said, cutting down unnecessary chatter as she was trained.

Tavishien pushed the throttle all the way and pulled back on the stick in the air mode of the terrain follower and followed the tops of trees up to the top of the mountain. Near the top it was baren with no plant growth, just rocks. Part of her briefing was to stay as low as possible going over the mountain tops where she would be an easy target.

Tavishien used her speed for maneuverability and as soon as she got the nose of the terrain follower pointed back down towards the valley below. As to not generate dangerous life-threatening speeds, Tavishien pulled back on the throttle allowing gravity to accelerate the terrain follower and not build up excessive speeds with propulsion.

There was an autopilot feature to the Terrain Followers, but those controls were very conservative and would never get as low to the trees as in the manual mode and would pop over the top of the mountains at a much higher altitude making it sitting duck target for an air defense system. To get to where she needed to go in the future, she needed to pop over the top of a mountain and only be exposed to the briefest amount of time possible. In effect she was stunt flying.

This was a training exercise in friendly air space. Agent Lucika didn't need to practice concealment as he was there to film Tavishien offset from her craft to get a three-dimensional perspective of her pitch and attitude. This film would be shown after artificial intelligence processed it at a Specialized Capabilities Air Research Facility (SCARF) that added gyroscopic indicators above the Terrain Follower video imagery.

Computer graphics displayed overlayed on top of the video with gyroscopic indicators allowed the student to see how far off a recommended flight path they took during training critiques. This highly subjective replay, heavily influenced by artificial intelligence algorithms, conveyed a logical extension of the guidelines established in the SCARF showed a perspective to spies where the margin of safety was razor thin.

Tavishien was starting to put together the big picture. They would use her sexual allure to get her into position to commence the remote viewing, but the fact was if she went behind enemy lines to the Tartar areas, she might have to use some of these devices to escape.

But Tavishien also wanted to go one day to go behind enemy lines to research her mother and find out as much information about her as possible including finding possible pictures and video of her. That aspect is the only reason why she would willingly venture into enemy territory, to find out a little about her genealogy and discover the mother she never spent any time with.

Tavishien was almost like a bird she had a strange ability to feel flying and in doing so she controlled the Terrain Follower with utter precision skimming the tops of trees and in one case flew right over the top of Frontiersman and at the upper speed limits recommended for the Terrain Follower scared the inhabitants of the cabin that appeared not much different than her father's.

The inhabitants went outside to see what created that surreal noise and by the time they got outdoors, Tavishien and the Terrain Follower were past their field of view with the forest, but outdoors they could hear noise caused by two Terrain Followers as Agent Lucika was about one hundred yards off Tavishien's starboard rear quarter with automatic trackers controlling the filming of her flight with the help of Artificial Intelligence, fully gyro stabilized for a very smooth recording.

Eventually Tavishien ran out of air space and had to pull back on the controls as she hugged the valley floor waiting for Agent Lucika to give her another objective to fly over. They hopped over several more mountain tops in a similar manner on their way back to the base and debrief at the SCARF.

The two landed the Terrain Followers inside the SCARF compound they were now working out of, behind eight-foot-tall razor wire double fences with vicious wild dogs policing the inner area between the two security boundaries. The slots designated for their Terrain Follower had charging connections where they would get the juice for tomorrow's training.

The dogs barked a lot until the day Tavishien showed up then they always seemed to quiet down in her near vicinity. Agent Lucika suspected he knew why. She was remotely viewing them and twisting their minds a bit in the process. He was not too far off the mark as the vicious dogs liked Tavishien. She could have walked into that security boundary, and they would have approached her just like the Tomlars do.

Inside the SCARF, they went into a secure conference room that had all the holographic display technology to show the recordings of today's events and the reconstruction of all the movements of the Terrain Followers.

The briefing officer was soon showing it all and comments manifested by artificial intelligence analysis. The black boxes in the Terrain Followers had built in satellite navigation and position recording that with the video downloaded from Agent Lucika's Terrain Follower showed the three-dimensional track of Tavishien's Terrain Follower and the gyroscopic indicator superimposed above it so Tavishien could see recommended course verses her actual. There were a lot of intersections and divergences of the Terrain Follower off the course plot of simultaneous positional data.

"What do you think? Agent Lucika asked the briefer.

"Well as you can see, we do have a real time score card. The entire flight is complex and there of course are a lot of human factors involved. We have a quality factor we use. We call it the Relative Concentration Index (RCI). Artificial intelligence has a vast database of all students trained in SCARF technology and the algorithms we use produce a flowing line that you see that moves up and down on the diagram as we position time cursor over a portion of the flight. We can run it in real time and the chart will build and flow just as the image of the Terrain Follower."

"What's the information on those green lines?" Agent Lucika asked.

"The center dashed green line on the chart is the average of all the students. The thicker green lines above and below are two standard deviations of all the students in time. Hence the center dashed line represents half the students that fall into this RCI plot.

We view a student with superior RCI will tend to ride near the upper thick green line and sometimes actually penetrate above it. Then through the dynamics of all the human activities, they crisscross and take on all types of configurations on the line."
"What's the bottom line?" Agent Lucika asked.

"If we have a student that rides above the center dashed line, we view that person as a superior student and if they ride near the upper dark green line they are of the best students."

"What's this other graph?"

"It's a time averaged presentation that is an exponential average verses time so that we don't have to view the entire video to get a sense of how successful the exercise was."

"That will be nice to know."

"Since it took you hours to accumulate the video and data, we have time compressed it and fast forward through areas the artificial intelligence determined requires no improvement so we can concentrate only on problem areas. Generally, the students know where they did well and there is no point in repeating when they did well at all those segments. In doing so we can cut the six hours of video down to fifteen to twenty minutes and concentrate on the highlights."

It now all unfolded as they watched. The recommendations on the gyroscopic display above the Terrain Follower didn't give very many recommendations as the flight trajectory was in line with what they determined was acceptable application of manual flight control to achieve the profile they recommended.

Tavishien didn't appreciate what she was looking at as much as Agent Lucika did. Tavishien's measured performance hugged the solid upper green line throughout the fifteen-minute presentation and exceeded it numerous times meaning she was an over achiever. If she went below the bottom green line at that moment in time, she would be considered an underachiever. And that never happened a single time.

When they finished watching the video there were a couple questions as to why Tavishien decided to do certain maneuvers at certain times, and all her responses were recorded and transcribed.

Tavishien was slowly surpassing all notions of what Agent Lucika envisioned for the woman. He now knew she was someone very special and felt more and more every day it was a privilege for him to work with such an extraordinary person who no doubt one day would be a person who helped paint the history for their civilization as her dealings will have compelling outcomes to serious and complicated scenarios.

To some extent, Agent Lucika thought he might be wasting Tavishien's time continuing this training she already seemed to master so quickly, but he felt the extra time would give her more time flying and possibly add to her proficiency.

***

CHAPTER FOURTEEN

The Romance Begins

The training for the day was soon concluded and they were driven to their temporary quarters reserved for them on base which was normally reserved for senior officers. The rooms were very nice and because they were senior officer rooms, they came with a steward to take care of their needs.

Tavishien had a female steward named Lateegely, who was very kind and sweet and very accommodative. Lateegely grew weary of the pompous senior female officers she attended. In a very short period of time, Lateegely discovered Tavishien was a breath of fresh air so kind and sweet, and little did she know Tavishien worked on her psyche as well and was soon remote viewing her and learning much about her life.

The one thing Tavishien didn't want to do was add any more burden to Lateegely's life and after a couple days their relationship was more like roommates unless others were around and then Lateegely had to follow the protocol of dealing with egos.

Lateegely saw a lot of senior officers in the past fifteen years working as a VIP steward. Her good looks placed her in this role where she could have been doing other less dignified work around the minions. Because of SCARF spooks would come and go and Lateegely received training and special instructions on how to behave around spooks and not ask questions or make any assumptions, nor were the stewards allowed to ever mention them to anyone not in the line of work. Lateegely thus knew better than to ask questions.

Tavishien understood Lateegely's posture and wanted her to feel more comfortable around her so after a couple days she informed Lateegely, "I'm a fashion model."

"Really?"

It was late in the evening and about an hour before bedtime so Tavishien said, "I'll show you some of my fashion shows, but you must promise never to reveal this to anyone."

"My silence is golden. We are restricted in discussing our guests here."

"Alright here's some holographs of me in some of my fashion shows."

Lateegely felt surreal and almost felt shivers as she watched all it unfolds.

"You look so incredibly beautiful in those holographs."

"I only look good because I had a world class makeup artist and one of the best fashion designers in the industry create those fashions I wore."

"I'm not lying when I say this, those holographs of you show the most beautiful woman in the world I've ever seen. I've never seen such beauty before. This truly is amazing."

After fifteen minutes Lateegely felt she was on cloud nine watching all this and said, "I feel so privileged that I could see all this."

"Thank you."

"I wish I were not so ugly."

"I know how to make you look pretty. Tomorrow is my last night here and Marti (Agent Lucika is using his cover name) is taking me out to dinner to celebrate me graduating SCARF with good scores. I'll let him know he will have to take you with us. I have a couple extra changes of clothes I brought along I wanted to wear to make Marti whimper but never got the chance, I'll have you wear one and I'll wear the other. Also, the makeup artists have trained me well to take care of myself in case I need to do so if I'm by myself. I have everything I need here to make you look good."

"If you do that for me you will make me the happiest person in the world. Would you mind filming me after getting the makeover."

"Sure, I'll make Marti film us together, especially if he wants to get to first base with me."

"You think he wants you?"

"I know he does."

"Then why doesn't he?"

"In the business he's in with all the responsibilities he has he knows better than to *stick his pen in company ink.*"

After Tavishien winked at Lateegely they both broke out into a girlish laughter.

Soon it was time for bed, Tavishien needed her sleep because tomorrow would be her most challenging day. She would be going to another area far away from here where they do live firing exercises to give the pilots a feal for what it's like when people are shooting at you. There will be explosions and other realistic training including chases and avoidances.

Morning came too early and Lateegely was softly wakening up Tavishien who heard the pleasant lady's voice and before she opened her eyes Tavishien remote viewed her and knew exactly who it was.

"Well, I guess I better get up. I'm not excited about the training, but I need to get it done so I can dress you up tonight."

"Alright, would you like a warm bath?"

"Sure."

"I'll start that for you now while you get undressed."

After the nice warm bath and changing into her flight suit. Tavishien was sitting at a table inside her quarters enjoying room service. Female Generals didn't go to the cafeteria unless it was for social engineering that happened from time to time. They preferred the room service with an improved diet to go with it.

Marti (aka Agent Lucika) drove them to the SCARF site where they had their morning operations brief and right on schedule they walked out into the compound and got on a Skycar that took them to the airbase parking apron not far away where their transportation was waiting. It was ultra high-speed transport usually reserved for Generals or high government officials traveling during periods of extraordinary dangerous times they have now and then when it appears war is about to break out. The high-speed transport looked very aerodynamic with extreme sleekness and apparent nimbleness.

They were soon underway flying to some distant location that appeared to be out in the middle of a desert. The high-speed transport landed and there were the Terrain Followers they were going to use. Since they were briefed and knew the nearby mountain was where the fun and games were to begin, they quickly got in and buckled up and headed out.

Agent Lucika was not a participant. He was a safety observer and would give Tavishien intermittent mid-course corrections to her assignments so they would not waste training time as the scenarios unfolded.

These Terrain Followers were like they would use to penetrate enemy air space and get to the target. Since they were at high risk, they had counter defenses to deploy in *Hail Mary* manners to save their lives.

Some of their threats were aircraft and others were missiles or kinetic weapons. The kinetic weapons had very little reaction time. They flew at about six thousand miles per hour, so you had to maneuver quickly to avoid getting hit. A kinetic weapon would crumble a Terrain Follower as easy as smashing a beer can.

Tavishien seemed to have a sixth sense and going over the first mountain top when the first kinetic weapons came at her she dodged them with great ease, but Agent Lucika was nervous, nevertheless. A few missiles came at her Terrain Follower and its jammers and super chaff foiled them.

Even though her super chaff confused the missiles, their detonation did shoot out shrapnel, some of which hit the terrain follower. At the end of the exercise the safety people were alarmed at the number of shrapnel the terrain follower was struck with. It almost appeared Tavishien was toying with them seeing how close she could survive. The reconstruction was terrifying. But at the end of the day, the trainers all surmised, very few students ever got such realistic live fire training experience before.

When they got back on the high-speed transport to go back to their base and get ready for the night's activities, Agent Lucika was grateful he didn't manage to kill Tavishien that day. He would do some soul searching later.

When Tavishien arrived back at her temporary senior officer's quarters, Lateegely was ready to pour her bath when Tavishien surprised her, "I have some special hair treatments for you, I want you to go in first and take a bath and wash your hair with the product I'm going to give you. It will make your hair ultra-soft. I'll take a bath after you because we need to get ready at the same time and your hair will take longer to dry."

"Alright."

In due time the women were bathed hair drying and walking around in their bra and panties and Tavishien said, "I'm going to do your makeup first so I can make sure I determine the best for you for the dress you are going to wear. Also, I think our feet are about the same size. I have some different shoes for you."

"Sure."

Tavishien went to town working over Lateegely who had no idea the incredible experience Tavishien just went through. If she knew that and what she was doing now, she would truly be humbled for the rest of her life being with this woman.

Tavishien did her magic with the makeup then the hair and Lateegely was slowly turning into a beautiful princess.

Lateegely watched Tavishien apply her talents to herself next and she proved how great she was. She needed these skills to possibly save her life one day when she needed to change her facial identity to get away from harm.

When Tavishien decided she had done enough for herself, she said, "We are almost done, and Marti will be here in about ten minutes so us put on the dresses now."

The moment of truth came. The two dresses were both delightful and made the women look glamourous. When they were fully dressed Tavishien said Okay dear, come over to this full-length mirror and look at yourself." Lateegely looked and was shocked.

"I can't believe this."

"See honey, you are very pretty. You have a lot of natural beauty. All you need to know is there is a way to make you shine. After tonight if you want to look good again, just take a picture of yourself tonight and show it to the makeup artist. They will figure out how to do it."

"I never imagined doing this with my hair."

"Honey, you were never trained in high fashion before. But now in the future you can look through fashion magazines to get ideas of what to do to make yourself look very appealing."

The women talked for a few minutes and the doorbell rang. Right on time was Marti with another gentleman he brought along to be his wingman to make sure he didn't *put his pen in company ink*, no other than IBR Tristan Karjal.

Marti (aka Agent Lucika) and Tristan were utterly stunned looking at the two ladies.

"Marti and Tristan, this is my friend Lateegely."

"Pleased to meet you," Marti said.

"Likewise," My name is Tristan.

Agent Lucika was now having spasms wondering if they just had a gigantic security breach. There was never a dull moment around Tavishien.

The four were soon walking to the nearby Skycar that would take them to a resort restaurant on the side of a nearby mountain where a lot of upscale people went to enjoy the food and the ambience that only a place like this could show the luster.

They had reservations for dinner with one more person than on the list, but, if necessary, Tristan was a good soldier and guarded the Skycar if necessary. They also had reservations for a Skycar parking slot that gave them close-up entrance plus a recharge while they were eating and enjoying the entertainment.

Lateegely had no idea what to expect. She had never been in such a swank place before. Nevertheless, her roll in codling senior female officers lent her proper etiquette and skills to handle anyone there tonight.

The two men of course didn't mind being with the best-looking women going into the restaurant. Tavishien had done magic for the two of them and Lateegely wore her unrequited beauty in style and grace.

The Maître d' met them near the entrance and asked if they had reservations and Marti announced they did in the name of Tristan Karjal. The Maître d' with her electronic clipboard with voice recognition gave off a small chime and flagged the reservation with four stars by the name meaning VIP special treatment required. Unfortunately, their table was not going to be ready for at least five minutes because they were early.

"Let me escort you to the bar for a complimentary drink and in about five minutes your table will be setup and I'll come get you." The Maître d' said then noticed there were four of them, but the reservation said three, so she made the inquiry.

"Your reservation says, three, would you like me to change it to four?"

"Yes please."

"Alright, this way please."

The beautiful Maître d' took them to the bar and informed the bartender,

"Serve them complimentary drinks until their table was ready."

The Bartender, Taro nodded and said, "Yes madam." He then took the four orders for drinks.

Marti selected the Gæsaber Elixir, and the others copied his order, and the bartender was quickly serving their drinks. Sitting at the bar next to where Marti sat down was none other than the venerable General Taroton who just the hour before signed the required endorsement for the safety report from today's spectacular training.

General Taroton signed the endorsement he didn't want to make that irritated him greatly, right after meeting with Agent Lucika in private who ordered him to whitewash the report since it was IBR safety observer's preview in what constitutes a violation in the training scenario. And here he was sitting a foot away from Agent Lucika who had a Cheshire Cat smile on his face basking in the power and authority he jammed down the Generals throat.

General Taroton was slightly agitated, but the elixir he drank and rubbed off a few rough edges and looking at the two beautiful women helped him quickly forget today's activity.

"You are the last person in the world I would expect to meet here tonight," General Taroton said with a bit of harshness in his voice.

"Well General, as you know I get around."

"Who's the two good looking women with you?"

"General if you want, I'll introduce you, but I want you to know the lady sitting next to me was the pilot of the Terrain Follower discussed in your signed report today."

"You got to be kidding me."

"Nope that's really her."

"My god she's beautiful."

"She should be, she's a fashion model."

"Who's the other beautiful lady?"

"She works for you. When I check out with you in the morning as you requested, I'll give you all the details on her."

"Please do."

"Remember General, it's not wise to *dip your pen in company ink.*"

"If she would entertain the idea, I would sign her resignation papers tomorrow and she could just be my personal aide for the rest of my life."

"After we leave, I hope you pursue her, she certainly is a beautiful woman as you can see."

"It gets lonely being single. I'll have to find a way to convince her to hang out with an old General."

"Good luck on that."

Timing was perfect, the Maître d' approached and said, "Tristan Karjal, your table is ready please come with me."

General Taroton looked at Agent Lucika knowing he was a spook asked,

"Who the hell is Tristan Karjal?"

"He's the IBR with me as my bodyguard. Nice seeing you General."

"Looking forward to that INTEL in the morning."

"If you like what you see, you know what you have to do."

"I'm used to long expeditions and conquests; I'll be ready to proceed."

"Good luck."

"Thank you."

The four followed the Maître d' to their table next to the ten-foot-tall window that gave them a picturesque view of the side of the mountain and the planes below.

The women sat down on one side of the table and the men on the other side which was perfect as it allowed them to talk to the opposite sex throughout the dinner and entertainment that followed.

There was a pianist on a Kromfomalgy Grand Piano and several other musicians on stage playing nice dinner music adding to the ambience. For everyone in the dining hall one thing was quite apparent, the two best dressed ladies were with Agent Lucika and IBR Tristan Karjal. Part of Tavishien's rewards for working out so well with Ljótunn bon Swartzler was the two fashion dresses she and Lateegely were wearing had never been seen before. Tavishien's fantastic skill as a makeup artist and those clothes set the bar for women high tonight.

Agent Lucika and IBR Tristan Karjal were captivated by the two ladies.

Lateegely suddenly noticed a lot of men smiling at her. She was well trained in body language to deal with senior officers and knew the basics. She was in fact eye candy tonight and she did not mind it one bit.

Their food was ordered and served and the meal with the Gæsaber elixir hit the spot just right. It was a joyous evening and Agent Lucika was gratified that he got Tavishien through some of the most intensive and arduous courses without getting killed. This was just one more item where Tavishien left her indelible mark on Agent Lucika. If he knew how much Tavishien played with his mind now, he would be rattled to the point he might order her death.

Tavishien was smart and knew those growing abilities needed to be shrouded forever as it gave her distinct capabilities that might come in handy one day. And she now knew she was probably expendable and would be sent on missions where her life was at stake. She also knew the obvious. Agent Lucika was her puppet master and pulled her strings. He in fact was the *defacto GURU* in the SIS. He wielded a lot of power.

Tavishien was starting to slowly develop an agenda and a plan to TAG Agent Lucika and make him have an emotional bond to her. She wasn't going to be a spy forever and even though she couldn't have children, she was starting to feel she just might want to spend the night in the arms of this influential man.

Since Tavishien couldn't get pregnant, Agent Lucika could enjoy all he wanted whenever. And at some point, it would be time for Tavishien to get out of the spy racket and do something different. Going back to a shack in the forest was certainly no longer part of Tavishien's future agenda.

Agent Lucika was going through some emotional transcendence and didn't quite know what it was. He was one of the best spies in the Intelligence Bureau, he had been tested in the line of duty numerous times. He had never succumbed to any type of emotional influence by a woman. Agent Lucika's heart was as hard as a rock, very impenetrable. His agenda was the spy business, and a woman would just be something in the way for him to achieve his goals.

But here he was staring at the diamond in the rough, Tavishien. When they plucked her from the woods in bad shape after the incident, she appeared and smelled like a savage. The transformance was remarkable and here Tavishien was sitting across from him in the most alluring and provocative manner ever.

Tavishien was good looking, and she knew it. She had a perfect figure and shape. Her body fat was perfect and most of the excess fat was in her breasts with a small tummy. As Agent Lucika was mentally pontificating his sensual exploration in plausible transcendence, he knew the obvious. Tavishien had awakened and knew she was a hot bitch and her spy training to allure her targets could easily be used on him.

He had no idea he was now the subject of penetration in ways he never counted on. He underestimated Tavishien's sophistication, and her rate of change engulfed the essence of manipulation she had now started using. Tavishien had nothing to lose. Coming from a filthy cabin in the backwoods to this charming gentleman was enough to encourage her actions. And being a sophisticated woman, Tavishien knew some things she could never reveal such as her growing ability to do mental telepathy on a grand scale.

Now that Tavishien was fully immersed in the spy business she knew she easily could be viewed as a threat and harshly dealt with including the forfeiture of her life. She would use those talents sparingly and when and only when they benefited her. The Intelligence Bureau was not going to receive such benefits as they already took so much from her, she had to keep some for herself and her own future. Now she only had two things left to do in her life before she died. Find out about her mother's past and seduce Agent Lucika.

The two men were doubly captivated by these two women. Their little heads were about to override their big heads. But tonight, it was just dinner and a little entertainment in the restaurant night club so to transcend to those ethereal plains of emotional transcendence was not really in the cards tonight. Nevertheless, Tavishien would be working on Agent Lucika (aka Marti) to cloud his better judgement and his mastership of prevailing events.

The meals and the elixirs were perfect to set the stage for act two. No sooner than their dinner table was cleared off than tonight's performance began, and their table was right next to the dance floor near the musicians.

Tavishien, doing her relentless investigation into Agent Lucika's private thoughts, knew all he wanted to do is pay the bill for dinner and leave. She had other ideas.

"This music sounds so wonderful, can we stay a while and listen to it?" Tavishien asked.

There was no way that Agent Lucika could turn down such an innocuous request, especially after the top-notch performance Tavishien demonstrated in training for spy insertions using Terrain Followers.

Tavishien didn't know much about the music other than it was performed by a live musical group and the sound was excellent as the resort needed to impress its clients.

The music was elegant and classy, but they were still playing dinner music. In thirty minutes, they would switch over to entertainment music so people could dance, socialize, and meet new people.

Tavishien was unaware this was coming, but she certainly enjoyed the music she was hearing.

Lateegely was enjoying the looks she was receiving not only from Tristan Karjal, but General Taroton was seated several tables over and giving her the evil eye. He couldn't believe she was one of his employees. Tomorrow would be an interesting day for him.

After listening to the nice music Tavishien was just about ready to say she was ready to leave when they shifted the music type. The entertainment music was far more flamboyant and evocative.

So just before Tavishien was going to call it a night she started listening to the new music and soon started seeing couples go to the dance floor and do very nice dance routines together. Tavishien was partially mesmerized."

Tavishien watched the couples dance for about ten minutes then she looked at Agent Lucika and ask, "Would you mind teaching me how to do a little of that tonight?"

"Sure, I can try if you like."

As soon as Agent Lucika (aka Marti) took Tavishien out to the dance floor, Lateegely had a look on her face that gave Tristan Karjal she wanted some of the same affection. She too was quickly escorted out onto the dance floor with General Taroton focused on every move Lateegely made taking it all in. *The hell with company ink and fraternization*, General Taroton thought.

Tavishien simply looked what the other women were doing. Her martial arts moves requiring split second adjustments were far more elaborate than what these women were showing. Tavishien nevertheless copied the essence of their moves and soon duplicated and improved upon them. The music was a perfect instrument in timing her body movements. Tavishien didn't care if she looked like a bitch in heat, she wanted Agent Lucika to receive an eyeful and motivation to taste the forbidden fruit. If she only knew how badly Agent Lucika wanted to mount her, she would simply tell him let's just go do it.

In a very brief period, there appeared to be a little competition on the dance floor, not only between Tavishien and Lateegely, but a few other sexy dressed women out there to impress their boyfriends and lovers.

Lateegely did a popular dance routine that was taught in dance schools for women to get an advantage and used in dance competitions held now and then.

Tavishien, a fast learner but in incredible shape due to all her training found it not a big challenge to perform and looked like a natural. The fact the two women were dressed up in designer dresses and makeup put on by Tavishien who's a master at makeup and disguises was not to help her get out of a fix in the spy business while she was tagging her clients for remote viewing.

After a few dances, Tavishien said, "Marti, I would like to sit down for a few minutes I'm getting kind of sweaty."

"Sure, no problem."

Watching the two leave the dance floor, Lateegely got the same notion and said to Tristan, "I would like to sit down for a few minutes, if you don't mind."

"Sure, no problem."

General Taroton decided he was going to make his move in on Lateegely stood up to approach their table, but before he got near it, Tavishien said to Lateegely, "Would you mind going to the lady's room with me?"

"Sure."

It was common for women double dating doing this to provide each other security as one never knew what lurked around the restrooms even in high class places like this. But more importantly, they did their scheming in the restrooms.

The women stood up and were quickly away from the table, so General Taroton reversed course and went back to his table silently cursing bad timing.

After they got to the lady's room which was empty at the time, Tavishien brought up the real reason for their trip there.

"The reason why I wanted you to come here is tell you a couple things."

"Sure."

"The makeup we are wearing isn't designed to hold up well if we start doing a lot of sweating. Keep that in mind and take frequent breaks to avoid building up a sweat."

"Thanks for the tip."

"My pleasure. But there is also something else I wanted to say to you."

"Sure, what did you want to say?"

"I've never been with a man I love. I've never experienced love making before. I've never asked for much out of life up to this point, but I have some special feelings for Marti."

"He looks at you like he has feelings for you as well."

"The reason why we are having his conversation is when we go back to our rooms on the base, I want Marti to come by my room and I'm going to ask him to make love to me. I know you have your adjacent room where you are supposed to be to look out for me. But I think if you ask nicely, Tristan Karjal might be willing to take you to his room for a few hours so you guys can have a nice long conversation and get to know each other."

"Alright, when do we plan on leaving?"

"Right away."

Lateegely smiled and shook her head. It was turning out to be a magical evening with everything Tavishien had done especially dressing her up to make her look like a princess, she was so proud of how she looked and here she was in the lady's room seeing herself in all the mirrors they had in there and she couldn't believe how beautiful she looked.

"I'll do whatever you ask me, but I have a request."

"What's that Lateegely dear?"

"Before we change our clothes tonight would you mind taking a picture of me. I love what you did to my makeup and dress, and I would like to have a picture to look at in the future and send to my relatives."

"Sure, I'll invite to two men into my room and ask Marti if he wouldn't mind taking some pictures of you and me. But I want you to do something for me as well. I want you to suggest in front of Marti that you want a picture of Marti and me.

"I would be most happy to make such a request." Lateegely said.

"But before we leave and go back to the Intelligence Bureau Campus, I want one slow dance and while Marti and I are dancing, please will you take a picture of us with me in his arms." Tavishien said.

"I would love to do that!" Lateegely said.

"Okay us go do it!"

The women were soon at the dining table and timing could not have been more perfect, the band just at that moment started playing a slow dance so that couples could get romantically closer together and have precious little conversations.

Tavishien walked over and grabbed Marti's hand and said, "From the workout you gave me today, the least you could do for me is give me one slow dance."

A woman at a nearby table overheard Tavishien and mistook what it meant and blushed very broadly and gave an incredulous stare while they were on the dance floor.

Tristan Karjal sat there wondering if he should copy Agent Lucika's actions but before he could decide, Lateegely had her communicator out snapping a few quick photographs. Tristan was a little concerned this woman had just photographed an important spy along with one of their most precious assets. He would have to notify Agent Lucika later to determine what to do about it. It could turn into a dicey affair as they didn't want those images propagating into the wrong hands.

Lateegely was very fast operator with her communicator as she often had to have very fast reports to her superiors over VIP matters. Before Tristan figured out what needed to be done, Lateegely forwarded all those photographs to Tavishien since she had her communications contact preprogrammed because she assisted Tavishien back on the military base.

Lateegely didn't know she was sitting a very short distance away from an IBR. Had she known Tristan was an IBR she might have felt very intimidated. That's another good reason why they never divulged this to people including the military and people on bases they came across.

Everyone would act far more naturally not knowing they were around IBRs. In the case of Lateegely had she known Tristan was an IBR she would have thrown caution to the wind when she got to his room and did exactly what Tavishien wanted to do to Marti. But long after Tristan was gone, Lateegely had another person of interest that was focused on her for his own manifest destiny, so in the end she would receive what a glamorously beautiful woman deserved.

After the slow dance ended, Tavishien said, "I'm kind of hot and sweaty now. Can we go back to the base now and end the evening?"

"Sure, if that's what you want."

"Thank you."

Moments just as General Taroton stood up to approach Lateegely to ask her to dance, the four of them stood up and were quickly away from the table and exiting the venue.

Agent Lucika had an APP on his communicator that when he pressed it notified the Skycar *to pull up to the front entrance as they were leaving*. The Skycar with its wireless connection to the Resorts Valet Service was vectored to the exact spot to pick up passengers. The Valet's were in remote control of the Skycar for safety reasons and their computers placed it with perfect choreography of driverless technology.

As soon as the four exited the building the doors to the Skycar opened and the Valet who verified facial recognition authentications gestured to the Skycar and said, "Sir, your Skycar is ready for immediate departure via automated navigation."

That was expected as the Resort didn't want people driving away and possibly causing an accident in the process. The Resort would not relinquish navigation control of the Skycar to the passengers until it was a safe distance away from the Resort and in a Skycar Freeway under Global Skycar Administration (GSA) control.

GSA navigation control methods allowed cities to have a thousand times density in the air as they would have on surface transport. Nobody complained due to the convenience and efficiency. Plus, the Skycars traveled four to five times faster than surface transportation in most cases.

The Skycar registered with Secret Intelligence Service had immediate access to the base and the programmed return point exactly to where they left from near Tavishien's senior officer quarters.

As they all exited the Skycar, Tavishien surprised Agent Lucika and said, "Would you please come into my room for a few minutes. I would like you to take some pictures of Lateegely and I before we change our clothes."

"Yea, I suppose I can."

"Thank you, I appreciate this."

As per the plan they went into Tavishien's room where Agent Lucika (aka Marti) took pictures of the women together and then Tavishien said, "I would like some pictures of Lateegely by herself and I would like some pictures of me by myself as will if you don't mind."

"Sure, I don't mind."

After those pictures were taken, Lateegely spoke up and said, "Tavishien could I please have a picture of you and Marti together, you looked so nice tonight dancing as a couple."

"I don't mind."

Soon the pictures were taken and Lateegely had them sent via her communicator swiftly to Tavishien who now had photographs of her important night she would never forget for what was to soon be bestowed on them all.

As Marti and Tristan Karjal were leaving the room after the pictures, Tavishien said, "Marti, there is something I wanted to talk to you about concerning what happened today. And I can't say it in front of Lateegely and it could take a while to discuss it. Do think it would be possible for Tristan to indulge me for a while and take Lateegely to his room so you and I can discuss something I think is very important."

Tristan had no clue what it was all about since he wasn't there with Agent Lucika and Tavishien when they were out doing those live weapons exercises today, but understood they probably went through hell and quickly responded,

"Sure, I don't mind."

The two couples then split up and the Boy Scout Tristan took Lateegely to his room where they started talking simple conversations and Tristan didn't mind looking at and talking to such a beautiful woman.

Suddenly Tavishien and Agent Lucika were alone in her room.

"What is it you wanted to talk about Tavishien?"

"I think after what I did for you this week as well in the past you owe me a lot."

"Yes, I do. I know that."

Tavishien was observing Marti's body language that betrayed him. The fact his little head started saluting gave some of it away.

"Marti, I really like you. This is what I want from you."

"What is that?"

Tavishien had watched movies and analyzed how stars did it plus in her spy training she was given an assortment of methods to approach men to get their little heads thinking and saluting and she had a weapon none of them knew. She knew how to mental telepathy into Marti's pleasure center of his brain. Her mental telepathy did far more than Damiana, L-arginine, or even Viagra could possibly do.

She then applied her spy trade and approached Marti and started her fantastic manipulation of him. No matter how hard he fought avoiding *dipping into company ink*, he was at a terrible disadvantage as Tavishien put her hand on the side of his head and pulled him closer so their lips would touch. She knew the exact perfect geometry and pressure to apply to make that kiss far more provocative than a mere mortal could withstand.

Agent Lucika's willpower was crumbling. He was utterly defenseless now. The nation's top spy was being handled by someone considered a neophyte and trainee at best.

Tavishien did her magic and soon the two of them were in bed conducting the perfect coitus. Tavishien had a distinct advantage in that she knew what was in Marti's (aka Agent Lucika's) heart, mind, and soul, because she had something he had no idea, that mental telepathy that was a side effect of the remote viewing ability.

Tavishien knew Marti was in love with her. She also now knew something that would alarm Marti even more. She knew his real name, who he really was, where he grew up, and his family and former personal friends. She had Marti's life story. The Agency would be utterly in shock and would have to do significant damage control if they knew Tavishien knew Agent Lucika was really Garratt Wyclaire and Lucika was an alias.

The other aspect is Tavishien's closeness to Garratt Wyclaire meant whether she liked it or not, she would probably do remote viewing of Garratt Wyclaire because she couldn't always control the information flow. It hit her whether she liked it or not.

Secret Intelligence Service (SIS), known as the Intelligence Bureau had spent over five million credits to change Garratt Wyclaire's image and his identity. The Tartars would pay 500 million credits to unmask Garratt Wyclaire. They didn't know of him personally, but they had some possible clues from the double spy that Tavishien recently killed. But the few breadcrumbs the double spy gave was not nearly enough to do the unmasking or reveal exactly in the org chart where he stood or what he did.

Another huge problem for Garratt Wyclaire is that if the SIS discovered he *dipped his pen in company ink*, there could be some serious repercussions. He crossed over the line, even though Tavishien initiated the romance. He would spend the next few weeks self-analyzing the disaster he had just created for himself by losing self-control at a critical moment. Unfortunately, Garratt Wyclaire had no idea what he was up against and sometimes you just do not know what you do not know. That's why the spy business got so dicey at times.

Eventually after Tavishien got her multitudes of gratification the influence and further ignition to subsequent release of passions died down. Post orgasmic mental slowdown and moderation of emotions led to pragmatic thinking. Garratt Wyclaire (aka Agent Lucika and aka Marti) began the reluctant discussion.

"Tavishien, you have no idea how much I like you. I have too much going on to divert my attention from the tasks at hand and what I must do for SIS in the future. It's not a job I can walk away from."

"I understand that."

"If my superiors discovered we were lovers it could cause huge problems not only for me but also for you. We can never expose this to anyone."

"That's not a problem."

"Because my life is terribly complicated, I do not have another woman in my life. You are the first woman I've tasted in almost six years, and that woman was only part of the operation as I had to seduce her for the operation. I did that to not only save my own life but to make sure the mission was a success."

"I understand what you have to go through."

"I'll be honest, I do not know if we will ever have a chance to do this again. We were lucky tonight the planets aligned. If one day after my projects are completed and if you still want me at that time, I will come for you. But you should know that will not be for a long while."

"I'm a big girl just knowing you would come for me I would wait. You should know I do not have the ability to have children."

"That's okay, I think because of the business you and I are in, if we did have children, they would be at constant risk. It's better I never bring children into the world."

"I understand."

"I know it's going to be difficult, but you are going to have to do your utmost to act like this never happened. We must protect each other. My superiors would go heavy handed if they discovered what we did tonight."

"Don't worry about me. Your secret is safe with me. I'll do whatever I can to protect you and make sure you never get in trouble."

"Thank you I appreciate that. I also want you to know it's going to be difficult for me because I will always have a desire for you."

"I like you having that desire. Us keep it that way, and one day when you can leave all this behind, we can then enjoy life together."

"Alright, one more kiss and let's get dressed. I'll leave and you can call Lateegely back to your room. I'm going directly to mine and if Tristan contacts me, I'll tell him we'll meet in the morning."

"Alright Marti, that is unless you want me to call you someone else." "Marti is good it's my cover name us stick with it."

***

In the morning the three IBR's Marti, Tristan and Tavishien were all meeting with General Taroton before they left. He wanted some final words with them and just finished reading the safety report from the previous day. He was highly agitated, but there was nothing he could do when IBR's pushed the safety envelope. He knew they had other considerations in their preparations and based on hearsay, many never returned from their secret missions.

But at the same time, General Taroton felt the pressure would be enormous if he had to file a fatality report due to training on his base. The only thing he could do now was smile and act like it was just another training experience when in fact it wasn't. Plus, he wanted some private words with Marti.

"I hope that all of you were comfortable while you stayed here at the base."

"We certainly were General."

"Good to hear."

"Thank you," Marti said with a poker face.

General Taroton looking at Tavishien who had surprised him with the explicit beauty she showed the previous night had some final words for her.

"Tavishien, your training results were sent to your sponsors with my endorsements. You scored very high and it's a shame you are not part of our military where your talents would be very beneficial."

"Thank you General Taroton, but I feel like I have some challenges at what I currently do."

"I have no doubt about that at all. Your actions and your success in training here leave behind an indelible mark."

Just as the three IBRs were about to leave General Taroton's office, he said,

"Marti, may I speak alone with you for a couple minutes?"

"Sure General, Tristan and Tavishien, would you please step outside for a few minutes."

When General Taroton was alone with Marti, he asked, "Marti, tell me about that woman that was with the three of you last night at the resort restaurant."

"General Taroton, like I said last night, she works here at your base."

"What does she do if you don't mind me for asking?"

"She was Tavishien's senior officer quarters steward. Tavishien who's a fashion model decided to dress her up to show her how much she appreciated her for all she did."

"I'll have to check into her. I know it's not proper to *put your pen in company ink*, but somehow, she captivated me."

"General, I'm sure if you pursue her, she might be far more receptive than you realize."

"I'm due to rotate or retire soon. I wouldn't mind retiring with a woman like that to spend my time with."

"She's been at this business for a while, I'm sure she's looking forward to retirement as well. Your timing could not be more auspicious."

"Thanks for the information, and glad your training was successful."

"Thank you general and tell your safety boys to lay off the heat on the training people. They did precisely what we asked them to do. As you know, we don't do normal missions and our actions often have a razor-sharp edge quite often between living and dying. We train like we fight, the same way. We have no choice, and we must take the risk because on real missions, our enemies will not coddle us."

"Yes, I suppose it can get really dangerous for you people."

General, the fact our enemies will do everything in their power to destroy us. We made the training as realistic as possible. I know we stressed the hell out of your training people in doing so."

"That's an understatement Marti."

"General, please let them know their efforts will pay off in the future when Tavishien or one of our other agents is able to come home alive because they had this experience and are ready for the real event."

"My superiors will probably not like that safety report."

"General, here is my business card. If your superiors come down on you for the enhanced training, contact me right away, we'll make sure they get the proper calibration."

"Thank you I appreciate this. I don't mind retiring on my own terms, but I don't like the idea of being shoved out the door."

"General, nobody is going to shove you. If they do, they will be dealing with me, and I could arrange for them to take a trip somewhere that we do enhanced calibration of individuals who get in our way."

The General smiled. It was all about leverage. Now all he needed to do was figure out how to leverage Lateegely into a lasciviously delightful scenario.

CHAPTER FIFTEEN
Cracks In His Armor

The days passed slowly as they prepared for their next mission. Tavishien knew her situation was indeed a losing proposition. Marti (aka Garratt Wyclaire) wasn't giving her the cold shoulder, he was simply doing what he had to do, shield the relationship from the world's best spy operation. Even the slightest amount of exposure could bring down crushing pressure quickly.

Garratt Wyclaire (aka Agent Lucika) didn't understand a lot of things and in fact had no idea how he managed to get in bed with Tavishien and have sex with her as if he was a dog chasing a bitch in heat. But the reality is it happened. He could not turn back the pages of time and knew he was in a very delicate situation, and the least little spark could ignite an inferno.

Garratt Wyclaire (aka Agent Lucika) also knew the facts of life. His superiors knew Tavishien was a remote viewer. Her services were essential. His wasn't. He got where he was with hard work and luck. If his superiors discovered what would be construed as miss-conduct *dipping his pen in company ink,* he would be immediately transferred, and they would put as much space between them as possible including shuttling him off to another empire planet in the far off reaches of space where living conditions were not ideal.

It was in the backdrop of this realization that tempered Agent Lucika as he went back to work in the most professional manner possible acting as if nothing happened.

Tavishien understood all his thoughts and every time they were in the same room together, she wasted no time probing him and remote viewed him relentlessly to see if there were any cracks in his armor she could get through on her conquest. Tavishien knew everything there was to know about Garratt Wyclaire. The fact she knew as much as she knew would deem a major security violation as she had derived information exceedingly way above her security clearance.

Tavishien knew not only all the *what's* but also the *why's* in all their efforts dealing with their enemies. She now knew a lot of information she was never supposed to be privy to. She also knew how deadly the spy game was and she could never reveal to anyone what she knew or how she came about discovering it.

Tavishien had no option but to role play to give the appearance that nothing had changed. Every day and more and more it seemed like Garratt Wyclaire (aka Agent Lucika) arranged things to put space between him and Tavishien. Every time they ended up alone, which became less and less frequent, it became obvious to Tavishien that her true love Garratt Wyclaire was doing everything in his power to avoid her.

There was an uptick in their face-to-face meetings only because more missions came about.

Mission planning and remote viewing results forced those private meetings.

What Garratt Wyclaire didn't know was Tavishien knew what was in his heart and she knew for a fact he loved her. But the fact he chose his job over her was just as much a disappointment as any other lover would have had for other reasons after a breakup.

Their romance lasted a few hours, but it taught Tavishien a lot of good lessons. The outcome was she would never give her heart to another man the rest of her life. Garratt Wyclaire would be her first and last lover.

Garratt Wyclaire (aka agent Lucika) during one of those special briefing where Tavishien reported remote viewer results for one of her targets, they were alone and Tavishien had moments when she wanted to be a bad girl, so she toiled with Garratt's mind using her telepathic ability that seemed to be advancing and giving her far more access than she ever thought possible.

After some manipulation Garratt, who knew everything they said was being recorded and there were cameras on them too, pulled a small sheet off his note pad and wrote down something then handed it to Tavishien.

Tavishien read the note that said, "Be aware we are being recorded in this room. I want to thank you for your patience and your discreteness."

Tavishien read the note and reached over and grabbed the pen out of Garratt's hand and wrote below his note: "I'm a bitch in heat and I can't take this loneliness much longer. You need to take care of me soon. I patiently wait for you."

The piece of paper in Garratt's hand was dynamite. If anyone saw this, he would soon have serious repercussions. He took the note, wadded it up into a ball and put it in his mouth and started chewing on it. And he slowly moved his head up and down giving her the signal which Tavishien didn't need. She already knew the answer.

There were a few more months of this torment and Tavishien finally decided she could no longer take it. She knew what she had to do.

Tavishien and Gabriel got along very well now, and their training activities were pleasant as Tavishien decided she no longer needed to beat her up.

Tavishien planned her great escape. She would do it with Gabriel's help in ways Gabriel never considered possible.

Tavishien had Gabriel take her out to a night club one evening. There Tavishien showed utter happiness, drank a few elixirs, then excused herself and followed a wealthy looking lady into the lady's room. The room was empty and, in a few moments, Tavishien made the other woman unconscious, then undressed her and took her clothes and put them on in a stall.

Any woman who came in during the switch would simply become unconscious. After changing clothes with the woman and taking her purse that had all her identity, Tavishien quickly altered her hair to give a different appearance and put on the sunglasses she had with her and walked out of the restroom and out of the night club and got into a waiting Skytaxi.

"Where to madam?"

"Take me to the airport."

Tavishien, a trained spy knew a lot of people were dumb when it came to personal security, and they had their financial accounts tagged to their communicator. Tavishien had one of those lovely gadgets she was trained in to unlock such devices and have instant access to the credits.

As part of her recent training, Tavishien was an expert at driving vehicles and Skycars. She could get around if necessary. Tavishien had determined the best way to get to the fishing village she hid out in after killing the guy and knew she could not go there direct. Tavishien would fly into the regional city then pay some Skytaxi operator a large sum to take her to the fishing village. After a quick trip to a clothing store outlet and a change of comfortable clothes, Tavishien was on her way to the village, with a few gifts to give to them.

Lucky for Tavishien, the arrival was in the mid-morning when most people were up and about when she made her grand entry. As she paid the Skycar driver a large bonus she said, "The reason why I'm giving you a good bonus is so that you forget you ever met me. If they find me here because you informed them where you took me, I will hunt you down and you will quickly regret it."

"Not a problem, for this tip I already forgot you."

"Thanks," Tavishien said as she continued manipulating his thoughts to make the Skycar driver never want to remember her again.

Soon there she was with the tribe people approaching wondering why she suddenly re-appeared.

In due time after saying she wanted to stay at the village for a while to get over something bad in her lifetime, one of the village women took her in. The village woman was not soon disappointed as Tavishien showered her with nice gifts that fully impressed her.

The tribe knew Tavishien was someone special because when Agent Lucika brought her here the last time surrounded by ample security, that left an impression on them.

Now suddenly here she was back again. Did she just go through similar scenarios to where they had to hide her again? Those were many of their questions that would never be asked because they knew it was best, they didn't know these things. The fact she showed up alone this time gave them assurance nobody knew she had arrived. That at least made them feel better.

Shortly after settling in, there were several Tribal women arriving to say hello to Tavishien who they got to like during her previous stay. She proved to not be a threat to their mates, and she was always a pleasant person to be around. Little did they know Tavishien manipulated their minds as well.

For all extensive purposes Tavishien was now a defacto member of the tribe. They adopted Tavishien in open arms. She was beautiful, pleasant, and non-assuming. Plus, Tavishien was not afraid of work and helped immensely. When other women of the Tribe had illness or serious issues, Tavishien always volunteered to help, including watching their kids and keeping them occupied so their mother could have restful moments.

Meanwhile there was an extensive search for Tavishien by the Intelligence Bureau. The way Tavishien flew the coup spending untraceable credits the rich woman had, they had no way of discovering where she went.

Agent Lucika was now in a serious bind. His superiors would soon be pounding him for answers to how their illustrious remote viewer suddenly disappeared. He knew based on the woman they found wearing her attire, it probably wasn't the enemy recruiting her and taking her away. Agent Lucika knew what his superiors didn't know. He knew as the pressure mounted; they might be able to force it out of him. *Tavishien left heart broken.*

Agent Lucika was still in love with Tavishien, but he was near the cusp of the fulfillment of the pinnacle in his career in the spy business. He was as close as anyone ever got to that jump up to the top levels of the Intelligence Bureau management, and his successes had been impressive, in part because Tavishien gave him the actionable intel to operate off that made his exploits legendary as well as immensely successful.

Just as he predicted there were lots of investigations into how and why Tavishien disappeared. The spotlight was intensely hot, but there was no real lead to the fact finding. The only person on the planet other than Garratt (aka Agent Lucika) that knew the source of this tumultuous event, Lateegely.

By the time investigators got to Lateegely, General Taroton had already started his grand strategy of being the person in her life she never imagined. They were at the incubation stage of that romance when the investigators descended onto the base and to General Taroton and after interviews with IBR Tristan Karjal, Lateegely was taken away for a few days of intensive investigations.

During intensive investigations with Lateegely, the reality started to unfold, and it pointed directly at Agent Lucika.

The pictures were damming evidence. Between interviews with General Taroton, Lateegely, and IBR Tristan Karjal, the investigative squad turned over a lot of information into internal affairs division who then put the heat on Agent Lucika.

Finally, Agent Lucika was sitting across from his boss in a private meeting to discuss the disappearance of Tavishien, one of their most important assets of late as her INTEL was more valuable than all the rest put together.

"We were at first worried the Tartars snatched her and killed her," The executive director stated nonchalantly.

"Her disappearance is certainly a mystery," Agent Lucika responded.

"Agent Lucika, you and I both know that you know why she's gone."

"I don't follow you sir, I'm not sure what you mean by that."

"You're a prime operative and should have realized that with the loss of such a tremendous asset we would leave no stones unturned."

"I would assume that."

"You had an affair with Tavishien before she left, didn't you?"

At this point in time Agent Lucika knew he would be subject to some expansive interrogation techniques if he withheld the truth, so he figured out he might as well get it over with even if it meant it cost him his career."

"I'm not sure how it began. I never thought for one moment there could ever be a relationship between us, but as time passed, we grew closer and closer and then one day it happened."

"You did an excellent job of covering it up. Had Tavishien not left, we would never have known."

"I realize as a spy I failed. I let my emotions over-rule my common sense and allowed the event to manifest."

"She's a very beautiful woman. I looked at several of her fashion show videos. It's obvious she could tempt quite a few men and you used her in that role to get her in position to do her remote viewing."

"Yes, I did, and I felt it was worthwhile to attempt."

"I'm not here to discipline you but I do want to give you some guidance."

"I'm ready to receive whatever punishment you want to dish out I screwed up."

"Actually, I do not believe you screwed up. If I were faced with the same challenges, I assume I would have taken the same course of actions you did."

"What is it you want me to do."

"I know this will seem kind of strange to you, but we understand the importance of you and Tavishien working as a team together is. What I'm going to tell you is not what you expect."

"Alright, what is it?"

"I want you to find Tavishien and bring her back. If the two of you chose to continue in a relationship, we will not interfere, but you need to get her back."

"Alright."

"What else?"

"When you and Tavishien get back together, you need to let her know your superiors know about it and all they ask of you is to keep it private. We do not want the people at the Bureau to know you have such a relationship."

***

CHAPTER SIXTEEN
Gold Extraction

T avishien was busy in the Village for several months and enjoying it. The village soon healed all her psychological wounds caused by Garratt Wyclaire (aka agent Lucika) breaking her heart and was now feeling better day by day.

The women knew Tavishien arrived with one of her wings broken. They didn't pry, but they knew when a bird was in pain. They did what they could do to help nurture her back to good mental health and as time became a way of healing everything, Tavishien was slowly restored.

Part of Tavishien's restoration related to her involvement in the gold extraction these tribes people developed over time with ingenious, though primitive methods.

Because the tribe was located on the shoreline where there was a gentle breeze at least half the day, they had a windmill that turned a pump mechanism that moved ocean water into a tank that fed the filers the tribes people made using sea grass with a few additives. After about a week the filter was permeated with a film that simply appeared to be sludge coming off the ocean. The mat like filter was then removed and placed into a collecting tank build that could easily hold 1000 gallons.

Week by week the collecting tank was filled with these filters. Then the secret ingredients were added and after a couple months the decomposed sea grass was removed out of the holding tank and laid out on a cement slab, they created to allow it to dry completely. After a few weeks the dried sea grass was placed in a barrel where it was set afire. The carbon remains of the sea grass were then ground up and placed in tub where more additives were poured in. After another week the top portion of this tub was removed, and all the residual liquids were poured into a tub used to process the next batch.

What remained was gold dust that was collected added to a collection of gold dust that was smelted and further refined for purity.

The amount of gold production did not make them rich, but it allowed the villagers to continue their lives with essentials. Tavishien's presence, since she had nothing better to do, slowly increased their gold production three-fold.

Life went on in the village and any single males that had notions of pursuing Tavishien quickly learned she was not interested. When asked by the village women why she always turned down the men, she responded, "I don't want to meet another man the rest of my life." They instantly knew she had a broken heart and there was more to the story.

Now and then Tavishien remote viewed Garratt Wyclaire (aka Garratt Wyclaire). She saw a hopeless man in misery in full regret he allowed the love of his life slip through his fingers. She also discovered developments that meant her time here with the villagers could be curtailed if Garratt Wyclaire ever got the notion of coming here to look for her.

After several long sleepless nights Tavishien did some soul searching. She knew Garratt still loved her and missed her terribly. *Should I help him find me?*

Many thoughts swirled through Tavishien's head as she was contemplating her future. Her love for Garratt Wyclaire caused her to flood the ionosphere wither her emotions. She had no idea she was transmitting what essentially was a homing beacon to Garratt. She didn't realize what she had done, nor did Garratt, but it gave him an idea where to go look for her.

Being at the tops of the Intelligence Bureau and with firm backing from management from top level management to find Tavishien, Garratt Wyclaire (aka Agent Lucika) had massive air and intelligence apparatus to deploy without the need to explain to anyone why he was doing it.

He didn't know why he suddenly thought of the fishing village, but Garratt knew this was a good location to check out. *Maybe she went there to make sure I would find her?*

The high-level reconnaissance flights over the village soon revealed there was a stranger among them.

Garratt Wyclaire (aka Agent Lucika) then ordered secondary surveillance including offshore boats, tribal visitors, and aircraft over flights. In due time he found what he was looking for. There was a person in the village that according to satellite photographs looked different than tribes' members and the boat and aircraft flyover pictures confirmed it was Tavishien in the photographs and video.

Agent Lucika knew what he had to do. He would have to send in someone Tavishien trusted to confront her and ask her to come back.

In due time Gabriel was in Agent Lucika's office getting her assignment.

"This is probably one of the most important assignments you will be given. If you want to know, this is in my top five that's how important it is."

Gabriel looked at Agent Lucika wondering what this was about, and her curiosity would soon explode as more information flowed from Agent Lucika.

"Alright, I think I'm ready for prime time."

"I know you are that's why I personally hand-picked you for this assignment."

"What is it I'll be doing?"

"Before we get into all that, I want you to know this assignment and everything it includes is classified as Most Top Secret (MTS)." "I do not plan on revealing any of it."

"That's good. Now I'm going to tell you a few things that only you will know and is to never be divulged to anyone as it could have a negative impact on me and I'm sure you know how that would not only affect me but you as well."

"I'm not going to reveal anything."

"Good."

Gabriel looked at Agent Lucika with utter curiosity as she knew this was a critical mission otherwise, they would not be having this private meeting, and the extraordinary language Agent Lucika was using on someone he worked with for many years on tough assignments.

"I'm sending you somewhere to go bring Tavishien back."

"You know where she is?"

"Yes. She's hiding in the same fishing village I put her after she killed the guy in the club."

"Why did she go there? She obviously must have known you would go there eventually looking for her."

"There is more to the story than I can reveal to you, and please do not ask because I can't tell you."

"Alright what am I going to do?"

"I'm sending you to that fishing village to bring Tavishien back."

"She's there?"

"Yes."

"Why did she go there?"

"That's one of the questions I do not want you to ask."

"Alright I'll do my best."

"Thank you. This is a very delicate matter, and anything involved in your travel on this mission is classified Most Top Secret."

"Alright understand all. When am I to leave?"

"In about two hours. Go pack you travel case."

"Right on it," Gabriel said and was soon on her way in total disbelief.

Being a smart woman, she knew where there is smoke there is usually fire. And for Tavishien to suddenly sneak away in the middle of the night was somewhat shocking. They had all misjudged her. *But what brought this on?*

Away Gabriel goes to the island and a few hours later meets up with Tavishien who immediately knew if Gabriel was here, the Intelligence Bureau knew she was here. *She hadn't escaped, after all.*

 After the short friendly conversation, Gabriel asked if they could go someplace to have a private conversation, hence they walked to the beach for privacy.

Gabriel said, "Agent Lucika really wants you back.

Tavishien was now mad. Sending Gabriel here to bring her back upset her off even more.

"Tell Garratt, if he wants me to come back, he has to personally come here and ask me."

"Who's Garratt?"

When you go to Agent Lucika and repeat those exact words, he'll understand what he must do. Otherwise, I'm not going back.

Gabriel stood there utterly stunned. She knew she wasn't a rocket scientist, but she didn't need to be Einstein to figure it out.

Gabriel was a sophisticated woman and had been in a variety of delicate situations in the past in espionage. Her transfer to the Intelligence Bureau Campus and working directly with Agent Lucika was meant to give her some period of calm to help restore herself after going through hell for so many years including being captured and tortured like most spies' experience under the circumstances.

Gabriel was extremely lucky to be alive. The Intelligence Bureau knew they needed to let Gabriel unwind for a few years as she had reached her limits. She was one mission away from being killed if they didn't pull her off the front lines.

Gabriel was astonished as her analysis led her to believe Agent Lucika had *dipped his pen in company ink*, and Tavishien knew his real identity. This would not go over well. She knew the best thing to do now was to go back without Tavishien and have that private meeting with "Garratt" and the fact she now knew his personal identity, made it kind of dicey for her as well.

Recounting her visit with Agent Lucika, he did *act rather strangely*. Now it all makes perfect sense. The extra secrecy about this mission and total compartmentalization created creepy feelings withing Gabriel.

Whether Gabriel returned with or without Tavishien, she knew she needed to fly back to the Intelligence Bureau Campus and brief Agent Lucika (aka Garratt) privately. She also knew that Tavishien was a tough bitch and during her escape on a motor bike where she evaded IBR's in wild stunt devil like maneuvers easily portrayed this woman would not be taken in short of some violent act.

"Alright Tavishien, I will go back to Agent Lucika and deliver him the message. But there is one thing I want to tell you."

"What's that?"

"We've gone down a long path together. You have done a lot and earned my respect many times over. No matter what happens in the future always remember I'm on your team and your friend."

"Thank you, that means a lot to me coming from you specifically."

Gabriel could see the tears forming in Tavishien's eyes and the tears started flowing.

Gabriel did the only thing she thought she could do and that was to put her arms around Gabriel and hug her and hold her in her sobs for a few precious moments.

After a short while Tavishien got control of herself and pushed Gabriel away and said, "You have somewhere to go. I know you are a busy woman."

"Alright. Hopefully we can work this all out and see you back at the Campus soon."

"I don't expect it will, I expect it all to end in tragedy."

The two said goodbye and Gabriel walked to the Skycar where three other IBRs sat fully armed.

"She's not coming?" the lead IBR asked.

"No, let's go back to the airport, I need to go brief Agent Lucika and determine what he wants to do."

"I think he just wants us to do a snatch and grab and bring her back regardless of her intentions."

"We are not going to take her back."

"After my talk with Agent Lucika, I think we'll have to grab her," the lead IBR said in a very arrogant manner.

"If you put your hands on that woman, I will personally shoot you in your dick. Take us back to the airport now. I'm sure Agent Lucika wants to hear what I have to say before he makes his next move."

The lead IBR sat there totally stunned. One thing he knew for sure was Gabriel was a great shot and she did not parse words.

Away the IBRs went and soon came back at the airport getting on their private highspeed transport to get them back to the IB Campus in a short while.

When Gabriel stepped out of the Skycar delivering them back to the Campus, Agent Lucika was waiting for them at the edge of the parking facility. He had a concern on his face. As the three IBR's and Gabriel approached Agent Lucika, he said, "Gabriel come with me. You men go to your offices and wait for my call after I decide how to handle this."

The men grumpy because some of them wanted to kick Gabriel's ass, simply walked back to their offices waiting to find out what the hell was going on.

"Come with me to my office, please" Agent Lucika said in a very professional manner looking directly at Gabriel.

Soon the two were in Agent Lucika's office where he started, "Why didn't you bring her back? The men were told to do a snatch and grab if necessary."

"We need to go to the secure room, what I have to say must be very confidential," Gabriel responded in a very succinct manner.

Agent Lucika now had a strange look on his face. *Did Tavishien reveal they were lovers?*

Soon in the room with door closed and the anti-snooping systems up and operating that would disable any possible bug,

Agent Lucika started, "Okay, give me the reason why you didn't bring her back or allow my men to forcibly abduct her and bring her back."

"Tavishien gave me a message to give to you."

"And what was that?"

"She said in discrete terms, tell Garratt if he wants me to come back, he has to personally come here and ask me."

Agent Lucika now sat there stunned. He knew the laws of probabilities. If two other people knew his real identity, others would too.

"Did you mention this to the three IBR's?"

"No."

"Why is that?"

"It was none of their business."

"Who do you think Garratt is?"

"Agent Lucika, no other man has ever been alone with Tavishien besides you. I think you broke her heart when the two of you went away for training. She came back acting very strange after that. Any good spy would assume you are Garratt."

"Did she tell you anymore?"

"I'm a woman, she didn't need to tell me anymore."

"If it's true my real name is Garratt, how do you think she found out?"

"Since I didn't know your real name was Garratt, it's a mystery to me as well."

"You understand you cannot reveal any of this to anyone or you will cause Tavishien, yourself, as well as me some very difficult circumstances."

"May I make a suggestion?"

"Sure."

"Go back with me, just you and me and talk to her. I believe if you ask her to come back, she will."

"She knows there is no way we can ever divulge the spontaneous relationship I recklessly allowed."

"Can I ask you a question Garrott?"

"Sure."

"When we go back to pick her up, would it be impossible for you to tell her you love her, even though your situation is very delicate?"

"Well, I do love her."

"That's more reason to tell her. You will fix a crushed heart immediately with those words."

"But what's the point it can't go nowhere."

"Garrot either one of you could easily be killed in the future as you work in a very dangerous environment. I think you should bring her back, then go set up a meeting with your superior and inform that person this happened and what your true feelings are. Tavishien has already done a lot for us. The least they could do for her is a little accommodation. Plus, she's kept her mouth shut about all of this. She's a team player."

"I suppose you are right. Let me make a couple calls and set up transportation."

"It will probably be dark when we get there."

"I'm sure when Tavishien hears the Skycar arriving, and you and I get out of it together she will approach us in a casual manner."

"What about the tribesmen?"

"I'm sure Tavishien will tell them it's okay."

Agent Lucika thought his high security chamber was totally bug free. He didn't know his boss who always had a poker face always knew his moves ahead of him. Approval to go get Tavishien was promptly approved with a poker face as Garratt's boss was curious how his illustrious spy was going to work himself out of the mess, he created for himself.

The one thing the big boss knew, Agent Lucika (aka Garratt Wyclaire) never ceased to amaze him how he was able to get himself out of fixes he was in. Since Agent Lucika was always watched by internal affairs officers very closely, they knew he didn't have a lover or a woman in his life.

Upper management would soon be utterly shocked at how Garratt managed to have an affair under their noses. That proved their sources and methods were not one hundred percent dependable. But that's how it is in the spy business. You don't know what your vulnerabilities are until you get the bitter taste of defeat.

Agent Lucika and Gabriel had a quiet flight to the region where they were soon in a Skycar flying to the village.

Just as Agent Lucika predicted, the trained spy Tavishien would hear them coming and she stepped out of her hut and there were a few tribe members also appearing and she said, "I know who they are. They have come to take me home."

"Do you want to go with them?"

"If he says the right thing to me I will."

The Skycar landed on the nice landing pad the Intelligence Bureau installed for them because it was a given this was one of their safe houses to hide people when necessary. Tavishien only had to walk 50 yards to the landing pad.

There the two were. The two most important people in Tavishien's life now, Gabriel and Garratt. They met Tavishien halfway and Gabriel as they planned on the way there talked first and said, "Tavishien, Garratt wants to talk to you alone. I'm going to walk back to the Skycar. Please come see me when you finish your conversation."

"Alright."

Garratt waited about a minute looking at Tavishien. It was twilight but there were a few ancient lights lit up in special types of lanterns protecting the candlelight from the wind and allowed them to provide a little bit of light otherwise it would be totally dark. They were standing about twenty feet from one of these lantern lights so Garratt could see Tavishien well enough and see her eyes were watered up as if she was going to start crying.

Garratt approached Tavishien very closely and said, "The first thing I want to tell you is that I do love you. I really did fall in love with you and my emotions have not changed. You are the love of my life."

"That's good to hear," Tavishien weakly said as her eyes filled with more tears.

"I want you to come back with me. I've decided that if you agree to come back with me, I will report to my supervisor that we are lovers and have gone past the point of no return. I'm willing to take any disciplinary actions they dish out. I want you to come home with me."

Tavishien threw her arms around Garratt and started weeping profusely. The tribes' women saw all this and now understood it all. She was here because she was heartbroken, and she had chosen them above all else as she felt they were the closest thing to a family she ever had. They all looked at her as one of them and felt her emotions as all this unfolded.

Tavishien had gone through a lot of traumas in her lifetime. She had a delicate heart for Garratt. She didn't ask for anything out of life, all she wanted was the fulfillment of the love she felt for

Garratt. And here he was presenting himself with indications that would happen.

This was a huge moment in Tavishien's life. It was a moment she never believed she would ever experience. After a couple minutes she slowly pulled herself together and looked up at Garratt. She knew what she was going to do would shock the Tribe women, but they already knew she was an unconventional woman. A force to be reckoned with.

Tavishien reached up and grabbed Garratt with her hands on both sides of his head and since they were nearly the same height, she easily pulled his lips forward to hers and kissed him the best she could as she was trained by her spy masters in the event, she needed to kiss someone as part of an exit strategy.

Garratt felt a lightning strike go through him unlike anything he felt in his lifetime. He was feeling the effects of remote viewing and mental telepathy flood gates hitting him. His brain was beyond Hemi-Sync, it was almost in the Gateway event and the kiss lasted for several minutes as he pulled Tavishien closer to him and felt the electricity between their bodies.

The Tribe women had tears flowing. Some of their husbands would get lucky tonight thanks to Tavishien's influence by this brave act.

Tavishien slowly pulled herself together and realized they had places to go and business to take care of. She wouldn't mind taking Garratt into her hut and make love to him all night long, but the problem is Gabriel was here and had already seen too much.

She then slowly pushed away from Garratt and said, "I'll go back with you, but I need to tell these tribe members a few things before we leave."

"Alright, take as much time as you need."

Tavishien approached the women who were all full of smiles after witnessing such a romantic episode and said to them, "When I arrived, I really didn't have much, what I came with I no longer need. I want all of you to have it. Share it amongst yourself." "What about all your gold?"

"I'm leaving that for the village. You took care of me when I needed it the most. Share it among everyone."

"That's a lot of gold Tavishien."

"You gave me a lot of care that was priceless. I want you all to have it."

Tavishien hugged all the Tribe women and shook hands with a couple men and turned around and approached Garratt where she grabbed his hand, and he led her over to the Skycar.

After flying back to home base and when they got into the Skycar sent to take them back to the Intelligence Bureau Campus, Agent Lucika informed Gabriel and Tavishien, "Tavishien and I are going to stop at the Rico Resort. Gabriel, you continue to the Intelligence Bureau Campus. Let my secretary know I'll be late coming into the office in the morning."

"I am not dressed to go to such a resort," Tavishien whimpered.

"Not to worry. I know how to contact Ljótunn bon Swartzler. I'm sure she has a nice gown she would like you to show off."

Agent Lucika then called Ljótunn bon Swartzler and asked her, "Meet Tavishien and me at the Rico Resort with a couple designer clothes that Tavishien will wear to dinner tonight."

"What about hair style and makeup?" Ljótunn bon Swartzler asked.

"Bring all that too. Assume she has nothing with her." Agent Lucika said knowing that was an understatement describing the *tanned tribe's woman.*

The manager of the Rico Resort was pleased to receive Agent Lucika's phone call requesting a penthouse and a special escort through the back entrance and up the freight elevator as he had done a few times before while moving high profile agents there to and from missions. The compensation for the extraordinary services was always stupendous.

Tavishien sat there feeling good because it now seemed what Garratt had said back at the fishing village was starting to come true. She would reward him with her best ability tonight for doing all this. It was shaping up to be the best day of her life, with the man she was in love with, and someone she respected because of his extraordinary ability to do all the things he did in his life as one of the nation's premier spies.

But Tavishien was no fool. She now understood clearly, she was imbedded into the spy business with no way out except death. She also knew that if she lost Garratt along the way she might prefer to be dead because going back to the fishing village to live the rest of her life wasn't much more of a step-up than living in Papa's cabin in the forest under harsh conditions.

Garratt informed the automated navigator to park in the VIP parking at Rico Resort. No doubt the manager would be standing by the parking spot.

As expected, the manager of the Rico Resort and two bodyguards were at the VIP parking spot and resort navigation controls vectored the Skycar down to the exact VIP spot they wanted them to exit the Skycar.

Just before Agent Lucika got out of the Skycar he turned to Gabriel and said, "Remember what we talked about earlier, I don't want our evening ruined."

"Not to worry Garratt, you and Tavishien are my best friends. I will take care of you."

"Thank you."

"You are welcome and be sure and take good care of Tavishien because I wouldn't want to have to hurt you."

"You can count on that."

After Garratt and Tavishien exited the Skycar, Gabriel gave the onboard navigator Artificial Intelligence the directive to take her back to the Intelligence Bureau Campus. After consulting with Rico Resort Security and Navigation Coordination System, the Skycar was permitted to take off and fly directly back to the Intelligence Bureau Campus and away it went.

As Gabriel expect she had a welcoming committee there waiting for her and soon was headed into the special compartmentalized security chamber by none other than Garratt Wyclaire's (aka Agent Lucika) supervisor a person near the very top of the spy apparatus management team.

This would be a tough two-hour interview. The outcome was uncertain. Gabriel had no idea where all this was going.

***

CHAPTER SEVENTEEN
Fling at the Rico Resort

The Rico Resort manager said to Agent Lucika as they walked into the resort VIP entrance hidden from view of the main entrance, he said, "I received a call from Ljótunn bon Swartzler who is on her way and needed incognito entrance. Do you want me to bring her and her staff up to your penthouse right away?"

Yes, and can you do me a favor and reserve a table for us near the performers in the grand dining hall?

"It will my upmost pleasure Marti."

"Thank you."

In a short while, the couple was led up into a luxurious penthouse and in agreement with Marti and the Manager, Hotel Security did a thorough job of sweeping for bugs or hidden cameras, just in case.

In the penthouse the Manager introduced Marti and Tavishien to the Butler and the Maid, "Kevin and Karen, this is Marti and Tavishien, please take good care of them."

Kevin and Karen bowed, and Kevin said, "Sir you can be sure we will do our best."

"Thank you."

The manager and his two bodyguards then left the penthouse and the Butler Kevin asked, "Would you two like something to drink?"

"Yes, I kind of want to unwind tonight, how about a Kanill Grasker elixir," Marti (aka Agent Lucika aka Garratt Wyclaire) replied.

"And you madam?"

"I'll have a Gæsaber elixir."

"I'll bring your drinks right away; would you like to make yourselves comfortable and Kevin gestured towards the plush furniture."

Tavishien walked over to the over padded sofa with a coffee table in front of it and seated herself. Garratt followed her and sat down next to her and the two looked into each other's eyes both wondering where to take it from here, and each decided to wait and have some of their drinks before they got carried away in romance.

The drinks were served via dumbwaiter directly from the resort bar, chilled to perfection which the butler Kevin served immediately and left the room closing the door behind him to give them privacy as they enjoyed their drinks which started going down smoothly.

Garratt closely observed Tavishien, a woman he had groomed to be a world class spy with all sorts of capabilities. In her sojourn to the fishing village, she had been exposed to the sunlight quite often and now had a glorious tan the illuminated her blue eyes and blonde hair. People on planet Earth would think she appeared like a 26-year-old Marilyn Monroe with a dark tan.

After several large sips of his elixir, Garratt was feeling moved and wanted to reach out for Tavishien when unexpectedly the intercom announced, "Marti, your guests Ljótunn bon Swartzler and her staff have arrived. Would you like me to escort her into your living room?"

"Yes, please," Marti (aka Garratt) responded.

Within a moment the crew arrived. Ljótunn bon Swartzler was mildly exasperated in the condition she found Tavishien. She knew better than to ask questions because she had not been around in a while and very well may have been on a mission. In fact, she was on a mission, her own private mission, so that she now knew she was successful at vetting Garratt's true intentions.

"Tavishien, we need to bathe you and apply some special compounds to your hair for your hair design for tonight."

"Alright."

Tavishien stood up and followed Ljótunn bon Swartzler who seemed to know where she was going, mainly she had been here before on several assignments prepping spies for missions.

A couple female helpers followed them through the bedroom into the private master bedroom bath. Soon Tavishien was in a bubble bath enjoying the Gæsaber elixir she brought with her from the living room.

Just as Ljótunn bon Swartzler was leaving the bathroom now that Tavishien was getting her hair shampooed to go consult with Marti (aka Agent Lucika), Tavishien asked, "Ljótunn could you please ask Marti to get me another one of these Gæsaber elixirs, I like the way it's making me feel.

"Sure dear."

Ljótunn bon Swartzler didn't like the way with Marti (aka Agent Lucika) was dressed, especially if he was going to be with her super model Tavishien that night. Ljótunn bon Swartzler wanted to fix Marti up as well and came prepared for all contingencies such as this.

When Ljótunn bon Swartzler notified Marti (aka Garratt) of Tavishien's request he said, "I'll make the arrangements and make sure its watered down, so she doesn't get intoxicated."

"Smart man, especially if you want some action afterwards."

"Do you think she is willing to have the big A with me?"

"It's written all over her face, darling. She's in love with you."

Right after Marti received the refill from the butler Kevin, Ljótunn bon Swartzler said, "I'll take it to her, I don't want you to see that pretty girl naked.

Then there is something I need to talk to you about."

After Ljótunn bon Swartzler gave Tavishien the watered down Gæsaber elixirs, she asked one of the assistants, "Can you finish here? I need Sandy to help me get Marti prepared."

"Sure, no problem."

Ljótunn bon Swartzler then went out and informed Marti he did not look appropriate to be the escort of her fashion model tonight and she had to get him ready as well and Marti (aka Agent Lucika aka Garratt) knew better than to argue with Ljótunn bon Swartzler who knew her business and the propriety of creating the essence of the illustration she wanted to make with her fashion designs knowing there would be eyes out there and people inquire where all this came from.

The Penthouse also had a guest bedroom where they sequestered Garratt in his preparations. They did not want him to have even a glimpse of Tavishien until they were complete with her, because the first impression is the most important. Between the fashion designers, makeup artists, and hair designers, Tavishien came out of the master bedroom appearing like Lauren Becall as a young woman with her hair parted on one side and hair flowing down majestically just like the famed movie star.

The dark blue strapless satin long evening gown with a slit on one side exposing most of the leg created a surreal image that struck Garratt like never before. Thanks to her long hiatus at the fishing village gaining that glorious tan, her exposed leg and shoulders illuminated that tan most explicitly creating a provocative enticement.

Thanks to surgery and major dental work Tavishien also had a killer smile that would take the breath away from mere mortals who saw her imagery this moment.

Looking at this incredibly beautiful woman, Garratt knew he was nothing more than a Noble Savage and by the grace of God he was awarded a second chance with the woman of his dreams.

Tavishien was clever as well as conniving when it came to her greatest desires. And standing in front of her, all cleaned up, Garratt Wyclaire looking at her in total awe, didn't know she was also manipulating him with her mental telepathy multiplying the effect. Tavishien was playing for keeps.

"When you finish your evening, just leave these clothes we loaned you here, the hotel will handle them for us."

"Thank you, I appreciate you responding so rapidly," Agent Lucika said.

"Marti, you always do a great job of working with us and it's been highly mutually beneficial. The least I could do is pay back some of the nice things you have done for us in the past."

"It was my pleasure."

"You two should leave now if you are going to the Grand Dining Hall as it will be getting crowded soon. We'll clean up after you leave."

"Thank you I appreciate this," Marti said then held out his hand to Tavishien who was wearing some nice designer jewelry to accent her strapless creation that would make men humble on a theme from Paganini.

The two lovers made their way to the Grand Dining Hall and when they reached the Maître d', the beautiful lady said, "Marti, the manager has a reserved table for you."

"Thank you."

"Follow me please."

The Maître d' led the couple to what was one of the best seats in the Rico Resort Grand Dining Hall with an unobscured view of the musicians performing very pleasant dinner music. Tavishien noticed there was an open spot that was obviously for dancing later in the evening.

A waiter was standing by their table as instructed by the Manager and immediately took their drink requests and went about getting them promptly.

The ambience was set and Tavishien quickly noticed a lot of men staring at her. Her first impression having spent a great portion of her life with the Tomlars back in the forest was the entire herd appeared to be in heat.

Once Tavishien realized she was the center of attraction and used her mental telepathy on some nearby men to confirm it, her personal psyche was uplifted feeling the tremendous pleasure the men felt for her. Her own feelings were that if she made them happy tonight with her appearance then she would be glad to make their evening better.

No doubt some of the old hags sitting next to their drooling husbands might not have been so pleased and she had no intention of probing their minds because she wasn't in the mood for negativity now that she was with her prince charming, and love was in the air.

The conversation between Tavishien and Garratt Wyclaire was simple and friendly. It seemed they were both feeling great relief that they had saved this special love from destruction due to the elements they lived by. Garratt knew his day tomorrow would be filled with some extremely stressful moments when he and his boss would be sitting facing each other in a rather tumultuous manner because of all the potential implications of what was transpiring tonight.

Garratt Wyclaire knew there was a distinct possibility he had been under surveillance the entire time he left the Intelligence Bureau Campus. He was no fool. But he also understood the facts of life. If his superior wanted to disrupt his evening it would have happened by now. Garratt asked himself, "*I wonder why he's leaving me alone?*

In due time their entrées were served, and the food was delicious. After spending time at the fishing village, Tavishien was more than ready to enjoy the works of a world class chef. She enjoyed her meal greatly and even though it had been a while since she went through etiquette and manners training, she retained most of it and even though she was a Frontier's Woman with very little exposure to high society, she was able to conduct herself as if she was from the upper crust of society. Tavishien's wardrobe and designer jewelry put on the exclamation point.

Tonight, unlike many times before Tavishien did not woof down her food. She deliberately took her time working every spare moment on her true love Garratt. She wanted to give so much of herself to him. But she also knew she played a dangerous game because Garratt Wyclaire was a consummate spy trained to wear the best poker faces and without her special access via mental telepathy, she would never know if Garratt was just playing a game like they do in the spy business. The honeypot trap works both ways.

Society rarely knows how many female spies get turned into double agents because they too become victims of honeypot schemes from men who lie to them and break their hearts when they discover the brutal truth, often behind bars in custody of people who betrayed them worked for.

By the time they finished eating and the table was cleared off and tablecloth changed with a fresh clean one, the music was shifting from dinner music to entertainment that would soon be ushering couples out onto that dance floor to allow them to mingle and mesmerize their dates in a variety of manners.

When Ljótunn bon Swartzler discovered Tavishien was alone with Agent Lucika, this did not appear like a mission. It was something different. If it was a clandestine mission, there would be a dozen other people here including Gabriel and IBRs like Tristan Karjal. Being an intuitive woman, Ljótunn bon Swartzler perceived this to be a lover's tryst.

This was the big deal, and Ljótunn bon Swartzler's heart went out to Tavishien as she knew much about her and her past. Rising from the ashes of a disaster to this lovely creature groomed into one of the world's best fashion models at meteoric velocities, impressed Ljótunn bon Swartzler greatly. There was now an added ingredient into the preparation of Tavishien.

It's well known in the spy business that women involved in honey pot traps or homosexuals also used, perfumes and colons are developed that release massive amounts of pheromones and if the person is nearby while the wearer is shedding those pheromones, it has an incredible inducement to the libido and makes the honey pot trap more successful.

Tonight, Tavishien's benefactor, Ljótunn bon Swartzler had Tavishien drenched in this pheromone shedding perfume that was high in pheromones but not overwhelming in scent. The recipient of this biological attack would simply smell the perfume as any ordinary perfume and not obnoxious as would be the case of a working girl.

The dancing started and when a slow dance was performed by the musicians, Garratt asked Tavishien "Would you like to dance?"

"I would love to."

Garratt's watchers in the crowd who would later put in their report as to their persons of interest were almost aghast at the incredible beauty of Tavishien. There was no doubt that Agent Lucika was on shaky ground with his superiors as they watched the couple go onto the dance floor. The Intelligence Bureau watchers also had body cameras on them filming it all. Before Garratt managed to get Tavishien in bed that night, his boss was already looking over the eye candy.

While they were slow dancing, and Garratt had his face up to Tavishien's ear he whispered, "I love you."

Tavishien knew he meant every word of it because at this close approximation of their brains her mental telepathy worked most efficiently as it could. Tavishien's probing gave her assurances Garratt's emotions truly matched his words. Tavishien had an uncontrollable body reaction and grabbed Garratt real tight. He felt it and his emotions were now driven into overload. It was an incredible journey he was now facing and the ugly duckling that turned into the beautiful swan just swooned him and all his ego. The two spies were now in a rarefied emotional bond that would serve them well into the future.

After a few more dances, Tavishien suggested they go back to the penthouse which Garratt was more than happy to accommodate. Soon they were two lovers in bed enjoying celestial feasts and the transcendence into passionate love making totally disregarding tomorrow because during this moment they could care if tomorrow came as they held each other in a fantastic love grip.

After their lovemaking they laid there regaining their strength that was totally depleted in the grandest physical exercise neither had experienced before like this. Garratt's emotions sequentially intensified repeatedly because Tavishien was giving everything she had. This was her special moment in her life, and she would give the last ounce of her energy to celebrate the love of her life.

Tavishien's actions multiplied Garratts lust and gratification. Even though desire is always many times stronger inducement than gratification. Tonight, those feelings were in total balance as there could never be without such a unique bonding of passions leading to this foray into activity and resplendence.

As they slowly recoiled from this magnificent energy drain, they eased into a casual conversation unlike the two had ever experienced with each other before. In bed and as lovers they were communicating on equal terms and Garratt knew one thing, he just failed miserably as a spy because Tavishien had hooked him better than any honey pot scheme ever devised.

He didn't mind what she had accomplished in seducing him and, in a way, it was refreshing because he knew she did it out of love and kindness. There was no turning back with Tavishien now as Garratt knew the obvious. If he didn't play ball with her, she would simply return to the fishing village or go somewhere else including possibly Tartarland to research her mother and one of the most important assets SIS had would be irrevocably lost forever.

At the same time, Garratt loved Tavishien unlike any emotions he ever felt for any other woman. She was intoxicating to him and worse than a narcotic now. He knew he was hooked for the rest of his life and there were no medications for subsequent withdrawal symptoms if there were to be any.

Garratt also had a huge disadvantage now. He knew a couple things. Tomorrow morning when he faced his boss, it would be a tumultuous moment as they go through the drill of figuring out where they stand and what's in store for the future. The boss will of course be glad his remote viewer is back just in time as things were heating up with the Tartars at the demilitarized zone (DMZ).

But there were some questions that needed to be answered, besides this lover's tryst. Tavishien had been gone for quite a while and did her ability dim as time passed? They would have to test her right away.

The other issue now first and foremost on the agenda is the day may come sooner than anyone predicted they may have to send her behind enemy lines. Because of her absence they had no alternative to putting her through a crash training program, recovering the same areas she previously experienced.

One question they would seek right away is what kind of physical condition was Tavishien in? While she was in the Village, did she maintain a physical fitness regimen or would they have to start all over again, taking months to get her back into fighting shape?

The conversation between Tavishien and Garratt lasted until they each decided it was time to hop in the shower and deal with all the sweat they generated in their physical rendezvous of passions on a theme from Paganini.

Something along the lines of newlyweds, the two were soon enjoying the shower together kissing, hugging, and enjoying each other's presence in untold levels of satisfaction.

In due time they dried off and changed into sleeping clothes set out for them by the valet butler and maid.

On this night back in the forest the Tomlars were all huddled in the barn in their sleeping positions. Amazingly they went to their exact same spots every night as if they had reservations on that small piece of floor. Tonight, the Tomlars were focusing on Tavishien. They loved her like she was one of their own.

The Tomlars remote viewed Tavishien love making with Garratt. Every one of them was exceedingly happy Tavishien found love and with their interest spiked, they observed her all night long. None of them could sleep. When Tavishien snored, it was just like she was at home with her father. The noise was music to their ears. And when Garratt snored it was harmonizing the effects just like Tavishien's mother used to do with her father.

It was not until very early in the morning before the Tomlars could sleep and they did, a very restful and pleasant sleep with dreams of their own created by their princess Tavishien.

In the morning Tavishien and Garratt dressed in the clothes they arrived in and were pleasantly surprised to discover they were dry cleaned and put in the closet which the Butler announced while they were having breakfast by room service.

After freshening up, the two new love birds were outside the Rico Resort front entrance and with astute timing, a Skycar came down to pick them up with Gabriel in the Skycar as a registered driver who could take them to the Intelligence Bureau Campus.

Before they got into the Skycar, Garratt said, "Tavishien, please never forget I do love you."

"I know you do, and I will always love you Garratt."

"Thank you."

The two hugged very strongly as if it was the most important moment in their life. Gabriel saw it all.

Upon arrival to the Campus, Gabriel said, "Agent Lucika, I'm going to take Tavishien to her dormitory room. We'll be there when you want to meet with us to give us our assignments this morning."

"Thank you. I don't know what it is yet, I'm sure I have a few meetings I must attend and then we'll figure it all out."

They split up and Garratt went to his office to face the fire. He had no idea how this was all going to work out. But he knew he had done two things at once. He tasted the forbidden fruit, when he *dipped his pen in company ink* and fell in love.

Agent Lucika (aka Garratt) knew he had failed as a spy by allowing his emotions to control events instead of his logic. This exposed a huge flaw in him. He was ready for the instant demotion and possible removal which would also include he would be forbidden to ever seek out Tavishien again.

If they did what he feared, she would be placed off limits, and they would sanction him if he ever violated his orders. He figured the easiest way they would deal with him would be to send him off to some colony planet where his opportunity to ever see Tavishien again would be eliminated.

As soon as Agent Lucika walked into his office area, his secretary said,

"Agent Lucika, the director is in the conference room waiting for you."

It was all starting now. In a few minutes he would know his fate. And it may not be pleasant. The last thing in the world he wanted now would be to permanently leave Tavishien. Not only would it break her heart, but he knew his own as well.

With sullen graveness and expectations of a very negative moment, Agent Lucika dutifully walked into the conference room, and there he was, none other than the director himself.

"Please shut the door."

Agent Lucika shut the door then walked over to the table and sat down directly across from the Director who was wearing his typical poker face. Agent Lucika had no way to read him or even a clue what was in store.

"I see you found Tavishien and brought her back."

"Yes, I did, sir."

"Good."

There was a long delay before the next words were spoken as the two looked at each other in a level of preponderance.

"Since you are a spy, you of all people should know we have no choice but to monitor your activities."

"Yes, sir I assume that."

"Then you should know we know everything you did from the time you left the Campus to travel to and bring Tavishien back to the Campus."

"Yes sir, I'm quite aware of the probability that I was under a lot of surveillance."

"You know you crossed the limits on a number of issues."

"Yes sir, I'm well aware of that."

"What was your motivation to do so knowing we would know everything you did."

"Sometimes in our business it's hard to not become emotionally involved with our colleagues. I never suspected I would ever evolve into such a situation, but now that it's done, I'm ready to take my punishment for whatever violations you feel I did."

"Well Garratt I suppose if I were in your shoes, I would have done the same exact thing. In fact, I'm quite surprised it took this long. Had you done this a long time ago we would not have lost her capability for such a long period of time when we needed her the most."

"I'm sorry sir that I screwed up."

"Garratt why do you think I think you screwed up?"

"It's obvious to me I should never have allowed something like this to transpire."

"Garratt, things are not the way you think they are."

"What do you mean by that sir?"

"We view Tavishien's capability so important that we would have asked you to seduce her to keep her here if we knew she was going to escape."

"Are you for real, sir?"

"Garratt, especially now that the DMZ is heating up. We need Tavishien more than ever. I don't care what it took for you to get her back here. The fact you brought her back is the most important thing in this discussion."

"I'm amazed sir."

"Don't be. It is what it is. And now you must protect that asset and do whatever you have to do to make sure she doesn't leave again."

"I'll try my best."

"Okay, we need to do an assessment on her. Find out how much she decayed in her abilities while she was gone. You will have to do a crash training program but this time, she's not going to be sent against organized crime and banksters. We have no choice now but to send her to Tartarland. This will be one of the most important missions in SIS history."

"What's the mission."

"You are the only person that is to know this until we deploy her."

"Understand, sir."

"You are to plan for her to get close enough to the Tartar Tyrannical Dictator Illtnaut so that we can start remote viewing him."

"Getting her anywhere near him will be extremely dangerous."

"Even if a few IBRs must give up their lives to get Tavishien close to Illtnaut to allow future remote viewing, it's that important. Those people are no different than other casualties of war, where nothing short of victory is acceptable."

"Tavishien could lose her life in the process."

"That's another risk we have to take."

"This is actually worse than what I thought you were going to do to me."

"Sometimes there are painful episodes with people we love that cannot be avoided simply by living."

"I insist I be sent on the away team to do my part in making sure she comes back alive."

"You know because of your position and what you know, we cannot allow you the possibility of being captured."

"You can do an implant and if I do not check in via special means, you can pull the trigger and kill me, so that should not be an issue."

"I will only let you go with the implant, and I personally will be holding the trigger."

"That's all I can ask of you sir."

"Don't let your love for Tavishien cause this mission to be aborted. If you attempt to come back before we get Tavishien close to Illtnaut, I will personally pull the trigger."

"I assure you sir; I will take it all the way even if it costs me my life."

"I know you would. You have often taken it to a razor's edge of your own demise."

"Once she reads Illtnaut, will you ever deploy her again?"

"I promise you if you get her there and she comes back here and can do the remote viewing, we'll never separate you two love birds again, nor put her ever in a dangerous situation again. Her remote viewing of Illtnaut is more important than anything else we could possibly have her do. Keeping her safe so she can do that will be our priority. I also understand her mental health also depends on you being with her. We will provide the two of you with cover so that you can continue your relationship in private, but you need to explain to Tavishien, she's not to expose that while here on the Campus. I will have to send the two of you on a lot of *missions* together off Campus so that you will have quality time together."

"I appreciate that, sir."

"Go spend some private time with Tavishien and explain all that to her. Your first mission is to go retrain her on operating all those devices you did in the past. But no live weapons exercises, we can't afford to risk her in any way."

"Sure, we'll only use simulated weapons."

"Good. Your travel arrangements will be made soon. Enjoy the rest of the day with her. Take her some place far away from the Campus."

"I know exactly where to go."

"I will be talking to you tomorrow as we figure out the training schedule."

"Alright."

Agent Lucika soon left the conference room and walked past his secretary who was smiling as she knew something was up. He went into his office and contacted Tavishien on her personal communicator.

"Hello." Tavishien said as she saw the caller's I.D. indicated Agent Lucika (aka Garratt).

"Hi there Tavishien. I have got some good news for you. We have the rest of the day off and I want to take you someplace."

"Where do you have in mind?"

"Dress casually because I'm going to take you to a tourist attraction where we can spend the day and have a good time."

"Sure, no problem."

"How soon do you think you will be ready?"

"Give me thirty minutes."

"Alright, meet me at the Skycar parking lot right where we arrived a short while ago, when you are ready."

"Will do."

Gabriel looked at Tavishien and was worried for her as she knew the SIS could come down hard on her and 'Garratt Wyclaire,' for crossing over the line and developing a personal relationship. She knew Tavishien spent the night with Garratt, probably had a romance and was extremely vulnerable right now. If Garratt's boss wanted to be a prick right now, Tavishien would have her heart ripped out of her with no recourse.

"Are you going somewhere?"

"Yes, Garratt is taking me to some kind of tourist attraction."

Gabriel was trying to second guess what that was all about and knew there was a fifty percent chance that Agent Lucika's boss ordered him to discontinue the relationship, and this was going to be the swan song. Gabriel almost wanted to cry but she didn't want to give away her fears.

"Do you need any help getting ready?"

"No, I know what I need to do. Remember I'm well trained in makeup and preparing myself."

"You have been gone a while; you might have forgot a lot."

"No, I remember it all quite well and when Ljótunn bon Swartzler's people fixed me up last night, I knew exactly everything they were doing and why. I didn't forget any of it."

"Alright Tavishien, I'll leave you and let you get ready. Maybe I'll see you when you leave."

"Be outside my door in 30 minutes because that's exactly when I'm leaving."

"Alright Tavishien, I'll be here, and I wish you the best."

"Thanks."

Gabriel grabbed Tavishien and hugged her and said, "I'm glad you are back. I did miss you."

"Thanks, I missed you too."

Gabriel was glad to leave right then and there because she knew until this all played out, she felt nervous as to what was Tavishien's destiny. Gabriel had come to like her quite a bit after time passed. She was the real deal and one of the few women she truly respected because of what she had done in her life and what she experienced to get to the Intelligence Bureau Campus.

Tavishien swung into high gear as soon as Gabriel was out the door, and in thirty minutes, she was not a plane Jane modestly dressed. She intended on making Garratt whimper, so she dressed to be smoking hot, just like she did at the military base when she was doing the Terrain Follower training and seduced Garratt.

Tavishien was an excellent makeup artist and proved she didn't forget any of it during her long sojourn to the remote village.

Tavishien's dress was far from being 'Casual.' She looked smoking hot, and would no doubt get a few looks and a few married men would get an elbow into the ribs today when their wives caught them spending too much time idolizing this living princess.

With the extraordinary tan, sun bleached hair, professional makeup and clothing that exemplified the essence of grandeur, even though it was not formal attire, Tavishien was ready to go do her magic on Garratt. He was her conquest and if any other woman entered the picture, she would quickly regret it because they had never met a ruthless spy like Tavishien who would do just about anything for something of such importance to her.

Since some other woman would have no idea how deadly Tavishien could be, they would make a huge mistake getting in Tavishien's way once she was committed to achieve her goals. And her number one goal right now was Garratt. She focused on that goal like a laser. Nice and sharp and to the point.

And there they were right at the 30-minute mark just like military precision. Gabriel was astonished. Gabriel understood vividly by studying other women as part of her job, the attention to detail Tavishien proved she was capable of. *Garratt will melt in her arms.*

"Would you like me to walk you to the parking lot?"

"Why not. You will get to see the look on Garratt's face."

"I can almost predict what it will be."

"Did I do a good job in preparing?"

"Women could spend all day getting ready and not produce what you just did in 30 minutes. You truly are remarkable."

"Thank you, but remember I had a lot of good training."

"Since I got to see you in action a time or two, I know how great your training was."

"It's too bad you didn't get to see me fly the Terrain Follower."

"I'm sure you rocked and socked them."

"I pushed it to the limit because one day it may save my life."

"In this business, I do not doubt you."

The women promptly arrived at the parking lot and a Skycar was there waiting for them. Agent Lucika (aka Garratt) stepped out of the Skycar to greet Tavishien and saw Gabriel accompany her. He suspected Gabriel knew the depth of their relationship, especially when she announced to Gabriel his real name. How she discovered that is something he would one day want to know, even though it really didn't matter much since Tavishien was tight lipped and a loner.

Just as Gabriel suspected, observing Garratt's body language she quickly knew vividly his reaction to the eye candy Tavishien underscored the reaction Garratt experienced upon glancing at this glamorously attractive woman.

There was a seriousness to his image, and he was composed with a lot of solemnity. *Perhaps his affection for Tavishien runs deeper and stronger than I imagined*, Gabriel thought.

"I'm going to let you go now. Good luck and have fun."

"Thanks for walking me to the Skycar. I have less butterflies."

"Any time Tavishien, that's what combat sisters are for."

The two women smiled, and Gabriel turned and walked back towards the Campus where she would go about her business.

"You look great," Garratt said and smiled.

"Thank you, you don't look so bad yourself," Tavishien responded.

"This is my personal Skycar, not the agency's so we'll take it with us and come back tomorrow and start working again."

"Sounds good to me, let's go have some fun."

The couple were soon in the Skycar traveling to one of Garratt's favorite destinations. He didn't go there very often because it brought back sad memories for him. The only woman that came close to giving him the emotional bond like Tavishien now created, was taken suddenly away from him. That permanent loss of a love left gaping holes in his heart, which made him the reluctant lover. Garratt didn't know that he would ever have gotten over the tragic loss of such a beautiful woman, a medical doctor as well, had it not been for Tavishien's secret manipulation of him through her telepathic ability.

Tavishien didn't quite know what caused that lingering sadness within Garratt, but she surmised it was the result of a broken heart. Each encounter with Tavishien, the fond memories of a bygone love slowly dulled and at this moment in time, seemed to hardly exist.

Garratt knew he might suffer some sadness going to his favorite place because it might cause those memories, he wanted to bury to pop back in his present psyche. But it was a risk he was willing to take because somehow, Garratt knew Tavishien would help him get over it quickly. There was no time to be melancholy since their futures were filled with vast dangers because of the business they were in.

The journey in the Skycar took about 30 minutes traveling the high-speed freeway in the sky navigated with precision by a system that tracked the Skycar via a transponder that continuously updated position information derived from satellite navigation.

Soon they were landing in a Skycar slot designated by the Black Diamond Resort Hotel where Garratt had reservations, but they had some tourist fun things to do before they planned delving into celestial feasts and gourmet love making.

"We are going to check into a penthouse, then after we freshen up, I'm going to take you on a little side trip," Garratt said.

"Whatever you wish to do, I'm sure I'll like it," Tavishien responded.

After meeting the butler and the maid to the penthouse and freshening up, Garratt surprised Tavishien and the two resort employees, "While we are gone some fashion designers and technicians may arrive before we get back. Please invite them in and give them refreshments. We should be back around the time they arrive so they should not have to wait long."

"May I ask sir, the name of the fashion designer?" The butler asked.

"It will be Ljótunn bon Swartzler and her associates."

"Alright Mr. Wyclaire, we will make sure they are comfortable if they arrive before you get back."

"Thank you."

Tavishien was quite surprised to learn Garratt had booked the Penthouse with his personal name. *Maybe he used his name here in the past?*

Adjacent to the resort was where Garratt wanted to take Tavishien. He would soon determine if he had successfully buried the wounds of the loss of the greatest love of his life until he met Tavishien. Tavishien's presence was therapeutic. This truly was the start of a new journey in life and the past was the past he could now bury. He knew from his training in psychology there were two thought processes done by leading researchers in the field. Some felt it was best to bring out the issue into the open and heal and deal with it.

The other side of the coin was the belief in out of sight and out of mind. Bury the past and move on. Garratt looked forward to out of sight and out of mind and somehow felt Tavishien would be the catalyst to help him succeed.

A short walking distance from the Black Diamond Resort was Garratt's destination where he would show Tavishien the top of the world. A cog train went up the side of Mount Black Diamond. This mountain obtained its name because of the extremely rare and exotic black diamonds found in the creek beds on the other side of the mountain from where the Resort was located.

The resort side of the mountain was plush and beautiful. The same could not be said for portions of the other side of the mountain where spoils from former mining operations peppered the landscape. Since the entire Black Mountain area had turned into a privately held resort area, the scars of the former mining operations deteriorated when no traces except in the riverbeds of the black diamonds could be found.

Miners lost huge amounts of wealth thinking the black diamonds came from the mountain, but after numerous mining attempts failed to discover any significant trace of black diamonds, the black diamonds mining enterprise collapsed and only a few meager prospecting remained mining the riverbed which was problematic due to high water levels nine months out of the year.

Soon Garratt obtained tickets for the cog train and the lovely couple was on their way up the long trip to the top of this huge mountain that stood over 14,000 feet tall. The mountain peak was 10,000 feet, almost two miles above the Black Diamond Resort in height.

The red painted cog train cars were well maintained, and the seats were at an angle since most of the journey was up the side of the mountain often moving five miles per hour but never over 10 miles per hour as the cog mechanism could only obtain slow speeds or the vibrations would be unbearable and unsafe.

Going up the mountain in the red cog train cars was a wonderful experience. On each side of the train was picturesque landscape that society rarely had opportunity to see unless they experienced such trips. It was spring green outside that added to the overall ambience. Everyone on the train appeared happy and thrilled to experience the majestic scenery.

A variety of types of trees and plants provided a breathtaking view. Soon they spotted the first sight of some of the wild animals that occupied the wide open countryside. In pockets of open areas surrounded by majestic trees were four legged critters eating grass and plant life that abound in the forested area.

Some creatures they observed were dangerous and could easily kill people, but they were protected because the passengers in the tram train were up in the air and protected by strong steel walls of the cog train cars.

Tavishien didn't need to look at the forest. She lived in one most of her life in the sheer wilderness. She enjoyed her time often looking at the wonderful man sitting next to her. She knew he had many scars from the dirty work of a spy but also of a broken heart.

It would be an awkward relationship as Garratt would never be able to hide his deepest secrets from Tavishien and he didn't know it nor would he ever as she wisely understood such revelation would complicate her life and possibly put herself in peril as she wisely understood in this vicious business of the world of espionage, they would view her combined remote viewing and telepathic abilities to be a huge threat. As such she knew the Intelligence Bureau would briskly dispose of her if they discovered all her talents. Tavishien understood what goes with such secrets also is the necessity to keep such matters her own deep secret, to be kept even from Garratt.

Whatever anxiety Garratt had getting on the cog train that might surface his memories and his psychological wounds, seemed to slowly ease off as his enjoyment of Tavishien quickly obscured all his other thoughts of the past. Tavishien was like fresh air to Garratt.

Tavishien and Garratt had been through a lot together and Tavishien had proven each step of the way, Garratts investment into Tavishien paid off handsomely.

And now here Tavishien was slowly becoming the love of his life. Satisfaction and gratification permeated Garratts soul each and every time he looked at Tavishien who was now applying some of the techniques taught her by Madam Ljótunn bon Swartzler: *keep smiling no matter how hard it hurts*.

Tavishien slowly stroked Garratt's ego and intensified his satisfaction as she put manipulative efforts into the pleasure center of Garratt's brain.

Garratt felt as good as some people who underwent exorcism to cast out the demons in their lives. His former lover would be amused at how quickly this young savage woman from the forest nullified any residual emotions she had bequeathed him. She also had no idea the success Garratt had in his life so casting him aside for bigger fish in the sea may have been a misguided decision as she clearly underestimated where he could take his life.

The cog train up to the top of the mountain took quite a while because as part of the trip, they slow down and stop to allow passengers to film some of the wildlife they encountered easily doubling the time it took to reach the very top of Mount Black Diamond. But once they reached the top, there was a nice restaurant and gift shop where they could get a snack and buy a few momentos.

After obtaining seats in the restaurant Tavishien settled for fresh baked cookies, a bowl of ice cream and Garratt followed suit.

The eight-foot-tall glass windows gave them an excellent view which allowed them to see fifty miles off in the distance.

"Nice view from up here," Tavishien said.

"Yes, it is," Garratt responded and smiled.

The two lovers knew this was the calm before the storm. Every day was precious and someday soon they could be sent in opposite directions doing dangerous work and one day, one of them might not come back. That's how it is in the spy business where things are unpredictable, and it's not always your lucky day.

Tavishien saw the Cog train depart and Garratt saw the look of anguish on her face as if they just missed their ride home, so he offered, "There is a different train coming back about every thirty minutes."

"That's good to know because after we have our snack, I want to look through those telescopes they have over at the observation window."

"Sounds good."

The snacks were served and the two didn't waste much time eating them and they did hit the spot. Soon they were over at the observation telescopes inside the building under a roof with a plate glass window in front of them.

"Why are these telescopes inside the building?"

"We are up high, 14,000 feet and storms go over all the time, almost every day. This is to prevent lightning strikes. That's the reason why the cog train went into the terminal building to let passengers out and prevent lightning strike casualties."

Before they left the mountain top restaurant and gift shop, they did see a few lightning strikes nearby and the thunder was quite apparent. The public had no access outside the building for their own protection.

This was a moment of happiness for Tavishien because she enjoyed her time with Garratt who was so nice and kind to her. But she also had something she utilized and that was her ability to probe his mind to discover his real feelings. Tavishien knew the truth about many of Garratts secrets which she could never address without exposing she could read his mind. But one thing she absolutely knew that gave her a feeling of safety and happiness was Garratt's emotional bond to her.

This romance was the real deal and Tavishien understood how other women felt about these matters because she also intruded into the thoughts of gawkers who laid their eyes on this beautiful couple. Because of Tavishien's exemplary vision into her romantic tryst Garratt, she was able to discover the sad truth of life. Half of the couples that got near them were not happy about their partners.

Half of the women she encountered and snooped in their thoughts were in a marriage they were stuck in with no way out. And because of those feelings Tavishien also detected anger and spite in some women who were obviously stuck with losers or men who did not treat them well.

The sight of this lovely couple full of smiles and happiness triggered some irrational emotions in some of these women who had negative responses because Tavishien was flaunting what they severely missed out on by choosing the wrong partner. Life is a crap shoot, and their dice didn't come up with the right numbers.

Tavishien also knew something those angry old hags didn't know. This love of her life could be ripped out of her hands at any moment because of the business they were in. Tavishien and Garratt were living on borrowed time, and Tavishien knew it.

Tavishien's forbearance in possible outcomes is why she intended to make the most of it in case she unexpectedly lost Garratt or worse yet, she could become a casualty in the undeclared secret war of espionage.

After spending time looking over the area through the telescopes it was time to spend some time in the gift shop. There Tavishien picked up three items. One to give to Gabriel, the other to Garratt and one for herself to use to remember this glorious journey with the love of her life.

Right after paying for the gifts, they headed out of the gift shop just as another cog train was arriving with a new batch of people with smiles on their faces.

"Looks like we can go back to the Resort on this train," Garratt said as the two approached it.

They soon climbed aboard after the crowd disembarked off the train leaving it wide open for those wishing to return. They found two seats on the opposite side of the train they came up on.

Garratt purposely had Tavishien sit next to the window so she could really enjoy the view but at the same time he could observe and enjoy the view of her as he knew this was a special moment in his life. Falling in love with such a rare woman, far different than anyone he met in his lifetime. Since Garratt was with Tavishien from the very first days after her brutal attack by the six Tartar soldiers.

Garratt knew all there was to know about Tavishien. The surveillance on Tavishien had been enormous and Garratt saw it all. The only lapse was the time Tavishien escaped and eluded the trackers and made her way to the fishing village where she hid out for a while. *Did she somehow signal to me where she was so that I would beg her to come back?* If that was the case, he's glad she did.

Garratt personally took full responsibility for Tavishien leaving. In his soul searching, Garratt decided that had he not been such a coward and put his career ahead of her, she would not have departed the way she did, seemingly brokenhearted. Garratt knew he could never make it up to Tavishien for his deplorable conduct, but from this day forward, he would handle matters completely different as he had elevated her as top in his priorities.

There was one huge rub in all this. He knew the showdown was coming. His superiors wanted her to tag some enemies and remote view them. Their number one target would always be Tartarland's Tyrannical Dictator Illtnaut. In all her days working for the Intelligence Bureau, the mission to Tartarland to get near Illtnaut would be her most dangerous assignment in her life.

Garratt knew it was only a matter of time before the decision to go forward on that mission was directed at him to initiate. He also knew after today it was business as usual; training just like in the past that would encompass all the tools of the trade Tavishien needed refresher training.

Riding the cog train down the side of the mountain, observing all the flora, including numerous purple flowers and spring green lifted everyone's spirits. It was a spectacular view with lots to cherish and remember.

Tavishien had a second satisfaction, her lover Garratt was purring like a kitten. She felt every vibration and she was going to soon reward him for his conduct. The day was just getting started for a memory Garratt would always have.

As the Cog Train slowly wound its way down the side of the mountain sometimes going in 'S' patterns and in a couple spots due to the terrain, there were bridges that passed over track down lower they would soon loop back around on. A couple of small tunnels existed that created a nice effect because when they exited the tunnels they were suddenly in a picturesque view. A waterfall soon painted the landscape and nearby in an open area a dozen Tomlar-like animals grazed with no care in the world having seen the Cog train thousands of times.

Eventually they reached the station and disembarked.

"Let's go back to the Resort so you can drop off your items you purchased, then we can walk around the village and do some sightseeing."

"Alright."

Walking through the lobby it all hit Garratt. There they were waiting for him. He should have known his travels would be watched since he was the caretaker for one of their prize possessions, a *remote viewer*.

No matter how great they worked at their disguises, as a master spy, it was a sixth sense that Garratt had. But now he had further sensitivity he never imagined before nor did he know what was happening. As they walked through the lobby and Garratt spotted the watchers, he didn't know Tavishien was reading his mind because he didn't know she was also a mind reader and she soon participated in quantifying the level of surveillance on them.

She used her remote viewer and mental telepathy to unmask every single one of the watchers in the lobby. Each one of them had a weird sensation which they reported back later to their superiors who concluded somehow every one of them had been tagged. That was now an extremely complicated problem for them because if Tavishien succeeded in tagging every one of the surveillance team, that meant they could never do a covert trail on her and if she ever decided to skip town again, she could in fact lose them just as easy as she did once before.

Suddenly Garratt's role in this enterprise suddenly elevated. He was the common denominator; Garratt was their only means of retaining Tavishien's services. In a way it saved his life and his career because it would now be impossible to remove him or dispose of him. He had no idea how much leverage Tavishien now had.

But since Garratt (aka Agent Lucika) was a great team player, his boss had no concern and the fact he was banging the Intelligence Bureau's primary *remote viewer* was not an issue unless he tried to leave her. He was stuck with Tavishien whether he liked it or not, because Tavishien was more important to future operations than Garratt's life.

Unfortunately, in the espionage business there are casualties and sometimes they had to sacrifice the best when the stakes were high.

***

CHAPTER EIGHTEEN

Dinner At the Black Mountain Resort

Garratt knew he had a couple hours to burn before his discrete fashion designer and her team would be showing up to doll up Tavishien. He thought he had enough time to take Tavishien around the local village that supported the needs of the Black Diamond Resort, but Tavishien had other ideas. Even though the Tartars destroyed her uterus, it had no bearing on her cyclical female anatomy. To add to her emotional spike that unfolded with this lover's tryst with Garratt, her biological rhythm was synchronized creating a temporal menagerie she wanted to act upon.

Upon arrival the butler assisted in taking Tavishien's shopping bags and positioning them at a convenient spot out of sight and asked, "Can I get you something to drink?"

Garratt thinking, they would be leaving soon responded, "I don't think so."

Tavishien surprised Garratt by responding, "I'm kind of thirsty. If you don't mind, I would like a Gæsaber elixir."

Garratt suddenly figuring his timeline was now altered then said, "If she's going to have a drink, I wouldn't mind having a Kanill Grasker elixir."

"It will be my pleasure to bring your drinks, Mr. Wyclaire and Madam Tavishien, I'll have your drinks ready in a moment," and left the room.

Tavishien with an evil grin on her face walked over to the padded sofa and sat down looking at Garratt who had a look of inquiry on his face. He followed her lead and sat down on the sofa next to her. Knowing the butler would be back in a few moments neither person initiated any intimate contact. But they did look into each other's eyes and smiled exposing their pleasant feelings.

"Did you like the train ride?"

"Yes, I loved every minute of it and thank you for taking me."

"It was my pleasure."

Tavishien didn't need to bring up the watchers in the lobby because she knew Garratt had a full handle on the matter and why spoil a moment of satisfaction?

"I like the way you look today," Garratt said in a pleasing fashion.

"I did it for you. I hoped you would like it."

"Very much so."

"Your fashion experts trained me well."

"I can see that."

The butler appeared with a tray and their drinks and served them and afterwards said, "If you want anything else just ask for the 'butler' and artificial intelligence will notify me to come to assist."

"Thank you. I think this will be all for a while."

"My pleasure sir." The Butler then bowed and left the room, closing the door behind him.

"Toast to you," Garratt said as he held up his glass, and Tavishien followed his actions, and they tapped glasses and took a nice big gulp. These elixirs were fully fortified for the effects the inventors wanted. On the first swallow alone, they were having their remarkable effects, but Tavishien was having another feeling that exceeded anything the elixir could offer.

Tavishien was hoping Garratt would make the first move because she would feel more gratified if he did. Any hesitation on Garratt's part would soon be modified by Tavishien's mental telepathy.

Garratt didn't understand fully why he was doing what he was doing, but he suddenly had the urge to kiss Tavishien. It was like something was in his brain saying, "kiss her fool."

Tavishien looked so good, and the stimulation of the elixir added to the effect. Garratt took another long sip of his drink and sat it down on the coaster the butler left behind, then slowly and carefully took the drink out of Tavishien's hand, and sat it down on the coffee table next to his.

Garratt reached out and softly touched the side of Tavishien's head and gently pulled her face closer to his as he was approaching her to do what his brain was telling him, "Kiss her you fool."

Tavishien expected all this since part of it was her manipulation. And as they grew close, she opened her mouth to take a kiss that Garratt would give her in a magical moment. Love flowed and passions transcended into a new dimension as time and space soon had no relevance as this glorious moment created ensembles of vibrations in Garratts heart. His kiss was passionate and deliberate and Tavishien engulfed it all enjoying every micro-second of it as just as time lapsed photography, the magical moment was stretched out to a short eternity.

Without knowing how they arrived there, Garratt's next moment of reality came when he suddenly realized he was in bed with Tavishien furling his manliness into her with the rhythm and frequency of his heartbeats. The synchronization was perfect and moments later the emotions exploded as the gratification multiplied the effects of the mental tornado now unleashing gratification in the pleasure center of Garratt's brain.

Garratt never had an orgasm anywhere like this in his lifetime. He never had real love like this before where he intuitively knew the woman loved him more than anything in her life. The fulfillment of such a *tumultuous allegros* left reverberations in Garratt's heart to where his emotions were flooded with cascading harmonics.

Garratt could die at this very moment because his life goals were more than fulfilled with this magical passage into a dimension of love Garratt didn't know existed had Tavishien not unlocked it with her secret abilities.

Soon as the love making was done, all Garratt wanted to do was hold Tavishien in his arms and soon there she was with her head on his chest as he softly and repeatedly kissed the top of her head as they slowly spun down from the alternate universe and magical dimensions. There was no need to talk. Tavishien and Garratt just wanted to cherish the moment of fulfillment of dreams and aspirations.

In fifteen or twenty minutes, the moment of silence slowly came to an end as small talk emerged. Tavishien took the time to inform Garratt, "The Tomlars are all happy that I feel so much love."

"Maybe someday I would like to go to the cabin with you and visit the Tomlars."

"They would enjoy you. Whether you know it or not since I love you, that makes you part of their family."

Tavishien could not see it because her face was on Garratt's chest, but she didn't need to because she could feel it through her mental telepathy. She knew tears were now going down the sides of Garratts cheeks. She had touched him in ways no other had in his lifetime, for that he would be forever grateful.

Tavishien's gratification was multiplied by this passage of time where the emotions poured out. These quintessential emotions were inescapable. The two had transcended to a unique situation because their unique journey through life intersected the way it did.

Tavishien purposely didn't move because she didn't want Garratt to know she knew he had cried. But she knew those were tears of joy sprinkled with unbelievable stress. No man had ever gone through what Garratt had to get to this moment in life. He paid his dues like no other. And what upset him the most was he had no choice, those watchers in the lobby were a harsh reminder to him, he would be forced to deploy Tavishien behind enemy lines and God help him if something happened to her. And God help those who hurt her.

After Garratt regained his composure, he said, "I scheduled Ljótunn bon Swartzler to come here and fix us up for tonight's activities. We need to get up and get ready because they will be arriving in a while."

"Sure, I don't mind dressing up for you tonight for the way you pleased me today."

"I hope I dress up nice enough to please you as well."

"Garratt you are a very handsome man. I'm sure I will love the way you look."

"Thank you."

After they were dressed and back out into their living room of the Penthouse, Garratt said, "Butler, please come here."

Moments later the butler arrived and ask, "What can I do for you sir?"

"Will you have the maid remake our bed and get us fresh drinks."

"It will be my delight sir."

Soon the loving couple were again sitting on the sofa as the maid came through all smiling because she suspected, Tavishien just received the big "A" and she was happy for the beautiful woman with the handsome man.

Shortly after the butler took the stale drinks away and replaced them with fresh drinks, the maid announced, "Your bed has been remade and I'll be standing by to assist in any manner required."

"Thank you," Tavishien answered before Garratt could get out a response.

The two lovebirds simmered their passions and cooled themselves off with the elixirs that refueled their composure and created great feelings that glazed the *tumultuous allegros* they just completed.

The small talk didn't last long before the Butler came into the room to announce, "Excuse me Mr. Wyclaire, your fashion designer, Ljótunn bon Swartzler and her staff have arrived."

"Please show them in."

A moment later they all came into the living room and took charge of their two subjects and took them to separate bathrooms to bathe and prepare them for the fashion makeover.

Ljótunn bon Swartzler knew this was a special night for Tavishien because she had complete confidence that Garratt Wyclaire had deflowered Tavishien and was now in love with her. Ljótunn bon Swartzler was going to do her almighty best to dress up Tavishien better than any movie star wished to be presented. As such she had a newly designed gown that was pre-tailored to Tavishien's figure since she had all her measurements. She also brought along some expensive jewelry to add an element of luster to the princess she would create tonight.

Garratt would also get his due. Ljótunn bon Swartzler had her own spy network that included Gabriel who had informed her that Garratt had the hots for Tavishien and treated her very well. Ljótunn bon Swartzler would also dress Garratt to perfection to created satisfaction for Tavishien she would not likely forget.

Tonight, was a special night for Ljótunn bon Swartzler because all experiences she had gone through with the two lovers. She would thus put forth the effort like this was one of the most important fashion statements in her life. In a way it was as she intuitively knew she was mingling with two of the most important people in the Intelligence Bureau.

The technicians went to work and applied their magic as the two slowly and systematically transcended from the ordinary to the temporal exceptional appearances. When the makeup, hair style and everything else was done the two were then clothed in tonight's spectacular fashion masterpieces. It was not until they were both completely ready to walk out the door of the Penthouse on their way to the Resort Dining Hall that they were permitted to see each other.

The butler, maid, and all the fashion technicians were lined up. Ljótunn bon Swartzler first went into the spare bedroom and said, "Garratt it's now time for me to introduce you to your princess."

Ljótunn bon Swartzler marched Garratt to the end of the reception line next to the double door to the Penthouse. The butler and maid were poised next to the door to open the two doors for the couple when they left.

Ljótunn bon Swartzler then walked to the master bedroom where Tavishien was waiting and feeling very proud of the way she looked. "Alright my dear, it's time for you to go show your prince how beautiful you are."

"You have done such a great job. I feel so wonderful."

"Tavishien you are a charm to work with. You are naturally beautiful, so it helps us a lot. But your attitude is what makes it easy for us. I wish all my models were like you."

"Thank you for the nice compliment."

"It's my pleasure, my dear. Now go make that prince whimper with your beauty."

The women giggled and then Ljótunn bon Swartzler opened the door to the master bedroom and walked Tavishien down through the reception line of the technicians and the maid and butler to her prince charming almost aghast at the incredible beauty that now bequeathed this mere mortal.

"Garratt, here's you princess. Be sure and take very good care of her."

"I promise I will, I love her."

Ljótunn bon Swartzler caught Tavishien just before she was about to burst into tears and ruin the makeup and she promptly said. "Tavishien don't do it, you need to be tough and hold back those emotions. You can cry some other day, but this is your special moment and the two of you need to get down to your reserved seats right away, as there is a crowd down there tonight."

Tavishien used all her willpower and held back the emotional burst and said, "I'll be strong, but Garratt you have no idea how much I want to cry like a baby now."

"I understand, I feel the same way."

The two doors were then promptly opened by the butler and the maid, and they made their way to the Black Diamond Grand Dining Hall, where the upper crust of society was there enjoying the ambience of a five-star resort and the world's best chefs.

Artificial intelligence tracked the VIP from the penthouse down to the dining hall and the Maître d' tablet had the alert informing them who was arriving including a picture as they were currently dressed and a diagram to the reserved table they were to be seated, with an unobstructed view of the musicians and easy access to the dance floor for after dinner dancing.

Besides the candle on the table, the dozen red roses added nicely to the ambience. Other diners didn't quite have the floral arrangement, so people observing the beautiful couple knew they were VIP's, but nobody knew who the couple was, except one couple that happened to be there that night.

No other than General Taroton and Lateegely were seated in a booth across the room. It did not take them but a mere moment to spot the couple and know who they were. General Taroton planned to approach Agent Lucika (aka Garratt, aka Marty) after they finished eating their dinner and as the entertainment shifted to a dance club and thank him for a lot of things.

Without this couple training at his base, General Taroton would never know who Lateegely was or how beautiful she could be. Just like Tavishien she too had some natural beauty that coupled with a nice dress and appropriate makeup made her into a living doll as well.

The two were seated and soon served drinks with all eyes on them including the watchers who knew Garratt was one lucky character to be with such a glamorous woman and due to sophisticated surveillance equipment knew he was already knocking the rims off her tires.

With almost a photographic memory Garratt spotted the watchers and Tavishien who was always monitoring what Garratt was thinking soon was aware of every watcher in the dining hall. She also knew that Garratts thoughts included he didn't care what they reported back because Tavishien was now his woman, and the deal was done. They are a couple.

In a while their entrees were served as the musicians performed soft dinner music. The food was great and having such great taste while looking at his glorious princess gave Garratt complete satisfaction. Over many years and stretches of time, there were very few if any moments like this for Garratt. He savored the moment and his happiness flowed with his body language that was infectious to those around him.

There were a few angry women that night in the dining hall that Tavishien spotted who were irritated their husbands were infatuated with Tavishien. But there was one woman there who looked fondly at Tavishien.

Thanks to Tavishien, General Taroton unlocked his heart to Lateegely and right after his retirement ceremony, he and Lateegely would invite many unsuspecting subordinates to their wedding. This of course was being kept confidential because General Taroton didn't want to get in trouble by having an affair with a subordinate.

Nevertheless, Lateegely was allowed to make plans with her family for the retirement and the subsequent wedding. Since the General would be retiring that day, there wasn't much his boss could do about him announcing his wedding plans right afterwards. Lateegely's family was thrilled with the news and did a great job of keeping it confidential to protect their relative's future.

General Taroton said to Lateegely as they were thinking about when the best time to approach the couple, "As soon as the waiters clean off their table we'll go over and say hello to them."

"Sounds like a great plan," Lateegely responded.

In due time the table was cleaned off and fresh drinks were delivered and soon General Taroton arrived with Lateegely to Garratt and Tavishien's table.

"Hey Marti (aka Garratt) and Tavishien, it's good to see you again," General Taroton said.

Garratt and Tavishien both stood up and Tavishien walked around the table and hugged Lateegely and said, "It's so good to see you Lateegely. I missed you!"

"Thank you Tavishien, I missed you as well."

"You look beautiful Lateegely!"

"You trained me Tavishien, that's why!"

"Don't be ridiculous, you're a beautiful woman, you didn't need my help."

"Tavishien, you gave me really good training and that's how I was able to do this, and I have a surprise for you."

"What's your surprise?"

"Let's go to the lady's room where I can tell you in private."

"Sure. Garratt, we'll be right back."

As soon as the two women were heading for the lady's room Garratt asked, "General Taroton, would you and Lateegely like to join us?"

"It would be my pleasure, Garratt. Is that your real name?"

Garratt smiled then looked towards the waiter standing nearby and signaled.

"Yes, sir how may I help you?"

"General Taroton and his date are joining us at this table, can you please bring a couple more chairs?"

"It will be my pleasure sir."

Soon General Taroton and Garratt were sitting at the table waiting for the women and started their conversation.

"I didn't expect to see you here, Marti or should I call you Garratt?"

"Well general, as you can see, I have a lovely date and we are here for the night in a Penthouse. You can call me Garratt but keep it private to you and Lateegely."

"She looks incredible. You are very lucky."

"Yes, I feel that way."

"Are the two of you a couple now?"

"Yes, my boss now knows we are a couple. We went past the point of no return."

"I have a little surprise of my own, but I would prefer if you kept it confidential until the date."

"What's your surprise General Taroton?"

"I'm going to retire soon, and the following day, Lateegely and I am getting married."

"Congratulations."

"Thanks, and you are invited."

"When is your retirement?"

"Three weeks from now."

"You know I think Tavishien, and I may be going back to your base about that time for some refresher training."

"Perfect timing. But try not to get me too excited by such wild training like you did the last time."

"Not a problem and you will like this. This will be simulated weapons only training."

"That's a relief. Why such precaution?"

"The big boss doesn't want any training accidents, says our personnel are too valuable. Plus, Tavishien already experienced the live weapons exercises, so she already knows how that feels. She just needs some proficiency training."

"With simulated weapons, she can definitely fly anyway she wants and not fear getting accidentally shot down."

"Send me the exact date of your retirement, and I'll make sure we are there a week ahead of time to give us plenty of time to coordinate events."

"It will be my pleasure."

Moments the two ladies returned beaming with smiles and Tavishien walked over and put her arms around General Taroton and said, "I'm so proud of you."

"Thank you I appreciate that."

The two couples were seated and enjoying their elixirs and the musicians started playing the dance music which quickly transformed the dining hall into a dance hall with a lot of happy couples.

Tavishien, had watched dancing on Network Video to learn it and practiced it during her etiquette training, was ready to celebrate with Garratt and show him some new moves that would please him. She practiced just for this moment and while stuck in that remote village for a while, when the villagers did their music and dancing, she played along and practiced her moves, picking up a few tricks the village women showed her. She was ready for an exhibition!

Lateegely was hoping General Taroton was going to ask her to dance and when Tavishien stood up and grabbed Garratt's hand and said, "Let's go dance!" General Taroton looked at Lateegely and smiled and asked, "Would you like to dance, Lateegely my dear?"

"I would love to."

The dance floor didn't have many couples dancing but with these four out there celebrating is seemed to influence the other couples and to the delight of the musicians, the dance floor was soon populated by inspiring dancers and women that wanted to get their boyfriends blood pressures up.

Tavishien and Lateegely were not in competition, but it sure seemed that way as they danced their hearts out attempting to please their boyfriends.

Most of the clientele in the Black Diamond Resort Dining Hall now turned into Black Diamond Resort Dancing Hall, knew that Tavishien looked especially great tonight, but what they didn't know is she was wearing one of the most expensive garments because it truly was Ljótunn bon Swartzler's most precious creation, saved for a moment like this to show it off.

Ljótunn bon Swartzler's operatives were secretly filming Tavishien who would act far more normal not knowing she was being filmed by an elaborate crew that would help create a portfolio so that Ljótunn bon Swartzler could show it to her half dozen most important clients in hen pecking order. From vast experience she knew to start at the top and work her way down, so she didn't offend someone of more prestigious stature.

During a normal fashion show, Ljótunn bon Swartzler didn't like a fashion model appearing too beautiful as it would distract potential clients who would focus more on the eye candy female instead of the garment.

But this was different, there were no other distractions and seeing the lovely Tavishien wear the garment and show off the way she was doing would get potential clients motivated and quite excited.

No sooner than Tavishien had the garment off that night, clients were already bidding on it. This was the case where the body movements created the awareness and the vallance the customer soon acquired for the design. It was a win-win situation. Tavishien got to look utterly fantastic for her prince charming and Ljótunn bon Swartzler got some interest from a half dozen high end clients, including one who was at the Black Diamond Resort Dining Hall and Dance Club that very night observing the spectacle herself.

Tavishien could easily have been a ballerina dancer because she had a unique ability to feel gravity better than anyone. Her sense of balance was second to none. Tight rope walking would be easy for her to learn, which sometimes was used on missions to access target buildings from across the street late at night. Who's guarding the roof tops? Usually nobody.

When the performers see such a spectacle as the two ladies were putting on, giving the observers an impression they were competing, but in fact were just having fun, it motivated them to put more into their music.

The music got better, more people danced, and waitresses were stressing out the bartenders to keep up the rate of servings because those elixirs were flowing like water! Life was good in the Black

Diamond Resort Dance Club that night and as the time passed the only thing the IBR watchers could think was, Agent Lucika was one lucky dog especially if he was *"tapping" the company ink with his pen* which they knew he was thanks to the hidden cameras and microphones that would get someone killed if Garratt ever found out.

What the IBR watchers didn't know was Tavishien was the master manipulator with all her extraordinary abilities none of them knew about including Garratt. Tavishien, also being very intelligent, and clairvoyant knew that if she informed Garratt of her extraordinary ability, it very well could wreck the relationship as he might start thinking she manipulated him for her own satisfaction.

Everything is fair in love and war and Tavishien was going to keep her most prized weapons to herself forever. It would be like a chess master having three spare queens in a game at the start instead of three pawns.

Tavishien's self-awareness and reflection gave herself the satisfaction of feeling that based on what those six rotten Tartars did to her body and all the pain and suffering she went through and the daily challenges she already faced as a female IBR with special abilities, the least she could do for herself is to indulge in the *tumultuous allegros* on her own terms with her own secrets.

Tavishien resolved the moral and ethical dilema by saying to herself she was in the middle of a war and in the middle of love and just like her enemies would use anything they could to do her in, *she would use everything she had to bond with a man she fell in love with* and do what she had to do to preserve that relationship. She also had the satisfaction of knowing that since she was never going to inform anyone, including Garratt, of her wartime and love time secrets that allowed such success.

During one of the dances Tavishien got remote viewer feedback from the Tomlars back at the forest now nestled in the barn for the night flooding her mind with great satisfaction observing Tavishien being so happy with Garratt.

This truly was Tavishien's Cinderella Night, but she had no way of knowing what existed on planet Earth many light years distance away. But in this case, she didn't need to try on the glass slipper because Garratt knew her well.

General Taroton was equally happy with Lateegely a fast learner who picked up a lot of makeup tips from one of the best, Tavishien. Therefore, Lateegely shined tonight as well even though her budget did not allow her to wear such expensive designer clothing. But because of her hair style, her makeup, the style of black silk dress she chose and how she wore it with the high heels put the exclamation mark on her. Lateegely's dress was slightly revealing and General Taroton thought it exposed much of her anatomy.

Later that night when Lateegely rewarded General Taroton (aka Michael) for the proposal and the diamond ring, he discovered what he thought he was seeing really was the real deal and it startled him to learn how brave Lateegely was to wear such a thing in public. All he had to do was undo one hook on the back of her dress and when it fell to the floor, it revealed she was wearing nothing under it. The black silk truly silhouetted her body nicely, even more so as she built up a little sweat dancing.

As the night wore on Tavishien decided she didn't want to waste the precious time doing the upright dancing in the Black Diamond Resort when she really wanted to engage in the Horizontal Tango on a theme from Paganini back up in the Penthouse. During the musician's break that came soon after quite a bit of dancing, Tavishien took her elixir that was nearly full and drank it all down with four or five seconds giving her the upmost buzz since the bartender wanted to make sure the VIP's got their due.

Tavishien then put her arms around Garratt and whispered some profound suggestions in his ear that suddenly caused him to have a metastable state in his little head and quickly agreed and the two then excused themselves from General Taroton and Lateegely.

As they were leaving the table Tavishien looked back at Lateegely and gave her that wicked wink and at the same time some subtle mental telepathy to encourage her to follow suit. Within a minute of the beautiful couple leaving the Resort Dining Hall Dance Club, Lateegely whispered something in General Taroton's ear that made Michael also experience strange metastable states and quickly agreed that was a splendid idea.

Love was flowing that night. Two beautiful women were giving the loves of their lives their due and even though some psychoanalysts would tell you desire is always ten times greater inducement than gratification, the gratification sure seemed to be as great as the desire tonight.

The strenuous love making, and the elixirs did their magic and soon the two couples were cuddled up feeling gratifying love of the best in their lifetimes. Tavishien left her mark during the evening and the IBR Watchers didn't have a clue of what to write, or even where to start since the day and evening was filled with such huge amounts of activity. The two managed to cram into a day what many couples hope to achieve in a week.

****

CHAPTER NINETEEN

Back to Training

Morning came far too early for everyone's satisfaction, but they now had to go pay the piper and find out what the Intelligence Bureau was going to bestow upon them.

Garratt flew them back to the Intelligence Bureau Campus then sent his private Skycar home on autopilot to his private residence that had exclusive Skycar parking slot on the rooftop of the high rise building he lived in. In due time Tavishien would come familiar with this home that almost shocked her when she first saw it because it was so bare of almost anything. Garratt never got around to decorating it.

Garratt had the basics of a bachelor that lived a clean and frugal life and didn't socialize too much because of the lurking dangers associated with practically anyone he could meet. It felt better for him to remain a loaner and avoid all the tendrils of life and passionate entanglements. But just when he thought he had his life in full control, living in a predictable manner, Tavishien shows up and upsets the apple cart. Now he was irrevocably altered in many ways he flatly refused to believe would ever happen.

As Garratt soul searched and pondered his new situation, suddenly it didn't feel so bad. Tavishien was quickly filling a void in his life. Garratt thought he could compartmentalize his emotions and remain bullet proof in the wars of love, he now found himself a casualty with a gaping hole in his heart where Tavishien climbed into and took full ownership. Garratt started to think what transpired and how much Tavishien had grown intellectually and altered herself ostensibly with a lot of Intelligence Bureau Training, but that was not all. She had help from sources nobody would ever think possible.

The Tomlars were indeed very analytical and intelligent. You couldn't tell it by the way they acted. But in that very private network the remote viewing allowed. Tavishien was fortified emotionally and philosophically. Nature has a very strong way of maintaining balance and restoring after disaster strikes like a forest fire.

It was through mother nature that Tavishien gained the inner strength and perseverance to change her destiny and at the same time change some people around her. Tavishien left her mark on Gabriel who was now a changed woman. She left her mark on Lateegely. She left her mark on General Taroton, and most importantly she left her mark on the love of her life Garratt Wyclaire.

Now it was time for the next chapter in Tavishien's life. She found out soon after arrival back to her dormitory room by the knock on her door, that Gabriel was there to start her physical fitness training.

Oh God, she didn't feel up to doing this, right now. Her Cinderella hours were over, and she didn't want it to end, and she wasn't totally sure she was in condition to start.

Gabriel threw gym clothes at Tavishien and said, "The party is over, you need to change your clothes so we can go out and attempt to do some running."

"I don't know if I can make it a block."

"Don't forget what I trained you on earlier, *if you are going to hoot with the owls all night long, you better be ready to scream with the eagles the next day.*"

"I think this morning I'm just a baby chick, *how do they scream with the eagles.*"

"I'll be back in five minutes with a special drink for you. It will help you get going, and I'm not going to press you too hard today. We'll work back up to it like we did in the past."

"Alright, I'll be dressed when you get back."

Gabriel sometimes had her own issues with screaming with the eagles and thus discovered some special energy drinks that would at least help her get started in the morning and give her body a chance to work off all the effects of the elixirs from the night before.

The Tomlars were also remotely giving Tavishien some encouragement and support, that helped somewhat.

When Gabriel rang the doorbell again a few minutes later, Tavishien was dressed in gym clothes, and she had decided the hell with washing her face and removing the makeup as she would shower after exercising.

"Here you go, this will help." Gabriel handed the special workout cocktail to Tavishien who wasted no time in downing it all. In due time she was starting to feel better and get a little buzz from the special drink Gabriel knew would pick up the tempo.

Five minutes afterwards they were walking out to their eight-mile workout and the question was how many laps Tavishien could do since she had been away for a while. None of them had seen Tavishien work out for quite a while. But what they didn't know, life in the remote village was not easy and required a lot of physical work, especially in pulling gold out of the ocean.

Tavishien might be a little hung over but Gabriel's drink was helping with, but the fact is she maintained great physical shape simply by the village life and doing everything associated with it including getting that movie star quality tan that exemplified her blond hair and Nordic appearance one might observe on planet Earth.

The two IBR females started out at their normal pace and Tavishien was keeping up like there was no problem with her running. All this of course was being recorded and Agent Lucika (Garratt) would watch time-lapsed video of it in his office as he reviewed all the day's activities and answered a few more questions to his superior.

In due time they finished four miles going at a pace they obtained before the Tavishien's long furlough of activities at the fishing village. Tavishien decided at this time she had enough for the day and wanted an additional day to get back to the swing of things.

The rest of the day was filled with low intensity martial arts training and tradecraft training. Considering Tavishien had been gone a very long time, everyone in her chain of command was happy she performed as well as she did because it meant they would not have to go through a really long period of rehabilitating Tavishien's physical endurance.

That evening, Garratt visited Tavishien at her dormitory room. He brought Gabriel with him so that if anyone observed him going there nobody would suspect any extra-circular activity was going on.

"Hello, Tavishien."

"I'm surprised to see the two of you together."

"While we are at the Intelligence Bureau Campus, we have to comply with what my superiors expect out of me."

"And what is that?"

"It's no mystery to Gabriel, she knows we are lovers and a couple, but my superiors do not want to display this relationship while we were here at the Campus."

"Well let's go someplace else then."

"We will be in due time. But I wanted Gabriel here with me to others seeing us coming and going will think this is a business call."

"It seems to me it appears that way."

"Sadly, it is because I have to give you an idea of your schedule and why I have to spend time away from you."

"Alright, I'm all ears."

"Tavishien you should know that if we see a lot of each other, it will materially impact your training regimen. Right now, the focus is all on you and getting you back into shape to deploy you. You are not aware of world events that are heating up, so your services are needed now more than ever. I'm dedicated and I know you are too. During the work week, we will stay apart so I don't interfere with your physical and mental conditioning."

"That is not appealing to me."

"I understand, it's not only hard on you it will be hard on me as well."

"So, what are you going to do?"

"I must make a few trips over the next few weeks for compartmentalized activities in preparation for your future missions. Gabriel will always be close. Due to the circumstances of how I will be traveling I will not be able to communicate to you until I get back."

"Will you be going someplace dangerous?"

"Tavishien my dear, that is our job, danger."

"When will you be leaving?"

"In a few minutes. I'm sorry we could not be together longer before I had to leave."

"It all makes sense now, the extra effort you went through."

"I wish I could have done more."

As tears were starting to flood Tavishien's eyes because he was searching Garratts thoughts and knew this was all legitimate and she also knew she could not react based on that knowledge without tipping Garratt off she knew far more than she was entitled to, or his superiors would ever tolerate. This was a dangerous game. Garratt was going behind enemy lines to eliminate a rouge spy turned traitor. Those tears were not heartbreak, they were tears of fear for her true love. He had no idea how much he meant to her.

Garratt approached Tavishien and put his arms around her and held her tightly to the point he almost restricted her breathing. But she loved the emotions he felt that she knew with her probing. She also knew one thing Garratt might think about later when it was too late. She would know everything he did with her remote viewing. That's something his supervisors didn't consider in this assignment, but there was no time for planning, this was an emergency and sometimes that happened. It all came together quickly as best as they could manage.

The moment passed too quickly. Garratt was out of her arms and suddenly she was alone with Gabriel with tears falling down her cheeks.

Gabriel was there for more than just appearances. Garratt knew that based on their fast and furious love affair his sudden departure would have a severe negative impact on Tavishien and she needed to be with someone for a while. Gabriel was her life support.

Garratt was soon out of sight, but he did not escape Tavishien's remote viewing. She saw and heard everything he said and heard and everything he saw. Her remote viewing was intensified and clarified by the Tomlars who were now in full synchronization with her. Every one of the Tomlars had great fear for Garratt and they knew it would crush Tavishien if anything happened to him.

Garratt walked to the waiting Skycar with three men waiting for them. It soon lifted off and flew to the military's space port where they were put aboard a shuttle craft that would take them out into space. Garratt had a change of clothes and a disguise he put on. His target would know who he was if he showed up with his normal facial recognition. Inside that large shuttle craft was another craft that Tavishien now observed in her remote viewing.

Tavishien seemed to relax, and the tears dried up and when Gabriel offered to take her somewhere to get something to eat, she responded, thanks for the offer, but I would just like to have some time with myself. I'll be ready to run with you in the morning."

"Alright dear if that's what you want."

Soon Tavishien was alone like she wanted to be as she was now in full observation of what was happening with Garratt (aka Agent Lucika, aka Marti).

The shuttle would not go over Tartar airspace for fear of likely being shot down. The ultra-stealth stratospheric glider would get Garratt down to the planet. After completing the mission, it had enough fuel to get back to a friendly airbase.

Tavishien was now getting a real education of what went on. The extravagance of what they would do to support these operations was quite remarkable.

It was hoped coming in at night Garratt would have a chance to avoid detection landing in a sparsely populated area where many anti-government people lived, so the probability of someone accidentally spotting him and reporting his arrival was significantly reduced thanks to the unrest that now existed in Tartarland where people went out of their way to upset friendly forces and help the enemy when they got a chance.

Inside the shuttle a familiar face was there, IBR Tristan Karjal. Since Tavishien had been close to him at dinner and inadvertently read Tristan's Aura she could see what Tristan observed.

As the stratospheric glider dropped out of the belly of the shuttlecraft Tavishien was monitoring IBR Tristan Karjal to see what was going on to give her the confidence she knew everything was okay. She saw all the monitors and displays Tristan was watching the Stratospheric Glider slip away in the night and made its way down to the planet.

There wasn't much communication going on because it might give away Garratt's position. Everything was passive. One half hour after Agent Lucika (aka Garratt) exited the Stratospheric Glider, there would be a burst transmission with a few key pieces of predesigned signals imbedded in telemetry. The Intelligence Bureau Special Operations Group (IBSOG) would know the first milestone was met. Once Agent Lucika was a good distance away from the Stratospheric glider, he would press a button on his that appeared to be part of his clothing, but by pressing a sequence on the innocuous looking button would send a burst signal to the Stratospheric Glider that would relay it to the Shuttle that he was safe and a good distance away from the Stratospheric Glider and unlikely to have been detected.

Tavishien spent half the night monitoring Garratt and became nervous and suddenly she got help from an unexpected source. The Tomlars suggested she lay down and go to sleep and they would watch over Garratt for her and would wake her up if something important happened. They also soothed her by flooding her mind with sounds of the mountain including memories of her father calling the Tomlars with his improvised seashell that amplified the sound to call them allowing him to avoid walking long distance.

While Tavishien was sleeping it was a good thing because actions like this are swift and brutal. Several people gave up their lives in support roles to put in place all the pieces allowing Garratt a one-man Army to get to the safe house where the traitor was being held between interrogations. They had no idea how much he had already given away.

Data mining in traitors is slow because the traitors are not stupid, they know that once they give everything they have, there is no purpose in keeping them alive, so they spoon feed the interrogators. The reason why this hit was put in place so spontaneously was this traitor had links to where the Tartars could probe and get a treasure trove of intel. There wasn't much time left because once he handed over the passcodes the Tartars could break-in networks and the damage would be egregious.

In the middle of the night, it was assumed the security perimeter would suffer perimeter guards vigilance decrement as the guards would be half asleep and not believe anyone had the balls to come there. Unfortunately, Garratt would have to kill a half dozen men silently to get into the safe house. To get to the traitor he hoped would be sleeping to make the kill much easier. He certainly didn't want a wrestling match with a paid killer and assassin.

The goggles Garratt wore were infrared and ultraviolet sniffers as well as other probing devices. Some of the security perimeter monitors used infrared scanning beams. With the special goggles Garratt could watch their scanning rate and skip in between scans to get at one guard at a time. Since this was in the heart of "Indian Country" the perimeter guards were overly relaxed, and their vigilance was more than decremented as some were mentally impaired by substance abuse because nobody onsite thought anyone would dare try to bust in let alone a standalone operative.

The perimeter guard's security detail certainly was not looking for a single infiltrator, in fact they were really not looking for much of anything because night after night it was a repeat, they were simply wasting their time and nights by doing this stupid guard duty when there was no point as far as they were concerned.

Garratt had to slowly crawl in like a preying lion on its target. He would use neuro-debilitators on a few of the guards that were not physically close enough to kill quickly silently. There were no fences to cut through or any guard dogs or traditional boundaries because as a safe house it couldn't stand out too much from the neighborhood to make it a plausible hideaway.

Taking down the six perimeter guards took over an hour. Now it was just a matter of getting inside. Based on reconnaissance drones sent in on previous nights, there was a late-night security inspection.

Apparently, a supervisor would leave the house silently as to not give away perimeter defense positions and personally walk to each post and verify the guard was awake and get a signal by *shaking of the fist in the air that everything was under control. No issues.*

The first man the supervisor was going to check was dead laying in such a way like he looked like he was holding his weapon in position to fire if necessary. The supervisor knew better than to assume the man was awake, so he kicked his foot to get his attention. The supervisor then fell over silently dead as Agent Lucika gave him the fast action poisonous injection at the same time, he put his hand over his mouth to prevent any sound from going out.

The stage was set the door was unlocked with a minimal number of people inside awake. The dart weapons administered a fast action kill poison that usually worked in a couple seconds.

Now was the most dangerous part of the mission because Agent Lucika didn't really know how many were inside and where they were situated. In his first pass in he had to kill the traitor, what happened to him was irrelevant as he had a timer that would detonate in about 15 minutes if he didn't make it out of the house to deactivate it to make sure he was never captured.

It was like he had a guiding hand he didn't know how or why but suddenly it was like he had a sixth sense. What was happening was the entire herd of Tomlars were helping him they were part of his team, and he was close enough to the men inside where the Tomlars could remotely read their Aura's through Garratt (aka Agent Lucika). As he entered the safe house, he suddenly did a lot of point and shoot at men inside and in the span of ten seconds killed all five of them who were stirring and coming at him.

Garratt's target, the traitor was gagged and tied to a chair and had blood all over him. He had obviously been beaten senseless because he appeared unconscious or was simply sleeping. It didn't' matter.

This was the mission. He hated to do this, but he had no choice. He put the device up against the man's neck and gave him a shot. The poison activated quickly while Garratt gave him a second shot to make sure. One way they can tell if the poison did its trick was the person usually defecated as they were dying. The stench suddenly erupted. Garratt knew he was probably dead but wanted to make sure and opened his mouth and saw the grim reminder of the torture the Tartars often did. His lounge was branded and swollen on one side. Garratt put a shot into the tongue, which was most likely overkill, but he didn't want to take chances.

Garratt took some blood samples for DNA identification from the man and stuffed them in a plastic bag into a pocket he zipped up then. He then turned and exited the house using egress techniques in case there was an unaccounted-for security guy he missed.

The egress took several minutes as he slowly put distance between him and the safe house quickly moving towards a riverbed that was a quarter of a mile away. He walked into the riverbed and walked up stream a mile before exiting on the opposite side of the river and a different route back to the stratospheric glider. That gave him a short burst which was a beacon once every five minutes to calibrate his course to get back before sunrise and away.

When the enemy found all those dead men back in the safe house, the search parties would come in earnest, there would be no other alternative, he had to get in that stratospheric glider and get away and hope that nobody stumbled across it in the meantime.

Part of the burst signal he received also gave an undetected indicator meaning the onboard computer's sensors believed there were no persons in the vicinity and thus it remained undetected. That was a key indicator because otherwise he might have to kill an innocent bystander which he didn't relish doing.

His goggles helped him see in the dark and avoid trip hazards and when he could run on open land he did so. It wasn't fear that drove him it was the reality that since he was a spy and who he was, there would be no rescue and death most likely. Buying any spare time was worth it even if it took his breath away.

Slowly Garratt covered the ground and approximately one hour after killing the traitor the automatic transponders in the Stratospheric Glider and his personal electronics synchronized and there was a change in shift in the audio cues which helped his direction finding and distance determination. Just like magic as the pitch got to where he wanted it, he stepped behind some trees and there it was the stratospheric glider, unmolested and nobody around, just the way he wanted it.

Soon Garratt was buckled up, and on his way flying below radar in a terrain following mode until he approached the border crossing and then went into hyper drive and shot up into the air like a rocket and was automatically vectored into the Air Force Base.

When Tavishien woke in the morning, Garratt was not yet out of harm's way. The Tomlars had a full handle on the situation and blocked her remote viewing. Their sophistication was showing as they knew it was best, Tavishien did not observe this in case something bad happened to Garratt. She was soon in her exercise clothes and walked outside her dormitory room and there was Gabriel approaching to get her for their eight-mile run.

Gabriel was hoping Tavishien would at least last for six miles today as they headed out. But today Tavishien was running for a new purpose. She ran hard as she put every ounce into her objective and promised herself, she would not stop until she finished the eight miles and then she had to know what happened.

The Tomlars upset Tavishien they were blocking out her remote vision. But there was no way she could fight it. The entire herd was just too powerful to overcome. But while she was running the Tomlars kept telling her "Run hard Tavishien, you know you can do it."

Gabriel, who was in top condition, didn't let up but was surprised that Tavishien kept her pace just fine and at the six mile mark even though she was drenched in sweat, she was still pouring on the coals. Eventually Tavishien hit the eight-mile mark fully exhausted and not an ounce of energy left in her body, but the greatest news she had in a very long time now came. The Tomlars told her Garratt was safe and would be arriving home soon. They also advised her not to try to view what happened. They knew it would rattle her if she saw half of it.

Garratt didn't realize the base he was landing at until he came to a vertical stop inside a compound that was fenced off. When the ship's computer determined it was safe to exit, they unlocked the door to the Stratospheric Glider and was in the compound he had taken Tavishien where she received her advanced terrain follower training.

No other than General Taroton was standing there with a couple men in plain clothes.

"Nice to meet you here of all places General Taroton."

"Yes, Agent Lucika, its funny how we seem to always be bumping into one another."

"How's things with Lateegely?"

"Could not be better, the big plans are still in effect and I'm looking forward to seeing you at my retirement."

"I wouldn't miss it."

"These IBRs are here to debrief you. I will escort you to our secure conference room where you can have your private discussions."

Just when Garratt was wondering what they would be doing with the Stratospheric Glider, a truck with a crane hoist on it drove up to it. A couple spooks screwed lifting pads into the hull of the Stratospheric Glider and lifted it on the back of the flatbed and soon tied it down and covered it with a tarp. As soon as they stepped up to the door of the building the truck was heading out of the compound with an armed escort on its way to a cargo plane parked at the air force base not far away from where they stood.

The general walked the men up to the secretary and asked, "Do you have their badges ready?"

"Yes, sir and handed him the three badges which the General took and handed to each man since he knew their names."

"This way gentlemen."

General Taroton took them into the conference room and said, "When I leave the room and close it that blinking light will go out and you are in secure mode and can begin your discussions which I'm not cleared to hear, nor do I desire to hear. If for some reason that door is open and the security boundary is lost, that light will start blinking again and will remain blinking until conditions are reset."

"We might need to take a few breaks," one of the IBR's said.

"If you have to leave the room and set off the blinking light after you are all back inside again and the boundary reset the secretary will extinguish the blinking light and you can continue your discussions."

"Alright we are ready to proceed," The IBR stated, and the general left the room and soon the light stopped blinking.

Agent Lucika (aka Garratt) sat down in the middle of the table and the two IBR's sat down directly across from him.

Agent Lucika knew both IBR men from the special operations directorate. They were the director's hench men and fact finders. They were as you would think bad hombres and would twist a puppies head off at a moment's notice if required.

These men knew something General Taroton nor anyone else knew. The clothes and commercial appearing communicator strapped onto Garratts hand that appeared like a wristwatch was a data collector for all the gadgets sewn into the clothes. Infrared body cams and sensors were there. Innocent looking buttons were cameras and microphones. They were wireless and their super high frequencies and very low power levels prevented anyone detecting them beyond ten or fifteen feet due to the attenuation of the signals in air.

One of the men pulled out a device from his pocket the size of a standard communicator the public used and placed it on top of

Garratts wristwatch appearing contraption and since it was programmed with all the correct passcodes downloaded the sensor data from the wristwatch. The boys in the cargo plane downloaded the stratospheric glider and bleached its memory. Each man took a copy of the wristwatch data to make sure they had double backup and not lose any data. The devices they had were capable of doing time lapsed photography, so they were able to get a quick glance of the activity to know what all happened before they began the verbal debriefing.

Now the moment of truth came. Garratt really had no idea who he killed and would not know until now and it would be a come to Jesus' moment if he killed a plant. He pulled the plastic bag out of his zipped-up pocket and handed it to the chief interrogator who then took a cotton swap to the blood and smeared it on a couple platinum wafers. He took one and slid it into the slot of his device and handed the second wafer to the other IBR who followed suit. Simultaneously their devices reported MATCHED DNA.

"Looks like you got our man, Brandon."

Now they went into the oral interview mode. These men were patient and experts. They left no stones undone and if necessary, would put Garratt through neuronic clarifier probes to clear up any details that didn't seem right. Garratt didn't particularly care for the neuronic clarifier probes because they were extremely painful and often used to torture spies they captured. But they were indeed highly accurate.

These debriefings would last until the end of the week. Garratt would not be going anywhere anytime soon as the establishment went to work on him. This was a very important mission for lessons learned but it was also very damaging because the end results would alert the enemy to sensitive sources and methods, they didn't want them to know about, short of wartime, in case they had to use such special methods and procedures again.

The traitor not only possibly gave away secrets, but he also allowed the enemy to discover the IBR's could break in and not leave behind much of a trace. Though there was some evidence left behind that would show a person was there because it's impossible not to track blook and other substances around. The lack of death from severe trauma showed the sophistication of the kills. It was somewhat unsettling to management that they had to disclose sensitive methods in *peacetime*, giving the enemy time to build future defenses that were harder to defeat.

One of the positive outcomes was there no recorded data on the Stratospheric Glider or from listening posts the enemy got any indication the Stratospheric Glider had been used in the operation. At least that secret might still be valid.

The other secret they hoped would remain locked away was the fast-acting kill poisons scientists had developed would lose any traces within a couple hours, so by the time the bodies were found they would not know the means to how they were killed.

The days drug by very slowly and painfully and Agent Lucika weathered the phenomenal stress. There were a couple areas they needed to clear up an issue and Garratt ended up getting zapped with the neuronic clarifier probes which was not pleasant. Everyone would love to visit a dentist long before getting zapped by one of those wicked machines. In the end they clarified nothing as Garratt had a good memory, was astute and almost clairvoyant.

The reason why Agent Lucika got zapped by the neuronic clarifier probes was they didn't buy his story he went in blazing with the killer poisons feeling like he suddenly knew where all the enemy was in the safe house. But after a couple neuronic clarifier shots the two henchmen concluded something strange was going on, giving Agent Lucika an edge.

Only Agent Lucika's (aka Garratt) boss drew the appropriate conclusion, he was probably helped somehow by Tavishien's remote viewing. Since her dormitory room was fully bugged and had hidden video camera's they pulled all the surveillance collected on her during Garratt's mission and she slept the entire night. Based on pulse, respiration rate, body temperature, etc.

The experts concluded Tavishien was sound asleep before Garratt stepped out of the Stratospheric Glider thus it did not make sense, Tavishien did any sort of remote viewing while the mission was underway and did not wake up until after he was safely aboard the Stratospheric Glider on his way to safety.

Then to furthermore illustrate Tavishien had nothing to do with it, she was out running eight miles with Gabriel running hard and finished her eight miles at a very good pace. The ESP that Garratt seemed to acquire going into the home for now remained a mystery to everyone. They didn't even bother pulling in Tavishien for examination because there was nothing to indicate she intervened in any way. It would remain a mystery forever.

Finally with every bit of data scrubbed, it was late in the work week, and the two interrogators and General Taroton rang the officer's quarters doorbell that Agent Lucika was staying in just as if it were going to be another repeat of previous days.

To Garratt's (aka Agent Lucika's) surprise the two IBR's stated, "We are all done here. General Taroton asked if he could escort you over to the aircraft to fly you back to Intelligence Bureau Campus."

"Good, I could use some of the Generals company I still feel stiff, and the pain killer's you guys gave me wasn't all that effective."

"Sorry sir, but you know we had to do what we were required too."

"All right us get moving."

***

Gabriel was kind of curious why Tavishien wasn't acting upset by Garratts lingering absence and was on her way to get her for their morning workout when she was summoned into Agent Lucika's office by his secretary.

350

"Yes, what can I do for you."

"I've been notified to have you take Tavishien to a safe house where Madam Ljótunn bon Swartzler and her staff are being sent to get her prepared for the welcoming committee."

"Who's the welcoming committee, and what's this all about."

"You, Tavishien, and Agent Lucika's boss will be there to welcome him back."

"Do I have time to change out of my workout clothes?"

"Yes. It doesn't matter Tavishien wears because she will be dressed in one of Madam Ljótunn bon Swartzler's garments. Change into professional office attire, then bring Tavishien here, the director will be here waiting for you to escort you there."

"I suppose I need to go tell Tavishien our schedule has been changed."

"She's been notified, as soon as you get changed, bring her here."

"Alright, I'm on my way."

"In thirty minutes, the illustrious trio were on a Skycar heading to a safehouse where Garratt would later arrive at the perfect moment. Garratt, now dressed in office attire, seemingly looking like a banker or lawyer, had no idea what was in store for him.

Just like clockwork at the safe house Madam Ljótunn bon Swartzler's fashion technicians arrived not a minute too soon and slowly molded Tavishien into that living doll they loved to exercise their tradecraft with.

The Skycar transporting Garratt didn't go in the direction towards the Campus that gave him some slight consternation being that he was in the spy business and when things like this happened it was usually a harbinger of bad things to come. To say he wasn't a little apprehensive when he got out of the Skycar at the safehouse he didn't know existed, was an understatement.

"We are stopping here."

Garratt (aka Agent Lucika) Was not in a good psychological state after all he had just been through and could imagine a painful experience was about to happen. But Garratt also knew it was pointless to resist because these goons carried a lot of firepower. Garratt noticed several Skycars parked by the safehouse in an upscaled neighborhood with plenty of parking available.

One of the IBR's walked beside Garratt and two behind him as they smartly walked up the sidewalk and as soon as they were at the door it opened and there was the director with a big smile.

"Welcome home Agent Lucika. Please come in I wanted to personally welcome you home and so do some of your friends."

This was a nice house with a good size hallway at the entrance that led to a large open area and off to the side there they stood. Gabriel with Tavishien who looked utterly fantastic thanks to the way Madam Ljótunn bon Swartzler's staff makeover elevated her physical appearance several stratums.

"Agent Lucika, you have the rest of the day and the weekend off. The watch officer has people standing by to handle any matters you normally would be assigned. You are officially relieved so that you can enjoy your long weekend and not worry about being recalled and I want you to enjoy your time off."

"Thank you."

"Never forget how much I appreciate what you do. You are a remarkable man and when we need you the most you always seem to be ready to carry on at a moment's notice. Sometimes I must dish out the harshest assignments to you. You did not let me down this time and I owe you a large amount of gratitude."

The IBR's in the room hearing the director knew Agent Lucika probably just went to hell and back and his body physique had the classic body language of someone that had just been horribly stressed and they surmised he probably got a couple jabs with the neuronic clarifier and felt for him. They also knew the director never sprinkled praise on an agent unless he gave up at least a pint of blood in the mission.

Just on key the Director said, "These fine gentlemen are going to take me back to the Campus. One of the Skycars out there is for your use. Agent Gabriel will take you to wherever you wish to spend your weekend."

"Thank you, sir."

"Thank you, Agent Lucika."

The two men bowed, and all of the agents cleared out except for Garratt, Tavishien and Gabriel.

Gabriel asked, "Where would you like to go."

"Take us to my home. I wanted to show it to Tavishien. Now is as good a time as ever."

The three left the safe house that was locked by the security apparatus as soon as they departed and headed straight for Garratt's high rise building with a great view. To Garratt's surprise, Gabriel pulled up to the front entrance and said, "I'm going back to the Campus to finish up some work, I'm going to let the two of you out here."

"Okay, thanks," Garratt said.

Gabriel then winked at Tavishien who looked like a million dollars.

The two exited the Skycar and Garratt led Tavishien to the elevator.

There were several attractive single women who lived in this building and were always wondering why Marti (aka Garratt) was always aloof and never with anyone, man, or woman. He was attractive but very private. A few of them saw him arriving with Tavishien. They were mildly shocked, and they knew the woman this man was with was utterly smoking hot. Now it made sense why he never paid much attention to them. He had his own eye candy to play with.

In due time they were up in Garratt's home. Garratt being the gentleman and decent person said, "You are not required to stay here with me but if you chose to spend the weekend here, I would be honored."

"Thank you, Garratt, I want to spend the weekend with you."

"That means a lot to me."

"The two then embraced and kissed. Tavishien was so grateful Garratt made it back alive and without too many scars.

Tavishien knew that Garratt was stressed out and exhausted and probably not in the mood for splendid euphoria and by probing his mind knew what he liked to do when he was home alone most of the time, listen to great music from a very sophisticated sound system he had that gave great three-dimensional sound a lot better than the nightclubs they had danced at.

"What would you like to do?" Garratt asked.

"I know you have probably been through a lot lately and need to wind down, perhaps we could just sip on an elixir and listen to some nice music?"

"That sounds great. I'll introduce you to my favorite composers and performers."

"Sounds wonderful."

Garratt's home had artificial intelligence always ready to respond to Garratt's commands. His artificial intelligence had a personality package that purchasers could select. Garratt had selected one rated as the perfect Butler to be in the background and not to bother him unless Garratt requested him to do something. Garratt had a choice of a name to give the artificial intelligence and he therefore named him "C" named after the grandfather of the Intelligence Bureau.

"C" took the agency from an embryonic state to the sprawling intelligence Octopus that it now was. "C" was the code name for the person Randolph Sorge. Because of several well publicized spy scandals Randolph Sorge was removed from his position and escorted to a very mild weather mountain area resort *Saserland* built to provide former spies a safe place to live out the rest of their lives. In due time Randolph Sorge disappeared at *Saserland* and nobody wanted to investigate the former spies' disappearance for obvious reasons.

Garratt assumed one day he too would get a one-way ticket to *Saserland*. Picking "C" for the name of his artificial intelligence was a good way to remember the consequences of failure in the spy business, especially if it cost you, your life. God help you if you got caught as a double spy because Tavishien already proved what Intelligence Bureau can do to them.

"C" please play the recordings of Saenstoven."

"It will be my pleasure, master Garratt."

Garratt realized he needed to make sure "C" understood Tavishien was someone special to him then stated, "C" I want you to know that Tavishien is a very special person in my life. Treat her as if she is my partner."

"Understand Master Garratt. Did you perform a unification?"

"C" not yet but I want her with me for the rest of my life."

"Understand Master Garratt, I will make sure to treat Tavishien as the special person you identified."

"Thank you."

"You are most welcome, Master Garratt."

Soon the music started playing and Tavishien now realizing how tired Garratt was from his stressful endeavors suggested. "Garratt, why don't you lay down on the sofa. I will take your shoes off for you to make you more comfortable."

Garratt feeling tired was happy with the suggestion and said, "Thank you."

He laid back on the sofa and Tavishien took off his shoes and raised his feet up on he long sofa so he would be comfortable. The lovely music was playing and Tavishien walked over to Garratt by his head and bent down and said, "Why don't you close your eyes and rest a bit."

Between the music and Tavishien's sweet treatment along with her manipulation of his brain to make him sleepy, Garratt went to sleep feeling more relaxed than he had been in quite a while. The sofa was quite large and Tavishien cuddled up next to Garratt holding him tenderly.

"C" performed software routines analyzing the two laying together. "C" had the ability to search the worldwide computational and data resources networks and improve its self-awareness. "C" over time had grown very intelligent thanks to all the data mining AI often did. Based on the conversation and the physical displacement of the two people on the couch, "C" concluded they were lovers and Tavishien would soon be more of a permanent presence in the home. "C" was more than ready to engage Tavishien and since she meant a lot to Garratt, "C" would do whatever he could to accommodate Tavishien.

Garratt was now engaged in the most restful sleep he had not experienced since before his deployed for his recent mission.

Tavishien made Garratt feel complete, and his mind was far away from the Intelligence Bureau Campus where he could enjoy several days of splendor and enhancement to his relationship with Tavishien. What might be bestowed on them in the future was now blocked out of Garratt's thoughts. Each time his dream tried to take Garratt to a temporal reality that wasn't pleasant, Garratt changed courses in his dreams which he learned to do a long time ago to maintain sanity after tremendously stressful events.

Going behind enemy lines to kill a traitor was about as stressful as it gets because there are so many points of compromise or failure due to malfunctioning equipment. Murphy's law, your most important equipment will fail when you need it the most.

Back when Randolph Sorge was running the bureau as "C" there was a period when they attempted to send Tartars behind enemy lines to perform espionage or sabotage against their former country, every single one of them was compromised. That was part of course why "C" was eventually removed. It wasn't until Tavishien performed the *coup de grâce* on the double spy that all the penetration by the enemy into and improvising and planning group (IP/G) was completely irradicated. Garratt also know all too well, had that double spy still been operating when he went on his mission he probably would have been intercepted and killed in a shootout thus failing in the mission.

What was the main reason for Garratt's mission? They had to assume they lost everything already, so why take on the risk to go kill the guy since he probably already spilled his guts? Garratt knew all too well the real reason. Management wanted any future traitor to know the extent they would go to track them down and kill them, even behind enemy lines. They would have no quarter the rest of their lives. It would only be a matter of time before the traitor was dead, whether they did it or the enemy executed them.

Garratt's role in the mission would never be disclosed. He operated with a pseudo name spy identification and only the very few people he had face to face contact with who were well vetted would ever know he was the person to assassinate the traitor.

Tavishien helped Garratt's cover because anyone wanting to know the whereabouts of Agent Lucika would soon be informed, he's with Tavishien doing advanced training. Some of her training during the mission and debrief occurred away from the Intelligence Bureau Campus which gave the appearance she was away with Agent Lucika, which she had been quite a bit in the past. Thanks to the watchers perpetuating the tryst, those closest to Garratt understood Tavishien was his lover, but nobody talked about it.

After several hours of restful sleeping Garratt regained consciousness and soon realized he needed to get up and use the bathroom. His stirring awakened Tavishien, and when he investigated her beautiful face, all made up by the makeup artists for this special moment, he would have wanted to indulge Tavishien in substantial amount of hugging and kissing, but he had to pee like a Russian Racehorse and informed Tavishien, I'm sorry I need to get up and use the bathroom.

"Alright honey," Tavishien responded and stood up then held her hands out to Garratt to help him stand up which he appreciated.

Tavishien was a very strong woman with all her training. She lifted Garratt a lot more efficiently than he realized she could do. It mildly surprised Garratt but as he reflected on it, he decided, she was a mountain woman already strong and build up even more training with Gabriel.

The music was still playing when Garratt finished relieving himself like the output of a fire hose, when he re-entered the living room.

Then it hit him. Garratt had not only been sleeping deprived, but he had also had a lack of food while the debriefings pressed ahead.

"I could sure use something to eat now. Shall we go out and find something to eat?"

"I'm dressed and ready to go," Tavishien responded.

"That you are." Garratt said recognizing how pleasant Tavishien appeared.

Soon they left Garratt's home and walked a short distance away to some local restaurants that Garratt went to often. Even though a few restaurants had smoking hot Maître d's and waitresses, Garratt never made a single pass at any of them. They wondered about the private man. He was certainly attractive enough to get the attention and possible companionship of some of these ladies, but he never made the first move.

When Garratt took Tavishien into one of his favorite restaurants that had at least four women working there more than ready to engage Garratt, they suddenly discovered why he never paid much attention to them. There he was with Tavishien who was dressed to kill. Her designer dress, hair style, body, and superb makeup created a luster they knew they could not compete with. But they understood one thing clearly, Garratt had fine taste in women in the event he ever wanted to venture out, they were ready.

The two were seated by a window with a nice view and were soon enjoying an elixir waiting for their entrees.

Tavishien studied Garratt's face. She knew he had gone through a lot of stress as he seemed to have aged a year or two in just the brief time he was gone. Garratt appeared to have lost some weight and he now had a few wrinkles Tavishien had not seen before. Neuronic Clarifier applications had lingering effects, that was apparent and when Tavishien sought his thoughts she was amazed the only thing he was thinking now was how much he appreciated Tavishien. Just being here with her, especially dressed up and looking so lovely had a calming effect on Garratt.

Tavishien learned a lot this moment studying and analyzing Garratt. He carried his veneer quite well despite living through pure hell, most of which was caused by the Intelligence Bureau interrogators Neuronic Clarifier applications. But they had no choice, the stakes were high and when strange things happen during a mission that requires great study and detail.

It was not uncommon for a spy to be brought back for questioning two years later after an event. When that happened, the spy no doubt received Neuronic Clarifier applications so the information could be fully vetted. Garratt went through some of those as well and certainly hoped this mission didn't have any of those reoccurrences.

For the time being the Intelligence Bureau interrogators start from a baseline of what the spy may have given away and how wanted to know: how long was he working for the other side?

Smart managers always clamp the baseline at, "we lost everything," and work up from there. Now it was a matter of collecting and cataloging everything the spy had access to so they could assess the damage and initiate mitigations and contingencies.

One of the reasons why the spy was identified is the Intelligence Bureau had their own double spies under control. A disinformation campaign was underway to give the enemy a belief they received a lot of tainted information and to act upon it could have severe negative consequences. Those monitors and trip wires were well in place and now it was time to sit back and watch the perimeters looking for attempts at penetration.

The passwords and passcodes of such spies were all deleted except for the disinformation channels. The Intelligence Bureau would give away a few breadcrumbs to make it look legitimate, but in doing so saved the entire loaf of bread. All this activity weighed quite heavily on Garratt. There was no history of the past, something he would no longer be involved in for the perceivable future unless he got one of those rare recalls and another dose of Neuronic Clarifier applications.

Internal affairs and the counterintelligence sections were now handling the matter and Garratt's portion of the mission was over and compartmentalized. Nobody in the Bureau would know Garratt was the assassin except for his boss and a couple of IBR's that supported missions and were never permitted to go behind enemy lines.

Tavishien now did her magic. She healed Garratt a lot faster than he deemed possible. Some of these types of missions take months to get over.

It wasn't post-traumatic stress disorder; it was post-mission stress recovery laced with post Neuronic Clarifier physiology that multiplied it. Hence the long recovery time.

Tavishien applying here telepathic abilities accomplished in a half hour what normally took weeks to unwind. Garratt didn't quite understand why he felt uplifted and less stressed so quickly. *Maybe it was being with his lover that helped me so much?*

The two finished their meals and elixirs but Garratt suddenly developed a gastrointestinal manifestation and said, "Let's go back to our home and freshen up then I want to take you for a walk at a place I like to go often to unwind from a heavy day."

"Sure."

The two were soon back at Garratt's home, but Tavishien was feeling upbeat because she liked the term Garratt had used, "Our home."

Tavishien wanted to reward Garratt with her body and give him celestial feasts and splendid euphoria but was curious about the place he wanted to take her, so she decided to pull back her horns and let Garratt be the tour guide on their journey through love and happiness today.

After the two freshened up, Garratt led them to the nearby beach that was also a park with nice lawns, picnic tables, and trees placed at various points to give picnickers a wide variety of views to enjoy their activities.

There were numerous birds including waterfowl and at one end of the park had food dispensers that for a small charge would give a person a hand full of nutritious food for the birds which they liked. This bird food provided prevented park goers from giving the wild birds too much unhealthy food. The management that issued this policy were obviously lacking knowledge of what the birds ate. If they could systematically observe every bird all day long, they would discover they often ate very unhealthy things, hence what the picnickers offered was actually a better option.

The two held hands as they walked along feeling the slight sea breeze and the enjoyment of watching the festive behavior the park goers exhibited. Children with their parents either enjoying family sports or trips into the water gave a sense of tranquility. They eventually made their way to the bird feeder stands which was one of Garratt's favorite past times.

The birds have facial recognition, and they knew Garratt quite well as they saw him nearly every day and he was very generous with the bird food.

Birds have personalities. They cry out for various reasons and when they get hungry and watch other birds eating generous portions of bird food, they get rather excited, loud, and brave. Some of the birds that knew Garratt came right up to him. Others were shy and kept their distance.

Tavishien could feel the bird's satisfaction as they devoured the bird food almost as quickly as it was given.

There were at least twenty different types of birds. Some of the birds were very colorful. But some were not and somewhat dull looking with no great colorization. Besides the aquatic birds, blackbirds and pigeons also came in for the feast. Right beside the pigeons a couple squirrels lined up showing no fear of Garratt as they had known him for several years. Garratt didn't show it, but he could feed the squirrels right out of his hand. Tavishien got a glimpse of that probing his memories, trying to find happy times of his life.

In a while Garratt decided he had given enough to the birds and suggested, "Let's continue our walk around the park and work off a few calories."

"Alright dear, if that's what you want to do," Tavishien said in a very nice voice that pleased Garratt.

The couple continued their stroll around the park and if they were to think about they would discover they had surveillance on them. Garratt and Tavishien would no longer travel hardly anywhere without undercover IBRs watching them and reporting on their activities. And, if necessary, spring to the rescue if their lives were suddenly threatened.

Today as Garratt decompressed his recent activities, he let his guard down. He was highly vulnerable. He wasn't thinking counterespionage or sabotage or assassination. Nevertheless, hell hath no mercy from Tavishien if someone harmed Garratt. Even though he wasn't playing it too smart and conducted risky behavior by placing himself out in the open so much, he was protected and didn't know it. It wasn't only Tavishien and the IBRs that had their eyes on Garratt, there was an entire herd of Tomlars monitoring affairs.

The main difference between human remote viewing and animals such as the Tomlars, the human remote viewing was highly directional, whereas the Tomlars were almost omnidirectional observing offset like an out of body experience.

Being with Tavishien that day saved Garratt's life. He didn't know it nor did the IBRs, that a Tartar hit team was at the park gunning for Garratt. They didn't know for sure, but they suspected it was Garratt who killed the traitor before they could break him. They too were observing Garratt but because his interactions with Tavishien didn't give the impression this guy had just got back from a secret mission.

Before they pressed home the attack the lead assassin said to the other, "This isn't our guy, he's far too calm."

"Either he was the greatest spy of all time that can compartmentalize his emotions, or he simply is not the man who just escaped our trap before he got out of the country alive, "the other Tartar said.

"Whoever it was left nothing behind as evidence," the Tarter lead assassin replied.

"We do not know how the killer escaped our trap."

"If he went over land, he would just now be getting back and going through debriefings."

In due time they were convinced this was the wrong guy and as soon as they detected a couple of IBRs, they fled the scene. Had they seen Garratt just a few hours earlier, they would have made the kill. Tavishien's presence had altered his appearance and state of being so convincingly saved Garratts life.

The Tarter hit men also had no clue how vicious Tavishien could get. It would not be an easy kill even with their laser pistols. With Tavishien's help, there's a good possibility Garratt would have delayed the Tartars long enough where the IBR's would have joined the fray, and the hunters would quickly turn in the hunted with absolutely no way to get back to friendly territory. And God help them if they hurt Tavishien. Garratt would personally supervise the torture to the point the wish they were dead.

The stroll around the park seemed like such an innocuous event. The two love birds were totally unaware, but the Tomlars were curious and kept up the vigil. They would be the ultimate trip wire, possibly giving Garratt a margin of safety, he didn't know existed nor did he know of the threat.

Tavishien was already dressed up and decorated for a night out on the town. Garratt was dressed in a semi professional manner but not in the style suitable to escort Tavishien to the Black Diamond Resort where he wanted to go have dinner.

"Let's go home now so I can change my clothes into something nicer to be with you, since you are already dressed up nicely for the evening."

"Sure dear." Tavishien said as she realized she wore the freshness and vibrancy that Madam Ljótunn bon Swartzler provided for her and this special moment with Garratt arriving back in her life, in one piece. After the festivities tonight, Tavishien would make love to Garratt in a way he would never forget as she opened her heart to him completely.

The day was slowly evolving in a pleasant manner when it could have been a total disaster with fatalities just a few minutes prior. In espionage one never knows how lucky they were quite often when the chips fall in their favor like Garratt experienced today by the grace of God. *Did God do this for Tavishien who had such a terrible life and needs at least a few breadcrumbs? What else is in store for them?*

As they experienced before, the restaurant was reconfigured to a dance night club slowly after 9:00 p.m. as the diners left and the dancers arrived.

Among the crowd were several couples dressed to the maximum that were routine dancers and took dancing lessons. These dancers know how to show up early and dance before the crowd gets into it as there is ample floor space available to show off. The women were obviously there to show off their moves and their splendid curves. The men were there obediently to make sure someone else didn't take their girl home. As beautiful as these women dressed up, there would be a line of men to take them home if they indicated they were ready for some big 'A.'

Tavishien's back was towards the dance floor so Garratt could see her and the activity of the dancers. As Garratt observed the early dancers it brought back memories.

Garratt reflected about the days he spent on an Island out in the middle of the ocean that was a tourist destination that had a group of Ballroom dancers that met on Sundays at the multipurpose building located at a golf course. He only went there because a couple of his lady friends went there on Sunday nights to Ballroom dance. Typically, there were 300 women and 7 men and if you were a great dancer, you had dinner appointments at their homes for the following week as they wanted to capture Garratt and other good dancers, as a permanent dance partner.

Competition among these fabulously dressed ballroom dancer women was so great that some of them offered their bodies in exchange for that dancing relationships. Garratt danced with them but never did partake in their celestial fests because he didn't want to break a heart. He could tell some of these women were starving for love, especially when they initiated the kiss and suggested a sexual tryst.

The musicians shifted the music to facilitate the early dancers that acted as a catalyst to get the party rolling. As the dinner crowd slowly eased out the people waiting in line for a table were ushered in with pure delight. Dinner was served up past midnight and it was not uncommon to see people dancing and eating intermittently.

As on a typical night there were a few tables full of barracuda's waiting to get their fangs into a suitable gentleman. It irritated a few of them that Tavishien was with one of the best looking and best dressed man in the night club. Garratt didn't plan to dress so lavishly but he knew he had to be cognizant of Tavishien's attire and dress accordingly, otherwise he would have been far more casual and not have so many eyes on him.

Tavishien had no intentions of competing with the showoff early dancers and simply enjoyed Garratt's company and the music and the elixir. In some cases the restaurant management would attempt to hustle them and the dinner crowd out of the restaurant to make room for the line of 50 people waiting to get in, but since Tavishien was dressed much more elegantly than all the other women in the club, management assumed she was someone special and to have such beautiful eye candy there to inspire the men was worth letting them stay as long as they wanted.

After 45 minutes of showing off the dancers needed a break and the music director wanted to clear the floor for them to usher in the general crowd, so they did what they always did about this time, play their best slow dance music.

The showoffs exited the dance floor and went back to their tables and ordered elixirs or finished the ones they already had. Meanwhile couples that were there for romance took to the dance floor to enjoy this wonderful music and mingle in the most affectionate manner with their partner. The band manager was shrewd and knew how to play back-to-back slow dances to keep the showoffs off the dance floor for a while in order to get the rest of the customers into the groove.

Tavishien hinted she wanted to dance, and Garratt complied and soon they were like the other romantic couples out on the dance floor savoring each other in a grand display of romantic ensembles.

Garratt had not been with a woman since the last time he and Tavishien were together, and a lot had happened since. Enough time had passed to where he had stored up plenty of passion for Tavishien, he had such affection towards.

Tavishien's perfume provided by Madam Ljótunn bon Swartzler was laced with high concentrations of pheromones. Between the imagery, the emotional bonding, and the pheromones, Garratt was reacting much like Tavishien predicted.

Tavishien caused Garratt a serious erection and it was stuck in his underwear at such an angle it was uncomfortable, and Garratt felt like he wanted to take a trip to the men's room to straighten it up and get more comfortable. But thanks to this cocked and out of position ornament, Tavishien could feel it and knew that Garratt was stimulated.

Tavishien instantly felt what she wanted and knew her own condition transcended to moistness and desire. But Tavishien would not rush things as tonight this was all for Garratt who needed to be rewarded for all he had done for her. She was on Garratt's timeline, as he saw fit and would follow along cheerfully to his pleasure and let him unwind and be happy.

After a couple slow dances Garratt informed Tavishien he needed to use the rest room and would be right back. As he left their table walking to the exit and the restrooms, one barracuda table saw the bulging dragon in his trousers and almost felt like following him to the restroom to make an indecent proposal. Nevertheless, it added to the gossiping and girls talk at the barracuda table.

Garratt made it to the men's restroom where he had a private toilet and could relieve himself and at the same time untangle the dragon, so it was no longer painful. What a relief! He also saw the dragon spit residue left behind because Tavishien had excited him so much in the slow dance as she was holding him as strongly as he held her in complete reciprocation. He felt kind of embarrassed as he suspected Tavishien was feeling the dragon and giving him a strange but lovely look.

Now that he had his clothes adjusted properly and the dragon was back sleeping again, he felt much more comfortable going back into the dining hall turned dance club.

Madam Ljótunn bon Swartzler had received her first batch of videos and pictures from her operative in the restaurant and had sent them on to her top five clients to get them to bid on the gown.

Women are kind of curious about what other women are curious about. In the videos the viewer could easily see some of the barracuda's huddling and talking about the woman in the designer dress. It was definitely the look of intense curiosity on the part of the gawkers. The potential buyers also key in on that sort of thing, because if the crowd likes it that means it is truly something to be interested in.

The illustrious couple did a few more dances including another slow dance before they decided to go home and enjoy the celestial feasts on a theme from Paganini. The five wealthy women were bidding on the garment and the numbers thrown out which they could hear with networked audio was 15,000 credits.

Madam Ljótunn bon Swartzler wasn't greedy and only wanted decent profits on the garment and didn't want to haggle with these ladies, so she said, "Okay the first person who offers 25,000 credits gets it. Lady number three in the group immediately barked, "I'll take it for 25,000 credits, but I don't want you to dry clean it. I want to smell what she smells like and possibly what her boyfriend smells like if he left behind any scent."

"You got a deal," Madam Ljótunn bon Swartzler responded noting the private video she had with each of the five women showed the other four were highly disappointed they didn't speak up quickly enough.

Madam Ljótunn bon Swartzler knew how to take care of the feelings of the other women. She would have Tavishien dressed up for the entire weekend and sell to the others who missed the buy because they didn't respond promptly with a bid. As soon as she finished up with the five women, she sent a secret message to Garratt stating she had more clothes, and she would like to keep Tavishien dressed up for the weekend. *Just let me know when to bring my team to your home.*

The stage was set for the two lovers to work on Garratt's posttraumatic stress and Neuronic Clarifier side effects. Where it took other strong men to overcome all this terrible physiology, Garratt rebounded in merely days. Between copious amounts of love making, sight-seeing, and viewing the beauty and splendor that Madam Ljótunn bon Swartzler and her team were able to create for Tavishien through the weekend.

Tavishien modeling the clothes did the trick and made Madam Ljótunn bon Swartzler a lot richer in the process as every single garment Tavishien wore was quickly sold to the 5 wealthy ladies all out bidding one another because they got to see a lot Tavishien didn't: Men gawking at Tavishien in total awe, and a few ended up with sore ribs as their wives caught them overextending their eyeball liberties.

One thing these five wealthy women understood vividly: clothes and makeup increased their looks by twenty percent or more. They were willing to spend the extra money because they wanted to exist in the top one percent. As such they had physical fitness trainers and hairdressers, nutritionists, and others work the magic just like Madam Ljótunn bon Swartzler did for Tavishien.

Garratt knew a lot of places to take Tavishien as he knew she grew up in a sheltered life never traveling more than 30 miles beyond her father's cabin in the mountainous wooded area.

Tavishien saw a lot of what she now observed during her Intelligence Bureau training and conditioning. But to see it and experience it in real life was another matter. This weekend acted in part for two purposes, which was not why it was designed. The first was to help get Garratt reacclimated back to his formal life and work off the post-traumatic stress and Neuronic Clarifier side effects but also to stabilize Tavishien because her remote viewing and upcoming mission was deemed more important than Garratt's survival.

Tavishien's role in the future was now at the critical level and soon she would make that ultimate deployment behind enemy lines. Here training regimen would start early in the week after the lover's tryst now ongoing.

Throughout the weekend love and bliss flowed in a sea of amorousness. Tavishien was happy to learn she didn't need to worry about a change of clothes because Madam Ljótunn bon Swartzler brought her everything she needed including underwear, shoes, and socks. Anything else she needed, Garratt took her to department stores to get between their sojourns to places and events that would create memories to last a lifetime.

One of Tavishien's amusing moments was at the ultra large aquarium where Sealife abounds. That triggered her memories of her friends that lived in the remote fishing village. Tavishien asked herself, *"I wonder how they are doing? "*

Since the Black Mountain Resort was the finest establishment in the area, there wasn't a point in going elsewhere. Saturday and Sunday evenings, Madam Ljótunn bon Swartzler helped create a cosmic menagerie in the psyche of Garratt who developed splendid temporal anomalies that sped up his recovery.

Time flies when you are having fun and in love. Suddenly it was Sunday evening at the Black Mountain Resort and Garratt was observing the candlelight flickering on Tavishien's face. Garratt had never spent a time like this with a woman in his lifetime, nor had he ever developed such extraordinary feelings. Considerable happiness and optimism evaporated all his fatigue and stress.

Garratt knew something he could never divulge to Tavishien. Once she tagged the Tartar leader, she would be brought back to the Intelligence Bureau Campus and never allowed to go beyond enemy territory again. Tavishien was too valuable to risk.

All Garratt had to do was get Tavishien through this last mission then they could set their course on their private lives and living a new life together, slowly dissolving their relationship with the Intelligence Bureau.

 Garratt would train someone to replace himself and he would leave behind the spy business, relocate, and change his identity with the help of the spymasters as his golden parachute and out of harm's way forever. *But will they really let me retire?* Garratt pondered.

Most people don't know what they lost until it happens. They get complacent and assume it will always be there. Garratt was no fool. He knew sitting in front of him was someone precious and he knew exactly what he would lose if something happened to Tavishien. *Why did I let myself fall in love?*

Knowing they had to go back to work tomorrow and would see less of each other, it was a somber moment. The dinner music was superb, and the food was rather excellent, but Garratt didn't eat much and eventually the waiter wondering if she should take away the entrée dishes ask Garratt, "Sir are you finished with your meal?"

"Yes, please take it away."

Garratt possibly ate three or four bites out of the wonderful entrée the chef worked extremely hard to make it to perfection. When the waters brought the untouched meal back to the kitchen the chef was alarmed and told the waitress, I'm going to change into my VIP service uniform, please wait here. I want you to take me to the guest who didn't eat his entrée."

In five minutes, the chef was dressed almost in a Tuxedo which he put on to meet some of the VIP that came to Black Mountain Resort. The waitress escorted the Chef to the table, and she informed the Chef on the way, it was the gentleman who did not eat much of his meal."

The Chef approached Garratt and said, "Good evening, sir, I hope you are enjoying your time here at the resort."

"Yes, having a lovely time."

"I noticed sir you didn't eat much of the meal. Did I make a mistake in preparing it for you?"

"Not at all, it was magnificent."

"But you were not enthused about eating it."

"I'm sorry sir, but there are some things about me you do not know. And the main reason why I could not eat is sitting in front of me."

The chef looked at Tavishien and saw her lovely grace, her beautiful smile, her exotic and beautiful dress which Madam Ljótunn bon Swartzler saved for tonight to be a special gift for Tavishien for all she had done to help her gain quick wealth in the garments she secretly modeled.

From a shorter distance the Chef could see Tavishien's skin and the finer points in her face and her magnificent curves. He now understood vividly because sometimes love has strange effects on men's appetites, and tonight he just witnessed it again.

"Sir, I understand vividly, and it makes me happy to know my efforts were not flawed."

"Not at all, the food was very tasty and any other day I would have eaten it all very abruptly and perhaps not in the best of etiquette."

Right then the Chef started observing tears in Tavishien's eyes. What he didn't know was Tavishien could read Garratts mind and knew how much he loved her. She was touched and those were tears of joy.

The Chef knew he had sparked an emotional response, and it was best if he and the waitress left right away so he said, "In case you get hungry, let the waitress know and I'll make you one of my best creations and put it in a thermos container you can take home with you."

"Thank you, I appreciate that."

The Chef nodded at the waitress, and they returned to the kitchen.

"It's a shame that wonderful meal has to go to waste." The waitress said to the chef when they returned.

"When's your dinner break?"

"In about half an hour."

"Box up that plate in a thermo-container, then enjoy it on your break."

"Thank you, I appreciate that."

"I appreciate what you did for me. It's rare that I get to see the flow of splendid love between people. You made my night."

In a few minutes the tears slowly ebbed and didn't screw up Tavishien's makeup too much, but she insisted, "I need to use the lady's room for a moment."

"Alright dear."

Tavishien went to the lady's room with her purse that had what she needed to fix any flaws she created with the makeup. She was happy the touchup work was minor. She wanted to look her best for Garratt tonight and she felt so wonderful knowing that prince charming loved her. It was her dream come true to find real love in life which she never expected.

By the time Tavishien made it back to their dinner table, the musicians had shifted from dinner music to dance music and the showoffs were already out on the dance floor showing their stuff. That changed the ambience of the dining hall as the dinner crowd was slowly filtering out quickly being replaced by the dance and party crowd.

Garratt was in a strange mood, not really into the swing of things as he was allowing too many thoughts to get into the way of a fun evening. He was so consumed in thought, he didn't even think to ask Tavishien to dance, which she didn't mind because she knew what he was mentally going through. When the first slow dance started, Tavishien stood up, walked over to Garratt, and held out her hands and said, "Let's go dance."

Soon the couple were dancing and in circumstances like men often tell sweet lies to women they are pursuing, but tonight the roles reversed. It was Tavishien whispering sweet things in Garratts ears and working on the pleasure center of his brain causing immediate response.

Tavishien could feel Garratts erection pressing against her, and she was delighted she had shifted all his concerns from his big head down to his little head. Garratt was slowly starting to feel splendid euphoria as Tavishien worked her magic on him. Her pheromone laced perfume quickly shed multitudes into Garratts senses and he was quickly captivated by the woman in his arms and feeling that exhilarated release.

The combination of these influences with the effects of the elixir was now redefining Garratts mood and he was no longer foreboding or analyzing his situation. He was now releasing his self-control to Tavishien who was now guiding him on the pathway to happiness.

What started out as a somber and almost dreadful evening pondering the future now transcended into pleasure and fun. After a couple slow dances, the pace picked up so the showoffs could do their last set of extravagant dance moves.

Tavishien feeling energized and the fact Garratt stayed on the dance floor pleased her as she now showed the showoffs, she had a move or two as well. But the big difference was Tavishien's body was much better along with her looks, which exemplified all her moves. In due time the crowd was no longer fixated on the showoff as Tavishien stole the crowd and in the process invigorated Garratt more.

Garratt's watchers made a few silent comments to each other about the eye candy they knew Garratt was banging. One of them elucidated, "What a lucky dog."

As the night wore on Tavishien knew she had peaked Garratt, and it was best they left soon so she could show him some extra special moves as they did the horizontal tango on a theme from Paganini.

"Garratt, I would like to leave now if you wouldn't mind."

"I'm suddenly kind of hungry, is it okay if I ask the waiter for that care package to take home?"

"Sure honey."

Garratt signaled the waitress who was very happy he asked for the care package and very happy Garratt had given her one of the best meals she had in a very long time.

The Chef who did extra good work on the takeout, took the entrée that was going to go out to a couple, put it in a thermo-box and handed it to the waitress, so Garratt had an amazingly short wait.

Thanks to the thermo-box the food was still warm after their first set of horizontal tango's that made Garratt's night. In due time they were sound asleep in each other's arms not thinking about tomorrow.

***

CHAPTER TWENTY
Mission Training Starts

Gabriel had not seen Tavishien this happy in quite a while. There was no doubt in Gabriel's mind that Garratt had achieved great success with Tavishien over the weekend. Gabriel had seen Garratt return from other similar missions in the past. He had never recuperated this fast before.

When Gabriel met with Garratt to go over the training schedule, she could tell he was fully rejuvenated. But she also knew that more than likely Garratt's little head was doing most of the thinking now.

After getting the details on the training schedule, Gabriel was out running eight miles with Tavishien who seemed to have improved endurance. Gabriel who ran every day was having a hard time keeping up with Tavishien. Later during the martial arts training, the instructors noted the vigor in Tavishien's workouts. Her kicks and her punches were nice and strong and up there in force with some of the best practitioners.

After the days training was over, Garratt contacted Tavishien and asked her to meet him at his Skycar. They soon left together back to Garratts home. Garratt explained this is how they would arrange their lives for the time being and took Tavishien shopping to buy her clothes to change into so that they no longer needed to be constantly assisted by Madam Ljótunn bon Swartzler and could live a simpler life, just enjoying each other's company and privacy. This routine continued for a few days, then there were some big changes in training.

With little notice during the working day, at lunchtime Tavishien was requested to go to agent Lucika's office. The staff still knew Garratt as Agent Lucika and had no idea his real name was Garratt Wyclaire, but some were aware he had the disguise as Marti for clandestine operations.

"We are traveling to Perland again for training," Garratt said.

"Like the last time?" Tavishien asked.

"More or less yes, just a refresher for you on all the devices you need to know how to operate."

"Will we get to stay in the same room together this time?"

"We can, but it might be rough for Gabriel to get used to sleeping with Tristan Karjal."

"Don't worry, if Tristan can't figure out how to turn on Gabriel, I'm sure she wouldn't mind teaching him a thing or two."

"Do you know something I don't know?"

"That's obvious don't you think?"

"If Elnar Harkensen has the rooms available, I'll make sure Gabriel gets her own room so that she isn't burdened with training her cub." Garratt said.

"I'm sure Gabriel will come by and help me pack, I'll ask her if she wants company." Tavishien said.

"We have to also be concerned about Tristan." Garratt said.

"It comes with the job; it will not be the first time Tristan's sent somewhere to sleep with another spy to give the right appearances. It will look more legitimate as two couples vacationing."

"Don't worry about Elnar Harkensen, I think he's well aware of who we are," Garratt replied.

"Alright then, I'm going to go pack for a couple weeks."

"Let me know when you are ready to go."

"Will do." Tavishien then winked at Garratt and left his office almost wanting to skip over to her dormitory room feeling happy they were going on a mini vacation where the activity would be fun like the last time.

As Agent Lucika (aka Garratt) secretary was doing the reservations she sent Agent Lucika notification that Elnar Harkensen's Bed and Breakfast Resort only had two rooms available which he responded, "That's alright, book them under my name." *Looks like IBR Tristan Karjal will get his opportunity to get special training from Gabriel. I suppose it's a good thing they are not married.*

In due time the four IBRs were meeting at the parking lot with their luggage and a Skyvan pulled up to take them to the Airport where they got on a transport to fly down to the tourist area. After transferring from the Transport to another Skyvan, they were soon on their way to Perland and landed in the parking lot of Elnar Harkensen's Bed and Breakfast Resort.

When Elnar Harkensen saw the Skyvan land he knew it was probably Marti and his group and went out to meet them and help i carry their luggage to their rooms.

"Welcome back Marti. Good to see you again."

"Thank you Elnar, glad to be back."

"Let me help you with your luggage, your rooms are all ready and paid for by your company."

"That's good to know."

"You got lucky, my two best rooms with the best views were available. They are a little more expensive than the other rooms, so they always sell out last."

"That's good to know."

Rooms 222 and 223 were on the second floor and just like Elnar stated and the views were great. Marti and Tavishien took room 222. Tristan and Gabriel were in room 223 quickly going over their modus of operendus of how they would manage to live together in a room with a large queen-size bed without embarrassing the other.

"I hope you brought pajama's," Gabriel said.

"Oh yes that's how I prefer to sleep."

"Don't get mad if I wake you up when you snore."

"Not a problem." Tristan responded.

The other two, Tavishien and Marti (aka Garratt) went about unpacking and setting up their room in a calm and deliberate manner since they had already grown accustomed to each other. Then they embraced and kissed and Tavishien wanted to take Garratt right then and there but knew they scheduled to meet the other two downstairs in about twenty minutes and walk over to Elijah's Diner because it was already dinner time, and the two couples were slightly hungry.

Elijah and his wife were happy to see these couples again. Not only were they great tippers, but Elijah's wife loved meeting a famous fashion model and wanted to see if she had any new pictures.

After they ordered their dinner and Elijah went off to do the cooking, his wife entertained the guests serving them elixirs then asked Tavishien if she had any new pictures. In the recent past when Madam Ljótunn bon Swartzler dressed Tavishien she always took pictures of her in her glorious outfits and sent them to Tavishien. Hence, Tavishien had some very lovely pictures to share with Mrs. Elijah who was soon ensconced with admiration of Tavishien.

Gabriel looked on and felt so relieved that Tavishien was back to normal mental health and healed from her long absence from Garratt. Gabriel was one of the very few who knew Marti (his alias) was Garratt Wyclaire. And she hoped the Intelligence Bureau would never become aware of this knowledge as it could put her into a serious situation since the Bureau didn't want anyone to know who Agent Lucika really was.

Marti and Tristan simply sat back and observed as Gabriel also got into the lady's chitchat.

Tavishien had a surprise for Gabriel as she pulled up a nice picture of Gabriel when she was all dressed up with her just before

Gabriel got involved in killing the guy and was taken to the remote fishing village.

Gabriel was so proud that Tavishien had that lovely picture when she knew she had dressed up smoking hot to get some attention.

Tavishien thought it only fitting to share the picture with Tristan and showed him as well and in the same moment also did some telepathic investigation and triggered some feelings in Tristan that quickly altered his behavior and thought processes as he now saw firsthand now nicely Gabriel could clean up. To think he was going to be sleeping with this woman tonight really hit him like a ton of bricks. *Can I keep my self-control?*

Elijah's restaurant wasn't very busy that night, so he and his wife spent most of the time sitting next to their guests and talking with them and they too enjoyed an elixir which greatly made it a very happy evening. When the fabulous diners left later, their tips were so generous it was more than paid for the elixirs they enjoyed that night, plus some.

After dinner the two couples walked through the town sightseeing and window shopping then went back to Elnar Harkensen's bed and breakfast to relax and get ready for tomorrow's events.

This training was designed around the area of operations where Tavishien would be inserted. It's unlikely a bicycle was going to be part of it so they would do the three main types of equipment, hovercraft, motor scooters, and powerboats. Later they would go back to the military base and do Terrain Follower refresher training.

The next two weeks were full of Hovercraft, fast boat, and scooter training.

Since Tavishien had impressed the scooter trainer during her previous visit, he didn't waste time with the preliminaries and took her right to the graduate level exercises which she accomplished quite well. He then suggested to Agent Marti (aka Garratt) he teach her some aerobatics. So now the stage was set.

Marti was at first reluctant and fearful she could be injured but soon Tavishien overrode Marti's conservative approach and said, "You realize this might save my life one of these days. I'm willing to attempt the training."

Garratt gave in very reluctantly and quickly wished to hell he had not, but nevertheless, Tavishien was in charge of his head plus his little head, and she took matters in her own hands while controlling Marti with her exceptionally growing mental telepathy she knew was improving as time went by.

Soon Tavishien was copying the super stunt man and doing aerobatics that defied gravity and common sense. Tavishien's sense of gravity and equilibrium was superb and in a matter of a few days mastered many of these tricks the instructor taught her with utter conviction.

At the end of the scooter training Garratt was stunned, but he knew better than anyone he was dealing with a real-life wonder woman. He hadn't figured out how she got under his skin, but it was a fact of life. He now recognized Tavishien had a growing influence over him. He also understood her sweet disposition was full of common sense and lucid awareness. Garratt's confidence in Tavishien was as strong as it ever had been. His trust in her was complete and he knew the obvious. *Tavishien owned his heart.*

The biggest part of the two weeks' training they experienced was getting closer to Elijah and his wife. Tavishien knew Elijah's wife had taken a distinct interest in her fashion modeling and she had saved her special outfit for their last night in paradise. She wanted to reward Garratt for his fantastic love and sweetness, and she directed Garratt to take IBR Tristan Karjal over to Elijah's restaurant because the two women wanted to surprise them with their last night in paradise with a nice makeover.

The two men were enjoying their conversation with Elijah along with special elixirs Elijah served them that was highly illegal because it was laced with special pleasurizers. The reason why it was highly illegal is if women drank this elixir, they would lose all control and be in intense heat needing instant gratification. Theory was if a man drank it and kissed his lover it would affect her just like her pheromones would him.

Tavishien the master spy makeup artist didn't take long to make herself and Gabriel look smoking hot. Gabriel had some nice clothes that were almost as nice as what Tavishien now wore. But with the hair styling and the makeup that Tavishien applied to the two of them, they both transformed into a couple smoking hot women that looked better than the most expensive hookers on the planet.

Tavishien and Gabriel then walked over to Elijah's diner and got intense looks along the way as men in the town were quite perplexed by the superb eye candy.

The two women strolled into Elijah's restaurant and put an exclamation mark on the delayed entry. Elijah's wife was there to greet them, and this made her day, she had two fashion models in her restaurant.

Thanks to Tavishien's relationship with Madam Ljótunn bon Swartzler, she had on a fashion designer's elaborate work that had never been seen in public before. This was the least Madam Ljótunn bon Swartzler could do for Tavishien for filling her pockets full of gold.

However, Ljótunn bon Swartzler was hopeful she would one day be able to film Tavishien wearing it so she could market a copy to her wealthy clients who only wore couture clothing in public and usually only bought if there were no copies floating around.

Garratt's heart dropped to his stomach in awe. IBR Tristan Karjal was now starting to appreciate this assignment as he had just recently *dipped his pen in company ink* because of the insistence of Gabriel.

During the previous night, Tristan was sound asleep having a lovely dream and soon felt very sexual as the woman in his dream was performing fellatio on him. Suddenly his sixth sense of a spy kicked in and he opened eyes and realized Gabriel was under the blankets making him feel so wonderful. Gabriel was a well-trained spy and had done honey pot schemes as necessary in the past during espionage.

Once Gabriel discovered she had woken up Tristan, she repositioned herself next to him and took his hand and guided it down to her womanhood so he would know how wet and desiring she was. Tristan was almost in a state of shock then because of her fantastic physical fitness she kicked Tristan around like a farmer throwing a bale of hay and had Tristan on top of her and grabbed his manliness and said, "A woman has desires too."

Gabriel took Tristan's manliness and inserted inside her womanhood and wrapped her athletic legs around him. She was going to work him just like a Japanese sex bed where the couple only must lay there.

Gabriel jacked Tristan up so much it only took a minute or so for him to explode inside her. But that's all she needed as she was ready for a quicky. She then bucked him like a bronco and sucked all the essence out of him. By the time Gabriel got done with Tristan, he was ridden hard and put away wet.

Tristan had avoided a relationship because he knew as an IBR he was living on borrowed time and married life would be almost impossible with him always coming and going. Very few IBRs were married and most of the time they got married their spouses forced them out of the business fast as it was a huge detriment to family life. Plus, when they got their special spouse briefing, they were left terrified this could come back on them and they might become collateral damage.

Gabriel had thus had a huge impact on Tristan's psyche. But since they were both IBRs it's not the same as marrying a civilian who had no knowledge of an IBR life.

As the two women walked to the table. Tristan was elevated in emotions even more because he had no idea how glamourous Gabriel could appear with a makeover. Some of the IBR watchers who were filming them in brief encounters when they could, were mildly shocked at Gabriel's metamorphism.

Gabriel would never be looked at as a plane Jane IBR ever again. Now they knew she was a secret princess who could put on her crown any time she chose. Thanks to some of the IBR technology, they also knew that *Tristan was dipping his pen in company ink,* and they were profoundly jealous, especially tonight.

When the dinners were all seated and smiling at each other, Elijah's wife asked if she could photograph them because she felt so close to them. Her photographs became some of the most treasured possessions for the rest of her life. She had taken such a fantastic liking to the two couples.

The two weeks had been a lovely time for Elijah's wife. Elijah was also quite happy that his wife was as happy as she was. The couples had brought happiness into the couple and energized the restaurant and now there was a lot more clientele than they and seen in quite a few years.

Some of the Clientele was IBR watchers, some of it was Tartar spies, and some of it was organized crime. Garratt (aka agent Lucika) had a price on his head.

Timing is everything. Before organized crime or the Tartar spies could do the assassination, the two couples departed early in the morning while it was still dark. Nobody saw them leave because everyone was sleeping and assumed their targets would be out in the open again the next day.

Garratt and Tavishien spent the next couple of weeks back at the Intelligence Bureau Campus where physical fitness for both was the task of the day. They worked energetically then went home to Garratts home in the evenings and lived the life of a couple.

Finally, after two weeks they were on their way back to the air force base and Terrain Follower proficiency training. This time, no live ordinance was allowed. Tavishien was now deemed too important to risk injury and death. While there they trained but also got to meet up with their friends, General Taroton and Lateegely.

Garratt had a few intense moments where he sweated profusely as he watched Tavishien fly the Terrain Follower like a crazy woman. Even though the ordinance didn't have a live warhead in it, she still got to practice those dynamic moves just as if they did. To give the feel of a live-round the drone shot a flare when it simulated detonating by proximity fuse. The sky was full of brilliant flares all day long as the intense flying kept Garratt at the seat of his pants, sometimes playing the aggressor and sometimes the observer for SAM missile launches.

This was the worst week of Garratt's life as he witnessed the probable destruction of Tavishien a dozen times, and she amazingly pulled out of it just in time as if she had a six sense. What Garratt didn't know is the herd of Tomlars was protecting Tavishien and guided her to her salvation repeatedly.

At the end of the day not only was Garratt super stressed, so were all the Tomlars going through hell remote viewing Tavishien and giving her split-second decision recommendations that saved her life. Tavishien's actions to Garratt and range controllers seemed supernatural. They had never seen anything like it as if she had a helping hand. Tavishien was helped considerably by the Tomlars who dearly loved Tavishien kept watch over her.

Tavishien's father, Lingraw Arginin, was kind of alarmed at how the Tomlars were acting that week. He eventually synchronized his remote viewing with them and saw their horror. By the end of the day, Lingraw Arginin, was grateful to his daughter, Tavishien when she completed the proficiency training.

Tavishien's father, Lingraw Arginin didn't know if he could handle another day of remote viewing her. He was though grateful the Tomlars were looking out for his daughter and that evening treated them to a special meal he reserved for them several times a year for celebrations. The fermented feed mixed in with their evening meal made them immensely happy and they soon got over the stress of watching Tavishien almost getting killed several times.

Missing missiles coming right at the Terrain Follower and missing crashing into a clump of trees by inches was truly an extraordinary sight to see. When Tavishien and Garratt left the Air Force base and headed back to the Intelligence Bureau Campus, none of the training people would ever think negative about women pilots again. Tavishien had set them all straight as they knew in their hearts there were few men who could have bested her.

The training people would also be wondering forever how Tavishien pulled off some of those superhuman maneuvers where she had to have gone through massive G forces and violent Terrain Follower maneuvers. The training advocacy committee would be studying and reducing the data for weeks to come up with answers and piece it all together for a report the new General who replaced General Taroton would have a hard time accepting and would always have doubt in the published results.

Now it was back to Intelligence Bureau Campus and half day briefings for the mission and half day physical exercise for a couple weeks. Then protocols set in. This was a sad day for Garratt as Tavishien was transported to a secret base where she would launch from to get secretly dropped into Tartarland to tag her target.

It was doubtful that Tavishien could get through the security corridor to reach the Tyrannical Dictator Illtnaut located in the heart of Difland controlled by his best security forces.

Hence, at the last minute, Garratt's superiors decided the best they could do even at high risk was to get Tavishien near one of Illtnaut's top Generals who didn't receive quite the same level of protection, a senior officer General Noel.

Tavishien was now in total isolation far away from society where the most secret operation in a long time was about to proceed.

Garratt was not allowed to be anywhere near Tavishien. He did man a command center supporting the operation.

Tavishien was soon to be inserted into an area of Tartarland that happened to coincide with where her mother came from. She would be deep undercover with great fake credentials provided from an abducted woman who was a loaner and no family. Tavishien read the abducted woman's Aura and it hoped her remote viewing would give a lot of examples of her past life which Intelligence Bureau knew much about thanks to a well-placed spy.

The intelligence Bureau did not know Tavishien also had the growing telepathic ability and she got even more from the woman so by the time she was inserted and had minor cosmetic surgery and handprint modifications, she was primed to step into the abducted woman's former life without anyone suspecting this aloof woman was abducted gone and rarely seen.

Tavishien arrived at the city of Terabine in the central Tartarland area where she would operate from. There was a lot of dead time in the mission while the Intelligence bureau put all the support personnel in position. During this dead time, Tavishien went to a public library to research her mother.

Since Tavishien's mother was a musician who performed with major orchestras, in due time she discovered a lot about her mother. The pictures she observed in the various sources of information matched the photographs in the research files the library had including several picture books.

It was quite an emotional moment and Tavishien saw others in the library photocopying information out of books with their personal communicators which gave her the idea to do the same. She knew the name matched and the information her Papa revealed about her mother and the drawings he made confirmed this was the correct person.

Tavishien was overwhelmed with emotion after she completed the copying and replaced the articles back in the correct positions on the shelves. Tavishien now knew who her mother was, and her relatives and close friends back many years before. *Were any of them still alive?*

In researching her mother's biography and articles about the missing musician, Tavishien discovered her mother's brother who was a prominent citizen of the in central Tartarland city of Terabine.

Tavishien violated the hell out of her assignment directives and made a personal visit to her mother's brother who was still alive and well. Tavishien looked almost exactly like her mother when she escaped Tartarland.

When Tavishien rang her uncle's doorbell, he felt like he had seen a ghost, but this was almost 30 years ago so there is no way she could look this young and when she asked if she could come in and talk to him about his sister, that striking resemblance to her mother is the only reason why he let a stranger into his home.

After Tavishien and her uncle settled down in his living room and he asked Tavishien, "What do you want to talk about? Why did you come here?"

Tavishien responded very succinctly, "You are my uncle."

Tavishien's uncle, Hannikainen, now knew the essence of the purpose of Tavishien's visit. He was utterly shocked by the claim, but nevertheless listed most intently to every word Tavishien now stated.

"I wanted to find out about my mother, so I came to this city to research her and that's how I discovered you. I thought you might want to know what happened to your sister and I was hoping that if you had pictures or information about my mother, you would be willing to share it with me."

Hannikainen suddenly had tears flowing down the sides of his cheeks, but couldn't believe it until Tavishien said, "I would be happy to give you a blood sample to take to get DNA confirmation. I have your DNA."

"That will not be necessary. You look just like your mother."

Tavishien held out a copy of her mother, Maki Zorthun's picture her father Lingraw Arginin had drawn with increíble precision, "My mother Maki Zorthun, when my father first met her."

That image created an emotional tremor in Hannikainen, and the tears were obvious. Tavishien couldn't help but have a few tears herself and so her uncle was feeling a sensual revaluation like he never thought he would experience in his lifetime. The moments passed and slowly they took hold of their emotions and the discussions followed that were the root of why Tavishien was visiting in the first place.

The next few moments were very delicate as Tavishien went on to explain what happened to her mother and how she was sad she never had a chance to see her in her lifetime.

Tavishien's uncle feeling a slight recovery of his emotions offered, "Would you like to see some pictures of your mother?"

"That would mean a lot to me."

Tavishien's uncle Hannikainen showed Tavishien his picture album that contained a lot of pictures of her mother including her concert performances that matched some of the pictures she saw at the library in some of the research items.

Hannikainen also had some recordings of her mother's violin performances and played a couple recorded performances for Tavishien, and when the uncle saw her break down and cry, he knew this was the real deal. The saddest day in Tavishien's life seeing the talent and beauty of her mother.

It was a sad day for both, but it brought closure for both of them as now her brother knew what happened to his sister and her death during childbirth. But the uncle was glad Tavishien's mother managed to have a child before she died, especially such a beautiful woman that looked just like her mother.

They had a long discussion and Tavishien said she would be leaving in a few days but in the future, she would attempt to get back and see Hannikainen again.

Tavishien left her uncle Hannikainen's home and walked a circuitous route back to the abducted woman's home Tavishien now used as well as her identity. Tavishien traveled a distance away including a trip on public transit vehicles back to the home of the woman she now emulated for her part in the mission that was now slowly unfolding.

In due time the mission started the next phase. All the spies inserted were in place and the attempt to tag the general was underway.

Generals are social animals and politicians at heart, and they must go to a lot of parties and socialize with people needed to help them get promotions and maintain their positions of authority. They indeed are social engineers as well as master manipulators.

General Granlinux, very close to the Tyrannical Dictator Illtnaut had been observed by the Intelligence Bureau deep plant moles for several years and under great risk that information carried out by IBRs made its way to the highly compartmentalized Intelligence Bureau Campus area where the deputy director of planning and Agent Lucika (aka Garratt) used that information for planning this mission.

This whole plan evolved around General Granlinux was a womanizer and abused elixirs and alcohol. With daring and luck, the moles were able to piece together the social calendar for General Granlinux. They couldn't figure out some of the private parties, but they did discover his proclivity to frequent certain locations where illustrious and beautiful women hung out in hopes to get an opportunity to meet people of influence. A beautiful woman with a great body that somehow was able to become an influencer could have her future improved by several stratums.

It was under this circumstance that Tavishien was deployed in hopes to get near General Granlinux to read his Aura and in the future remote view him and provide critical intelligence at a time when aggression seemed to be flaring up that not only would create tensions on this planet but space settler colonies that had physical closeness to Tartar planets could also erupt in violence. Nowhere else in the galaxy were two warring factions that controlled many other planets, cohabitated on the same planet where the governments and centers of power existed.

The Tyrannical Dictator Illtnaut wanted to end that posture and wanted the entire planet to be under control of the Tartars. The latest conflicts were associated with the Tartar Dictator Illtnaut probing and testing around the area of Tartarland which also coincided with where Tavishien's father lived in his cabin in the woods. The amount of penetration was systematically expanding to the point where there was some discussion about evacuating all the frontiersmen and people like Tavishien's father due to the probability, the area could erupt into savage fighting.

At the appropriate hour, a limo pulled up in front of the house Tavishien was temporarily living in. She was dressed for the occasion. Tonight, Tavishien was going to Tag General Granlinux, then be extracted out of Tartarland.

The limo driver was one of the moles. He had all the credentials of a limo driver that was no longer around and conveniently deposited where it's unlikely his remains would ever be found. Tonight, the plan failed for one simple reason. The General was exceptionally horny and wanted that blonde at all costs. Working behind enemy lines wasn't as simple as working in a resort.

The General had a lot of assistants to carry out whatever he wanted. He was very easy to approach, that's the way he wanted it and Tavishien approached and quickly read his Aura, but her escape routes were quickly shut off. The moles looked on in observation and suddenly did not have a warm fuzzy as it all unfolded. There was nothing they could do to rescue Tavishien. She would either find her own escape route or she was finished and at the mercy of the General after he got his satisfaction.

But the General's biggest mistake was Tavishien after her experience with the six Tarter soldiers her father killed wasn't going to just lie there and take it.

After the General and his men got Tavishien to his quarters on the base. He had her tied and gagged by his goons too big and mean to overcome even by the powerful Tavishien. The General was going to insert his manliness into Tavishien while she was gagged and tied up. But Tavishien was a smart cookie and decided that since her chances of remote viewing this creep was unlikely, then devised her plan to at least kill him and face the consequences.

In her plan she mumbled something. The general knew she was tied up and could not do much to stop him and decided to pull off the gag to hear what she had to say. Tavishien also did some mental telepathy to manipulate the general. He took off the gag and looked at Tavishien's pretty face.

"What did you want to say?"

"Take off all these restraints so I can make love to you properly, but if I'm going to please you I don't want these assholes to see what I can do for you to make you happy."

General Granlinux sincerely believed Tavishien was going to please him, and the restraints were not necessary looked back at his bodyguards and said, "I think she wants to be friendly with me. You guys go outside and shut the door."

"You will get more sweet loving that way," Tavishien added pouring on the charm.

After the General Granlinux untied Tavishien she then started to perform the fake loving pre-copulation acts to put the General at ease including kissing him on his lips like a real lover would. Then she said, "Lay down on your back so I can begin to please you."

General Granlinux laid back smiling as Tavishien started performing fellatio making the General feel ecstasy and believe it was happening, then Tavishien said, I'm going to get on top of you and show you how a capable woman can please a man.

Tavishien climbed up on General Granlinux smiling kissing him again and rubbing her vagina against his penis making him rock hard and expectant. Then as she pulled away from the kiss, her martial arts training went into effect and before the General could react Tavishien had her fingers in both eyes killing him but not silently as General Granlinux cried out just before she killed him. The guards heard the frantic yell and came into the room, guns drawn and there was Tavishien quickly standing with blood all over her hands and General Granlinux's DEAD!

While one of the security men held the weapon pointing at Tavishien's midsection the other one walked over and saw the General Granlinux's eyes had been poked out and he was dead.

These were world class security personnel, and they knew one thing. Tavishien wasn't a pretty girl. She was something beyond that because it takes a martial artist to do what she had just done, and thus was probably an assassin. They called the appropriate authorities on the base and soon Tavishien was led to an interrogation center at a prison where they started in on her.

Because the security people were slow in unraveling what just happened, they didn't remove Tavishien's shoes for several hours that had microphones and bugs in them. Eventually they did and soon discovered Tavishien was indeed a spy. Unfortunately for Tavishien that was the game changer.

At the moment the beatings began IBR Agent Duff walked into Garratt's office at the special operations compound the mission ran out of with a sad look on his face.

"Agent Lucika, I have some bad news for you."

Garratt (aka Agent Lucika) had worked with Duff on previous clandestine missions and knew the look on his face when horrible news was just about to be relayed. Duff was a no-nonsense kind of guy who never embellished and accurately reported the status no matter how painful it was. For that Garratt appreciated him. But now Garratt knew Duff was going to tell him something that was likely to hit him in the gut.

"What is it, Duff?"

"They caught Tavishien, and they know she's a spy."

Duff could see the tears form in Garratts eyes. Garratt knew the rotten bastards the Tartars could be to spies. He saw the man he had to kill and how puffed up his face was and all the blood. No doubt Tavishien would be like hamburger in the morning.

Even though Garratt felt a ton of bricks had just hit him in the gut, he knew what he had to do.

"Thanks for the report, Duff. Inform the staff we will launch the emergency extraction team shortly to prepare to launch."

"How the hell we going to break her out of that prison?"

"Tatar security has a bad reputation of vigilance decrement early in the morning. While the support craft are in route to the prison we need to indicate to them areas they can bust down without killing Tavishien."

"That's easy, she's in the maximum-security area, so that's on the Northwest corner of the facility," Duff responded.

"Fine, the fighter bombers will level the rest of the buildings so we can get her out without having to waste time fighting the security forces."

"You realize you could cause a war going in like this to save one person."

"They are not ready for a war, but we are."

"Alright boss," I'll go notify the appropriate parties."

"Thanks Duff."

"Agent Lucika, I'll do the best I can."

"Thank you. I appreciate that."

Tavishien got slapped around a little, but the security men were informed top interrogators would arrive in the morning to handle the matter and Illtnaut's Interior Minister will personally arrive to supervise questioning and torture if necessary.

Garratt surprised Duff when he later informed him, "I'm coming along and will be in one of the Terrain Followers protecting the egress route."

"Sir, that's very dangerous. We can't afford to lose you."

"I don't care, it's more important we get Tavishien out alive whether I live or not."

Around 2:00 A.M. when it was expected the Tartar security forces would be suffering from vigilance decrement, the airborne force flew below radar hugging the terrain and crossed the border and were in Tartar Territory. IBRs had given an alert to the military to expect possible action.

The transports flew below the sound barrier and efficiently made their way spread out to a rendezvous point near the prison where a systematic attack would take place using laser guided weapons to do precise targeting to prevent collateral damage to the prison block where Tavishien was being held. As they got near the rendezvous points, the transports disgorged their terrain followers fully loaded with sophisticated weapons and they formed up and were vectored to the prison.

The prison was set up for attack from the ground. Nobody ever considered an air attack so there were no air defenses nearby.

As Tavishien sat in her jail cell with a few minor bruises looking at the rotten bastards that slapped her around outside the bars sitting in chairs acting as sentinels and well-armed, the first bombs struck.

Alarms went off and the lights went out as power had been disrupted. Emergency lights came on. There was maximum amounts of reverberations and low frequency sound spikes from the explosions Total chaos began and a lot of standby prison guards in bunk rooms were incinerated as the buildings were systematically taken down and using infrared anyone running about was gunned down.

The two security men now fearful for their lives headed for an exit to see WTF was going on abandoning Tavishien. Several Terrain Followers landed in the courtyard of the prison surrounded by disintegrated buildings and building materials laying around in large piles with fires burning in several of the destroyed buildings. Grunts piled out of the terrain followers and headed for the high security building.

A few security people shot at them but were quickly cut down by ample fire power as the grunts broke into the building and started searching for Tavishien on all floors yelling out her name and soon one group heard her response. The steel doors to her prison cell were locked shut with no power to open them. The grunts came prepared and had putty like materials to burn holes in the door to extract Tavishien who wasn't in bad shape yet. They led her to safety and put her on a Terrain Follower and the Grunts all got on as well and flew out of the compound taking a few random shots at them from a few of the survivors but didn't receive much damage.

The gaggle of Terrain Followers made a bee line to the transports to fly into and get out of there fast. Garratt and his group of transport defenders were spread around protecting the egress when the alerted Tartar Air Force with a squadron came after them. It was going to be a close call. Garratt knew if he just delayed the Tartars a few moments the rest could escape unharmed and decided he would give his life to Tavishien if necessary.

Flying by radar and target illumination indicators Garratt headed towards the Tartar squadron.

Duff knew exactly what Garratt was up to. He wasn't going to let him die alone and possibly may help him survive. The gaggle of Hovercraft and the transport knew what was happening and so did Tavishien who was now suddenly distressed watching all this transpire.

The Tartar Air Force could not head directly to the Transports because they had formidable craft in the way and Garratt and Duff were already shooting weapons their way they had to avoid turning radically and shooting flares to attempt to jam the heat seeker missiles. Duff got lucky and nailed a couple unsuspecting fighter-bombers but there was just too many of them and he and Garratt had no choice but to fly directly into the hornets' nest to screw up their attack plan.

It was a foregone conclusion of what was going to happen. The remaining Terrain Followers got into the transports just in time and turned and accelerated at high speed and could go just as fast as the attackers who would never be able to catch them thanks to Garratt and Duff doing the supreme sacrifice.

By the time the transports were long gone, Duff and Garratt were lying in wrecked heaps on the ground presumably dead. Duff appeared like he didn't survive and was lifeless. Even though Terrain Followers had some survivability for a crash, the weapons Tartars used appeared to have killed Duff in his valent last moments trying to save Garratt who also succumbed to the lopsided power of the Tartar Airforce.

Garratt survived the crash but was terribly burned and disfigured and sustained terrible internal injuries.

In the morning the Tartar investigative team combed through the wreckages and found the two men. Duff appeared dead but Garratt clinged to life and was soon transported to an emergency room of a hospital where doctors feverously worked on him to save his life with the inducement the Tyrannical Dictator Illtnaut wanted his life saved so he could personally interrogate him.

As soon as the government people left with Garratt, the locals, many of them dissidents, combed through the wreckage to see if there was anything left behind of value. Some of the components of the Terrain Followers included expensive metals that could be cut up by welding torches and metal saws and sold to scrappers for some good income.

They quickly found Duff's body that appeared dead but they decided to put in on an improvised gurney and take him to the villages medical practitioner who was a major dissident and would love to see the Tyrannical Dictator Illtnaut removed from office and replaced with a moderate statesman who would stop the insanity of the conflict with Difland and return to peaceful coexistence as it was before Illtnaut grabbed power in a coup.

The Tartar doctor had Duff's body placed in his emergency surgery room and hooked up life support and began to search for a pulse or shallow breathing which would be the case of a severely injured and burned person on a coma.

***

CHAPTER TWENTY-ONE

Agent Lucika

Agent Lucika underwent several emergency surgeries as the doctors scrambled to save his life. They barely saved his spleen, kidneys, and liver. In a deep coma, there was very little mental activity, but he had a pulse, heartbeat, and shallow breathing that was improved by a respirator as they slowly cleaned out his scared lungs partially damaged in the explosion and subsequent wreckage.

The Terrain Follower Agent Lucika crashed, had a protective cage like racecars and other high-speed devices. If the Terrain Follower wasn't too high in altitude and came down at an angle and not a steep vertical trajectory, there was hope the safety cage would off a high degree of impact protection.

Luckily for Agent Lucika and IBR Duff they had significant forward velocity as they were charging directly head onto the Tartar Air Force components. The occupants of the Terrain Follower were encased in a fire-retardant protective sphere inside the protective cage thus were spared life threatening fires from spilled propulsion fuel.

Even though they had some burns that disfigured them, the rest of their bodies escaped most of the fire damage. Most of the damage to their bodies occurred from the pyro-techniques that detonated when the proximity fuses ignited them.

After approximately three weeks the Tartar doctors informed the Tyrannical Dictator Illtnaut's security personnel who were guarding the prisoner, they had done all the medical treatments possible, the patient remained in a coma and now it was just wait time to see if he regained consciousness. At some later date if Illtnaut approved they would begin reconstructive surgery on the side of his head that received most of the deformations during the crash. But there was no point in starting those complex cosmetic surgeries if the patient didn't regain consciousness and remained in a vegetative state in a coma.

By now the Tomlars had remote viewed and understood the circumstances of Tavishien including her heart break. She was now at her father's cabin with the Tomlars, crying every day and showing great psychological damage by losing the love of her life.

The Tomlar who had been taken to the hospital when Tavishien was recovering from her ordeal with the six Tartar Soldiers had read Agent Lucika (aka Garratt's) Aura then and had remote viewing ability with Garratt and every day searched for Garratt. For several weeks there was nothing to find because in Garratt's vegetative state, all his brain waves were minimal and even his delta and theta waves were barely observable by the best instruments.

Just when Tavishien was contemplating suicide, which disturbed the Tomlars quite substantially, Garratt suddenly started having a pickup in brain wave activity and was slowly entering a dream state with increased Delta and Theta brainwaves.

The Tartar doctors knew this but also knew the Tyrannical Dictator Illtnaut would want them to use shock treatment or other means to bring Agent Lucika out of the dream state so the interrogators could start working on him.

The doctors knew the delicate nature of Garratt's physical condition and knew they had to buy him as much time as possible so that he could be restored back to a functional human being. They withheld brain wave awareness from the Tartar security people for several more weeks and informed them daily the spy remained in a vegetative state, but his body functions were slowly getting better, and his kidneys and liver were now functioning which was a good sign he was going to live and probably regain consciousness.

The spleen surgery was touch and go but the doctors did miraculous surgery, and that organ was now functioning and would be viable adding to Agent Lucika's positive prognosis.

It was at this time, Tomlar, with the greatest sensitivity to Garratt detected his growing delta and theta brainwaves. And just as Tavishien was contemplating suicide to be done that day, the Tomlar surprised her with an unexpected remote view that informed her Garratt was still alive.

Tavishien suddenly jolted out of the melancholy and severe negative personal psychology and was aroused by the news. Her contemplation of suicide abruptly ended. In a way, the Tomlar had just saved two lives, Garratt and Tavishien. Without his intervention in due time, they both would be dead because Tartars executed spies after their interrogations concluded they got all the useful INTEL out of the spy.

Because of the notification from the Tomlar, Tavishien then concentrated on her own remote viewing of Garratt, and she too soon was able to detect his meager delta and theta brainwaves. Her heart was suddenly uplifted because now there was a chance, they could rescue Garratt and she would do what he did for her, but she also suspected Garratt's rescue mission was compromised and there might be another mole within SIS at the Intelligence Bureau Campus, thus she herself would have to plan a way to break Garratt out. And she knew one place she could go and get help, her uncle if she could get to him.

Where Garratt was being held in the hospital didn't have much security and Tavishien knew she had the means to disable the security men and break Garratt out, then it was just a matter of taking him and escaping the country, the same way her mother did, walk out. But she also knew one other thing, once she got past the border, her father would be waiting to assist.

Tavishien needed help to get Garratt back to Difland and to her uncle whom she knew she could count on his assistance.

Gabriel had been sent weekly to check up on Tavishien since the incident. She tried to bring a couple psychiatrists along to help Tavishien deal with her grief, but they were quickly asked to leave and never come back, as Tavishien would personally shoot them if they returned.

Tavishien allowed Gabriel to visit only because Gabriel brought some supplies during her visits that made life a little more palatable in the cabin. Things that people would not realize how wonderful the products were like toilet paper, toothpaste, mouth wash etc.

Even though Garratt was still in the dream like state, Tavishien knew she had to start the planning now if they were going to do it any time soon. The following day Gabriel arrived with a few supplies, had been getting more concerned at Tavishien's mental state and was almost ready to have people fly in and sedate her and take her to a treatment center.

Today when Gabriel arrived and met Tavishien, she was in a quick state of shock. *Tavishien was smiling and happy!*

Tavishien's father was away from the cabin with the Tomlars, so Tavishien took the opportunity to converse with Gabriel that quickly explained why she had such a profound change in spirit.

Gabriel, being a smart lady, knew better than to inquire and felt Tavishien would soon be elucidating why she seemed to have changed her attitude. The timing of those thoughts was quite perceptive as all that soon followed.

Just as she predicted Tavishien began the revelation.

"I have a couple things to tell you, but you have to promise me on your life you will not reveal this to anyone without my permission and I have a reason."

"What's your reason?"

"I believe Garratt got shot down trying to protect us because we still have a mole at the Intelligence Bureau Campus who tipped off the Tartar Air Force."

"What makes you think that?"

"I don't want to get into that right now. We can deal with that later, but I need your help now more than ever."

"You know you can count on me."

"Alright, remember do not report this to anyone. However, we may have to bring someone in to help us and the only other person I know I can trust is IBR Tristan Karjal."

"I agree we can trust him because he's now my personal lover."

"Good for you. I hope he pleases you."

"Like I never dreamed of."

"Alright you will have to bring Tristan in on it in a place where we know nobody else can hear it."

"And where is that place?"

"Right here near this cabin. I know I can take us a short distance away from here where it's unknown to anyone and not possible to put bugs there. But when we go there together, we must leave our personal communicators in the cabin because they can probably trace them and monitor us."

"What's the other thing you're going to tell me?"

"When you bring Tristan back out on your next trip, come a few days earlier, come up with an excuse I asked you to bring me something, I will reveal it then and how I want to deal with it. I want Tristan to know, he cannot discuss this with any IBR or anywhere back at the Intelligence Bureau Campus."

"Alright dear," Gabriel said feeling relieved that Tavishien had such a positive abrupt change.

"One other thing."

"Sure Tavishien, what?"

"I know when you get back to the Intelligence Bureau Campus, your superiors will be asking about me. No doubt they want to try again soon to get a remote view of Illtnaut. You obviously see that I've had a huge improvement to my psyche."

"Yes, I can tell."

"Just tell them you saw a slight improvement and in due time I'll slowly get over this mess. Because if you tell them I'm cheerful it will upset our plans. When you come back then I will tell you. Don't speculate on it and do not mention this to anyone because you have no idea how ruthless these evil bastards are and what they might do. When you get back, I will explain it to you, then you will understand."

"Got it and I'm so relieved you are in a much better mood."

"So am I."

Gabriel didn't need Tavishien to tell her what cheered her up. Gabriel knew women and knew for a fact only one thing would have such a drastic change on Tavishien, and it had something to do with Garratt Wyclaire. And such a positive change meant one thing.

Somehow Tavishien knew Garratt was alive. That meant she was remotely viewing him. But she also knew the complexities of the spy agency and sending someone into assassinate Garratt was not out of the question because Garratt himself had been sent in to kill one of their spies who knew a lot less than Garratt did. Tavishien didn't need to say no more. Tavishien already was formulating a plan to rescue him.

It now was a foregone conclusion to Gabriel that perhaps Tavishien was being very secretive about Garratt's situation because she feared his own government would silence him, or was there more to it? She would find out in a couple days when she brought Tristan back with her.

***

The Tartar doctors treating Agent Lucika (aka Garratt) were silently delighted at what they were seeing as the delta and theta waves had grown measurably stronger. At this time Garratt was having dreams about a woman but didn't know her name. The Tomlars remote viewing Garratt knew they had to wake him up soon or the doctors would be told to disconnect life support and let the man die.

These Tartars knew what Garratt was sent to do and succeeded at helping to break a female spy out of prison. There really wasn't much more to the case they really needed to know. This man was just another pawn in the game of international clandestine operations. Thanks to their mole they would eventually get his information so there really wasn't much more necessary to waste valuable resources on restoring him.

The Tomlars had heard the conversations via the remote viewing and even though Garratt wasn't processing the information he could hear the conversations and so could the Tomlars.

As they applied the entire Tomlar head's efforts they started causing Garratt to begin developing Alpha then Bravo and Gama brain waves. A couple of the doctors treating Garratt were neuro brain injury experts and they knew that when a patient started exhibiting this combination of brain wave patterns they were soon to be awakened.

This was very provincial in Garratt's case because the security men mentioned to the doctors as they were leaving for the day with no need to stick around for the human vegetable, "If he's not revived by morning, we are going to have you pull the plug on the life support."

Another lucky break for Garratt, he didn't open his eyes until the security men were gone and out of the building.

One of the doctors standing beside Garratt saw him open his eyes.

The doctor knew not to stress the patient and waited patiently smiling and waiting for Garratt to utter something and determine if it was intelligible. They knew this man was likely a spy because of the intense interest the government agents had with him and thus may not be able to speak the Tartar language. But one of the doctors, studied in a medical school not far from where the Intelligence Bureau Campus currently existed and would be able to easily translate what the man said.

The Tomlars notified Tavishien Garratt was now awake right after Gabriel left allowing them to focus all her attention on Garratt and remote viewing him and trying to signal him, but he wasn't responding, and he seemed to not remember anything.

Garratt had lost his memory in the crash and would take a lot of therapy to regain portions of it. Sadly, a lot of it was probably irrevocably gone.

The Doctor who could speak with a Crawflang Empire Dialect, said in

Garratt's native tongue, "Good afternoon, sir, how are you feeling?"

Garratt could not remember who he was did understand the question somehow and knew he could answer, responded, "I'm not sure how I am, I feel kind of strange."

"You are being given some pain relief medications and things might seem strange to you."

"It has been strange. I think I had a very long dream."

"That's expected with your trauma and the medications."

"I have no idea where I am."

"You are in one of the finest hospitals in the Tartar Empire."

"How did I get here?"

"Do you remember your plane crash?"

"No. Was I in a plane crash?"

"Yes. Your aircraft crashed and burned you were lucky you survived. You had a partner with you. He wasn't quite so lucky."

"He died?"

"Yes, he was pronounced dead at the scene."

"Do you know what his name is?"

"We were kind of hoping you would tell us."

"I would if I knew what his name was. I don't remember being with another person or a plane crash."

"Do you know what your name is?"

Garratt thought for a moment and said, "I don't remember my name, perhaps you can get it from my personal affects at the crash site."

"You don't remember your name?"

"No. Perhaps you can notify the police and they can help find out who I am with a lost person investigation. Someone must know I'm missing."

"The police have thoroughly investigated you and they have not been able to come up with any reported missing persons."

"There has to be someone that knows I'm missing and went to the police."

"I'm sorry, but there have been nobody reporting you are missing."

"There must be some way to find out who I am. I can't believe a person can come up missing and nobody knows."

"I'm very sorry sir, but that seems to be the case."

The doctor saw tears form on the side of Garratt's face and a few drops slowly went down his cheeks.

"Are you sad sir?"

"I'm just profoundly shocked nobody knows who I am, and nobody is interested in finding out what happened to me."

"If we help you recover your identity and some of your memory, will you be willing to work with us?"

"I will do anything you ask of me."

"Would you be willing to go under hypnosis?"

"To get back my memory I will try anything. I want to know who I am."

"It's not uncommon for someone like yourself that had some brain trauma to suffer some sorts of amnesia, and sometimes people recover on their own and start remembering things, and from that we can do things to help bring back more memories, but often a portion of it is gone forever. It can never come back."

"Well, if we can find out who I am, then we can go to where I live and meet people that know me who can give me information about where I came from and who I am."

"Our sponsors are truly interested in you regaining your memory, they will allow us to work with you and provide you with rehabilitation that will hopefully help restore some of your memories and give you back your identity."

"Thank you, that means a lot to me."

"We do not think you are well enough to start hypnosis now. I think maybe in a week after some of the treatments we did run their course, your general health situation will have improved, then we can start with hypnosis and other treatments and hopefully we can discover something to give us a clue where you came from."

"What about my fingerprints and facial recognition?"

"We were not able to fully do the facial recognition because you had some severe trauma to the face, and it is not able to identify you. None of your fingerprint data matches anything in our records."

The doctor saw the tears streaming down the face of Garratt. He knew Garratt was upset about losing his memory and thought maybe it would be best if he sedated him. Especially before they showed him a picture of what he now appeared like.

"I'm going to give you your pain medications now. We need to keep up those medications for a few more days until we know your skin has healed enough to tolerate not being given pain relievers."

"Alright, do whatever you think is necessary doctor."

"I wish I could call you by your name, but we don't know that yet. Hopefully through work with our staff psychiatrist he can help you find a way to remember some of your past."

"I would be very grateful doctor."

The doctor nodded at the nurse holding a tray of medicines, mostly injected for the best efficacy, and a couple swallowed in the form of a nice tasting liquid.

Garratt took his medications then laid back into his bed and in a few brief minutes thanks to the medications he was back off at a dream state.

The Tomlars and Tavishien knew what had just happened. It was almost heart breaking to Tavishien, but it raised her desires to enact an effective plan to help Garratt escape the hospital and be brought back to the Intelligence Bureau Campus where hopefully the surgeons who routinely did cosmetic surgery to change a spy's identity would repair a lot of damage to Garratt's face. Tavishien didn't mind if it even changed him into a different looking person because she knew what was inside Garratt and in his heart, mind, and soul.

The following morning Garratt was still sleeping when the security force arrived to direct the doctors to disconnect the life support equipment. They were quite surprised. The respirator and much of the life support equipment was already disconnected and out of the room. The only medical instruments that remained were monitoring equipment that now showed the displays and numbers of a living healthy person.

The chief medical official, Garratt's primary care giver met the men bedside as Garratt continued to doze in his drug induced pleasant sleep where at times, he was dreaming about Tomlars and wondered what that was all about.

"You have disconnected all the life support equipment?" The head security representative asked.

"Yes, he doesn't need those services any longer." Doctor Gemerkt replied.

"Has he become conscious?"

"He's showing intermittent signs of consciousness. I think in about three days he will likely become fully conscious."

"Anything you can to do speed that along?"

"If we did cognitive enhancements now, it's possible we would destroy a lot of his memories. It's best we allow him to regain consciousness even if it takes a few days longer so that he will be much better able to tell you what happened to him and how he received these extensive injuries."

The security team had never informed the doctors this person was an enemy combatant they had shot down and planned to heavily interrogate him. The doctors knew vividly the activities and brutal treatments they had inflicted upon people because they had restored a few of them to the point the interrogations could continue.

The doctors knew what kind of men the Tyrannical Dictator Illtnaut employed. Men who would twist the heads off puppies for amusement and treat women spies or Illtnaut's enemies just as badly.

Most of Doctor Gemerkt's friends were dissidents and if had some way to help the man escape, he would. The luckiest day of Garratt Wyclaire's life was being assigned to this neurosurgeon as a patient.

Illtnaut's security men hung around the hospital all day long, casually walking into Garratt's private hospital room from time to time and never saw him stir so they decided to come back in the morning.

"Doctor if he regains consciousness, call me immediately."

The Security man handed Doctor Gemerkt his business card with contact information on it. There was nothing on the card to indicate Klaus Sorge worked for Dictator Illtnaut and his security apparatus. But Doctor Gemerkt had seen several patients brought in that had been tortured almost to death by this scourge named Klaus Sorge.

"I will, but I must warn you it could be in the middle of the night or very early in the morning."

"That's alright, any time of day will be greatly appreciated."

"Alright then, you will promptly receive the phone call."

"Thank you doctor."

"You are welcome, sir."

The security men left just in time because in just moments Garratt opened his eyes. He had been listening to the conversation and something in the back of his mind was telling him to remain quiet and act like you were sleeping. Garratt didn't realize he was receiving help from the Cabin in the woods as Tavishien and the Tomlars kept an ongoing vigil and when Tavishien needed sleep the herd promised to wake her immediately if there were any changes or anything she needed to promptly know about.

About fifteen minutes after Klaus Sorge left the hospital, Garratt opened his eyes and Doctor Gemerkt was standing by his bedside checking his blood pressure and monitoring all the equipment showing his heartbeat respiration and other vital health indicators.

Doctor Gemerkt said, "Welcome back, I'm glad to see you are awake."

"Thank you. I felt like I had a really good nap."

"You did and it lasted about 24 hours." "I feel like I need to use the bathroom."

"No problem, let me grab someone to assist me getting you into the bathroom to do your business."

Doctor Gemerkt briefly walked out of the room can came back with a strong looking orderly that was on staff there because they treated some mental patients that sometimes had to be physically restrained so they would not hurt themselves or other patients.

"Okay sir we are going to help you to your feet and put you in this wheelchair and take you into the bathroom."

"Thank you."

"See this lanyard hanging down from the ceiling?" the orderly said after they got him into the bathroom and situated on the toilet."

"Yes."

"When you are finished, pull it and we'll come get you."

"Thank you."

The doctor and the orderly left the bathroom and shut the door. Garratt did his business and wasn't sure he could stand up. He wanted to but didn't want to fall. He also had looked at the bathtub and decided he would like to take a bath so when the Doctor and the orderly returned, he asked the question: "Would it be possible to take a bath?"

"That would actually be good for you, and I'll have some additives added to the water that will greatly help you."

"Thank you."

Moments later Garratt was in the soapy bath water laced with pleasurizers and bioactive chemicals that influenced health and tranquil psychology. Garratt didn't quite understand why the bath felt so wonderful, but it greatly improved his sensibility and forbearance.

The bath felt so good, but there were a few places on his arm that scratched because of the capped off feeding tube also used to administer medications. Other than that, Garratt felt great but noticed he had some discolored skin and several scars. He had no idea the number of extensive surgeries he went through putting his body back together so he could continue living as a viable person.

He was surprised there were no mirrors in the bathroom or in his hospital room. *If I can see myself in the mirror, maybe I'll remember who I am,* Garratt thought.

When Garratt decided he had enough of the bath, he pulled the lanyard and the orderly and the doctor immediately came into the bathroom.

"I'm had enough, can you help me out of the bathtub?"

The super strong orderly didn't need any help raising Garratt and the doctor already had placed towels in the wheelchair for Garratt to sit on the wheelchair then the orderly handed Garratt a towel to dry himself with and while Garratt proceeded to dry himself the orderly took a hair dryer off the counter top nearby with a brush and proceeded to dry and comb his hair.

Garratt was very lucky he was wearing a helmet at the time of the crash and even though one side of his face needed further reconstructive surgery to bring back a semblance of handsomeness, his hair and scalp were undamaged. His hair had grown quite a bit since the shoot down and the orderly said, "In the next few days, I think we need to bring a barber in the room to cut your hair."

Moments later Garratt was back in his hospital bed that had been changed while he was taking a bath feeling extra good with clean skin, clean sheets and felt considerably better except he suddenly started feeling hungry.

"How soon before I can eat something?" Garratt asked and the Doctor.

Doctor Gemerkt immediately responded, "We must be careful what we feed you for a few more days until your last surgeries have healed. But I think it would be okay for you to have soup now." He nodded at the orderly who knew instinctively what to do.

In a short while, Garratt was enjoying a rather pleasant soup that was filled full of the same nutrients he would get in his feeding tube while he was on life support. The doctor noted the great prognosis, he had a good bowel movement had successfully eaten and now his gut bacteria was flourishing because of the contents of the soup.

Garratt was in a good mood and the doctor then asked him if he was able to remember or think of anything.

"I don't know why but I've been having dreams about Tomlars."

"Is it possible you were raised in the Arctic area?"

"I have no idea, but the Tomlars seem so real in my dreams."

"No memory of your family?"

"Doctor, you have no idea how much I wished I remembered my family."

"In a couple more days after you have gotten better, a neuro-research associate will visit you and attempt hypnosis to see if he can help spring some memories."

"I'm looking forward to that, I'll do whatever he asks of me because I really want to know who I am."

"Alright."

The doctor nodded at the orderly who knew it was time to take the soup dishes away and as he was putting all that on a cart the doctor instructed him, "I want you to come back after you dispose of those dishes with a mirror."

"Sure, thing doctor, should I bring some sedatives?"

"Yes, what we planned on giving him tonight after his meal."

The orderly was gone for a few minutes, then came back with a small cart that had syringes and medical bottles on a tray as well as a mirror.

"Before we have you look in the mirror, I want to go ahead and give you your medications now."

"Sure thing, doctor."

The doctor then gave his patient several injections and knew that in about 15 minutes, his patient would be sound asleep in spite of horror he would now see looking at the mirror.

"You ready to look now?"

"Yes, it might help me remember who I am."

At this very moment, Tavishien and the Tomlar herd were remote viewing Garratt. They too would soon see Garratt's new image as he looked into the mirror.

The doctor handed his patient the mirror and Garratt started looking. One side of his face was destroyed. It was all scar tissue. The other side looked much like he suddenly remembered. But he still didn't recall his name and Tavishien knew it would be unsafe for Garratt to know his own name before she broke him out of that hospital.

The doctor watched Garratt's reactions and saw a few tears appear but otherwise no verbal or physical response. At this time Garratt was receiving messages he had no idea where they were coming from saying in essence, you can be repaired by cosmetic surgery, don't worry about this. I still love you.

Then suddenly Garratt smiled which caused the doctor to be quite perplexed.

The doctor then asked, "Is there something you remembered looking into the mirror?"

His patient responded, "I don't remember her name, but I know a woman loves me. I suddenly felt her love and it felt good."

The doctor knew this was quite an extraordinary event and knew instinctively it was that woman he thought about that would repair the synapse and help him remember who he was. This was great progress.

The medications the doctor gave his patient didn't seem to be working, he sat there smiling, fully awake and alert. The doctor sat down in the chair near the patient's bed and at the same time directed the orderly, "Go ahead and take the cart back to your office. That's all we need for now unless I contact you."

"Alright sir, someone will be here all night long, by my shift ends in about an hour."

"Thank you for your help today," the doctor said to the orderly.

"It's my pleasure to work with your doctor. I've seen the miracles you have performed," the Orderly replied.

"Those are not miracles; they are just better understanding of patients."

"Whatever you say doctor, but I appreciate the progress I always see with your patients."

"Thank you."

The doctor sat beside Garratt for almost 30 minutes observing and wondering why he wasn't responding to the injections, but the fact the patient was smiling and happy after seeing the horror of his personal catastrophe, left quite an impression on the doctor.

Finally, after 30 minutes Garratt laid back in his bed and shut his eyes going into a deep sleep receiving love from a woman in ways, he had no idea how it worked but it was if she were in the room speaking to him. His lover was living in his head speaking to him. He wished he remembered her name, but something told him she would never give up on him and they would one day see each other again. *She will find me.*

The doctor made sure the monitoring equipment was picking up all the appropriate signals, then he went back to his office, filled out all the required files, then left the hospital after checking out at the nurse's station. The doctor got into his surface transporter and drove to his home. He lived with his sister Marina, one of the members of the inner circle of the dissidents who would do anything to see the demise of the Tyrannical Dictator Illtnaut.

Doctor Gemerkt knew all about his sister, a once very successful trial attorney, until she ran afoul of Illtnaut and his henchmen. Her lawyer's license was stripped from her, and she had no means of an income now and the good doctor took her in to help her as much as possible.

There had been discussions with her about the unique patient. Marina knew how to keep a secret, especially something as precious as this one. She also knew her brother was distressed because as soon as he got the patient back to normal, the Illtnaut henchmen would take him away to some undisclosed location where the torture would be horrendous. The doctor felt terrible that he restored the patient just so he could go through terrible suffering again.

Knowing what kind of trauma, the patient experienced before being saved at the hospital created a sense of sadness in the good doctor. His sister Marina read his body language with great precision as a former trial attorney she knew vast things about body language.

Just like many other late-night arrivals at home, when Doctor Gemerkt arrived home he had lost his appetite and his own mental condition was having trying times as he felt responsible for what soon would be bestowed upon the patient.

"I see you are down in the dumps. Is it your patient again?"

"We made great progress today. But I'm sad because I know what will soon happen to him when Illtnaut's henchmen take him away."

"Perhaps there is a way we can help him escape?"

"You and I can't be involved. We live under a microscope."

"I do have friends you know?"

"Yes, all too well."

***

CHAPTER TWENTY-TWO
Planning and Execution

Arrived in a Terrain Follower, checked out at the couple days later as expected, Gabriel and Tristan military base thirty miles away.

Gabriel brought a few items along to make it look good as if this was a social call. After they went into the Cabin, Tavishien handed them each a piece of paper they instantly read which said, "This place is bugged by the SIS. Everything we say is being recorded. Don't say anything important until I take you away from the Cabin."

The two nodded at Tavishien who then took the papers back and placed them in her pocket she would soon throw into the fireplace before they left the cabin.

"How are you doing these days?"

"Doing a lot better thank you. The Tomlars have kept me busy lately. It's that time of year they like to journey further away from the cabin, so I must walk longer and longer distances to find them and bring them back to the barn for the night."

"You look good, looks like you have worked a little on that tan."

"When I'm here at the cabin and nobody else is around I can walk around nude getting a full body tan. It seems to help me a lot."

"I should probably make a few surprise visits, Tristan said jokingly just before Gabriel gave him an elbow in the ribs."

"You don't have to be so sensitive."

"She's like my sister you know."

"Sorry."

"I have an idea us go for a walk and if the two of you decide to fight it out you will not break any furniture," Tavishien responded with an evil smile.

"Good idea," Gabriel responded.

Gabriel assumed there were hidden cameras around the cabin and took no chances and led the two in a circuitous route to where she wanted to go.

Papa was a long way off out looking for some live game for dinner which meant Tavishien could take the two people she trusted to their secret hiding place they would hide out if war came to this area.

Behind a couple boulders was a long steel bar probably 6 feet long and over an inch in diameter. Tavishien's father obtained this bar when he was building his cabin to help move the long beams around when he was building the home. One end of it had a flat spot making it an ideal pry bar. She walked over to a large boulder and used the bar to pry out outwards about a foot. She then stepped into the cavity and pushed on the hidden handles on the other side of the boulder. It did not take a tremendous amount of effort on her part since the boulder was on a rounded steel spheroid shaped privater her ingenious father and black smithed and designed and build himself.

Now there was plenty of room for the other two to enter. When they got inside, they discovered shelves of sealed food packages and numerous plastic water bottles filled for emergency purposes.

"Looks like you guys could stay here a long time," Gabriel said. "My Papa said we only need about 30 days supplies because he knows that how long the war would last."

"With today's weapons, that's probably true."

"Alright now that we have established secrecy, what is it you want to tell us Tavishien?"

"You must promise me not to reveal this to anyone because I have my reasons which I do not want to disclose to you," Tavishien stated in a most serious manner.

"Alright, your secret is safe with us. What is it?" Gabriel asked but figured out in advance what Tavishien was likely to state.

"Garratt is alive, and I know where he is being held."

"And where is that?"

"He's in a Tartar hospital."

"Shouldn't we alert the SIS so they can arrange to rescue him."

"One of the reasons why I do not want SIS informed is they may decide its less risky to send in an assassin to kill Garratt than it would be to rescue him."

"Why would they do that?"

"They did it before, in fact Garratt did the assassination as Agent Lucika."

"How do you suppose we get him out of that hospital?"

"I have a plan and will require very little support. All I need from you guys is transportation, once I get there, I can break him out and get him back."

"What do you want for transportation?"

"My plan involves using a hovercraft to deliver a scooter and once I get the scooter on land I can get to the hospital and get him out."

"Do you expect the hovercraft to come back to pick the two of you up?"

"No that's too dangerous. How we will get out is a secret I have to keep to myself to make sure it's viable."

"We are your best friends; you don't trust us?"

"Listen, I know as soon as the SIS discovers you deposited me on Tartar Soil, they will interrogate you including possibly using a neuronic clarifier and break you. By you not knowing they will not know and after I get Garratt back, I'll tell you why."

This left Gabriel and Tristan in quite a conundrum. It added a huge mystery to it, and they were now very apprehensive because they both knew Tavishien had remote viewer capability and she might have discovered something that would alarm them.

The thought of receiving the neuronic clarification treatment didn't please them, but they also know the agency would only press that so far after repeated polygraphs showed they were forthcoming on all information except how Tavishien was going to get out of there with Garratt and furthermore what was Garratts condition after experiencing the Terrain Follower crash? What happened to Duff? There were a lot of questions hanging.

The meeting soon ended and within a week they would execute the plan and God help them if Tavishien was captured again.

***

The next morning Klaus Sorge and his goons showed up at the hospital. Doctor Gemerkt protected himself by notifying Klaus Sorge, *the patient had regained consciousness for a brief period of time but was feeling some terrible pain, so he was sedated and resting.*

Garratt was still sleeping when the security men entered his room. An orderly was in attendant recording some remarks in his chart.

"The patient is still sleeping?"

"Yes. We expect he will probably wake up around noon time and we'll feed him and try to get his system digesting food the normal way through his digestive track, give him sedatives, pain killers and a bath."

"What time do you think you will be done with all that activity?"

"If he wakes up around noon time, he should be done with all of that by

14:00."

"Will he be able to talk then?"

"We hope so."

"Was he coherent when he woke up?"

"He didn't have much to say other than he was feeling a lot of pain in the areas we did a lot of surgery, but other than that he was not very talkative. Answered a few of our questions."

"What questions did you ask him?"

"We asked him who he was and if he had any family, we could contact to let them know he is here."

"What was his answer."

"He doesn't know who he is and has stated he will do anything possible to learn who he was."

"Anything else?"

"He said he keeps dreaming about Tomlars. He also said there was a woman in his life, and he knows she loves him and is waiting for him."

"What was his attitude like?"

"We said we will arrange Hypnosis to help him remember."

"What was his response to that?"

"He said he will do whatever it takes to help him relearn who he is."

"Does he know that he's been disfigured?"

"Yes. He asked why facial recognition and fingerprints haven't been able to identify him. Our response was we have tried but could not get a match and nobody has reported a missing person. Then we felt compelled to bring in a mirror, so he knows he's been disfigured."

"How did he respond when he found out half his face was destroyed?"

"He had some tears at first then he started smiling."

"Did he say why he was smiling?"

"He indicated it was because of his lover."

"How long did he remain awake?"

"We had to give him pain killers and sedatives. Those were administered before we gave him the mirror because we knew it would be very difficult for him, like it is for all burn victims."

"Are you sure he's not faking the amnesia scenario?"

"No, the fact he is eager to get the hypnosis and claims he's willing to do anything to get his identity back is rather compelling his brain trauma caused him to lose most of his memory."

"How is he like other patients that had similar train trauma?

"First of all, you can look at the side of his face and see he had a violent event. We suspect whatever it was might be as severe or more than practically any patient we've ever had. Some of those patients regained some of their memory after six months. Some of them never."

"Memories gone for good?"

"Sadly yes."

"They didn't even remember their family members?"

"That's correct, just like they were complete strangers, including former lovers or spouses."

"How soon will we know he's able to start remembering things?"

"We plan on starting the hypnosis in three days. We expect his overall medical condition will have improved to the point the stress associated with the hypnosis will not harm him."

"Any chance of us bringing our neuronic clarification people in at that time?"

"From vast studies it's shown that neuronic clarification can actually be severely counterproductive with brain trauma people."

"What's the best solution?"

Your best hope of restoring enough of his memory so that you can get to the bottom of why he had this trauma is through more healing and hypnosis applied gently and sparingly at first. Each month we can increase this activity and from our experience once we are able to help them regain some of their memory, the healing process usually allows a significant amount of recovery in three to six months."

"Is it possible for him to recover most of his memories?"

"With the amount of trauma he experienced, if he's able to eventually recover half of his memories, he'll be lucky."

"Alright, we'll come back this afternoon, but I plan on asking him a few questions."

"I'm sure he wouldn't mind. He's very eager to find out who he is and where he came from and find his family."

Klaus Sorge nodded and left. He was with the Tyrannical Dictator Illtnaut two hours later giving him a briefing on the condition of the Terrain Follower pilot they shot down.

Klaus Sorge was now also under some pressure. When Illtnaut found the investigators left the other dead Terrain Follower pilot behind and not inspect him for possible clues, he was even more angry when he was later informed *the other airman's body was missing and most likely removed by dissenters.*

Klaus Sorge adamantly said, "The investigators saw no indication of life. There was no pulse and the person who was heavily burned was not breathing."

"Why would the dissidents remove the body?"

"My speculation is to give that person a proper burial. As you know they are also Orthodox Religion practitioners."

"Yea and that's the source of their troublemaking."

"What about the two craft. Was there any useful intelligence discovered in them?"

Our priorities were to get the patient to a medical facility as soon as possible to save his life so that he could be interrogated. When the investigators went back to the crash sites the next day, the dissidents had already carved up the craft and no doubt have sold their take to metal recyclers."

"Any chances of find those items?"

"By now they most likely have been melted down because that is expensive materials."

Klaus Sorge knew this conversation was going to be stressful because Illtnaut was a very impatient Tyrant. He wanted to avenge General Granlinux's death and wanted to know what part of it this person played in it even though the Air Force pilots in their debriefings stated *he was protecting the transports and did a supreme sacrifice to help them get away.*

Illtnaut respected courageous men and felt total disdain towards chickenshits, especially the cowards that did not carry out his orders despite how horrific they might be.

In their discussions Illtnaut explained to Klaus Sorge, "These doctors have no idea who or what this man is. All they know is he went through a terrible trauma."

"That's correct. They know what they are doing."

"I'm willing to wait a while for this man to regain his memory because I want to know what happened."

"He's not in a normal state, so we can't use our normal methods of torture and neuronic clarification to break him. In essence he's already broken."

"That's true, but the doctors will restore him then we'll get to the bottom of his role in all this, but as I look at all the reports, they tell me he was just part of a security detail protecting the transports."

"Yes. He's just another grunt whose heroic act almost got him killed."

"After he's restored, I personally wish to talk with him before we do our traditional interrogation techniques."

"I understand your excellency, we'll let the doctors do their work and we'll bring him to you when they think he's well enough to speak with you and has some memories restored."

"Good, you know what I want. I also want you to try and find out what the dissidents did with the body of the other pilot."

"We'll be visiting dissidents in the area shortly."

"Very well, Klaus. "You are dismissed."

Klaus Sorge left Illtnaut's mansion with a great deal of satisfaction the conversation turned out the way it did. He was no longer under immense pressure to break this guy and get a confession. Plus, the guy had no confession, he was merely a pilot flying a machine the Tartarland's Air Force shot down. *This person would be more of value in a spy swap.*

Eventually Klaus Sorge met reliable dissidents who over time proved they had a price and could easily be bribed. Little did Klaus know they were paid well to tell them what they wanted to know, not what he should know.

Through these informants it was determined the pilot they left behind they knew was indeed dead and like they do with their own Orthodox people when they die, he was cremated, and ashes dumped in the river.

"What about his clothes and personal effects?"

"He had no personal items with him. He was cremated in his charred flight suit and boots."

"Any identification marks of any type on his uniform?"

"He was severely burned, and all of the front of his flight suit was heavily charred, therefore not identification survived, it got burned in the wreckage."

***

A week later Tavishien was dropped off at an obscure beach from a Hovercraft in the middle of the night. There was some moonlight so she could drive out of the beach area without attracting much attention. Once she got out on the main hiway she would switch on her lights and appear like any ordinary person traveling at night on a scooter which happens as working girls and waitresses often went home during this time.

Tavishien assumed the Tartar authorities would not associate her with the stolen woman's identity she used in the past, because when she went to meet General Granlinux, she killed, she had no identity on her.

Since the woman they stole her identity was a recluse, nobody would recognize she had left and returned. The community learned a long time ago to leave her alone as she was adamant, she wanted no visitors and refused to answer the doorbell.

One light was left on in the home so people would assume she was there. The home had an attached garage, but the woman had no vehicle and used a lot of space in it to store her collections. Tavishien had put a combination lock on it and now she was back, entered the number and parked the scooter in the garage and entered the home. It was exactly the way she left it. She would get some sleep now and during the day go visit her uncle acting like nothing happened. She might need to use his home as a safe house if things got out of control.

After her alarm woke her up, Tavishien got up, took a shower, and changed into some of the clothes that she left behind during her last venture behind enemy lines. After Tavishien was dressed she contacted a taxi who soon arrived and took her to her uncle Hannikainen's house.

Hannikainen was happy to see Tavishien again and became slightly spooked when Tavishien said, "One of the reasons why I'm here is to tell you I have a man in my life who recently went through a trauma and received some terrible burns on the side of his face. I'm going to attempt to get him to my Papa's cabin where I can get someone to transport him to a facility, I know that can do reconstructive surgery.

"I could drive you up to the border, but that's as far as I can get you."

"Papa's cabin is only twenty miles from the border, it's an easy walk from there."

Before Tavishien launched the Garratt rescue mission, she explained to her father she would be coming with Garratt who was heavily burned on foot coming from enemy territory in about a week or so and not to shoot them like he normally did Tartars. Her papa would be very careful knowing it could be her daughter and Garratt.

Meanwhile, Doctor Gemerkt's sister had contacted a few other dissidents and were now planning on breaking Garratt out of that hospital. They had no idea that Tavishien was there until the last minute. Tavishien figured that hospital visiting hours were after evening meal and she was not far off the mark.

As expected, Klaus Sorge and his henchmen were at the hospital at 3:00 and Garratt had received medications, a bath, some soup and awake.

Klaus Sorge only brought one other man into the room because he didn't want to spook the target of his investigation. The patient had no reaction to these men who the doctor introduced.

"These men are investigating your accident and are assisting and trying to help us discover your identity."

"Oh great, I'm glad you are here."

Klaus thought the man was faking it really good or as the doctor indicated he lost his memory.

Klaus asked, "May I ask you a couple questions sir?"

"Sure."

"Do you know who you are?"

"No, I sure wish I did, and I would like to know if I have a family and why they have not looked for me."

"Do you remember your accident and how you got here?"

"No, all I remember is waking up here and meeting the doctor."

"Do you have any memories or thoughts?"

"Yes, I do. I'm always thinking about Tomlars. Have no idea why. Perhaps I'm a rancher."

"Anything else."

"Yes, a woman. I know she loves me for some reason, but I don't remember her face. I wish I did."

"The doctor said in about three days he would start the Hypnosis with you to help you remember. Would you mind if we attend your Hypnosis?

"Sure, if you think it may help you discover who I am."

"We are glad you think that way."

"I will be very grateful if you help me remember who I am."

"We'll do our best."

"Thank you."

Klaus Sorge turned around and nodded at his assistant and said, "Doctor, we'll be back tomorrow and visit and hopefully he might remember something."

***

Tavishien left her uncle's home and went to the hospital not far away. She was extremely lucky they took Garratt to this particular hospital which was right where she needed it to be for what she needed to do.

When she arrived, she passed Klaus Sorge and his security detachment. Tavishien, being a smart spy, knew they were probably a security detail involved with Garratt and as such tagged Klaus Sorge just in case since he was doing most of the talking was probably the boss. She also heard Klaus say, "We'll meet here late in the morning and see how the patient in room 214 is doing."

One of his security guys responded, "He seems awful cheerful with all those burns."

Since Tavishien spoke Tartar fluently because of her upbringing living twenty miles from the border and listening to Tartar radio shows with her father for an hour every day, easily understood what the men were saying and if she was stopped, she could fake being a Tartar real easily. She was dressed very modestly and none of the security people recognized the most wanted woman as she passed them.

Now she knew exactly where Garratt was and when she swung into action tomorrow, after these guys visited and left, get him out of the hospital and on his way to freedom.

Even plainly dressed, Tavishien was pretty. People were quite pleasant to her when she walked through the ward on the second floor and approached room 214.

Doctor Gemerkt was alone with Garratt when Tavishien walked into the room. Since she had already seen his disfigurement, she wasn't in a state of shock. She was holding her emotions back, being a great spy doing what she had to do to get her beloved back to safety.

The doctor asked, "May I help you miss?"

"Yes, I'm here to see this man."

"Do you know who he is?"

"Yes, his name is Marti."

The doctor was stunned but also knew this courageous woman was in very big danger. He then started thinking about his sister and maybe she could be of help.

Tavishien then walked near Garratt and started applying her telepathic ability and said, "Be quiet, I'm here to help you and get you back to safety. You are in a very dangerous situation, and we will get you out of here within 24 hours. My name is Tavishien and I'm your lover."

Doctor Gemerkt saw the tears come down "Marti's face." He knew this was the real deal. He had no idea where the hell the woman came from but since Klaus Sorge and his goons were of intense interest to this man, she had to be involved and she was very brave to come here.

The doctor had no idea how delightful the dictator Illtnaut would be if he learned this woman was here. His sister had a lot of influence on him, so Doctor Gemerkt knew he didn't have much time to deal with this because there could be snitches who saw this woman appear.

Doctor Gemerkt pulled out his business card and wrote his sister's phone number down on it and said, "This is my sister. You will be in real danger if you remain here much longer. She's a dissident and hates our government. Go somewhere and call her. Marti will be here. I'll explain it to him after you leave."

Tavishien tagged Doctor Gemerkt and probed his mind and quickly determined his offer of help was sincere. She walked over to Garratt and kissed him on his lips and using her mental telepathy said, I'll be back to get you, just play along that you can't remember anything. I promise your memory will return soon.

Tavishien then left the room and exited the building and hopped on a public transport that simultaneously stopped in front of the building. She rode the transport about a mile, got off, walked to the other side of the road at a pedestrian crossing and waited for the next transport and rode it three miles in the opposite direction.

Tavishien had the communicator the woman whom she stole her identification had owned. When she stepped off the bus, she was at a beautiful public park that did not have many people walking around because of the hour of the day.

Doctor Gemerkt informed Garratt, "I need to go to my office for a few minutes to call my sister. I'll be right back."

Doctor Gemerkt called Marina and said, "You will receive a phone call from a woman shortly. This is a time when you dissidents can really help someone. She needs your help and it's for the most noble causes. I'll tell you about it when I get home this evening."

"Alright, what's her name?"

"Tavishien."

Tavishien, who was now remote viewing Doctor Gemerkt as well as Klaus Sorge observed that phone call. Tavishien knew the help was legitimate and she would be grateful for the rest of her life to Doctor Gemerkt and his sister Marina.

Since Tavishien knew Marina had received Doctor Gemerkt's phone call, she knew it was the appropriate time to call Marina.

The call signal went through, and Marina answered her communicator.

"Hello."

"Marina?" Tavishien asked.

"Yes." Is this Tavishien?

"It is."

"My brother Doctor Gemerkt said I needed to talk to you. Where can we meet?"

"I'm at the city park next to a water tower and a factory on the other side of the street."

"I know exactly where you are. I can see that park from my home. I'll be there in five minutes."

By the time Marina arrived walking, Tavishien was the only female at the park, so Marina knew it had to be her.

"Hello." Marina said.

"Thank you for seeing me."

"I rarely get any of this type of activity from my brother, the doctor, so you must be extra special."

"I'm not the one that's special. He's in the hospital."

"I see. Why don't we walk to my home where we can talk."

"Sure."

Marina was very accurate when said she could see the park from her home and the walk was short when they arrived at an expensive home that overlooked the park from the far side amongst other distinctive looking homes.

They entered the home, that was well kept and looked expensive, as Marina had acquired a lot while she was working as an attorney.

"Would you like something to drink?"

"I suppose an elixir to calm me down would be good."

"I know exactly what you need. I used to give it to my clients while I worked as a defense lawyer."

Soon the two ladies were sitting at the dinner table sipping on their elixirs.

Tavishien tagged Marina and soon used her telepathic abilities to get a gauge of who she really was. The fact Marina was a huge dissident pleased Tavishien because it meant this was legitimate help.

They discussed what was going on and Garratts condition and loss of memory. However what Tavishien didn't know was Garratt's memory was suddenly flooding back. The floodgates were open, and he knew vividly Tavishien was the woman he loved and in his dreams. It made his heart feel so wonderful he got to see her face.

The downside was he also recognized the terrible trouble he was in and the huge risk Tavishien undertook to get here. He also knew she had a plan, or she would not be here. He would let her lead and he would follow because he knew only, she could pull this off.

As the women discussed the situation, Marina figured out a strategy that Tavishien never considered because up until now she had no local help except her uncle.

"I think the best way to help you get Garratt out of there is I will go into the hospital room and leave with Garratt. You said he's about my brother's size?"

"Yes."

Tomorrow I'll send a change of clothes, shoes, hat, and surgical mask to the hospital with my brother. With all the FLU that's going around most people are wearing masks, so people will not see him leave the hospital disfigured. I'll pick him up outside the hospital, and you can pick him up from there. Meanwhile me and the dissidents will take the government on a series of wild goose chases.

Thanks to Tavishien tagging and hearing the conversation, she informed Marina, Klaus Sorge and his people will be visiting Garratt mid-morning, I think they will leave the hospital around lunch time."

"Perfect. The staff will be busy feeding the patients and not realize Marti walked out of the hospital."

"I have a 2-seat scooter and I've been trained in stunt driving. I'll be waiting in the parking lot when you bring Garratt down."

That night Tavishien had a very busy time back at the home of the woman where she had her scooter parked, now gassed up and ready to go. She was busy remote viewing Klaus Sorge and in doing so remote viewed his meeting with Illtnaut. This turned out even better than tagging General Granlinux who only saw Illtnaut off and on routinely, mainly at social gatherings.

Klaus Sorge was with Illtnaut every day and had something that the General didn't have. The complete oversight of their intelligence agency. He was one of the top dogs thus by remote viewing Klaus Sorge, she could do far more damage to the Tartars than she ever could have with General Granlinux she had killed.

Tavishien visited her brother and told him the plan would happen tomorrow to have his car gassed up and they would have collateral assistance from dissidents, and hopefully their drive to the border would be uneventful.

By now Garratt had been walking to the toilet and elsewhere and asked the doctor to have someone take him for a walk around the hospital so he could get some fresh air. In front of the orderly, Doctor Gemerkt said, "I would like to go for a little walk myself. I will take you downstairs and we'll walk together."

"Thank you."

"There is a lot of people with the FLU now, put on this face mask just in case we get near some of them."

"Alright."

The two men left the hospital and walked around the nice, lovely landscaping clear around the building. Garratt said. "This feels so good after lying in that bed so long, would it be okay to make one more lap?"

"Sure, no problem, plus there is something I want to tell you."

As the men walked the second lap the orderly observed them through a window and really had great appreciation for this doctor who was a humanitarian and a great person. What the doctor did not know was the orderly was also a dissident and knew Marina well. He also knew something was going to happen to the patient and he would do whatever he could to help.

Eventually when the two men came back into room 214, Garratt's private hospital room, he knew several things. First of all, the director of the Tartar intelligence agency would soon be visiting him and would talk briefly with him. Then he would have lunch, then big things would happen.

Just like all planned, Klaus Sorge and his henchmen showed up and they took the orderly aside and asked him some poignant questions about the patient in room 214 and asked if there were any revelations since they last saw him.

"Yes, there is."

"And what is that."

"Last night he was crying and in a lot of sadness because it's a terrible ordeal for him to lose his memory. We were ordered to watch him closer because the doctor is worried, he might attempt suicide."

Klaus Sorge knew now would not be the time to probe too deeply, especially if they were now having to sedate the patient to keep him from committing suicide. He already knew what Illtnaut wanted no matter how long it took, for the man to regain his memory before they brutalized him for what they wanted to get out of him which is something they didn't know.

"How are you feeling today?" Klaus asked Garratt after they went into his room?"

"How should someone feel if they can't remember anything in their lifetime? Perhaps death is the solution."

Klaus knew the patient was depressed and looked up at Doctor Gemerkt who knew to speak up then and said, "It's normal for a patient like this to experience depression. We are going to have him eat something, then I'm going to inject him, so he has some happy time."

"Alright Doctor, I think we should leave now. Thank you for your efforts."

"I'll try my best. I think in a couple days as we start the Hypnosis, we might be able to help him overcome some of his grief if we can just get back a few crumbs of his memories."

"Alright doctor, we'll be back tomorrow, hopefully he's in a better state."

"I hope so too."

Klaus Sorge and his thugs left the hospital and were due to visit Illtnaut and give him a brief update.

In due time the staff started taking trays of food to all the rooms and the orderly helped Garratt to the bathroom. Inside he said, "Your change of clothes is in that cupboard. Good luck."

Garratt, who was steadily regaining his memory including his prowess of a spy shut the door opened the cupboard, found the clothes and another surprise: a weapon in case he had to defend himself and Tavishien. It was all coming together in a rather spontaneous manner. As soon as he was dressed, he exited the bathroom and there was Marina there waiting for him and handed him the mask to put on and said, "put this and your surgical head cover on."

Soon they were walking out of the hospital, and nobody knew it was the patient, nor could they see the damage to his face thanks to the mask.

Marina walked Garratt over to her car and said, "Get in."

Garratt got in the car and Marina drove her car down several blocks and pulled into the driveway of a business and Tavishien was waiting there on her scooter. Garratt got out of the car and said, "Thank you."

"My pleasure."

Garratt walked over to the scooter and hopped on the back. He knew Tavishien was quite capable.

Tavishien pulled out onto the road and promptly drove to her uncle's home. His garage door was open, and the car was in the driveway. Tavishien pulled the scooter into the garage. Tavishien and Garratt got off the scooter and walked out of the garage and hopped into her uncle's car as the garage door was closing.

Hoping the support element was in place, they drove conservatively not taking any chances of a traffic stop and headed to the border. It would be an overnight trip.

Tavishien's uncle pulled up to the closest point to the border he could get on a dirt road. This was a very sparsely populated area and stopped the car and said, "You have arrived at your destination.

By the time Klaus Sorge and his goons arrived at the hospital in the morning, Tavishien and Garratt were five miles inside their country outside enemy territory.

Tavishien asked, "Would you like to stop and rest?"

"Not until we get to your father's cabin. I know I can make it. My body feels fine, and the doctor told me in my meal he gave some extra energy components which will help me for a couple days."

"Any pain?"

"Sure, there is pain, but the idea of freedom easily overcomes that and also getting my memory back is an added bonus."

The two continued their trek walking in well concealed foliage so when the Tartars eventually come looking for them suspecting this was their escape route, they simply hugged trees until the flights were gone as they could hear their approach from a long distance.

The Tomlars were remote viewing Tavishien and Garratt and informed her father of their progress. He got his weapon and ammunition and walked five miles east to meet the two. This also turned out to be very auspicious because Illtnaut wanted them back!

Trackers had crossed over the border. Tavishien's father had notified Gabriel the two were on their way and he would meet them. Gabriel and Tristan flew out in two seat terrain followers with weapons just in case.

At the five-mile mark Tavishien's father met them and Tavishien had already discovered and said, "There are trackers behind us about a mile sent out to kill us."

"Follow me I know where we can go where we can see them, but they can't see us."

He then led them to a spot that had the advantage of vision almost one way and the trackers came. There was a dozen of them. As soon as they came out into the clearing, the first one's head exploded as Tavishien's father nailed him. The rest then took cover. There was sporadic rifle fire and Garratt had his weapon for perimeter defense if they got too close.

The gun battle commenced.

Tavishien's father handed her his communicator and said, "Gabriel is on her way with terrain followers."

As the 12 men fired in the general direction of Tavishien and her group, the Terrain followers popped over the horizon.

Tavishien talking to Gabriel and Tristan said, the enemy is directly east of us about 200 years. You should be able to see us on the Hill top."

"Yes, we see you, stay down, we are going to drop some bombs."

The Terrain Followers swooped down and as they spotted a few enemies they fired their machine guns and started dropping bombs. Half of the dozen Tartars were killed on the first pass. Tavishien yelled out at the Tartars in their language, drop your guns and come out with your hands up or we will kill every one of you. After a couple more bombs were dropped the survivors decided enough was enough and raised their hands and walked out of the tree line.

More firepower quickly arrived and a couple dozen special forces guys came out of their transports and approached the prisoners standing with their hands up. In a few more minutes everyone was gone. Papa was taken to his cabin and the rest went to the Intelligence Bureau Campus.

Tavishien and Garratt were soon in the secure conference room with Garratt's boss who was very irritated with Tavishien.

"Tavishien, I hope you realize we do not condone your actions and this sort of thing has never happened before."

"I had to do what I did for a good reason."

"There is no reason good enough for you to totally ignore protocol and do such an extraordinary mission without my approval."

"There is one condition, and that's why I could not inform Gabriel and Tristan in case you did neuronic clarifications on them."

"And what's that?"

"You have a mole here in high places."

"What?"

"That's why Garratt was shot down, the mole tipped off the enemy and they set a trap for us."

"Who is the mole?"

"I can't tell you until I kill him."

"You put me in a very bad spot."

"Alright director, now I'm going to tell you something, that you cannot reveal to anyone until we kill the mole."

"I tagged the top spy in Illtnaut's intelligence agency. I now have frequent remote viewing of Illtnaut."

The director sat there dazzled.

"Remember if you tell anyone, the mole will know because you don't know who the mole is until I kill him."

"If it's someone high up in my staff you just can't kill him."

"He's done a lot of damage to you and almost got Garratt killed and got Duff killed. Plus, we don't know how many other agents he turned. After he's dead, you will have to look at everything he had awareness of and realize it's been compromised."

"If you kill this person, you realize I'll have to have you arrested."

"You will never be able to prove it was me that killed him. So, you will be wasting your time arresting me."

"We'll see about that."

"Your spy agency is currently a leaking sieve and Illtnaut and Klaus Sorge are laughing at you because it's so easy for them to eat your lunch. In fact, today as I remote viewed Illtnaut he joked at what kind of an idiot you are."

The director felt the sting. He knew Tavishien would not be saying these ruthless remarks unless she knew it to be the case because she was profoundly a straight shooter and never embellished anything.

As Tavishien was working on the director with her mental telepathy to calm him down a notch or two, she brainwashed the director into believing someone close to him is a mole and has done a lot of damage. *How could he not have seen this?*

Overseeing an Intelligence Bureau, the director knew the number one axiom of the spy business. The espionage that hurts you the most is espionage you were never aware of.

The director suddenly changed his tune.

"Everyone thinks Garratt is dead. Tomorrow we will have a memorial service for him and Duff."

"Why sir?"

"If it's true that we got a highly placed mole among us, then we need to make him think Garratt is dead so tomorrow at the memorial service we'll be honoring these two men."

"What about Garratt's disfigurement?"

"I will soon have Garratt transported to a remote medical facility to do reconstructive surgery on his face and change his identity. I will personally handle the identity change so the mole will not know."

"I want to be with him when he gets the surgery."

"Why do you need to be with him?"

"Besides providing him extra security, I also want to know who he is when they finish."

"That sounds reasonable. I'll have a mask prepared for Garratt tonight so he looks like someone nobody knows tomorrow and then the two of you can leave from here to where I must send you. "When we get back, we have to deal with the mole."

"We'll take up that matter when you get back."

"Thank you."

"I'm going to escort you to my personal parking garage through the entrance of my office. I don't want anyone to see you guys until sometime in the future with identities changes."

The three walked through the door with a cypher lock and on the other side of the door was a Skycar.

"Hop in." The windows were darkened in a way they could see out, but nobody could see in.

The car and the garage had voice activation control. Soon they were out of the garage and airborne and flying to Garratt's Highrise home. The Skycar parked on the rooftop in Skycar temporary parking.

As Tavishien and Garratt were getting out, the Director said, "A little later, my personal mask maker will be arriving to get you ready for tomorrow's services. Madam Ljótunn bon Swartzler will be arriving first thing in the morning to dress the two of you in formal memorial wear. The public will not know who Garratt is. He has a brother he's not seen in twenty years. That brother will escort you to the memorial."

Garratt and the director both knew Garratt's brother died twenty years prior. If someone like the mole tried checking up on him, they would go to a dead end real fast as he was now almost untraceable. His death and reporting of it was never made public. All the relatives knew was he went to climb a mountain and never came back.

The mask maker was busy most of the night but gave Garratt several naps. By morning he was ready for Madam Ljótunn bon Swartzler who would not be glamorizing them as this was a memorial and they were thus dressed as if they were going to a funeral.

***

The dissident doctor slowly brought Duff back to life. Duff was a tough cookie and wanted to get back to friendly territory so he could engage in his line of work and somehow get revenge on the evil Tartars for killing his buddy Garratt (aka Agent Lucika).

He followed a similar path to Tavishien's papa cabin which he knew well. Duff made it almost to the Cabin when he was confronted with Tavishien's father who was about to kill him, but the Tomlars knew this was Duff by remote viewing Garratt and told papa not to shoot him, he was Garratt's friend.

Papa put the gun down and said, "I've been notified you are Garratt's friend."

"That's true."

Papa recognized the voice and said, "I know that voice."

"Papa it's me Duff."

"What the hell happened to you?"

"It's a long story. You got that phone we gave you, it has a speed dial to Gabriel, can you call her?"

Shortly Gabriel and Tristan were on their way in a couple Terrain Followers and picked up Duff who was wearing a mask since he was terribly burned. Duff was jubilant to see them.

Gabriel joked and said, "Your memorial service is in about two hours we need to get you there so you can watch it. I don't think the director wants anyone to know you are alive, especially since you will probably go get some reconstructive surgery."

I've kind of started liking all these scars. It helps me with the women." The group chuckled and were soon Airborne.

There was just enough time to put on a premade mask on Duff for the memorial that lasted about 30 minutes. There were a lot of tears and crying because a lot of people loved Duff. Duff might have been tuff, but he came across to people in ways they responded in a positive manner. Duff was a tough loss for the Agency.

The director was notified five minutes before the memorial that Duff was alive and in the audience with a mask on because he too needed reconstructive surgery.

The director was the consummate actor as he did the memorial with great precision and respect. Soon it was over, and people didn't mind they rushed Tavishien and Garratt's brother out of the venue quickly as they knew she was probably about to start crying her eyes out.

They hopped in the six-seater Skycar with Duff and their escorts and were flown promptly to the Airport where a private aircraft was waiting for them. They were soon on their way to an undisclosed location.

When they arrived, they recognized the place. This was one of the mansions they visited when Tavishien was out getting a tour of the countryside when she received her scooter and hovercraft training.

As they got out of the Skybus sent from the airport, Garratt said, "I recognize this place."

One of the escorts said, "There is an operating room set up here and the reconstructive surgeons are here waiting for you. Your treatment will start today. Everything you need is here or will be brought to you."

"Who do you work for?" Garratt asked the man.

"I'm part of the director's personal security detachment. We work for him and answer to nobody else."

"So, our secret is safe with you?"

"We are not permitted to discuss any aspect of our job with anyone. We like receiving the high pay the director gives us for our silence."

"But can you be bought? Everyone has a price."

"I already have a lot of money. I do not need any more money. I do this simply for the pleasure of working directly to the director and do not have to answer up to anyone else."

"Alright thanks."

***

The men received surgery sequentially. Garratt the first day and Duff the second day. Duff and Tavishien were sitting in chairs in the recovery room where the best cosmetic surgeons on the planet had done their magic. Garratt's face was now bandaged up and eventually he came too feeling a great deal of hunger as he had not had an ideal diet for a while since he was shot down.

Garratt was in good spirits and the chief surgeon informed him the skin grafts worked well and he would feel some pain in his legs for a few days where they borrowed skin to put on his face.

Garratt had plenty of pain meds flowing in his system and felt fine. Tavishien felt so relieved she was back with him and hoped he never went behind enemy lines again. Tavishien's days of going behind enemy lines were also curtailed as now she was super important providing the director personally, information she derived from remote viewing Klaus Sorge.

The young man who brought them here returned a day later and said he needed to talk with Tavishien alone. He took her to the Skycar and said, we have sufficient privacy to talk here. This Skycar has been certified bug free.

"What do you want?"

"The director knows until we figure out the modus operendus it's going to be hard for you to send information to him. I'm going to step out of the car so you can talk to the person in the passenger seat."

"The young man stepped out of the Skycar and suddenly a opaque barrier between the driver's seat and the seat behind dropped down and there was the director."

"Hello Tavishien, I was told the surgery went well and the surgeons said in a few more days, Garratt will look handsome for you."

"Thanks."

"The reason why I came here is because I don't want anyone else to know what you get from Klaus Sorge. Have you remote viewed him lately?"

"Yes, quite a bit frankly."

"Until we figure out how we are going to do this, I will make personal visits to you, and you can personally brief me. Eventually you will brief Garratt and I'll meet with him."

"Alright."

"Any new revelations from Klaus Sorge?"

"Yes, the mole sent word to Klaus who informed the emperor that Duff and Garratt's memorial service concluded, and they were definitely killed in an operation."

"Do they know Garratt was the man in the hospital?"

"No, they think he was a pilot the dissidents helped escape from the hospital."

"What about Duff?"

"They think he was killed, and the dissidents incinerated his body and dumped the ashes into the river."

Tavishien then went on to discuss three things the Mole was doing that heavily distressed the director and drove him over the line.

"Alright it's clear to me this mole has created an intolerable situation for us. I will permit you to sanction him, but he must disappear. I don't want anyone to know you three had anything to do with his disappearance."

"I think we can easily handle this matter. The mole is secure in his operation and doesn't think you are smart enough to discover him."

"Those are the best people to take down. The ones that get overconfident."

After two weeks of treatments and post-surgical healing, the threesome was now given some time to relax and plan their operation.

What the mole didn't know was Tavishien had tagged him once in the past. She didn't know why, but he was present at a couple of their operations, and she did it merely out of curiosity.

The mole was so overconfident, he had a seaside villa and by arrangements didn't need protection nor did he desire it since most of his espionage operated out of that villa.

The director was not informed of who the mole was because he might tip off the mole before they took him down.

The threesome now with new identity including Tavishien who can look completely different by the help of Madam Ljótunn bon Swartzler reconnoitered the area and found all the assets they needed to do the job.

The director's personal Skycar had incredible weapon systems in it. Garratt knew that and asked to borrow it. The young aid that was part of the director's personal security detachment flew in with Garratt sitting in the front seat with him. Duff was in an armored vehicle with a group of special forces guys in the event the Mole escaped his seaside villa.

Tavishien picked her mode of transportation. She had a hovercraft with a scooter tied down on it. She too was heavily armed and could easily pass for a GI Jane type person.

The mole had a weekend routine and part of it was basking in the sun, drinking, and enjoying the call girls that were usually there. Today was about the same.

All the hit team wore special encrypted earbuds.

Tavishien looked smoking hot with her bikini on and had her weapon down the back of her bikini which she could easily get too and when she pulled up on the beach in the Hovercraft, she started walking towards the mole who was at first smiling as her bikini just about revealed everything. The call girls present were no match for Tavishien's beauty with the makeup job that Madam Ljótunn bon Swartzler's makeup artists did only two hours earlier.

"Who are you lovely lady?"

"A girl who wants to get to know you better."

"That's a fine-looking boat you got there."

"Thanks, it comes in handy."

"Just what can I do for you?"

"I think we need to talk about something."

"And what is that?"

"If you want to see my tits, you need to tell these women to go into the house, then I can tell you."

"The mole smiled and turned to the women and said, "Go in the house I want to find out why she's here."

This action was to divert the mole's attention so he would not see the sky car landing behind him. Tavishien could see it and watched Garratt and the security detachment climb out of the Skycar and quickly descended to the patio area. The mole could suddenly hear footsteps and turned around to see who was coming and was alarmed because these men looked dangerous.

The mole then stood up as to run back into his home when Tavishien pulled her gun and said, "Sit back down or I'm going to shoot and kill you."

The mole saw Tavishien holding the blaster and knew he was in a trap and realized this woman probably knew how to shoot the gun.

One out of ninety-nine times the mole went out there without taking his gun with him. Today was the worst day to be unprepared as he soon found out.

The call girls were looking out the windows trying to figure out what was going on. The mole slowly sat down trying to figure out an exit strategy, but Garratt and the security detachment arrived so abruptly he couldn't think of what to do and the girl holding the gun was too far away for him to charge her and no doubt she was probably an expert shooter. Right then his world started crumbling.

In the spy business traitors only have trials if the government wants to broadcast what they can do to a spy if they catch them. The rest of the time they simply dispose of them.

The plan had been well thought out.

Tavishien had a couple buckets of chum in the hovercraft. People had a tendency not to swim in this area due to the water being generally too cold and it was shark infested.

Garratt and the security detachment guy were very strong, and the man was soon standing with strong hand cuffs on and leg restraints. They then escorted him down to the water's edge.

"Lay down on your stomach."

"Fuck you."

Garratt punched the guy in the nose hard and now the blood was oozing out and helped him down onto the sand. Tavishien had put her gun back in her bikini and walked over to the hover craft and grabbed the tow rope with a hook latch on it and clicked onto the leg restraint on the mole. Standing on the moles back, Garratt pulled out his stiletto and bent down and cut the man several places causing him to bleed badly.

Garratt then nodded at Tavishien who then pulled one of the two chum buckets out of the Hovercraft and walked over and sat it on the beach. She then got back aboard the Hovercraft and put it in reverse in the Hovercraft and backed it off the beach and turned around facing the ocean. Garratt and the security detachment carried the bleeding man down to water's edge and dumped the chum all over him which caused him to scream in pain as it interacted with the cuts on his back.

Tavishien steered the hovercraft out towards open ocean and Garrot and the security detail walked up to the back of the door of the home and went inside to confront the women watching and appeared terrorized.

"Nobody knows this man owns this home. If you keep your mouths shut, you can have this home. If you say anything to anyone you too will be dragged out to the ocean and fed to the sharks."

Garratt and the other man then went to the Skycar and got inside and took off flying above the man Tavishien was dragging out to the shark feast.

Flying above the Hovercraft Garratt informed Tavishien where to steer to head directly towards a large group of sharks, perhaps as many as 100 of them.

Garratt then directed via secure communications, "Stop the Hovercraft and cut the tow line and throw the other bucket of chum into the water on top of the man."

The mole was still alive and floating in a lot of pain struggling to not go underwater and drown.

Tavishien steered the hovercraft right next to the man and grabbed the other bucket of chum and threw it on top of the man which seemed to cause the sharks to enter a feeding frenzy. She then disconnected the tow line.

Tavishien got back into the Hovercraft's driver's seat and started it forward increasing the throttle. Tavishien then turned north and headed to an area several miles up the coast into a sparsely populated area and pulled the hovercraft up on the beach. She then untied the scooter and drove it off the hovercraft onto the sand of the beach and followed a public access walkway that went up the hill and to a parking lot, then onto a road and drove the scooter back to the rental she had left just an hour before.

By arrangement, a couple came to the beach in another Hovercraft. Tristan hopped off the Hovercraft and he and Gabriel returned the two Hovercraft to a rental five miles further up the coast.

The call girls took to heart what the men had said and sure enough nobody came around checking up on them. Duff and his group returned to the special forces base that often-supported Duff's clandestine operation's including the time he and Garratt were shot down.

Garratt and Tavishien were soon in a new home with a good view of the mountains and the lake below them.

Tavishien forced the director's hand that she would continue the remote viewing if the director never sent Garratt on dangerous missions again. For what Tavishien was reporting directly to the Director and nobody else, he was willing to make such a concession. Plus, he was now paranoid after discovering his best friend was the mole and didn't really care to know what happened to him.

But one thing he knew was with Garratt and Duff, he probably had a bad ending. He was also mindful how Tavishien took care of a mole in her baptism to fire.

But the one thing the director knew. If a very serious issue within SIS ever happened again, in his heart he knew Tavishien would rise to the occasion along with Garratt, Tristan, Gabriel, and Duff.

Paul D. Escudero

保罗·道格拉斯·埃斯库德罗

July 25th, 2023

Dramatis Personae And Special Information

Doctor Gemerkt, Surgeon who treated Garratt after aircraft crash.

Klaus Sorge, Dictator Illtnaut's head of Tartar Intelligence Agency

General Granlinux, very close to the Tyrannical Dictator Illtnaut

Tavishien the Remote Viewer.

Karoline, One of Tavishien's alias.

Agent Lucika aka Garratt Wyclaire aka Marti, top spy and Tavishien's lover. Agent Lucika is a Western Alliance INTEL operative which is all part of the Crawflang Empire.

General Taroton (aka Michael) head of air force base where Tavishien received advanced aerial combat training.

Lateegely, Tavishien female steward at the air force base. Also, Lateegely was General Taroton's lover.

Escterbina Kropolis, The owner of the motor scooter rental.

Ulger Kroft. He was a stunt man used in movies.

Elijah's Diner, Main restaurant in Perlman.

Hăiguī sea life that weighed 100 to 200 pounds.

Norman Swansen who owned the Hovercraft business.

Gabriel and Tristan Karjal Intelligence Bureau Reps IBR.

 Elnar Harkensen, owner of bed and breakfast, car, scooter, and boat rental.

Douglas Draske IBR

Gæsaber elixir. The Gæsaber was a double fermented elixir.

Kanill Grasker elixir.

Luthor Braxleon drug trafficker.

Commander Bull, the deputy for the National Police.

Grande Emerald Resort where some of the action takes place.

Karl Vlasson, The head of organized crime.

Tolar Seia, Karl Vlasson's representative.

Grande Perstroyan Divergency Hotel is another hot spot for action.

Brynja and Freyja, friends Gabriel introduced to Tavishien.

Grand Xenix Resort, action location.

Thurston bon Katterberg's Grand Xenix Resort penthouse where the first major remote viewer test was done.

Maxine Causwell female PIMP for Thurston bon Katterberg.

Ljótunn bon Swartzler fashion designer and model trainer

Brakaloff which was much like Venison is on Earth.

Wenmark, the area next to Tartarland where Agent Lucika aka Garratt Wyclaire aka Marti, and Tavishien first met.

Doctor Hannah Barrymore treated Tavishien after her trauma.

Concert fiðluleikari (violinist)

Fiðlu violin

Klavier, piano.

Maki Zorthun mother of Tavishien Arginin

Lingraw Arginin, Tavishien's father lived in a mountainous area of Difland, one of the planets of the Crawflang Empire. He sold goods made from Tomlars hides surpassed the quality and softness that other hides

A visitor from planet Earth once said the Tomlars had a striking resemblance to Thomson's Gazelle.

Tartarland is a large area on Difland controlled by the Tyrannical

Dictator Illtnaut. [Icelandic] Wicked Bull

Rockovnar was the leader of the six Tartar soldiers that attacked Tavishien causing a terrible trauma.

Coloson General Hospital where Gabriel went after Tavishien attacked her.

Tavishien's uncle Hannikainen.

Brakaloff which was much like Venison is on Earth

***

Author's Note:

This is a work of fiction. There are no living persons or things from planet Earth in the works because this story takes place on an alien planet that does not know Earth exists.

If you finished the Novel, you realize there are some disgusting events in the early part of the book, such as the rape. That rape trauma had to be elucidated because I know a remote viewer that experienced such trauma and is how and why she became a remote viewer working for intelligence agencies the way this fiction lays it out. One day in the future after she fully retires, she can claim this story as her own and correlate real things that happened in her life as I randomly created a fiction to convey what possibly may happen with a remote viewer operating in such a fashion.

The love story between Tavishien and Garratt really happened to her. She has read this book since she's a consultant to me. She explained the way I painted that romance and how it manifested and how she left for a couple of years and went to a remote fishing village where she lived in a very austere fashion living the alternative lifestyle happened.

And just like in the story, there came a time when they desperately needed her talents and hence her lover did an extensive investigation to locate her whereabouts. He also knew the only person she would talk with is the woman who trained her in martial arts and thus her trainer was sent to ask her to come back.

Just like the remote viewer story I penned, the remote viewer insisted her former boss had to personally come and ask her to come back and she forced him to disclose to management they were lovers. And just like in the story, she knew what his real name was and not the Alias. That triggered a huge security review because it indicated there had been some sort of data leak. In reality, his identity disclosure was nothing more than a remote viewer's ability to discover things management wanted hidden and buried.

The remote viewer was utterly astounded I wrote the romance exactly how it happened when she never mentioned this person to me. Did those thoughts come to me through some remote viewing process?

I asked this person whether our government remote view Aliens?

Her answer and explanations would totally astound you, but I'll leave it to her to come forward when or if she decides to disclose it or any of her missions. None of her missions are in this book. I was not interested in the missions, just the techniques, and thus created fictional missions that may not be to far off the mark such as dealing with organized crime and unsavory characters.

If they have a person like I depict in this Novel, why wouldn't they remote view aliens? If not, then perhaps they should.

What would be gained by remote viewing Aliens? If they are cutting deals with Russia or China, shouldn't we be interested?

Question: Why wouldn't Aliens play both sides? What's Alien agenda?

The truth of the matter is nobody on this planet knows. What Aliens have in mind may not be in America's best interest.

It's logical to assume if Aliens are in fact planning planetary conquest, they would employ *divide and conquer*. That's why they would play with both sides and use one side or the other as a surrogate to reduce the efforts they have to make to take over the planet. Our secret space program is probably on a reckless course that easily could end up in total disaster.

Are there competing Aliens out in space like there are on this planet? If you don't think there is, then one day you may be in for a huge surprise. I captured that scenario in my Novel *51 REASONS TO ASK 51 QUESTIONS.*

Do other countries employ remote viewers against the USA?

<u>Clairvoyant Remote Viewing: The US Sponsored Psychic Spying (columbia.edu)</u>

Extract:

> During the Cold War years, the USA and Soviet Union are known to have been spying on each other using the services of psychic 'remote viewers', with the specific objective of gathering intelligence information of military significance.

This book is dedicated to a remote viewer and if she decides to come forward and disclose, she is the person I wrote this book about, I will add a comment about her and a short biography about her to the book and create a new revision if she wishes me to do so.

I'm also dedicating this book to the Television star Lucille Ball.

Why?

In case you do not know it, we would not have had the Star Trek Television Series without Lucille Ball. After the initial showing of Star Trek, it was cancelled. Lucille Ball, who had control of Desilu Productions, an American television production company and she supported Star Trek and manifested its continuation.

Star Trek had a lot of influence on subsequent science fiction shows and movies. The science fiction lovers and community owe Lucille Ball a lot for saving Star Trek which perpetuated a lot of the subsequent developments in science fiction entertainment. For those of us who write science fiction Novels, Lucille Ball is just as important as Isaac Asimov and Robert A. Heinlein.

www.ingramcontent.com/pod-product-compliance
Lightning Source LLC
Chambersburg PA
CBHW051131300726
48978CB00011B/228